# LOVE LIES BLEEDING

8/11

# LOVE LIES BLEEDING

JESS McCONKEY



wm
WILLIAM MORROW
*An Imprint of* HarperCollins*Publishers*

This book is a work of fiction. References to real people, events, establishments, organizations, or locales are intended only to provide a sense of authenticity, and are used fictitiously. All other characters, and all incidents and dialogue, are drawn from the author's imagination and are not to be construed as real.



HarperCollins books may be purchased for educational, business, or sales promotional use. For information please write: Special Markets Department, HarperCollins Publishers, 10 East 53rd Street, New York, NY 10022.

FIRST EDITION

*Designed by Diahann Sturge*

Library of Congress Cataloging-in-Publication Data has been applied for.

ISBN 978-0-06-199968-0

11 12 13 14 15 OV/RRD 10 9 8 7 6 5 4 3 2 1

*To my editor, Emily Krump, and my agent, Stacey Glick. This book never would've been written without your encouragement and support!*

# LOVE LIES BLEEDING

# One

*Oh God, they're in the house!* How had they found her? Were they here to finish the job? The bitter taste of fear clogged the back of her throat, her heart pounded, and a scream tried to fight its way up from deep inside. *No, you can't scream. They might hear you.* She swallowed twice.

Run. She had to run. She had to find Jackson, but her legs wouldn't move. Why wouldn't her legs move?

Her eyes flew open and she stared wide-eyed into the darkness. *Where were they? In the living room? In the hallway?* A soft moan escaped her lips as a cold sweat dampened her upper lip. She felt as though she could smell her terror lingering in the air.

Suddenly the darkness vanished. She winced and jerked her hands over her eyes, trying to block the blinding light. Footsteps hurried across the bedroom floor. Her breath came in short, swift gasps as she felt the bed dip and her hands were slowly pulled away from her face. A quiet voice pierced the roaring in her ears. Jackson's voice.

"Sam, Sam, wake up. You're having another nightmare."

Images of men chasing her . . . hurting her . . . circled in her mind as she tried to raise herself from the bed. She couldn't move her legs. Thrashing, she pushed with her hand while she fought to sit up.

"Easy, Sam. You're tangled in the sheets. Let me help you," Jackson said from where he sat on the side of the bed.

Her eyes locked on his face and the images faded. *Nightmare . . . it was only a nightmare.* Reality finally penetrated her sleep-soaked mind.

Inhaling sharply, she stopped her tossing and willed her body to relax while her fiancé pulled her upright and began to slowly unwind the sheets binding her legs. Awake but disoriented, she shoved her limp auburn hair out of her face while her eyes darted around the room, searching for something familiar.

This wasn't their bedroom. Their bedroom walls were a perfect shade of Martha Stewart mocha, not knotty-pine paneling. In this room, plaid curtains, not sheer linen, hung over rough, slatted blinds. Where the hell was she?

Panicked again, she felt her heart kick up a ragged rhythm. *Not the hospital—please, not back in the hospital.*

Wait. The walls in the intensive care unit were a cold, sterile green, not wood-paneled. She cocked her head and listened, but the only sound she heard was the pounding of her blood in her head. No whoosh-whoosh of the respirator. Her hand flew to the base of her throat. No plastic tube forcing sustaining oxygen into her lungs—only a small raised scar. Okay, so she wasn't in the hospital. The thumping in her chest slowed.

She stared blinking at Jackson while the last remnants of shock lingered in her mind. He sat on the edge of the bed, leaning toward her, a book clutched in one hand. A lock of dark brown hair had fallen forward across his high forehead. Reaching up, he pulled his fingers through it repeatedly, brushing it back as he watched her.

"W-w-where are we?"

"Sam, we're in Minnesota, remember? Renting a cabin at Elk Horn Lake for the summer?"

That's right—away from the city, to rest, to help her battered body heal. Now she remembered.

Scrubbing her face with her hands, she tried to rub away the memory of the dream. Every night she feared sleep. Every night some variation crept out of the recesses of her mind to torture her.

"Did I scream?" she mumbled into her hands. "Did I wake you?"

"No," he replied, setting the book down, "you didn't scream this time. You moaned. I was still up reading. I thought you were having spasms again."

He'd been reading in the guest room, she thought with a stab of guilt. Since her "accident," as her mother liked to call it, Jackson couldn't share her bed any longer. They'd discovered that his sleeping in the same bed only made the nightmares worse. In the beginning they'd tried to rationalize them away. Just the aftershocks of the trauma she'd suffered. They kept telling each other the dreams would eventually stop, but they hadn't, and now she felt powerless as the intimacy they'd shared slipped away.

Dropping her hands, she caught Jackson staring at her legs. In her tossing and turning, her long nightgown had worked its way up her thighs. Her shriveled left leg now lay bare and exposed on the cool, cotton sheets. His eyebrows knitted together, and she watched as the corner of his mouth curled downward.

She grabbed the sheet and yanked it over her leg, hiding it.

With a shake of his head, he raised his eyes to her face. "It was a bad one this time, wasn't it?" he asked in a low voice. "Do you want to tell me about it?"

"First, I heard a window break, then voices. They were talking while they ransacked the house," she said, plucking at the sheet covering her left leg. "They said they were going to kill us. They were laughing about what they'd do to us." A shudder shook her shoulders, and Jackson's hand reached out for her, but stopped short of touching her. "I thought they'd found me again," she finished in a whisper.

A soft sigh stirred the air between them. "It was just a dream. Those assholes aren't looking for you. The attack happened because you were in the wrong place, at the wrong time. A hundred and twenty miles from here . . ." He paused. "They didn't know your name then, and they don't know it now."

"How do you know? They're still out there, aren't they? The police never made an arrest."

"Sam, you're safe," he said, lowering his head and pinching the bridge of his nose. "Your father's influence kept your name out of the press, and your credit cards and ID were still in your purse."

"But—"

He held up a hand, stopping her, and his voice took on a hard edge. "Again, Sam . . . it was just a dream. You can't continue to let your fears torment you."

She threw off the sheet and scooted across the bed to sit on the opposite side, making sure to keep her leg covered with the corner of the blanket.

"But it seemed so real. Just like the ones I had in the hospital." She looked over her shoulder at him. "The voices stopped, and all I could hear was my heart. I didn't know if they'd found you. I tried to get up, but my legs wouldn't move."

Jackson shifted his position to face her. "Have you discussed this with Dr. Weissinger?"

Dropping her chin, she stared at the floor. "Of course."

He braced his arm on the bed and leaned closer. His brown eyes, once full of charm, were now full of concern as he tugged on the corner of his mouth before speaking.

"Have you really?"

*Here we go again*, she thought. *Sam, are you taking your meds? Sam, did you do your exercises? Sam, you need to try harder.*

Irritation shot through her and she stood awkwardly. "What? Now you want to add lying to the list of grievances against me?" She walked to the window, her left leg dragging slightly on the hardwood floor.

"I never said you were a liar," he replied gently, "but I don't believe you're always honest with Dr. Weissinger. He's your psychiatrist, Sam, but he can't help you if you don't tell him what's going on."

"I know that." Suddenly chilled, she rubbed her bare arms. "I'm not stupid."

Jackson gave a soft groan. "I never said you were. But Dr. Weissinger might be able to give you some different meds that will help with the nightmares."

"Right, *Dr.* Van Horn." She twisted around to look at him. "That's the answer you doctors have for everything, isn't it? Write a scrip, make it all better—better living doped up on meds," she said in a rough voice. "That's what the antidepressants are supposed to do, isn't it? To make it all better. But they're not working, are they?"

"You have to give it time, Sam. You suffered a serious trauma. You'd be dead if the security guard hadn't acted so quickly. You need time to heal."

"Time? Ha, what do you call eight months?" She felt the bitterness snake through her. "Eight months since they made me beg, on my knees, for my life." Her voice rose. "Eight months since that son of a bitch cracked my skull with a tire iron."

Jackson shook his head as his eyes traveled to the nightstand and the array of pill bottles. Seeing a picture frame lying face-down next to them, he picked it up.

Sam felt her heart squeeze. It was a picture of them on the ski slopes at Vail, taken the week Jackson had proposed. He'd put it in an expensive walnut frame and had insisted that she keep it on her nightstand.

"Why did you turn this over?" he asked, holding the picture frame toward her.

Looking away, she shrugged one shoulder. "I must've knocked it over during my dream."

"Then why aren't the pill bottles—" He cut himself off. "Never mind," he said, setting the picture back on the nightstand.

Her eyes returned to the smiling faces in the picture staring at her from across the room. Smiling faces now surrounded by pill bottles. The woman in the picture had never taken pills to stop her dreams, pills to stop her fear. She'd been strong and capable.

*And you'll never be that woman again*, jeered a voice inside her head.

Unable to bear looking at the person she'd been, she turned away. She felt Jackson wrap his arms around her. "It'll be okay," he whispered. "We'll get through this."

She jerked away from him and limped toward the bed. Why did Jackson and her parents think a simple pat on the head with a "Don't worry, Sam" would make it all go away? They didn't get it.

As she sank to the bed, her eyes flashed with anger and with a wave of her hand, she brushed Jackson's book off the bed. "Oh yeah? Easy for you to say—you weren't the one in a coma for months—all the time dreaming one terrible dream after another, unable to wake up and escape the dreams." She hugged herself tightly, and drawing a deep breath, let the frustration pour out. "You don't have a leg that doesn't work right because of nerve damage. You're still the same person you were a year ago. I'm not."

"You—" He clenched his jaw and stopped abruptly. "You're upset and, well, never mind. If you're going to be okay, I think I'll go back to bed. I'll leave the door of the guest room open in case you need me."

Sam's hand shot out as she felt the tears gather. She'd hurt him again. Something she'd been doing a lot lately. "Wait . . ."

Pausing in the doorway, he turned, his face calm and his expression unreadable.

"I'm sorry," she said, clearing her throat. "I don't mean to be such a bitch, Jackson. I—"

"I *do* understand, Sam," he said swiftly while he held up a hand to stop her. "Dr. Weissinger told us to expect these mood swings." He paused as if he were carefully picking his next words. "But it might help if you'd remember your life isn't the only one that's changed." With a shake of his head, he turned and walked out of the room.

She stared at the open doorway for a moment. Great, he was not only hurt, but angry. What would she do if he finally got fed up with her and left, not only her bedroom, but her life? He'd become her anchor and there were days when only the dream of their future together kept her going. Until Jackson, her focus had been her work, and she'd never met anyone who'd made her want to change. She had avoided commitment, but he'd changed all that when he breezed into her life at a concert, one of her mother's many charity benefits. Both of his parents had been patrons of the arts, devoting time and money to help struggling musicians, and since their deaths, he'd continued their good works. After the concert, he'd wooed her relentlessly with flowers, dinners, and thoughtful gifts.

Her eyes filled with tears again as she looked down at her left hand and the three-carat diamond Jackson had so proudly placed on her finger. It was all going to be perfect. After the wedding, they were moving into his family home, a wonderful Victorian, nestled in the woods and newly restored to her precise specifications. She dashed away the tears and rubbed the muscle in her left thigh. The work that the carpenters had done on the staircase with its curving walnut banister had delighted her, but now it reminded her of Mount McKinley. How could she negotiate the high risers when she had trouble walking across the room?

If Jackson did leave her, what would her family say? Her father had been thrilled when they starting dating. He was proud of the fact she was marrying a successful plastic surgeon. He said he couldn't have chosen a better match for her if he'd have picked Jackson himself. He'd even agreed to a donation for a new wing at the hospital as an engagement present.

She had to stop being such a bitch. She had to change . . . but how? Every time she tried to show him how much she loved him, her fears, her resentment over the way her life had changed, strangled every word, every action.

Rising, she limped back to the window. Lifting her hand, she let it linger over the cord used to raise the blinds. She wanted to open them. She wanted to see the starry night sky, but she was afraid, afraid that someone might be out there in the night, in the woods, watching the cabin, watching her.

Letting her hand fall to her side, she crossed to the bed and sat. Her left leg felt stiff and she rubbed her thigh absentmindedly. Only thirty-five, she felt more like eighty. Leaning back and using her elbows for balance, she slid her feet forward until her lower legs were away from the bed. Even with her nightgown covering them, she could see the difference between her right and left legs. The right looked normal . . . the left, shrunken with wasted muscle. She took a deep breath and lifted them, just like the therapist had shown her. Her right leg rose to a foot off the floor, but her left wavered only inches above it. Closing her eyes, she concentrated on her brain making the connection with muscles in her leg. A thin sheen of sweat dampened her forehead as the leg rose another inch.

*Yes*, she thought triumphantly, *just a little higher.*

A spasm hit, sending pain shooting up her leg. With a groan, she let both feet drop.

A sense of weariness swamped her. Would her leg ever be strong again? She was tired of the whole thing, tired of trying, tired of everyone's quiet voices giving her the answer she didn't want . . . *"It takes time—just be patient."*

Well, how *much* time would it take? Would she ever be able to walk normally? Would she stop jumping at sudden noises? Would she enjoy the warmth of the sun on her face ever again without the overwhelming fear that someone was lurking and waiting to pounce? Would the dreams go away?

Time was running out. Not only on her relationship with Jackson, but on her career, too. Her dad had already given her old job at his advertising agency to her former assistant, Dan Borden. Dan was now her father's right hand, not her. What if he proved himself indispensable? Lawrence Moore wasn't a fool. He wouldn't replace a valued employee with her just because she was his daughter. Nepotism didn't go that far with her dad.

*No Jackson—no career.* The thought made her stomach clench.

From the corner of her eye, she spied her cell phone lying on the nightstand next to the pill bottles and the picture. Flipping the picture facedown, she picked up the phone and stared at it. If only she knew what was happening at the agency, she'd feel that she wasn't out of the loop. That she had something waiting for her at the end of her struggle. She could focus on the future, and not the now.

Using speed dial, she called Dan's private number. So maybe it was past midnight, but Dan was a night owl, and in the past they'd shared many late-night calls. He'd been not only her assistant, but her friend. He wouldn't mind.

"Hey, Dan," she said with forced brightness when the groggy voice on the other end answered.

"Samantha!" he exclaimed, suddenly wide-awake.

"I know it's late," she said, the words rushing out.

"Is something wrong? Are you okay?"

"No, nothing's wrong. I'm fine," she replied, trying to keep the need out of her voice. "I'm sorry. I thought you'd still be up. I didn't mean to wake you."

"That's okay . . . it's . . . um . . . well . . . we've been busy lately. I've put in some pretty long hours, so I've been turning in earlier when I can."

"I'm sorry," she apologized again. "I'll let you go so you can get back to sleep."

"No, really, it's okay. What's up?"

"Nothing . . ." She hesitated. "I was just wondering how everything's going."

There was a long pause on the line

"Fine . . . good," Dan answered cautiously.

"Did you land the Schwitzer account?"

"Yes."

"Is everything going well in the art department?"

"About like normal," he replied, not really answering her question.

She plucked at the blanket and felt her desperation rise. "Having any problems with Marcus? Maybe I could give you some advice on how to handle him." She tried to chuckle. "You know how those artsy types are. Always going off on a tangent and ignoring the client's wishes."

"We've had a few disagreements, but not bad."

"Nothing like the time he wanted to use a purple-and-pink background in the ad for the sporting-goods company?"

She heard him hesitate.

"No, nothing like that," he said finally.

"That's good. How about Ed? Is—"

"Let's not talk about the agency," he said, cutting her off. "How are you doing? Are you enjoying the lake? Your dad said Jackson had spent a summer there when he was a teenager and loved it. That's why he suggested they send you there," he said, suddenly talkative. "It must be beautiful this time of year."

Sam thought about the darkness waiting outside the cabin windows, thought about what lurked in the woods ringing the property.

"Oh, sure," she lied. "It's great up here; really, ah, peaceful."

"Is Jackson staying up there with you?"

"No, he has too many patients to take the whole summer off. He'll be driving up on the weekends."

Dan laughed. "We ought to know . . . it's all about image, isn't it. A plastic surgeon's life has to be pretty hectic. All those women who want it nipped, tucked, and sucked." His tone grew serious. "It's good your dad's hired someone to look after you while Jackson's gone. It's going—"

"What?" she broke in, frowning. "Dad's hired someone to stay with me?"

"Ah, well," he stammered. "Lawrence mentioned that they've hired a woman, a physical therapy assistant, to help you."

"A nursemaid," she stated flatly.

"He—he didn't say she'd be living with you. I'm—I'm—"

Sam sighed into the receiver. "Don't worry, Dan. I'll talk to Dad about it. You just caught me off guard, that's all."

"You won't tell him I told you, will you?" he asked with a twinge of fear in his voice.

"No."

Dan cleared his throat and his tone became stronger. "With you being alone during the week, I know he's worried . . ."

*About her mental stability*, she thought, filling in the blank.

"He's only trying to protect you," Dan finished.

*Protect her?* A realization hit her. "Dad told you not to talk to me about work, didn't he?"

"Um, well . . ." His voice trailed away.

Dan always blushed easily, and Sam could imagine the pink infusing his pale face.

"He wants you to concentrate on your recovery," Dan blurted out. "He doesn't want you to worry about what's happening down here in Minneapolis."

"But, Dan," she pleaded, "I need—"

"I agree with him," he forcefully interrupted her. "You know how much stress there is down here, and your dad knows that you don't need it."

Great, everyone knew what she needed better than she did. She closed her eyes and shook her head. There was no point in arguing with him. Dan was a company man, and there was no way he'd ever go against Lawrence Moore.

"He's probably right," she said, defeated.

A soft chuckle sounded in her ear. "Lawrence is *always* right."

"Look, I've kept you long enough. Sorry for waking you."

"Not a problem, Sam. I miss you." He paused. "One last thing—the paintings in my, er, *your* office?"

"The cityscapes that I did in college?"

"Yeah. Lawrence had *your* office redecorated—"

"Really?" she asked, not hiding the irritation in her voice.

"Yes, but he had a good reason," Dan said, rushing in. "He wanted it to have a fresh look when you came back." He hurried on before she could respond. "He suggested we donate them to the charity auction that they're having for the Minnesota Museum of American Art, but I thought you might want them. I'll ship them to you."

A thousand thoughts cruised through her mind, but she knew Dan wouldn't understand them any better than Jackson or her parents did.

"Thanks," she said simply.

"You're welcome. I knew it was the right thing to do," Dan said proudly. "You'd better get some sleep, Sam. Great talking to you," he said before he clicked off his phone.

"Bye, Dan," she said to empty air, feeling like a door had just been slammed in her face.

# Two

Anne Weaver never walked, she marched. Today, her long legs ate up the distance between her car and the small house she shared with her teenage son, Caleb. She stopped midstride as her eyes took in her yard with its thin blades of grass fighting for a toehold in the sandy soil and the white trim around the windows, badly in need of a new paint job.

Where was Caleb? He should be helping her lug all these groceries inside. With a shake of her head, she hoisted the bags higher in her arms and mounted the steps of the porch. As she yanked the screen door open with one hand, her ears were assaulted by the loud voice of a TV announcer assuring her for only $19.95 his product could tackle any laundry problem she had.

Guess she knew where Caleb was—plopped on the couch, his size-eleven feet dangling over the arm. That kid would lose his hearing if he didn't start turning down the volume on the TV.

Groaning, she continued her way down the short hallway to the kitchen located at the back of the house.

"Caleb!" she yelled over the sound as she set the bags of groceries on the counter. "Turn the TV down!"

The TV continued to blare.

"Caleb!"

"What?" a voice whispered in her ear.

Jerking her hand to her chest, she spun around to see her son grinning at her. "That's not funny . . . sneaking up on me. I could have had a heart attack," she said with a stern look.

Dressed in a navy T-shirt and cutoffs, Caleb rolled his eyes while his grin widened into a smile.

Watching him, she was struck by how much he'd grown over the past year. Why, he could look her straight in the eye now.

Her expression softened, and without thinking, she brushed a shock of blond hair off his forehead. "Where were you?"

"Out in the garage," he said, pulling one of the bags close to check out the contents.

"And you left the TV—"

"Okay, okay, I'll shut it off." Caleb lumbered out of the kitchen. A minute later, the living room fell silent.

"Finally," Anne muttered to herself while she unpacked the groceries.

Returning to the kitchen, Caleb grabbed one of the bags again and started to rummage through it. "Get anything good?"

Yanking the sack toward her, she removed a bag of carrots and waved them in front of his face. "These."

"Oh, yum," he shot back as he foraged through another sack. "No chips or salsa?"

"Carrots are healthier," she said, placing them on the counter. She didn't add the words *and cheaper.* Ever since that kid had hit puberty, it was impossible to keep food in the house. Anything in the fridge was fair game, just as long as it hadn't turned green and fuzzy. And even then, she suspected he scraped off the fuzz and ate it anyway.

Caleb jumped up on the counter, his long legs dangling, and

ripped open the bag of carrots. "So, are you excited about your new job?" he asked between chomps.

"Oh, I don't know," she replied, opening the refrigerator and placing the ketchup next to the bottle of mustard. Moving the bottle of mayonnaise to the left, she placed a jar of pickles by the mustard. "I haven't met the patient yet, only her father and fiancé."

Caleb didn't speak for a moment while his mother rearranged the contents of the fridge. Finally, he broke his silence.

"Why are you nervous?"

"I'm not nervous," Anne replied, glancing over her shoulder at her son.

Caleb hopped off the counter and crossed the short space between them. "Hmm." He pointed to the straight row of condiments. "Ketchup, mustard, pickles, mayo. All you're missing is a hamburger and bun." Placing his hands on his knees, he leaned forward and peered at the second shelf. "And here we have milk and Hershey's chocolate side by side, then on the next shelf—"

"Okay, okay," she said, swinging the door shut. "I get it. I'm grouping again."

He relaxed against the fridge and cocked his head. "At least this time you didn't alphabetize everything."

Lifting an eyebrow, she gave him a wry look before moving to the sink. She picked up the dishcloth and began wiping down the clean counter.

Caleb followed. Laying a hand on his mother's, he stilled her swift movements. "So? What's bugging you?"

With a sigh, she let go of the cloth and turned, propping a hip against the counter. Crossing her arms over her chest, she shook her head. "I don't know . . . during my interview with Mr. Moore and Dr. Van Horn, I couldn't help thinking that they were leaving things out."

"Like what?"

"I'm not sure. Maybe her injuries are more severe than they were letting on." She gave a slight shrug. "The whole conversation was just 'off' somehow."

He dropped a hand on her shoulder. "You worry too much, Mom."

"You know, Caleb, you would, too, if . . . oh, never mind." She pushed off from the counter and walked over to her purse sitting on the kitchen table. Taking out her checkbook and pen, she quickly deducted the grocery check from her balance. With a frown, she slapped the checkbook shut and tossed it and the pen into her bag.

"Not good?" he asked, noticing her expression.

Feeling Caleb's eyes still on her, Anne forced a smile. "Ah, it'll be okay," she replied with a wave of her hand. "I'd hoped Mr. Moore would offer more, but I'll still be able to sock at least part of it into your college fund."

Caleb looked away. "What's the deal with this lady?" he asked, snagging a handful of carrots. "Everyone at Esther's was talking about her."

"Samantha Moore?"

He nodded.

"As she was leaving work, she was attacked in the parking garage by a group of young men—"

"A gang?"

Anne nodded. "It sounds like it. They really don't know. She was beaten and, during the beating, sustained a head injury that put her in a coma. When she came out of it, she couldn't give the police much of a description, but a security guard saw her attackers running away. He thought they were wearing gang colors."

She eyed her son. What if they'd been forced to stay in the

Cities? In some crummy apartment. Would Caleb have been sucked into that life, too? The thought made her shiver. They'd been so lucky . . . her getting a job as a physical therapy assistant at the county hospital in Pardo and inheriting this house from her grandmother. It had been a struggle. Raising a kid alone. It seemed that there was never enough money, but they got by. And now, in another year, Caleb would be off to college to major in prelaw. He wouldn't make the same mistakes she had. His life would be better, easier. She was determined to make it so.

Lost in her thoughts, she missed the remark Caleb had just made. "I'm sorry. What did you say?"

"Um, well." He traced a seam in the worn linoleum with the toe of his tennis shoe. "I said I ran into Teddy Brighton today, and—"

"Caleb!" she exclaimed, cutting him off. "That kid's bad news. How many times have I told you to stay away from him?"

"Jeez, Mom, he's not that bad."

Anne's eyebrows disappeared under her fringed bangs. "Really? Tell that to the Abernathys, Greg, Fritz Thorpe," she said, her fingers ticking off each name, "the Mich—"

Caleb grasped her hand to stop her. "It was just a harmless prank. No one was hurt."

"You're right, no one was injured, but untying all those boats last summer and setting them adrift was *not* harmless." She squeezed his hand that was holding hers for emphasis. "It not only inconvenienced those people, but their boats could've been damaged, floating around the lake like that."

"Mr. Brighton took care of it," he argued. "He pulled all the boats back in and made Teddy apologize to everyone."

"Humph," she snorted, releasing his hand. "One of these days, Teddy's going to do something that his dad can't fix."

"No, he won't. He's changed. I think military school straightened him out."

"I don't care if that school named him student of the year, I still don't want you hanging out with him."

"But just listen." His voice took on a note of excitement. "He's going to be up here all summer and his folks are letting him have a party in a couple of weeks. He asked me if my band would play—"

"Caleb—"

"Mom, come on," he pleaded. "He said he'd pay us."

"Right. And you'll be using the money to bail yourself out of jail." She drilled him with her eyes. "Do you remember the last party Teddy had? The cops busted it and several kids got hauled in for underage drinking. You're almost eighteen now. Soon they'll be able to arrest you and print your name in the paper."

"Mom," he argued in a determined voice, "it's just a job. I won't be partying with Teddy and his friends."

"You'd better not," she said with a quick nod. "The Brightons have always let Teddy run wild, and I'm not—"

"Look," he interrupted, "it's not only a chance to make money with the band. Mr. Brighton's got connections and—"

Her eyes narrowed. "What kind of connections?"

Caleb dropped his head and wouldn't look at her. "With a recording studio in Minneapolis," he mumbled.

Exasperated, she crossed the kitchen and, grabbing the dishcloth, began to furiously wipe off the counter again. "It's a pipe dream. For every band that makes it, thousands don't. I'm not going to let you throw away your education to go chasing after something that'll never happen."

His head shot up. "You mean like you did?"

Tossing the cloth in the sink, she whirled on him. "Yes. Exactly like me."

"But I'm good, Mom, *really* good." Lifting his chin, he looked her square in the eye. "Even Mr. Thorpe says so, and you know how picky he is."

"I should've never sent you to him for piano lessons," she muttered.

"Wouldn't have made a difference. Mr. Thorpe didn't teach me guitar. I taught myself," he replied defensively. "I can do it, Mom, I know I can. Just because you didn't make it as a model in New York doesn't mean I won't make it as a musician. It's different!"

Fisting her hands on her hips, Anne glared at him. "We're not going to discuss this now," she insisted. "You still have another year of high school. You need to focus on school."

A mutinous look pinched Caleb's face. *God*, she thought, *he's so young. He doesn't have a clue. He doesn't understand how life can chew you up and spit you out.*

"I don't want to argue," she said, passing a hand across her forehead. Dropping it, she turned and opened a cupboard door. "Dang it, I forgot bread." With a sigh, she grabbed her purse off the kitchen table and fished out her car keys. "I've got to run down to Dunlap's," she said, referring to the small country store and gas station located two miles from the lake. "I'll be back in a minute." She glanced over her shoulder at Caleb, leaning against the counter, and stopped.

His face still wore a defiant expression and his eyes were angry and hard. Without a word, he shoved away from the counter and brushed past her as he strode into the living room. A moment later, the TV blared.

The argument with Caleb still troubled Anne as she pulled her car into the small parking lot at Dunlap's and stopped. She hated fighting with him, but she couldn't let him pursue this cockeyed dream. Resting her head on the steering wheel, she took several deep breaths. She had to play it smart. She knew from experience that the more she hassled him about going to college, the harder he'd resist her. It had been so much easier when he was four and she was bigger than him. When he didn't listen to her, all she had to do was give him a "time-out." Unfortunately, time-outs didn't work so well with eighteen-year-olds. The sudden image of Caleb's now-lanky frame folded onto his little desk chair that he'd used as a kid made her smile.

Raising her head, she shut off the car and pocketed the keys. They'd work it out. Somehow she'd figure out a way to show him the foolishness of his plan. Somehow she'd convince him her way was better.

The sound of cars whizzing by caught Anne's attention.

Dunlap's sat at the intersection of two main highways. Head north and you'd wind up in Duluth . . . head west and you'd find yourself in North Dakota. It was a prime location and Esther Dunlap made the most of it. A grocery store/motel/gas station; she fleeced not only the local residents and vacationers with her inflated prices, but also weary travelers by offering something other than convenience-store fare. Homemade sandwiches, pastries, fresh baked pies, premium ice cream. So what if you paid twice what you would in a larger town? So what if the gas was at least a nickel more than at the Shell station twenty miles down the road? Esther had a corner on the market and she knew it.

The gas station/grocery store sat in a graveled parking lot, with the motel sitting by itself a few yards away. Around to the back of the five units, there was a view of a small bay, located just off the main part of the lake. The Dunlaps—Esther and her son, Edward—lived on the second floor of the main building, right above the grocery store. Very little mention was ever made of Mr. Dunlap, who had died when Edward was a baby. According to rumors, Esther felt he had served his purpose by providing her with a son, and once he was gone, there was no need to ever think of him again.

Anne exited the car and crossed the parking lot, past the two gasoline pumps. Mounting the steps of the wide porch that surrounded the building, she paused at the doorway to let a couple of vacationers pass by on their way out of the store. She acknowledged them with a small smile and a nod. Once inside, she immediately saw Esther on her perch behind the counter.

Like a queen surveying her kingdom, Esther kept a sharp eye on all the customers milling about the store. God forbid someone should rip her off by taking a five-finger discount on any of her goods. Anne watched Esther lean forward on her stool and her face tighten when she spotted the Baxter twins, a pair of towheaded eight-year-olds who were perusing the candy bars. Her fixed look stayed on them until they moved away and joined their parents in the next aisle. Crossing her arms over her ample chest, she settled her short, squat body on her perch before focusing on the next potential thief.

On her way to the shelves holding the bread, Anne noticed Kimberly Brighton, Teddy's mother, and her mother-in-law, Irene. Not wanting to engage in conversation, she looked quickly away, but not before taking in how Kimberly was dressed. It was Saturday morning at the lake, yet Kimberly looked as if she'd been at a spa. Her whole look was polished, and Anne knew that her simple, tailored blouse probably cost more than Anne's monthly grocery budget. Add in her Capris, gold bracelets jangling at her wrist, and woven leather sandals, and Anne could make her car payment with the money that woman was wearing. She looked down at her own clothes—T-shirt, shorts, and flip-flops picked up on sale at Walmart. Nope, nothing polished about her.

With a wry grin, she snagged a loaf of bread and wove her way past the other customers to the counter.

"Will this be all?" Esther asked, picking up the bread. "Don't you need anything else?"

*Not likely*, Anne thought sarcastically. Like she'd part with any more of her hard-earned money on Esther's overpriced wares.

Giving her a bright smile, Anne ignored Esther's obvious disappointment. "Nope, this is it."

"Well then." From behind her thick glasses, Esther's gaze fell on Anne's purse. "I'm sure you'd like to settle your charges."

"What charges?"

"Caleb's." She reached under the counter and withdrew a recipe box containing sales tickets. After thumbing through them for a moment, she pulled one out. "Here it is. For ten gallons of gas, a box of Ho Hos, and a Mountain Dew."

"May I see that, please?"

Reluctantly Esther handed over the yellow sales slip.

As Anne skimmed the spidery writing, her heart sank. Forty dollars out of a weekly budget that was already stretched too far. She stopped at the last charge. "What's the extra five dollars for?"

"Service charge."

"You tack on—" Anne stopped herself. It was pointless to argue with Esther about the bill, but wait until she got home . . . Caleb would hear about running up charges without her permission.

Anne extracted the money from her billfold and handed it to Esther. "I'll talk to Caleb, but from now on, I don't want him charging."

"That's between you and him," Esther said as she swiftly hit the buttons on the antique cash register, ringing up Anne's total. "I hear you have a new patient."

"Yes."

"You're not still working at the hospital?"

Tugging on her bottom lip, Anne's gaze fell to the counter. Everyone around the lake had heard of the layoffs at the hospital and she knew Esther was no exception. Esther must want the details, but Anne had no intention of giving them to her.

Raising her head, she met Esther's speculative look head-on. "I'll be going back this fall," she replied curtly as she mentally crossed her fingers.

"Good thing you have a new job, isn't it?" Esther asked, sacking the loaf of bread. Pushing her glasses up on her nose, she leaned against the counter and angled her head. "Jane McGill said that your new patient is staying at the old Jones place."

From behind her, Anne heard a gasp. She glanced over her shoulder to see Irene Brighton glaring at them. Looking back at Esther, she watched as the woman's attention traveled to Irene. A small satisfied smirk hovered at the corner of her mouth. "That cabin's cursed," she said smugly. She paused dramatically, her focus never shifting from Irene. "If those walls could talk—"

"Kimberly, let's go," Irene interrupted. "I just remembered the last gallon of milk I bought here curdled within two days."

The smirk fell away from Esther's face as the Brightons strode past, the scent of their expensive perfume following in their wake.

Esther's whole face puckered as she stared at their retreating backs. "Uppity woman. She's not half as good as she thinks she is," she muttered, shoving the sack across the counter.

Choosing not to respond, Anne took the bag and made her own way out of the store. Just like everyone else living in the small lake community, she'd heard the stories. Heard all about Blanche Jones and her wild ways . . . the parties . . . the affairs, but my God, it had all happened years ago. Blanche was long gone. According to gossip, she'd run off with one of her lovers, abandoning her much older husband, Harley. A short time later, he'd left the lake, too, after selling the cabin to an insurance agent in Pardo who'd used it as a rental property off and on ever since.

As Anne stepped off the porch, she caught sight of a red shirt ducking around the corner of the building.

"Edward," she called out as she rushed after him. "Wait."

Rounding the side of the grocery store, she saw Edward patiently waiting for her. He stood with one arm clasped across his stomach, staring out over the water. Even at this distance, Anne could see the redness of the skin on that arm, the swelling, and the way his fingers curled like a claw.

He turned toward her and a shadow of a smile eased the lines of pain bracketing his mouth.

"Hey, I missed you on Thursday," she said, striding up to him.

Edward's gaze traveled down to the arm resting at his waist then back to Anne's face. "Sorry I stood you up for my appointment. Mother had a long to-do list and I couldn't get away."

"Your therapy is important, too, Edward," Anne chided. "It helps with the pain, doesn't it?"

He turned away from her, watching a duck cruise the lily pads looking for water bugs. "Some, but after twenty-five years, Anne, I doubt there's a lot even you can do."

"If you don't think the ultrasound is helping, there's more we can try," she insisted. "Dr. Osgood might prescribe a nerve block or a drug pump. Maybe spinal-cord stimulation would help." She caught his eyes. "And if you'd consider talking to a psychiatrist . . ."

Taking a step away from her, he shook his head. "I'm not talking to a shrink," he said with determination.

"But, Edward—"

The sudden slam of a door and the sound of heavy steps crossing the porch stopped her.

"Edward! Edward!" Esther's shrill voice rang out, startling the duck. With an indignant quack, it took flight.

At the sound of the duck, Esther's head popped around the corner of the building. Seeing Anne talking with Edward made her jaw clench and her lips form a thin line.

"Edward," she said in a brusque voice. "Quit lollygagging. We've got customers waiting for that bait." Not pausing for him to obey, she spun in her sensible shoes and lumbered back to the store.

He began to walk swiftly away. "I got to go."

"Will you keep your appointment this week?" Anne called after him.

"I'll try," he said over his shoulder before disappearing inside the bait house.

Discouraged, Anne trudged off to her car. Pulling out of the parking lot, she couldn't get over Esther's attitude. Edward suffered from complex regional pain syndrome, a fancy name for a disease that caused him constant pain. One would think Esther would support her son in his attempts to find relief. But no. It seemed all she did was interfere.

Anne shook her head as she turned down the lane leading to her house. Why? Was Esther afraid that if Edward learned to control the pain, he wouldn't be dependent on her any longer? She couldn't understand it.

# Three

Tiny points of yellow glow from in between the tall pines. One by one they flicker out as the night deepens and the witching hour approaches. Finally, the last one extinguishes and peace descends.

At last I'm alone in the dark.

*No*, says the voice inside my head, *you're not alone . . . she's still here, waiting for you.*

"Stop," I whisper aloud to silence the voice. "I'm not going to think about it now."

I cross the deck and open the screen door, heading for my private stash. A bottle of Glenlivet single-malt Scotch. I pour three fingers and swirl the deep gold liquid around in the glass. The rich floral scent fills the air around me. Taking a small sip, I close my eyes and savor its mellow taste. Content, I walk to the stereo and hit play. The poignant strains of Debussy's "Clair de Lune" soar from the speakers. My fingers move in time with each haunting note, as if I were playing.

A satisfied smile plays at the corners of my mouth, and after adjusting the volume, I return to my place on the deck overlooking the lake. Pulling up a chair, I prop my feet on the railing and tip my head back, letting the music carry me away.

*Far, far away*, coaxes the voice in my head. In my solitude, I can imagine I'm anywhere in the world except here. New York, Paris, London . . . cities with sophistication and class, cities with excitement and energy. That's where I belong. Not here in the woods, part of a sleepy backwater community whose biggest thrill is a weekend fishing tournament.

My grip on the glass tightens.

It's not my fault I'm here. If they'd give me the opportunities that I deserve, if *she* didn't hold me back, I could be in one of those cities right now, engaged in witty conversation with important people.

My eyelids drift shut as the scene plays out in my mind. Me, at a party surrounded by elegantly dressed men and women. They're smiling as they hang on my every brilliant word, and I know they're thinking, *My, how clever he is!* Below us, the lights of the city sparkle, and in the distance, the hum of traffic drifts through the concrete canyons. The atmosphere is so *alive*. Electric. It energizes me and I see myself achieving every dream.

I open my eyes and the image vanishes. Reality. I'm not surrounded by bright city lights, just stars shining overhead, and the only sound I hear over the music is the call of a loon.

*Silly birds*, I think, downing my Scotch and standing. *They say loons mate for life.* The image of her battered face flips through my mind. Nothing lasts forever?

# Four

The thud of running shoes echoed. They were closing in. Part of her wanted to stop, turn around, and confront her pursuers. Tell them to go away and leave her the hell alone. Another part of her—the one concerned with self-preservation—said, *Run . . . faster.*

She turned restlessly in her sleep, no more able to escape her nightmare than she'd been able to flee the parking garage.

Hands suddenly dug into her shoulders and spun her around with a force that made her head snap. The clip holding her hair in place smashed on the floor. Her Coach bag flew out of her hands and skittered across the concrete floor.

A young man, dressed in work pants slung low on his hips and a dark blue jersey, pressed his fingers into her tense muscles. "Hey, baby, whazup?" he asked.

Her eyes flew to his friends standing behind him. They chuckled. They all wore the same kind of pants. A couple of them had blue handkerchiefs hanging from the pocket. Their shoes had a Nike swoosh. But it was their eyes that made the sweat trickle down her spine. In the cold flickering light, their eyes, sharp and cunning, were the eyes of predators.

"Please, what do you want?" Sam pleaded, and tried to pull away from the young man.

The young man smiled as his hands gripped her tighter.

Wincing with pain, she stammered, "Please don't hurt me . . . I'll give you all my cash."

"Give?" He chuckled low in his throat. "You don't *give.* We take." His eyes caught the flash of her engagement ring. "Hey, this fine lady's getting married," he called over his shoulder to his buddies.

"Come on, man," one replied, shifting back and forth. "Quit fucking around. Grab the purse and the ring and let's go."

The young man holding her jerked his head toward his friend. "We go when I say we'll go." He looked back at Sam with pupils so dilated, his eyes were black. "I think we should give her a test run." He took a step closer and put his face next to hers. "Is that your car, lady?" he whispered, his hot breath tickling her ear.

*Oh God, they're going to rape me*, her brain screamed as her body turned boneless and she started a slow slide to the floor.

The young man's hands gripped the flesh of her upper arms and yanked her upright. When he saw her fear, the spark in his black eyes flared, as if her terror fed him. His excitement swirled around them, and she could smell it over the noxious fumes of the garage. Sour and musky.

"Please, please don't hurt me. I'll give you anything you want. Just let me go—please." The boy's face wavered as sudden tears blurred her vision.

The young man snickered. "Did you hear that? The fine lady's begging." He glanced at his companions. "Let's see if she'll beg on her knees."

Laughter followed while hands from behind forced her to her knees. The concrete felt cold and the chill traveled through her skin to settle in her bones. Her muscles trembled, but she couldn't tell if it was the cold or her fear that made them shake.

Sam's eyes flew to each face in the circle now gathered tightly around her, looking for sympathy and finding none. One boy, holding a tire iron in his fist, winked. *This can't be happening.* Beyond fear now, her shaking stopped while her brain disconnected from her body. She felt as if part of her were drifting away. Her gaze fell to the gray concrete.

"Okay, lady, start begging," said the young man standing in front of her.

"Please, please, I don't want to die," she whispered, each word rasping from her clogged throat.

Her head was wrenched back until she had no choice but to stare up at the young man standing over her.

"What's that? I didn't hear you."

She choked. "Please . . ."

A sudden voice rang out, reverberating through the empty garage. "Security! What the fuck are you doing!"

The hands fell away as their eyes flew to one another's faces in silent communication.

Slumping back on her heels as they released her, she gasped with relief.

The young man holding the tire iron took a step forward, glaring at her. And as if in slow motion, she saw him raise the tire iron high over his head . . .

Sam opened one eye slowly. The sun peeking through the slats cast thin horizontal bars across the wooden floor. So Jackson hadn't entered while she was sleeping and opened them. No one had been able to watch her while she slept.

She raised her head, shutting her eyes tightly against the dizziness she always experienced first thing in the morning. Her senses were foggy and her whole body felt wrapped in cotton. A slight headache gnawed at the base of her skull. Always the same. The dream. The headache. Would it ever end?

Opening her eyes, she struggled out of bed and headed for the bathroom.

Leaning against the sink, she forced herself to look at her face in the mirror. Dark circles ringed her eyes and her shoulder-length auburn hair looked as lifeless as she felt. She ran her fingers through her hair, pausing to trace the scar running down her scalp. Another lasting souvenir of her attack. Left by the incision the doctors had made to relieve the pressure caused by her brain swelling. She tugged at the hair sprouting around the puckered skin as if pulling on it would suddenly make it longer. *No, still short and still sticking out like a cowlick.* She hated the way it looked.

She dropped her hands and her gaze traveled downward. She'd gained back some of the weight she'd lost in the hospital, but she still looked like a refugee from a concentration camp. Underneath her nightgown, her breasts seemed to sag like sacks above bony ribs and hip bones that jutted out. Yup, she thought, all in all she was quite a looker. Glancing back at the mirror, she stuck out her tongue. Well, at least that looked normal.

As she turned on the faucet, the sound of rattling pans and the smell of brewing coffee drifted through the doorway. That's right . . . her parents were making the two-hour drive up from Minneapolis for brunch. A long drive for just a meal, but after her conversation with Dan, she knew her dad had an agenda. He and Jackson were going to tag-team her into agreeing to a babysitter. Well, it wasn't going to happen. Just because her left leg didn't work perfectly didn't make her an invalid.

She splashed cold water on her face and rubbed hard. No way

was she going to allow a stranger to take care of her. They hired this woman . . . they could just as well fire her. Drying her face, she opened the medicine cabinet to grab her brush. Maybe today, and with enough gel and hair spray, she could tame the cowlick.

Her brush was gone.

*Where is it?* She shoved the assortment of pill bottles out of the way, knocking several over. They spilled out of the cabinet, rattling as they rolled down the porcelain sink. It wasn't in the cabinet, she thought with a rising sense of panic.

It was always in the cabinet. Ever since returning home from the hospital, she'd been careful about placing her things exactly in the same spot every day. Her brush on the second shelf; her slippers on the right side of the bed; her robe draped across a chair. It gave her a small sense of control over a life that had changed so dramatically.

She ripped open the top drawer with enough force to pull it off its rollers. The end tipped downward, dumping washcloths and hand towels onto the tiled floor.

"What are you doing?"

Sam shot a glance over her shoulder to see Jackson standing in the doorway, watching her.

Grabbing the edge of the sink for balance, she squatted down and began to pick up the towels. "I couldn't find my brush."

With two steps, he was beside her. He grabbed her upper arm and hoisted her to her feet. "There's no need to turn the place upside down trying to find it," he said. "Maybe you left it in the bedroom."

She shook her head. "No, I *know* I left it in the cabinet." Turning toward him, she saw the expression on his face. *Sam's losing it.* "Okay, I'll go look."

With uneven steps, she went into the bedroom and began

searching. Jackson followed and stood in the doorway watching her. With a sigh, he turned and left, only to return a moment later.

"Is this it?" he asked, waving the brush at her.

She grabbed it out of his hand. "Where did you find it?"

His lips tightened in a frown. "On the second shelf in the medicine cabinet."

"But . . . but," she stammered as her fingers gripped the smooth wooden handle. "I looked . . . I swear, it wasn't—"

A loud knock on the front door of the cabin interrupted her.

"It doesn't matter, Sam," Jackson said with a glance over his shoulder. "Your parents are here. Hurry up and get dressed. Brunch will be ready soon."

Alone, Sam sank down on the bed and stared at the brush in her hand. She didn't care what Jackson said, the brush hadn't been on the shelf. She would've seen it. Tipping her head back, she stared at the ceiling. *Unless her eyesight was beginning to betray her, too.*

"Let it go," she murmured to herself, "and calm down."

Leaving the brush on the bed, she stood and crossed to the closet. If she wanted to convince her father and Jackson that she would be okay staying alone, she didn't need to be acting hysterical over a missing brush. She pulled out a pair of jeans and took a moment picking out the right shirt. Something flattering. Appearances had always been important to her parents. If she looked more like her old self, they'd be more likely to listen to her.

Makeup might help, she thought, touching the side of her face. In her past life, she would've never considered going without it, but now it had been so long since she'd worn any, her skills at achieving that flawless look were rusty.

She dressed as quickly as she could. As she slid her feet into a pair of black flats, her heel hit something lying at the edge of the dust ruffle. Bending over, she picked it up. The book Jackson had been reading last night. She remembered knocking it to the floor. Turning it over, she studied the title: *The Minnesota Guide to Haunted Locations.*

Puzzled, she stared at the cover. *What is this? Jackson's taste has never run to the paranormal.*

"Never mind," she whispered to herself. "You have more important issues than pondering Jackson's reading material."

With a sigh, she placed the book on the nightstand and went back into the bathroom. Jackson had already cleaned up the mess she'd made. Grabbing her makeup bag, she quickly brushed on mascara, a little eye shadow, and concealer to cover the dark circles under her eyes. Stepping back, she gave herself the once-over in the mirror. Not as good as she once looked, but it would have to do. At this point, she really didn't have much to work with. Her eyes strayed to the chunk of hair sticking out. She grabbed the can of hair spray and tried smoothing it down. It popped right back out. Hopeless.

Setting the hair spray down, she braced her hands on the edge of the sink and stared into her own eyes in the mirror.

"You can do this," she whispered to herself. "Be calm . . . be in control."

With a nod, she turned and slowly walked out of the bathroom and down the hall to face her parents.

They were gathered in the living room, holding mimosas, her mother's favorite beverage.

Her parents made a handsome couple. Dressed in navy slacks and a white starched shirt with the sleeves rolled back, Lawrence Moore managed to look as distinguished in the living room of a lakeside cabin as he did in a boardroom. His silver hair waved back from his high forehead and his green eyes were as sharp as a broken bottle. With his military-straight posture, he could intimidate by the sheer force of his presence.

Her steps faltered. He wasn't going to intimidate her. She stiffened her spine. Not today.

Nancy Moore was the exact opposite of her husband. All soft with rounded edges. Blond with delicate blue eyes, she was a perfect counterpoint to her husband's hardness. And while her dad attacked things head-on, her mother would take the roundabout way in dealing with unpleasantness. The end result was the same—they both managed to always get what they wanted.

"Jackson," she overheard her father say, "you're a doctor. Prescribe—"

Her mother's delighted shriek interrupted him.

"Samantha!" Her mother placed her glass on the table and quickly crossed the room to gather Sam in a hug. Stepping back, she looked Sam up and down.

"My, don't you look . . ." Her voice trailed away as her eyes focused on the errant hank of hair. " . . . nice."

Self-consciously, Sam tugged on her cowlick. "Thanks, Mom."

"Would you like a mimosa?" she asked.

"She can't, Nancy," Jackson said swiftly. "The meds, you know. No alcohol. She'll have straight orange juice."

"Hey, Princess, don't you have a hug for your old dad?" her father's voice boomed out, drowning her mother's response.

With a smile, Sam wrapped her arms around her father. He smelled of starch, cigar smoke, and English Leather. She closed her eyes and let the scent carry her back to her childhood when she was "Daddy's little girl." Oh, to be seven years old again and have her only fear be the monster lurking in the closet of her bedroom. A monster her dad always banished.

But he hadn't vanquished them eight months ago and she was no longer a child. She had to convince him to quit treating her like one. Releasing him, she moved back and gave her father a tentative smile.

With one hand resting lightly on her shoulder, the fingers of his other hand stole to the side of her head. As he touched the strands stiff with hair spray, a frown crossed his face. "You should've let Renaldo," he said, referring to her mother's hairstylist, "fix that."

Sam brushed his hand away. "It looks better than it did. At least I don't have a bald spot anymore," she replied, trying to keep her voice light.

"Nancy," her father said, his attention shifting quickly to her mother. "When we get back to the Cities, call Renaldo. Get him up here." His eyes returned to Sam's head. "He can fix it so it's not . . ." He paused, searching for the right word. ". . . noticeable."

"Lawrence," her mother said, "he won't want to drive two hours for one haircut."

"Humph," he snorted, "he will."

"Dad," Sam said, crossing to the couch, "it's okay. It's growing out."

She eased down onto the couch as Jackson handed her a glass of orange juice. Taking a sip to wet her suddenly dry throat, she stared up at her father, now towering over her.

"Dad," she began.

He held up a hand, stopping her. "Samantha, the three of us," he said, motioning toward her mother and Jackson, "have discussed this and we think it best if someone stays with you during the week. We've hired a woman named Anne Weaver. She's a physical therapy assistant. She'll not only assist you day to day, she'll help you with your therapy," he announced. "Jackson is also prescribing a different medication for you to take before bed to help you sleep better. You can start tomorrow."

Sam shot a look at Jackson. As he caught her eye, his chin dropped and he stared at a spot on the polished tile floor. Without asking him, she knew he'd told her parents about her latest nightmare. Annoyed, she rubbed her palms on her pants. Why hadn't he talked to her before blabbing to her parents?

"Anne will," her father said, "be here—"

Sam held up a hand, stopping him. "No."

"What do you mean, 'no'?" he said, taking a step back in surprise.

"I'm tired of all the pills and I'm tired of everyone hovering over me." She paused and cleared her throat. "No meds . . . no babysitter," she finished firmly.

Her father crossed his arms and glared down at her. "Samantha, you listen to me—"

"No, you listen. The meds aren't working and I'm tired of feeling drugged all the time. And as far as having a keeper, I don't need one."

"But your therapy? What are you going to do about that?"

"I can still drive. Without the medications, I won't be restricted." She turned toward Jackson, hoping for support, but he remained silent. "They surely have therapists at the hospital in Pardo. I'll go there," she continued.

"That's unacceptable," her father said, pivoting and striding over to the table. He mixed another mimosa and gulped it down before speaking further. "We're not going to leave you up here alone."

"Fine," she fired back. "One of you stay with me. I don't want a stranger here."

She looked at her mother, standing by Jackson, nervously

twisting her heavy gold wedding band. Her eyes traveled to Jackson. With his eyes focused on her father, it was as if he were waiting for Lawrence to tell him how to respond. With a slight shake of her head, she returned her attention to her father. His lips were clenched and she could see a vein throbbing in the side of his neck. Suddenly his face relaxed, and he smiled tightly.

"You know we can't do that, Samantha," he said as if he were talking to a five-year-old. "We all have obligations in the city. I can't leave the agency; Jackson has his patients; and your mother has her social—"

"Right," Sam said bitterly. "We'd hate for Mom to miss one of her charity benefits."

"Samantha," he said harshly, "you're being cruel. You know how important—"

She surged to her feet, taking a moment to get her balance. "Me, cruel? What do you call shoving me off on a stranger like I'm some unwanted burden?"

Her mother reached out to her. "Sam, dear, don't—"

"Don't what, Mom?" she asked, her eyes filling with tears. "Argue? Sorry. I can't help it." She dashed away a tear trickling down her cheek. A spasm suddenly shook her left leg and she sat down hard on the couch.

Her mother gave a little gasp, but stayed rooted at Jackson's side.

"Are you happy now?" her father demanded. "You've upset your mother."

A surge of anger stopped Sam's tears. "What about me? Are you concerned that I might be upset? That you've made these decisions without talking to me? I should have a say about what happens in my life."

Lawrence's chest puffed out as he took a deep breath. "I

don't mean to be unkind, but the brutal truth is that since your accident—"

"Attack, Dad," she broke in, "I was attacked."

"*Accident*," he continued with emphasis, "we don't believe you're capable of knowing what's best for you." He took a long pause before resuming, his eyes wandering to the side of her head before returning to her face. "You've been making poor choices beginning with that day." He shook his head. "We can't allow them to continue."

Sam's forehead creased in a deep frown. "I don't understand. What do you mean 'that day'?"

A heavy silence fell in the room while the clock ticked away the seconds. Finally her father spoke. "You should've never stayed late at the agency. After Dan's car was broken into and everything of value stolen, both Jackson and I cautioned you about being alone in the parking garage, but you didn't listen."

At her father's words, Sam felt the tears gathering again. *No, she wasn't going to cry.* Slowly she rose to her feet. "Have you always blamed me for what happened, Dad?" she asked in a flat voice.

Her mother rushed to her side and threw an arm around her shoulder. "Oh, Sam, your father doesn't blame you." Her eyes shot to Lawrence. "Do you, dear?"

He didn't answer.

"That's what I thought," Sam said, shaking off her mother's arm and limping toward the hallway.

"Wait, Sam, don't leave," her mother called out. "Let's forget this unpleasantness. Let's sit down and have a nice meal . . . We'll talk about this later."

As she reached the door to the bedroom, she heard her father.

"Let her go, Nancy."

Turning, she called over her shoulder, “Yeah, Mom, let it go. Have another mimosa,” she said, slamming the bedroom door.

Leaning against it, she let the tears fall. How long had her father blamed her for her attack? He was right—they had warned her about staying late, but she’d been working on a presentation for a difficult client at Lawrence’s request. Was he right? Was she responsible? Should she have run faster, screamed louder, fought harder?

Her hand strayed to the chunk of hair on the side of her head and she tugged at it nervously. She noticed her manicure bag lying on the dresser. Stumbling over to it, she removed the pair of scissors.

*He didn’t like the way my hair looked, huh?* She lifted a lock of hair and snipped off the end. Then another and another. Soon the dresser was covered with a mass of auburn hair.

The bedroom door suddenly flew open. Her hand paused as she saw Jackson’s horrified reflection in the mirror.

“What are you doing!”

# Five

At the sound of Jackson's cry, both her father and mother came rushing down the hallway. Three shocked faces stared back at her in the mirror. Her father's mouth tightened in a grim line and her mother's eyes filled with tears as she began to cry softly. Jackson simply looked sad.

Her father placed a comforting hand on her mother's shoulder. "Nancy, I'll handle this. You and Jackson go ahead and start brunch. Samantha and I will join you in a little bit." He turned his attention to Sam. "Let's go out on the deck. I want to talk to you."

Tossing the scissors back into the bag, Sam took one last look at herself in the mirror. Her hair now stood out in spikes all over her head. *Well,* she thought defiantly, *no more cowlick.*

Head up, she limped past Jackson and her mother as she followed her father down the hallway and across the living room. He flung the French doors open and stepped outside. She made a move to join him then stopped.

The deck, jutting out from the side of the cabin, overlooked the lake. From the doorway, Sam saw birch trees with their leaves shivering in the light breeze and wispy clouds trailing across the blue sky. From a distance, she heard the roar of a speedboat. The sun's warmth invited her to take one more step, to walk to the edge of the deck and peer down at the clear water shimmering in the light.

She hesitated. Her gaze darted from the lake, to the trees, to the underbrush. She'd be exposed, out there on the deck. What if someone were hiding in the brush watching her? She wanted to shrink, grow smaller and smaller, until she was no longer a target for prying eyes. Wiping her damp palms on her jeans, she caught her father staring at her with a frown playing across his face. She stiffened her spine and walked slowly out the door. Pulling out a lawn chair, she sat as quickly as she could.

With a shake of his head, her father moved a chair closer to where she was sitting, joining her. He sat back and stretched his legs. For a moment he didn't speak as his eyes focused on the distant shore.

"It's lovely here, isn't it?" he finally asked, turning his attention to her.

Sam nodded.

"Restful."

She nodded again.

Drawing his legs in, her father bent forward and lightly touched her knee. "It's why we picked this place. We're trying to help you, my dear."

"But, Dad, I need to be independent. I need to do things for myself."

His eyes strayed to her head. "Like your haircut?"

Sam pulled at the short spikes. "You were making a big deal out of it. I simply fixed it."

"A pretty childish reaction, wouldn't you say?"

She dropped her hands and gripped the arms of the chair.

"You want to stay alone." Leaning back, he studied her. "How do we know you won't become frustrated or upset or angry again, and do something equally childish?"

"Like what?"

"Harm yourself."

She crossed her arms over her chest and glared at him. "I'm not going to hurt myself."

"Maybe not on purpose, but after what I saw today, I don't know if I believe you, Samantha."

Sam opened her mouth to argue, but in the distance an engine suddenly backfired. She shrank down in her chair.

Seeing her reaction, Lawrence shook his head. "Look at you . . . the slightest noise has you jumping like a scared rabbit. How can you expect us to leave you alone?"

She sat up in the chair and drew her shoulders back. "I don't need a babysitter," she insisted.

"Quit referring to Anne as a babysitter. She's trained in physical therapy and comes highly recommended. Of all the candidates we interviewed, she was the most qualified."

"You and Jackson *interviewed*," she stressed, "not me. I haven't even met this woman. How do you know I'm going to like her?"

A smug smile tugged at the corner of his mouth. "Of course you're going to like her." The smile vanished. "Don't you trust me to make the right choices for you? Haven't I always done what was best? While you were in the hospital, I made sure you had the top doctors in the country. When you finished art school, I gave you a job at the agency . . ."

Her chin went up a notch. "Yes, and I've worked hard for you."

"Us . . . you've worked hard for *us*," he emphasized. "You've made me proud, Princess, and someday it will all be yours, but you need to get well first."

"I know," she hedged, "but just because I need therapy does not mean I can't make my own decisions—"

His eyebrows shot up, stopping her.

Dropping her hands into her lap, she lowered her head. "Look, I know I have some problems . . . the nightmares, the vertigo, the panic attacks . . . but I'm still capable of living my own life. I know what's going on."

He remained silent.

Looking up at him, she saw doubt written on his face. "I do," she protested. "I'm getting better at differentiating between my dreams and what's real."

"What about last night?"

She silently cursed Jackson for not keeping his mouth shut.

"It's been a long time since I've had an episode like that."

Sitting back in his chair, he watched her for a moment before shifting his attention to the lake below. "You agreed that it's restful here." His focus returned to her. "Staying here and letting Anne take care of you is much better for you than living in the Cities and doing your therapy there." His eyes strayed back toward the lake. "Up here, you won't be running into our friends all the time. You won't have to deal with their endless questions about your accident. You can concentrate on getting better."

"And if I'm away from the Cities, you and Mom won't have to deal with their curiosity either, will you?"

"Samantha, what on earth is that supposed to mean?"

"It's got to be hard not having the *perfect* daughter anymore, isn't it, Dad? If I'm up here, you won't have to be reminded of how things have changed. Out of sight . . . out of mind. Isn't that part of it?"

"Don't be ridiculous." He huffed. "We're only thinking of what's best for you."

"I can think for myself."

"No, you can't." He focused on her hair. "You proved it this morning. Look at what you did to yourself," he said, disgusted.

Not meeting his eyes, she ran her fingers through her short hair. "It doesn't look so bad," she said defensively.

"Samantha." He rose to his feet. "I'm done arguing. Anne Weaver will be staying with you and that's it."

Sam let her body sag, feeling drained. She should've never let her temper get the best of her. How could she have been so stupid? She'd played right into their hands and now she didn't have the energy to fight him. Great. Another stranger hovering over her, telling her what to do. *Time to get up, Sam. Take your meds, Sam. Eat your broccoli and carrots, Sam. Time to go to bed, Sam.* Any hope she had for privacy would be gone.

Her father pivoted on his heel and moved toward the French doors.

"Wait," Sam cried out, jerking forward. "Couldn't we compromise?"

Turning toward her, he arched an eyebrow. "What kind of compromise?"

"Let me stay alone at night."

"I don't think that's a good idea." He shook his head slowly. "What about the nightmares?"

"Didn't you say Jackson was prescribing a new medication that's supposed to stop the dreams?"

"You've refused to take your medications."

From inside the cabin, Sam heard someone knocking at the door. Anne Weaver. Time had run out.

"If I promised to take them?" she asked in a rushed voice. "Look, if they work like Jackson said, I'll go to sleep and not wake up until morning."

Her father eyed her skeptically. "Will you cooperate with Anne?"

"Yes," she said, wringing the word out.

"Hmm." He looked at her, unconvinced. "I'll need to discuss it with Jackson."

Sam rose to her feet and reluctantly followed her father into the cabin. Once inside, she saw Jackson standing in the middle of the living room and talking with a woman dressed in blue jeans and a sleeveless top. A thick blond braid snaked down her back. God, she was tall, a couple of inches taller than Jackson. At first impression, she seemed willowy, but then Sam noticed that her arms were corded with muscle.

She felt weak and helpless next to her.

The woman's attention shifted from Jackson and landed on Sam. Immediately her eyes focused on Sam's hair.

Cocking her head, Sam silently dared the woman to comment.

Her mother noticed Sam's defiant stance and rushed to her side. "Samantha, darling, this is Anne Weaver," she said in her best society voice.

"Hi, Samantha," Anne said, holding out her hand. "It's good to finally meet you."

Conversation stilled and it seemed that her family held their collective breath as they waited for her reaction. Sam knew what they were thinking. Would she play nice? Or would she be rude? If she wanted her father to agree to give her at least some privacy, it was in her best interest to be polite. She tamped down the urge to tell them all to go to hell and leave her alone. With a tight smile, she took Anne's hand. She could almost hear their collective sigh.

"Anne," she said curtly as she tried to return Anne's firm grip and failed.

Releasing Anne's hand, she limped to the table and snagged a piece of bacon off a platter as the conversation resumed.

Jackson and her father poured on the charm while they explained their expectations. They began to go over the list of Sam's medications; her therapy; her injuries. Every time they said the word *accident*, Sam cringed inside. Trying hard not to limp, she carried her bacon over to the couch and sat down. She broke off a small piece and popped it into her mouth while the talk flowed around her as if she were invisible. It tasted like sawdust. With a grimace, she swallowed hard and placed the uneaten portion on a napkin lying on the end table.

Anne had a small notebook in her hand and was taking notes. She paused and glanced over at Sam.

"Would you like a glass of water?"

"No," Sam replied, rising slowly. "I feel a headache coming on. You really don't need me, so I'm going back to bed."

As she stood, she caught the look passing between her father and Jackson. But she didn't care what they thought. They'd all ganged up on her and she'd lost. No matter what she said or did, she was going to be stuck with Anne Weaver. She might as well retreat to the bedroom and let them hash it all out. Once in the bedroom, she slipped out of her flats and crawled under the covers. Spying Jackson's book, she picked it up and began thumbing through the pages, the words not really penetrating her brain. Suddenly the title of one chapter caught her attention.

"'Lake Country Ghosts,'" she murmured.

"Do you really have a headache?" Jackson asked from the doorway, startling her.

"Yes," she lied as she slammed the book shut and tossed it on the bed.

Noticing the book, Jackson crossed the room, and picking it up, ran a finger down the spine.

"Not your usual reading," Sam commented drily.

His shoulder rose. "I was bored, and found this in my room." Placing the book on the nightstand, he sat beside Sam. "Look, I know you're unhappy with this arrangement, but it really is for the best."

"According to you and Dad."

He shot her a dark look. "You need to trust us." Abruptly, the darkness fell away. "You're going to like Anne. She's highly qualified and I *know* she's just the person to get you on track."

"I'm not a derailed train," Sam replied in a voice tinged with sarcasm.

"Darling." Jackson's hand moved toward her cheek.

Sam froze, fighting the desire to scoot away from him.

With a sigh, he let his hand drop without touching her. "By the end of the summer, you'll be back to normal," he said with a firm nod of his head.

She didn't know if his statement was for her benefit or his.

His eyes strayed to the clock on the nightstand. "Look at the time. Lawrence wanted to leave by one." He stood and looked down at her. "I'm leaving the car here. Anne has the keys along with a spare key to the cabin. That way she can come and go without disturbing you."

"I don't like that."

"Why?"

"How do you know she won't make copies?"

"She's not going to make copies," he replied with a snort. "We wouldn't have hired her if she couldn't be trusted."

"What if she loses the key?"

"Sam, you're being silly," he said, blowing her off. "Are you going to come out and say good-bye?"

Easing down in the bed, Sam pulled the covers up to her chin and curled on her side. "No."

With a sigh, Jackson sat back down on the bed, careful not to crowd her. He was silent for a moment while a mixture of emotions flitted across his face—irritation, disappointment, and finally resignation. When he did raise his head, Sam caught the sadness in his eyes. "Samantha," he began slowly.

She drew in a sharp breath as her fears from the night before came crashing back. *Here it comes . . . he's had it . . . he's going to break off the engagement.* Part of her longed to throw her arms around him and beg him to stay.

"Samantha," he said again, "I hate seeing you and your father at odds."

She exhaled in a rush and waited for him to continue.

Turning his face away from her, he stared off into space. "I've told you how my childhood was filled with family strife . . . my mother . . . my father . . . the affairs . . . the constant conflict. That's not what I want in our life."

Surprised at the mention of his parents, Sam rose up in bed. "Jackson, he's not allowing me any independence."

"He agreed to let you spend the nights alone."

"As long as I'm a good girl," she said bitterly.

"I'll talk to him—"

"No!" she exclaimed. "I think you *talk* to him a little too much. Why did you tell him about the nightmare?"

"He had a right to know."

She felt her temper flare. "And you took it upon yourself to tell him. You say I need to trust you, but how can I when you report everything to my father? Exactly where does your loyalty lie?"

"My loyalty?" he sputtered, his face turning red. "After I've stood by you through this horrendous ordeal, you can question that?"

Too late she realized that she'd gone too far and leaned toward him. "Jackson, I'm sor—"

Shooting to his feet, he stared down at her. "Loyalty? Ha! It's a question of love. Your father loves you, and you take it for granted. You don't know how lucky you are. Try having parents like mine!" he exclaimed. "You've never had to suffer the embarrassment of watching your mother carry on with young men. You've never been a pawn in a marital tug-of-war."

"But—"

He whirled and paced over to the window. He shoved his hands in his pockets and his shoulders drooped. "I can't *stand* this fighting. Between us—between you and your father. Is it too much to ask for a little peace in my life?"

Sam struggled out of bed and crossed over to him. Hesitantly she placed a hand on his shoulder. "I'm sorry. I don't like fighting either. And I'm sorry if it brought back bad memories."

He turned and Sam saw the stress on his face. Silently she promised herself to be more understanding. Jackson had suffered an unhappy childhood. His mother had died when he was sixteen and left him with a storm of conflicting emotions. He'd loved his mother, but he'd also hated her for the way she'd used him against his father. And any time conflict erupted between Samantha and him, he always brought up the bitter experiences of his past. She rubbed her forehead. Now she did have a headache.

Jackson's face cleared. "You'd better take something for your headache. I'll get you a glass of water."

Moving to the bed, Sam crawled under the covers and waited.

He returned a few moments later, but instead of a glass of water, he held the picture from the nightstand.

Sam sat up. "What are you doing with that?"

"I found it hidden in a drawer." He jabbed the picture toward her. "Why did you hide it?"

The muscles at the base of her skull tightened and her head began to throb. "I didn't hide it."

"No one else has been in the bedroom, so how did it get into the bathroom?"

"Ah . . . ah," she stumbled, "Mom was . . . after I cut my hair . . . maybe she moved it."

"Sam, I was with her the whole time . . . She never touched the picture."

Drawing her knees to her chest, Sam rested her forehead against them as the blood pounded at her temples. "Then I don't understand how it wound up in the bathroom."

"Neither do I," he said in a tight voice.

She raised her head and stared at him.

His lips tightened in a thin line. "Obviously you don't want it, so I'll take it with me." He glanced down at the picture. "I think Dr. Weissinger needs to know about these periods of forgetfulness."

"I remember exactly what I did this morning and it doesn't include—"

A sharp rap at the door stopped her.

"Jackson, we need to leave if we're going to beat the traffic back . . ." Her father paused as he picked up on the tension in the room. "What's wrong?"

Jackson glanced down at the picture in his hand. "Nothing." His gaze moved toward Sam. "I'll call you this evening." Pivoting, he left the room.

Her father's eyes followed him. "Do you want to explain?" he asked Sam.

"No," she said, lowering her head and massaging her neck muscles. "I'm sure Jackson will tell you all about it on the way home."

He moved to the bed and stood looking down at her. "Don't worry, Princess," he said with a pat to her head. "Once you're better, things will smooth out with Jackson. I'll reason with him."

Sam raised her head. "I think it would be better if you left it alone."

"Nonsense." He gave his hand a careless wave. "Jackson is perfect for you, and if I can help you two through this rough patch, I will."

"Dad—"

"Shh," he said, bending down and placing a kiss on her cheek. "Everything will be fine." He straightened and wagged a finger at her. "Remember your promise, Samantha. I expect to get good reports from Anne."

Too tired to argue, Sam simply nodded.

Crossing the room, he turned at the doorway. "Get some rest. Anne will be here if you need anything."

After her father softly shut the door, her eyes traveled around the empty room. Maybe he was right. All she had to do was cooperate and everything would be fine. The nightmares would be gone. Her relationship with Jackson would be back to normal and they could finally proceed with the wedding. She'd have her old life back. Working with her dad . . . married to Jackson. It was what she wanted, wasn't it?

But what about the picture? How did it get into the bathroom? Did she pick it up without realizing it and carry it in there with her? The thought scared her and made her head pound. Her gaze settled on the antianxiety pills sitting on the nightstand. She did need to calm down. Opening the bottle, she shook one of the small pills into her hand and stared at it. She really hated these little blue pills. She hadn't been lying when she'd told her father they left her feeling numb, but maybe numb was better than the way she felt now. Popping the pill into her mouth, she swallowed it without water.

Sliding back down in the bed, she closed her eyes and let oblivion claim her.

*Whispers . . . I hear whispers.*

The thought woke Sam up with a jerk and her eyes flew open, staring into the darkness. She glanced at the illuminated clock. Midnight. Was Anne still there, talking to someone? Was the TV on? In the glow from the clock's lighted face, she spied a piece of paper propped on the nightstand. Flicking on the light, she scanned it quickly. Anne had been gone for two hours. She was alone. It had been another dream.

Then she heard it again . . . the soft, sibilant whisper that had jarred her awake. She scooted up in bed and quickly shut off the light. A pulse throbbed at the base of her throat. *Anne forgot to lock the doors.* The spit dried in her mouth and she wanted to cough, but didn't dare. She didn't dare alert whoever was in the cabin. She listened hard as she grabbed the pillow and squeezed it tight to her chest.

The sudden call of a loon echoed across the lake, and Sam shoved her face in the pillow, stifling her cry. She couldn't stand the uncertainty and lowered the pillow, craning her neck as she struggled to hear. Nothing. The overwhelming urge to bolt from the bed and tear through the cabin, inspecting all the windows and doors, fought with the need to stay still, stay safe. The muscles in her left leg twitched while she battled the need to move.

She lost.

Grabbing the Maglite lying on the nightstand, she crept out of bed and across the room. With the light in one hand, she slowly turned the knob with the other and opened the door a crack. Holding an ear to the small opening, she listened.

Silence.

Carefully, she eased the door open and slipped into the hallway. The tile on the floor felt cool beneath her bare feet as she flattened her back against the wall. Slowly, with her hands trailing the wall for balance, she edged down the hall toward the living room. At the end of the hall, she half turned and sneaked a look around the corner.

Moonlight filtered through the sheer curtains covering the patio door, casting silver light across the floor. She drew back while anger melded with her fear. Damn, Anne hadn't pulled the heavier drapes closed. She had gone off and left Sam exposed. Shutting her eyes, Sam inhaled deeply and steeled herself to take another look. Slowly she shifted until she could peek into the living room with one eye. No shapes lurked in the room, but shadows obscured its edges. Someone might be waiting in those shadows, waiting just beyond the moonlight, ready to pounce if she made a move. Clutching the light with sweaty palms, Sam caught a faint whiff of cigarette smoke and snapped back around the corner. The intruders had taken the time for a smoke while ransacking the cabin? In spite of her fear, the idea seemed ridiculous.

She looked again. Nothing had changed. No glow of a burning cigarette bobbed in the dark. And the scent of smoke was gone. Still huddled in the hallway, she felt along the edge of the living-room wall until her fingers found the light switch. She flipped it up.

In an instant, the shadows disappeared and soft light filled the main part of the cabin. The room looked exactly the same as it had always looked. The pillows on the plaid couch facing the fireplace were right where they'd been earlier. The dark wood doors of the kitchen cabinets were shut and the drawers were closed.

Sam limped from the hallway, across the living room to the doors leading out onto the deck, and snapped the drapes shut.

"Better," she breathed softly. No one could see into the cabin now.

She crossed to the kitchen door and rattled the doorknob. It was firmly locked. She checked the catch on the window above the sink. Still in place.

Hobbling back to the living room, she went to the French doors and lifted the drapes back just enough to check the lock. The door was latched and the safety bar was in place along the bottom track. She found the other switch and turned off the lights, throwing the room back into darkness. Grasping the edge of the drapes, she stayed half hidden in its folds and stared out over the lake.

The reflection of the full moon glowed on the quiet surface of the lake, while the tall pines ringing the lake masked the far shore in inky black. To the north, the hulking shape of a small island guarded the entrance to the bay where her cabin was located. From her position, Sam saw the boathouse and the dock protruding out into the lake. Its weathered boards looked pearly in the moonlight.

Her hand tightened on the drapes.

At the end of the dock a lone woman stood with her back toward the cabin. The moon seemed to act as a spotlight shining down on her. Too short to be Anne, she had red hair that cascaded down her back and over white, white shoulders and arms. She was dressed in a long lavender nightgown, thin enough for the light of the moon to reveal the shadow of her legs even at this distance. Sam saw the bright red ember of a cigarette move in a lazy arc toward her head as she lifted it to her mouth. A thin plume of smoke drifted above her and out across the lake when she exhaled.

Had she been the one Sam had heard whispering? Had she been close enough to the cabin for her cigarette smoke to drift inside? The thought made Sam's breath hitch. The drapes had been open. She could've been standing on the deck, watching, and Sam would've been oblivious to her prying eyes. She dropped the drapes and clutched her hand at her side. What in the hell was some woman doing wandering around the lake in her nightgown at this time of night? And on *her* dock?

She inched the edge of the drape aside.

The moonlight still reflected off the placid water and the dock still looked shaded in soft grays, but the woman had disappeared.

Dropping the drape, she flicked on the Maglite, then grasped it with both hands like a weapon and shambled back to the bedroom. Once over the threshold, she shut the door, locking it. Crossing the room, she crawled into bed, pulled the covers up to her chin, and turned on the bedside lamp.

She fell asleep clutching the Maglite to her chest.

# Six

The lights of the city spread out below me and a beautiful sense of freedom bubbles deep inside. I've escaped, at least for a little while. The opera I'd enjoyed tonight had made my spirits soar, and now I'd finish my perfect evening with a perfect late-night supper at one of the finest restaurants in Minneapolis. When I'm seated, I'll order the best wine they have to offer, a thick steak, and asparagus done just right. My mouth waters at the thought and a faint smile tugs at my lips. Moving away from the plate-glass window, I turn to where the maître d' waits at his station, in his starched white shirt, black jacket, and impeccable bow tie. He gives me an appraising look, and suddenly nervous about my own appearance, I flick an imaginary piece of lint from my sleeve.

Picking up a menu, he gives me a smooth smile. "Will anyone be joining you?" he inquires with a note of superiority in his voice.

I resent it. *Who does he think he is? He's nothing more than a glorified waiter.* If she had allowed me to follow my destiny, this man would've been fawning all over me. He would've been honored to have someone of my stature choose his establishment. Instead he looks at me as if I were ordinary.

Masking my irritation, I assess him with a cool eye. "No, I'm alone."

His shoulders sag under the weight of my stare, and turning, he motions toward the half-empty dining room. "Right this way."

I follow two steps behind as he leads me to a table near the doors to the kitchen area. Placing the menu on the table, he pulls out a chair.

"Your waiter will be right with you," he says as he begins to glide away.

With a light touch to his arm, I stop his retreat. "This table is unacceptable," I say in a low tone, and point to an empty one by the window. "I want to be seated there."

"But due to the late hour, that area is closed," he replies swiftly.

"Then open it," I say, turning away from him and moving toward my selected table.

I hear a slight hiss as he follows in my wake, but ignore it. Reaching my destination, I wait patiently for him to pull out my chair. He does, and with a nod of my head, I smile tightly and take my seat.

"I'll send someone right over."

Satisfied, I pick up the menu to peruse the selections. Glancing over the top of it, I see the maître d' engaged in a hurried discussion with one of the waiters. The man frowns as his eyes settle on me, while the maître d' spreads his hands in a helpless gesture. With a shake of his head, the waiter picks up a water pitcher and heads my way. Returning my attention to the menu, I allow myself a triumphant grin. Maybe now they'll see I'm not ordinary.

I make my selections quickly, then settle back to enjoy the view of the city. I belong here . . . I really do. If only there were some way to escape . . . to have this sense of freedom every day instead of satisfying myself with these stolen moments. Suddenly bands of tension tighten around my chest. If I tried to leave my old life behind, it would hurt financially.

*At what price freedom, eh?* I think bitterly, and take a big gulp of my Merlot, not tasting it as I swallow.

My steak arrives and I try to shove my dark thoughts away and enjoy these last moments. I cut into the tender meat with the precision of a surgeon, and as I do, a thin, watery line of red oozes across the pure white china plate. Stabbing the meat with my fork, I place the morsel in my mouth and chew, but it seems to have no flavor. I wash it down with wine and try again. Dry as dust.

Snapping my fingers at the waiter, I point to my now-empty glass of wine. He scurries over and refills my glass.

"Is your steak to your liking?"

"It's fine," I answer, waving him away and grabbing my wine-glass. Another long drink while I stare at the red liquid seeping over the plate.

One stupid moment of violence . . . and a life is ruined. And through no fault of mine. It was her . . . she was responsible for what happened, not me. Why should I continue to pay the price? I stare out the window at the lights. Somehow they don't seem as bright as they once were. Disgusted, I throw my napkin on the table and down the last of my wine. I signal for my check, and after settling the bill, leave my half-eaten meal sitting on the table, the bloody juice now congealed on the plate.

I stride past the waiter, past the maître d', and out the dining-room doors. As I stab the elevator button, my anger sizzles. Another evening ruined by her. It can't continue. I've earned a better life than this . . . I *deserve* a better life than this. There must be a way out.

All I have to do is find the key.

# Seven

Anne sat in her car and stared at the cabin. Yesterday did not go well. Sam had shut herself in the bedroom for most of the day, claiming weariness. At first Anne had wondered if it was avoidance on Sam's part. It had been obvious Sam didn't want her there and resented her parents' and fiancé's interference.

They'd left that part out during her interview, she thought wryly. Neither the father nor the fiancé had mentioned that Sam was less than thrilled with the idea of in-home therapy. Anne's lips curled downward in a frown. What kind of reception would Sam give her today? Would she spend the entire summer struggling to win Sam's cooperation? Didn't Sam realize how lucky she was? She had people in her life who cared, who would do anything to help her.

Disgusted, Anne shook her head. *She'd* never had that kind of support in *her* life. No one had ever stepped up to the plate to help her. It had always been up to her, and her alone, to shoulder the burdens, to make the decisions, to solve the problems. It was a miracle that she hadn't been crushed by the weight of it all.

She laid her head against the seat and shut her eyes for a

moment. Instead of acting like a spoiled brat, Samantha Moore should be overcome with gratitude.

Straightening, she opened her eyes and blew out a long breath as she stared at the cabin door. What she thought of Samantha Moore wasn't important. She had a job to do. During the interview, Lawrence Moore had made his expectations clear, and in not so many words, he'd let her know that failure was not an option.

Her thoughts shot to the pile of bills lying on the kitchen table. A pang of anxiety squeezed her chest. What if she did fail and he fired her? Laid off from the hospital and no money coming in—it wouldn't take long for her savings to dwindle. Her carefully laid plans for Caleb's college would be shot to hell. All those years of scrimping, wasted. She rubbed a spot on her chest as if to loosen the knot around her heart. She couldn't let that happen. Whether Samantha Moore wanted her help or not didn't matter. She'd do whatever it took to keep Lawrence Moore happy.

Flinging the car door open, she got out and strode across the sandy yard to the front porch. She'd taken one step when a plant growing at its edge caught her eye. Had it been there yesterday? Anne moved closer to take a look.

Stalks with deeply veined, green leaves shot skyward and were beginning to arch toward the ground. Looking closer, Anne saw tiny clusters of buds forming. She'd driven by this cabin for years, but she'd never noticed this bush growing by the porch. The landlord must have planted it.

"Ah, who cares?" she mumbled to herself, fingering the leaves. "Time to quit dithering and get my butt in there. I've got a patient who resents me." Taking a deep breath, she squared her shoulders. "But I've faced worse."

With firm steps, Anne crossed the porch and unlocked the

cabin door. Swinging it open, she peered into the semidark room. The silent atmosphere was stifling. *This won't do*, she thought. Quickly, she moved to the French doors, and flinging back the curtains, jerked one open. Immediately sunlight flooded the cabin, chasing away the darkness, and the air lightened as a breeze from the lake fluttered in.

Anne took a deep breath and let it out slowly. "Better."

Moving back to the kitchen, she began making preparations to cook breakfast. She'd wait until it was ready before waking Sleeping Beauty. As if the young woman had been summoned by her thoughts, Anne turned to see Sam shuffle into the kitchen.

Squinting against the sunlight, Sam ran her fingers through her butchered hair.

Glancing at Sam over her shoulder, Anne decided that was the worst haircut she'd ever seen. It looked like the woman had used a Weedwhacker. Maybe she should gently suggest a trip to Alice's Beauty Barn in Pardo?

"Good morning," she said, schooling her face into a cheery mask. "What would you like for breakfast? How about eggs and sausage?"

Sam tugged at her errant spikes of hair, looking first at Anne then glancing toward the open door to the deck. "Nothing—just coffee," she mumbled.

During the interview, Lawrence Moore had shown Anne pictures of Sam, but looking at her now, she was amazed at the difference between the woman in the photos and the one who stood there, pulling at her hair. In the photos, she'd been smiling and confident, but now? It was like she'd been stripped to the bone. Light pouring in highlighted her hollow cheeks and her almost skeletal frame. And her eyes—shadowed and haunted—darted around the kitchen with uncertainty. At that moment Anne thought she'd never seen anyone *less* confident than Samantha Moore.

Catching Anne watching her, Sam dropped her hand away from her hair and gave Anne a defiant look. "What are you staring at?"

"Nothing," Anne replied quickly, pulling the eggs and milk out of the fridge. "You don't look like you slept well. Did you have a bad night?"

Sam gave a rough bark. "You might say that." She looked back toward the door to the deck. "There's too much light in here. And," she called over her shoulder as she limped across the room, "don't ever leave here again without pulling all the drapes and blinds." Reaching the door, she closed both the door and the drapes, plunging the room back into gloom.

Breakfast forgotten, Anne was beside her in an instant. "It's as dark as a tomb in here," she said, opening the drapes. "A little sunshine will make you feel better."

Sam shut the drapes. "No, it won't."

Anne opened them. "Yes, it will."

Sam's hand wavered on the curtains while her eyes narrowed. "I like it dark."

"I don't. The curtains stay open," Anne said, drawing herself up to her full six feet and staring down at Sam. As she looked into those troubled eyes, sympathy tugged at her, but she tamped it down. She couldn't let this little wisp of a thing get the upper hand.

Emotions flitted across Sam's face—defiance, anger, and finally resignation. Her shoulders sagged, and she pivoted awkwardly. "Whatever," she replied in a voice dripping with bitterness. "I'm going back to bed."

Anne's hand stopped her. "No, you're not. You're going to eat breakfast, take your meds, and start your therapy."

"Who put you in charge, Nurse Nancy?" Sam shot back, hugging herself tightly.

"Your father."

Sam's arms dropped to her side. "Oh, that's right." She shambled over to the couch and plopped down. "You're here to care for his crippled daughter," she finished sarcastically.

Anne placed her hands on her hips and studied her. "Do you want to get your mobility back or not?"

Sam's chin shot up. "Of course I do," she exclaimed, "but I don't need you to do it. I'm tired of everyone treating me like an invalid."

"Then quit acting like one," Anne fired back, returning to the kitchen.

Sam surged to her feet and with halting steps followed her. "Excuse me? You've known me what? Less than twenty-four hours? How do you know how I act?"

"And during those twenty-four hours, you've spent most of your time hiding out in the bedroom, sleeping." Anne cracked three eggs in a bowl and beat them with short angry strokes. "That's not the behavior of someone who wants to get better."

"You don't know anything about it," Sam insisted.

"I know what I've seen and what your father and fiancé told me during the interview."

Sam yanked out a chair and sank down. "Did you ever consider that their perspective might be a little skewed? That they have their own reasons for sticking me up here in the boonies?"

"Such as?"

"Such as my mother doesn't like dealing with 'unpleasant' situations." Sam leaned back in her chair and gave Anne a long look. "Remembering what happened to me is unpleasant."

"My impression was that your parents and fiancé want to do what's best for you."

"No, they want to do what's easiest for them. And shoving me off on you is easy."

A comeback sprang to mind, but Anne clamped her mouth shut. *Nope,* she thought, *I'm not going to get involved in a debate about her relationship with her parents.* Instead, she calmly laid the whisk in the sink and turned her attention to Sam. "What difference does it make what their motives are? Isn't getting your strength back the important thing?"

"Don't you think I've tried?" Sam cried. "I've taken every pill, every potion they shoved my way, until I've felt so woozy it's been hard to tell what's real and what's not."

Anne let her expression soften. "It takes time for the body to heal and—"

"Right," Sam snorted, cutting in, "like I haven't heard that one before, and while you're at it, why don't you explain to me how fortunate I am?"

Sam's remark echoed Anne's earlier thoughts and Anne felt a stab of guilt. She watched Sam's anger and misery shimmer around her like an aura, and she couldn't help thinking that maybe Samantha Moore wasn't so fortunate after all. But before she could frame a response, Sam continued.

" 'Really, Samantha,' " Sam said in a spot-on imitation of Lawrence Moore. " 'Look around the hospital—how many of these people will never walk again?' " She suddenly slumped in her chair. "I'm supposed to be thankful they only bashed in my skull."

Turning away, Anne struggled for the right words to say. This woman probably had more money than she herself would ever see in her lifetime, yet Samantha Moore couldn't buy what she needed most—determination. Anne had to find a way to break through the girl's bitterness. If she didn't, she'd fail and Lawrence Moore would fire her. Grabbing the bowl, she felt a small sigh escape before she could stop it. Rolling her shoulders, she tried to release the building tension while she plastered a smile on her face.

"Look, just sit there and relax while I make breakfast," Anne said, sliding the toaster toward her and popping two slices of bread into the slots. "After you're finished, we'll go out on the deck and start on some exercises."

Sam rose to her feet and took a halting step toward the living room. "I told you . . . I'm going back to bed."

Anne's smile vanished. Great. What did she do now? Hog-tie her and haul her out onto the deck? Lawrence Moore would love hearing about how she manhandled his daughter.

"No wonder you're not making progress," Anne muttered, and slammed the lever down on the toaster.

Sam whirled. "What did you say?"

Pivoting, Anne leaned against the counter and met Sam's angry stare with one of her own. "I'm not surprised at your condition. You say you don't want to be treated like an invalid, but that's exactly how you act." Frustration sharpened her voice. "You don't have what it takes to work hard."

Sam's head reared back. "That's not true. Thanks to me, Dad's agency is one of the best in this country."

"That was then. What about now?"

Sam's gaze broke away from Anne's face and slowly traveled down her own body. Her focus settled on her left leg. She stared at it a moment before stiffening her spine and returning her attention to Anne. "How long?" she asked, her voice soft.

"What do you mean?"

"If I promise to cooperate, how long before I'm back to normal?"

"You want a time frame?"

Sam nodded mutely.

Should she make false promises in order to ensure Sam's cooperation? She'd never lied to a patient before, but if it meant hanging on to this job . . . Looking at Sam standing there—her chopped hair, her thin body—she wanted to help her. Feeding her a bunch of bullshit wasn't the way to do it.

"I can't give you one," she said finally. "All I can give you is a promise. I'll work hard if you do."

Inside she prayed it would be enough.

Sam barely touched her breakfast, but Anne had at least one victory. Sam had dressed in loose sweatpants and a T-shirt and was now lying on a chaise longue while Anne massaged the wasted muscle in her left leg. She'd almost gone into shock when Anne had insisted that they do the exercises on the deck overlooking the lake. Even now, as Anne kneaded her leg, Sam's eyes were scrunched shut while tension vibrated through her small frame.

Those eyes suddenly popped open and Sam's leg jerked.

"Did you hear that?" Sam whispered.

Anne shifted as her eyes scanned the area around the cabin. "I didn't hear anything."

"Rustling," Sam replied, flinging an arm toward the deck railing. "Over there in the trees."

Anne resumed her massage. "It was probably just a squirrel. Try to relax."

"I want to go back inside," Sam said as she tried to sit up.

"It's okay," Anne answered, gently pushing her back. "We're

staying out here. The fresh air and the sunshine will do you good."

"I said I'm going back inside," Sam repeated firmly.

"No, you're not." Anne kneaded Sam's thigh muscle in swift strokes. "You promised to cooperate and that means we stay out here."

With a disgusted sigh, Sam plopped back against the chaise and closed her eyes again.

Perplexed, Anne shook her head. It was a beautiful day. The sun beat down on them, warming her back as she leaned over Sam's leg. And bees, drawn by the heavy scent of the lavender oil she was using, buzzed lazily at the corner of the deck. How could Sam prefer being cooped up in the cabin? She moved her hands down Sam's thigh, pressing firmly on the tightness gathered beneath the skin. Slowly, she felt the knots begin to ease. A smile tickled at the corner of Anne's mouth.

Another small win. If she could only gain Sam's trust . . . Not only would it please Lawrence Moore, but it would allow her to really help this woman. The smile vanished as Anne's lips pursed. The damage was more severe than she'd imagined. Her hands paused, and as they did, Sam's eyes opened.

"Something wrong?" Sam asked, raising her head.

"No, no," Anne replied quickly, her fingers digging into the muscle.

Sam's head fell back against the chaise. "How long is this going to take?"

"Not long. I want to loosen the muscles before we begin the exercises."

Sam's eyebrow arched. "*We?* You're going to do them with me?"

"Nope," Anne answered with a grin. "You're going to be the one doing the sweating."

"That's what I figured." She rested her hands on her stomach and closed her eyes. "I don't care. As long as it works, I'll sweat buckets." Her eyes shot open and drilled into Anne's. "This is going to work, isn't it?"

Anne's fingers played over the damaged muscle again. Would the therapy work? It depended on what her expectations were. After feeling the extent of the deterioration in Sam's leg, she doubted Sam would ever walk without a limp, slight as it might be. She remembered the photos Lawrence Moore had shown her. Specifically the one of Sam flying down the ski slopes. That would never happen again. Would Sam or her father accept less than a one hundred percent recovery? She dug into the muscle with her thumbs, making Sam wince.

"Sorry. Your fiancé told me you were an artist," she said, not answering Sam's question. "Do you have any supplies with you? The scenery up here is fantastic and—"

"Humph," Sam replied with a soft snort, and closed her eyes. "I haven't painted in years."

"It might be a good distraction for you. Give you a focus outside of your therapy, and a mental break. Maybe you want to—"

"No," Sam said curtly, shifting uneasily on the chaise. "Your job is to work on my leg, not my head."

Frowning, Anne grabbed a towel and wiped the oil from her hands. Fine; Sam was right. She was a physical therapist, not a psychologist, but it didn't take a doctor to see Samantha Moore had more issues than just a damaged leg. Not her problem, though. Her job was to help Sam build the strength in her leg. Moving to the end of the chaise, she pulled the leg of Sam's sweatpants down, and lifting Sam's ankle with one hand, she placed the palm of her other hand on the arch of the girl's foot.

"I want you to push against my hand with your foot, hold it for five seconds, then release. We'll do it—"

Sudden footfalls coming around the corner of the house stopped her. Sam jerked her foot away and sat up in alarm. Together she and Anne turned as a man strolled across the deck toward them.

Wonderful. Fritz Thorpe. Anne had wondered how long it would take for him to show up. Today he was dressed immaculately in white linen pants and a navy polo shirt and his silver hair peeked out from beneath his captain's hat. Stifling a groan, Anne looked down at Sam to gauge her reaction to Fritz's sudden appearance.

Distrust shadowed Sam's eyes as they darted from Anne to Fritz and back again. Her muscles tensed.

Noticing Sam's reaction, Fritz held up a hand and stepped back. "I'm sorry. I didn't mean to startle you." Pointing over his shoulder, he smiled at them. "I knocked, but no one answered. Anne can attest to the fact that I'm perfectly harmless."

Anne leaned forward and pressed a firm hand on Sam's arm. "Sam, this is Fritz Thorpe," she said, her voice calm. "He lives right across the lake."

"What Anne didn't add is that some consider me an old busybody who has to check out all the new residents in our little community," he replied with a chuckle as he pulled out a chair and sat. "Personally, I see myself as the unofficial welcoming committee of Elk Horn Lake."

Sam's fingers stole to her hair and plucked at the short strands. "Ah," she said stiffly, "I'm Samantha Moore."

"Lovely to meet you, Samantha," Fritz replied with a broad smile. "How long are you going to be staying with us?"

"Not long," Sam answered, swinging her legs off the chaise. "Anne, I'm tired." She rose awkwardly to her feet. "I'm going back to bed." With a nod toward Fritz, she limped across the deck and disappeared into the cabin.

Anne watched her leave with reluctance. Now that Sam was back to hibernating in her bedroom, she felt the small victories won this morning slip away.

After Sam had closed the patio door, Fritz turned to Anne. "Oh dear," he said with a rueful look, "she is a bit skittish, isn't she?"

Frowning, Anne picked up the towel and scrubbed it across her hands. "Sam's wary of strangers. She's been through a lot."

Fritz leaned back, steepling his fingers. "Esther Dunlap told me that she'd suffered some type of trauma. What happened?"

"I don't gossip about my patients," she replied curtly, tossing the towel into her bag. "If you want to know—"

"What *is* that smell?" Fritz exclaimed, cutting her off.

Glancing over at him, she saw him waving a hand in front of his nose. She picked up the bottle and held it out. "Lavender oil."

His lips curled in distaste. "Ugh, I never could abide that scent."

"Sorry," she answered in a neutral tone, capping the bottle and throwing it on top of the towel. "Most people find it calming."

Fritz gave his head a quick shake. "Not me." His attention turned toward the cabin. "Does your patient know about this place?"

"Not you, too," she said, rolling her eyes.

A hard look stole across his face. "I remember Blanche and Harley quite well and I was here that last summer. Blanche poisoned everything she touched." Tugging on his bottom lip, he shook his head. "It was a sorry day when Harley brought her here. All the lives she destroyed." He shook his head again. "It wouldn't surprise me if her evil lingers on."

Anne snorted. "Oh, come on. They left the lake years ago. Whatever happened back then is old news."

His eyes narrowed. "Tell that to Edward Dunlap." His face suddenly relaxed and he leaned forward. "Since my attempt at welcoming Ms. Moore fell flat, while I'm here, let me broach another subject with you."

Anne tilted her head and studied him suspiciously. "What?"

He gave her a charming smile. "I'm putting together a little quartet for the annual Fourth of July celebration and I'd like Caleb to join us."

She stood quickly, grabbing her bag. "He's busy working and getting ready for school this fall."

Fritz chuckled softly. "He told me you'd say that."

"You've already talked to him?"

"Yes," he said, rising. "Caleb is a very talented young man. He should be encouraged to develop his gift."

"He's going to make something of his life." She turned on her heel and headed for the French doors. "He's going to college."

"That's what you want . . ." Fritz paused. "What does he want?"

Anne whirled. "He's my son, not yours. It's up to me to guide him, not you."

He lifted an eyebrow. "Guide or force?"

"My son is none of your business," she replied in a curt voice. "Now, if you'll excuse me, I have work to do."

With two angry strides, she left him standing on the deck alone.

# Eight

What was she doing here? Sam thought as she paused in the doorway of Alice's Beauty Barn. This wasn't part of her therapy—just another situation in which she'd been prodded into complying. She passed a hand over her eyes. Honestly, she was so tired of being forced into things. The same hand then strayed to her chopped-off hair. What difference did it make how she looked? Why couldn't everyone leave her *alone*? If she had the strength, she'd get the hell out of here and walk back to the damn cabin.

Anne, as if sensing Sam's thoughts, suddenly took her arm and led her over to one of the cushioned chairs in the tiny waiting area.

Two of the chairs were occupied by women—a mother and daughter possibly. They reminded Sam of her mother's friends—glossy and smooth with an unmistakable air of wealth and privilege. When their eyes met Sam's, the older woman leaned close and whispered something to her companion. They were talking about her, Sam thought as a wave of panic hit.

Anne's grip on Sam's arm tightened for an instant as she

glanced over at them. "Irene, Kimberly," she said with a quick smile as she guided Sam into the chair.

Murmuring "Hello, Anne," the women returned her smile then resumed their whispers.

Unfazed by their cool response, Anne released Sam and picked up a magazine, shoving it in her lap.

"Here. Read this," Anne said, then turned and marched over to the receptionist's desk. She leaned forward and, in a hushed voice, began to talk to the young woman standing behind the desk.

A thin veil of envy settled over Sam as she watched Anne. She took in her long, tan legs, the well-muscled forearms and biceps, the long blond braid snaking down her back. Anne wore her strength and beauty without artifice. Sam slumped in her chair. With her damaged leg and her bag-of-bones body, she felt nondescript and insignificant compared to Anne. Tilting her head down, she glanced out of the corner of her eye at the two women next to her. Their voices were so hushed that she couldn't make out the words. Were they measuring her against Anne? Her grip on the arms of the chair tightened. Were all the women in the shop doing the same?

Clouds of hair spray and the smell of ammonia, along with other chemicals, seemed to drift toward Sam while she tried to focus on something other than the two women. Part of her wanted to scoot closer and hear what they were presumably saying about her, but another part of her wanted to run and not look back. She shifted uneasily in her chair, causing the magazine to slide across her lap. Grabbing it, she began swiftly thumbing through the pages while she tried to calm her thoughts.

*Think about the last couple of weeks*, she told herself. She *had* promised to cooperate with Anne, but her therapy had started to feel like boot camp. Nurse Ratched, as she now thought of Anne, had worked her butt off. Every time Sam had tried to let things slide, Anne called her on it. With her no-nonsense approach, Anne had driven her, pushed her. Her eyes moved from the magazine to her left leg.

*You don't like her methods, but they are working*, said a voice in her head. Her leg was stronger—not a lot, but a little. The sessions with Anne had brought more results than the months of therapy in the Cities. She wouldn't admit it to Anne, but she was pleased even though she'd fallen into bed each night exhausted, so exhausted that half the time she'd forgotten to take the new medication Jackson had prescribed. The only bonus of her negligence had been a lack of nightmares—she was too tired to dream, she supposed.

Forgetting the magazine, she let her gaze roam around the small beauty shop. A couple of elderly ladies with their hair tightly twisted on minuscule rollers sat under hair dryers perusing the latest scandal sheet. Two stylists were busy working at their stations. At one, a little girl sat perched high in a chair as the stylist snipped her bangs. At the other, an older woman's blue-gray hair was being styled. That stylist, her own bleached locks giving a new definition to the term *big hair*, kept up a steady stream of chatter while she plucked and picked at the top of her client's head. Behind her, littering the counter in front of the big mirror, were small figurines of poodles. Big ones, small ones, and not only at the woman's station, but on the receptionist's desk and on the shelves displaying haircare products as well. Pictures of the dogs lined the wall. Everywhere Sam looked she saw poodles.

The words *oodles and oodles of poodles* sprang into Sam's mind as she felt her anxiety spike. It was too much. Too many poodles; too many women; too many whispers. In her mind's ear, they became louder and louder until the sound seemed to ricochet around in her skull. She didn't belong here with all these women getting cut and curled. She needed to be back in the safety of her cabin. Gripping the arms of her chair, she began to rise until she saw the receptionist and the bleached-blond stylist staring at her. Instantly she plopped down, squirming at the unwanted attention. A moment later, Anne joined her.

"Alice," Anne said with a jerk of her head toward the stylist, "is going to take care of you as soon as she finishes with Mrs. Albright."

"Whatever," Sam mumbled in response while, out of the corner of her eye, she watched the stylist called Alice.

With a flourish, the blonde whipped the plastic cape off her customer's shoulders. "There you go, Mrs. Albright," she said, smiling. "I'll see you next week." Expectantly, she faced Sam and Anne, her smile still firmly in place.

"Come on," Anne said, taking Sam's arm.

Sam jerked away and crossed slowly to the waiting stylist.

"Alice," Anne said, making introductions, "Samantha Moore."

"Nice to meet you," Alice answered with a bob of her head, and motioned toward the sink. "Let's get you fixed up, shall we?"

*Shall we?* Sam thought. It would take more than a haircut to fix her up, but she bit back the sarcastic remark and followed Alice to the waiting chair. Moments after settling in, she felt warm water cascading over her head and smelled the soothing scent of herbal shampoo while Alice's expert fingers massaged her scalp. It felt wonderful. Sam's eyes slowly closed, and her tight muscles relaxed. The panic that had been nibbling at her since she'd entered the shop faded away.

"Say, honey, that's quite a scar—what happened?" Alice suddenly asked.

Sam's eyelids popped open as she slid lower in the chair. "Um—well—I," she stumbled.

Alice wiped a hand on a towel and grasped Sam's arm, pulling her upward. "That's okay, honey. None of my business." Her fingers continued rubbing Sam's head. "You have nice thick hair. I know just how to cut it so the scar won't show."

Having finished shampooing, she escorted Sam to her station. When she removed the towel, Sam got a good look at herself in the mirror.

With her wet hair plastered to her scalp, every bone in her face seemed to stand out in the harsh fluorescent light. Her lips curled in disgust. She looked like a death's-head.

Noticing her expression, Alice spun the chair around, putting Sam's back to the mirror. Picking up a comb, she gently ran it through the tangles. Anne crossed the room and joined them.

"So, Alice," she said cheerfully, "how's Pumpkin?"

The comb paused over Sam's head. "Fine, just fine," Alice replied. " 'Course she still misses Miss Fifi."

Sam's gaze stole to the pictures lining the wall, settling on one in particular. A poodle, sitting regally on a chair, stared out at her from a frame draped in black ribbon. Miss Fifi? Before she could ask, Alice waved the comb toward the picture.

"That was my baby," she said to Sam, her eyes misting. "My first Miss Fifi. I had her the longest—thirteen years."

Sam felt Alice's remark deserved some kind of acknowledgment, but she was at a loss. "Um . . . um . . . you breed poodles?" she asked lamely.

"Oh no, honey, I'm not a breeder, but I surely do love them." She picked up her scissors and began snipping. "Do you have a dog?"

"No. I've never had time for a pet."

"That's too bad." Her scissors stopped as her gaze stole back to the pictures. "I've had poodles for . . . oh, twenty, thirty years now . . . and I don't know what I would've done without them. They're a lot easier to live with than my ex ever was." She let out a raucous laugh. "They don't argue and they never leave the toilet seat up."

"Maybe I should get a dog," Anne said with a chuckle. "I've never asked, but how did you get started with poodles?"

Alice's smile faded while she turned her attention to cutting Sam's hair. "An old friend."

"Really? Who?"

"Oh," Alice said, her attention suddenly darting to the two women who were still waiting for the other stylist, "just someone who lived around here. You wouldn't know them."

"But—"

"How's Caleb?" Alice suddenly asked, changing the subject.

Sam listened to their banter and tried to tune it out. Who cared about dogs? Or what Anne's son had planned for the summer? As her thoughts drifted, she realized that Anne's remark about painting had bothered her more than she'd let on. It had been so long since she'd held a paintbrush in her hand, but if she closed her eyes, she could remember how it felt. The way her fingers had curled around the smooth wooden handle while the scent of turpentine surrounded her. The excitement of staring at a canvas that seemed to beg her to fill it with color. How the images had danced through her mind and flowed through her brush onto that canvas, and she'd become so lost in what she was creating that she'd completely lose track of time.

*No.* Sam shoved the thoughts away. As her father had pointed out, art was fine as a hobby, but one couldn't make a living from it. She'd been much better off listening to him and joining the advertising agency. So what if she hadn't had the time to indulge herself by painting. She'd enjoyed more success than she'd ever dreamed of having, and by God, she wasn't done yet. Thinking of Dan and the way he was sucking up to her father, she clenched her hands beneath the plastic cape she was wearing. She'd fight her way back into her job if she had to.

And if she lost the fight? Forgetting Alice and her scissors, Sam gave a quick nod. She'd start her own agency and she'd give the old man a run for his money. Jackson wouldn't approve. He wouldn't want any bad blood between members of the family, but too bad. He'd just have to deal with it. She'd start work on her business plan as soon as she got back to the cabin. Then if her father refused to give her her job back, she'd be covered.

Her mind still racing with ideas, Sam looked up and found both Anne and Alice staring at her with a puzzled expression. "Ah, sorry, did you say something?" she asked, feeling a blush stain her cheeks.

Removing the cape, Alice spun the chair around so it faced the mirror. "There," she said, winking at Sam's reflection. "How do you like it?"

Sam's eyes widened. The ragged locks were gone. Instead, her auburn hair was arranged in a shiny cap around her face that seemed to mute and soften the gauntness. She began turning her head this way and that, and the strands bounced and glistened in the light. Sassy . . . she felt sassy, she thought, grinning at herself.

She looked up at Alice and her smile widened. "Thank you," she replied with sincerity. "It looks great."

Pleased, Alice helped Sam to her feet and, with one last touch, fluffed the hair on either side of Sam's face. "Come back in six weeks for a trim."

Sam sobered. *Not likely. I'll either be back at my old job or launching my own agency by then.*

"In six weeks, I'll be back in the Cities," she said, shooting a determined look at Anne.

Anne looked down at her feet, refusing to meet Sam's stare, and Sam felt her pleasure slip away. The other woman didn't believe that she'd be better in six weeks.

What had she been thinking? She gave herself a backward glance in the mirror. A new haircut hadn't changed anything, she thought as she limped across the beauty shop. It wouldn't get her job back, and it wouldn't make the muscles in her leg stronger. And who was she kidding? If she threatened her father with the possibility of opening her own agency, he'd only laugh at her.

Useless, she was still useless.

Sam slammed into the cabin. "I'm going back to my bedroom," she called over her shoulder as she headed toward the hallway.

"Fine, I'll come get you when I've finished straightening up the kitchen." Anne flung her purse on the table and crossed to the counter. "We're going for a walk today."

The stress caused by the women at the beauty shop whispering about her and by being asked questions that she didn't want to answer was more than Sam could handle. She stopped short and turned back around. She didn't care what Anne wanted. She wanted to be alone, even if it meant locking herself in her bedroom. Narrowing her eyes, she studied Anne's biceps. Probably not a good idea. The woman looked more than capable of dismantling a door.

"I need rest," Sam cried with a stamp of her good leg. "You've been dragging me around all day. Can't you leave me alone for five minutes?"

"No problem," Anne replied pleasantly. "That's about how long it's going to take me to put away these dishes . . . then we'll go for that walk."

Sam crossed her arms over her chest and glared at the other woman. "I don't want to go."

"Sure you do. It's a nice afternoon and a short trip up the lane will help strengthen your leg. Then, when we get back, I'll do another deep muscle massage."

Her self-assured tone had Sam gritting her teeth as she struggled to come up with a response. "Don't you ever get tired of giving orders?"

"Don't you ever get tired of trying to hide out in your bedroom?" Anne fired back.

"I'm not hiding out."

"You would if I let you."

"I've done everything you've asked—no, wait, *told* me to do."

"And bitched about it the whole time."

It was no use. Anne was like an immovable object and arguments bounced off her like raindrops on concrete. She didn't listen to Sam any more than her father and Jackson did. Sam felt hopelessness threaten to swamp her.

Suddenly a woman's squeal drifted up from the lake followed by the sound of a deep baritone voice.

"Just touch it."

Her attention flew to the open patio door.

"No," the woman shrieked. "It's wiggling."

"Oh, come on," her male companion said. "It's not that big. It's only ten inches."

Out of the corner of her eye, Sam saw Anne's mouth twitch with a grin. "My God, I hope he's talking about a fish."

An absurd image flashed through her mind and something rose inside Sam like effervescent bubbles, driving away the hopelessness. Something so foreign, she'd forgotten what it felt like. For the first time in as long as she could remember, she laughed.

As Sam walked down the gravel path, the sun did feel good on the back of her neck, but she wouldn't give Anne the satisfaction of admitting it. The breeze blowing off the lake carried with it the smell of pine and honeysuckle. Ahead of them, a cloud of gnats whirled in the air. If Anne hadn't been with her, she might have stopped and let the sun soak into her body to warm the constant cold spot deep inside.

But if Anne wasn't with her, she'd be alone, outside, no longer protected by four safe walls. Out in the open, where anyone could find her. The cold spot inside grew and her steps faltered.

Anne noticed and halted. "Are you doing okay?"

She didn't answer and kept walking.

In two long strides, Anne came even with her and took a deep breath of the pine-scented air. "Doesn't this make us feel better?" She sounded like an adult talking to a little kid. "Being outside in the fresh air and sunshine? Instead of cooped up in that old cabin?"

"Look, Nurse Nancy, don't patronize me," Sam grumbled. "There is no 'us.' There's you and there's me."

Anne shook her head, slowing her pace to match Sam's. "You are a prickly one."

"I have the right," Sam shot back.

"Maybe you do," Anne said as her gaze wandered to the stand

of pine trees growing along the road, "but a good outlook can help the body heal."

Sam lifted an eyebrow. "Another lecture about my attitude? You really do like playing amateur psychologist, don't you?"

"No, but I've worked with patients who've suffered trauma and I know how it can mess with your mind," Anne replied calmly. "Dr. Van Horn told me about how you were attacked."

"At least you didn't call it an 'accident,'" Sam muttered, lowering her head.

"What?"

"Nothing." Sam kept her focus on the ground. "I don't want to talk about it."

Anne ignored her. "He said it happened two weeks before your wedding, and—"

Sam's feet skidded to a stop on the pea gravel. "I said I didn't want to talk about it."

"Talking helps. It's not good to keep it all bottled up inside."

"Ha," Sam said with an angry snort. "How would you know?"

Anne lifted a shoulder. "I've had my share of problems . . . maybe not like yours . . ." She paused, as if weighing her words. "Before we moved here," she continued, "my son was running with a bad crowd and—"

Sam's hand flew to her throat. "Bad crowd? What does that mean? Your son was in a gang?"

A gang had ruined her life, and now here was a woman whose son was just like them. Her heart pounded. She had to get back to the safety of the cabin.

Spinning on her heel, Sam stumbled, but Anne's hand shot out and steadied her.

"My son wasn't in a gang, yet . . ." She faltered. "A friend—a coworker at the hospital—took the time to listen to me." Anne dropped Sam's arm. "She suggested we move to the lake, and coming here saved us. Maybe it will save you, too."

"It's not that easy . . ." Sam's hand strayed to her weak leg. "I've lost everything."

"You're still alive, aren't you?"

Sam felt the bitterness crawl out of the cold spot inside. "If you call this living—I don't." She took a step forward. "I want to go back to the cabin."

"Nope," Anne said, gently taking Sam's arm again and turning her around. "See that cabin down the road? Today we walk that far . . . tomorrow a little farther."

"Why do you have to keep pushing me?"

Anne gave her arm a little tug. "I was hired to help you and that's what I'm going to do."

"I've had enough help for one day."

"I don't think so," she replied, giving Sam's arm another jerk. "Come on; keep moving."

Sam shrugged away from Anne's grasp. Another battle lost. Okay, fine, she thought, she'd walk to the neighbor's damn cabin. Maybe she had promised to cooperate, but she had to draw the line somewhere. Anne was taking complete control of her life, and she'd had enough of that from her father and Jackson. Anne wouldn't win the next fight. With a sense of purpose that she hadn't felt for a long time, Sam took a firm step. The other woman followed.

As they approached the cabin, two dogs rushed toward the chain-link fence surrounding the cabin, startling Sam. She stopped while the dogs danced around barking. Behind them, back in the far corner, she spied another dog, cowering next to a tree. Two black ears lay flat against its head while it stared at the world with haunted eyes, as if at any moment it expected a blow to fall. Pink patches of skin showed along its haunches, and even at this distance, she could see the poor thing's ribs. She thought of Alice's pampered poodles. This dog had never been pampered in its life.

The dog's eyes suddenly locked onto her, and in an instant, her mind flashed back to the parking garage, and she saw herself on her knees, begging for her life. Humiliated and afraid to move—just like that dog. *It's not fair—no living creature, not even a dog, should ever experience that kind of terror.* Her breath caught in her throat as the dog's eyes seemed to plead for help. The blood rushed to her face and all the anger bottled up inside her burst. She hadn't been able to save herself, but maybe she could save this dog. With determined steps, she limped past the fence and headed toward the small deck that extended from the front of the cabin.

"What are you doing, Sam?" she heard Anne call from behind her, but she ignored her.

Grasping the railing, she hauled herself up the steps, one at a time. She crossed the deck and pounded on the front door. From inside, she heard the soft strains of a saxophone.

Suddenly the music stopped and a man wearing jeans—no shirt, just jeans—answered and stepped out on the deck. Above his narrow waist, dark hair trailed across his tan chest. From what Sam could see, and she could see quite a bit, he didn't have an ounce of fat on him.

"Yes?" he said as his dark brown eyes questioned her.

Shaken by the vision of a half-dressed man standing in front of her, Sam felt her words die in her throat. Then she remembered the dog with the frightened eyes and her anger flared again.

"You ought to be ashamed of yourself," she lectured, jabbing a finger at the man. "That poor dog out there. He needs help, and—"

"It's not a 'he'; it's a 'she.' Roxy. And I know she needs help," he interrupted, studying Sam. "You're not from around here, are you?"

Sam squared her shoulders and glared at him. "We're not talking about me—we're talking about that dog. And if you don't take better care of her, I'll report you to the ASPCA."

He crossed his arms over his chest and leaned a shoulder against the side of the door. "Go ahead."

Her eyes narrowed. "You don't care if I turn you in for cruelty to animals? They'll fine you and take your dogs away."

"I know." Straightening, he reached into his back pocket. "Here's my card. You want to make sure you get my name right when you turn me in," he said, and handed her the card.

In the shade of the porch, she squinted to read the words.

The blood rushed to her face again, but not in anger—in embarrassment.

The card read *Greg Clemons, Animal Behaviorist, Scott County Animal Rescue League.*

"You—you," she stuttered.

His mouth curved in a smile. "Yeah, I foster abused dogs—"

Sam turned away before he could say anything else, but he reached out and, touching her arm, stopped her.

"Hey, I'm sorry. I didn't mean to embarrass you. I was only yanking your chain a little. Truthfully, I admire your passion," he said with laughter in his voice. "Would you like to meet Roxy?" He looked over at Anne and waved.

"No, no, thanks," Sam said, jerking away from him. Putting her head down, she hurried across the porch. She heard Anne cry out to be careful, but in her haste, she missed the first step. With a squeak, she pitched forward, and thudded to the ground at the base of the steps.

Her right leg crumpled beneath her and both Anne and Greg rushed toward her. Rolling over on her bottom, she pulled up into a sitting position.

Crouching, Anne ran her hand gently down Sam's ankle. "Are you hurt?"

"I'm fine," Sam replied.

Anne looked up at Greg. "Nothing feels broken, but it's starting to swell."

"I said, it's okay," Sam argued as Anne and Greg helped her stand. A small groan escaped as she tried to put weight on her ankle.

"Wait right here," Greg said, holding up both hands and backing away. Turning, he ran to the house, leaving Sam leaning on Anne. A moment later, he returned, now wearing a T-shirt and carrying keys in his hand. He hurried up to Sam and scooped her up as if she weighed nothing.

"Wait—stop." Hating this stranger's closeness, Sam struggled against him. "Put me down. What are you doing?"

"Taking you to the emergency room," he answered, and gripped her legs tighter. "You need an X-ray."

Sam squirmed harder. "No! No hospitals!" she cried with a helpless look back at Anne.

Anne came up even with them and placed a hand on Greg's arm. "Wait. I'm pretty sure it's not broken. It's probably just bruised. Why don't you take her inside and I'll give Dr. Miller a call? See what he has to say about bringing her in."

With a shrug, Greg reversed his position and carried Sam inside his cabin. Striding over to the couch, he deposited her on it, propping up her legs.

"I'll get an ice pack," he said, turning away and heading for the small kitchen off the living room. Anne followed, dialing her cell as she went.

Alone, Sam took a deep breath and let it out slowly. How could she have been so stupid? Yelling at a complete stranger then taking a header off the porch. If her father and Jackson found out about this, they'd have a fit. Looking down at her legs, she was more concerned about her father and her fiancé's reaction to her fall than she was her ankle.

Her attention shifted to the small living room. A large sound system dominated the wall to her left and, in the corner, sat a basket full of what appeared to be chew toys. *At least those dogs weren't forced to spend their entire lives outside*, Sam thought, spying several dog hairs littering the couch. Plucking at one, she turned as Greg and Anne entered the room.

"Well?" she asked, her eyebrows lifting.

"Dr. Miller said to wrap your ankle and ice it," Anne answered.

"No X-ray?"

"Not now. But he'll want to see you if there's much swelling or if it isn't better by tomorrow."

Sam breathed a sigh of relief. "It will be," she said, swinging her legs off the couch. "I think you're making a lot of fuss over nothing."

She made a move to stand, but before she could, Greg swept her off her feet.

"Not again," she cried, pushing against him.

"I'm driving you back to your cabin," he stated flatly as he carried her toward the door.

"I can walk."

"That's not a good idea," Anne said from behind them. "Dr. Miller wants you to stay off of that leg as much as possible."

"But I can walk to the car," Sam argued, squirming in Greg's arms.

"You heard Anne," Greg said, his tone short. "And, lady, if you don't stop wiggling, I'm going to wind up dropping you." He leaned his head closer to Sam. "Then your ankle won't be the only thing that's bruised."

# Nine

Anne stomped into her house and threw her bag on the nearest chair. She'd had it. Samantha Moore was impossible. She'd overlooked the young woman's contrary attitude while she used every ounce of experience she had to help her, and what does Sam do? Ignores her pleas for caution and falls off a porch, wrenching her right ankle. Anne tugged at her thick braid in frustration. Then she had the audacity not only to argue with Greg as he carried her in and out of the car, but to kick Anne out after she'd settled her in bed.

How in the hell did she think she could manage? Anne had half a mind to let her try. Call Lawrence Moore and tell him she quit. Working at a bar and handling drunks had to be easier than dealing with that woman. No, wait—the care facility over in Hankton. Sure—the salary wouldn't be as high, and the cost of driving the eighty-mile round-trip would take out a chunk, but it would be better than putting up with Samantha Moore's drama. She'd drive over there tomorrow and at least check it out.

She paced into the kitchen and yanked open the refrigerator. No, she couldn't do that. She'd never abandoned a patient before, but God, it was tempting. She'd go back to the cabin tonight, but keep the idea of resigning in mind. It wouldn't hurt to ask around. Maybe she could find another patient. Hearing the front door slam, she turned to see Caleb stride into the kitchen. He took one look at his mother's face and skidded to a halt.

"What's wrong?"

Anne blew out a long breath. "Sam fell," she said, shutting the door, "and—"

"Is she okay?" Caleb's eyebrows shot up. "Did she fall during therapy?"

"She'll be fine. It's a minor injury and should be okay in a couple of days. And no, it happened at Greg's . . . long story."

"You know, Mom, people around the lake are talking about her."

"Who?"

Caleb shrugged. "Esther Dunlap—"

Anne cut him off. "You haven't been charging at Dunlap's again, have you?"

"No. I paid cash," he replied defensively. "But I ran into someone down there and they were asking me all about Miss Moore. They said they'd heard stuff about her from Mrs. Dunlap and Mr. Thorpe."

*Figures,* Anne thought with disgust. If Fritz mentioned his encounter with Sam to Esther, she would've passed his tale along to everyone she knew. And once the story hit the rumor mill, the degree of Sam's antisocial behavior would've grown with each telling.

"Who wanted to know about her?"

Caleb's gaze wandered around the room as he refused to meet her eyes. "Just someone."

Anne knew immediately who'd been quizzing him. "Teddy Brighton."

"Yeah," he said quickly, returning his attention to her, "but I wasn't hanging out with him. I just ran into him at Dunlap's."

She eyed him with skepticism, making him squirm.

"Honest. I only talked to him for a couple of minutes."

"I hope that's true, Caleb," she replied sternly. "And I hope you didn't tell him anything I've told you about Samantha Moore."

"Nah, he seemed more curious about where she was living. He said he'd heard something about the woman who used to live there and his grandfather. He said—"

*Blanche Jones and the first Theodore Brighton.* Anne held up her hand, stopping him. She'd heard those stories, too, but she didn't intend to discuss old gossip with her teenage son. She had enough to think about dealing with the present; forget about something that happened decades ago.

Anne reached up and tousled Caleb's hair. "I have to go back and I'll probably be spending the night," she finished, trying to keep the dread out of her voice. "You'll be okay here alone?"

"Ah, Mom," Caleb replied, dropping his chin. "I'm not a little kid."

"I know, but I don't want you doing anything stupid."

His head lifted. "Like what?"

"Like inviting Teddy over."

"Mom, forget about Teddy," he argued. "You told me to stay away from him and I have." He scuffed a tennis shoe across the floor. "Besides, Teddy's too busy entertaining a bunch of his city friends."

"Good," she replied emphatically. "Let them get in trouble instead of you."

"Mom—" He cut himself off and chewed on his lip. "Why didn't you tell me you talked to Mr. Thorpe?"

Anne looked away, missing the sudden light in Caleb's eye.

"He said you don't want me to play in the Fourth of July concert," he continued.

She waved away his words. "I didn't think you'd have the time to practice, what with your job and getting ready for your senior year."

"But—"

The sudden ringing of the phone interrupted him. Happy to end the conversation, Anne grabbed it on the second ring.

"Hello."

"Ms. Weaver?"

"Yes."

"I'm Joseph Marshall with Scott County Bank—"

Anne's hand on the receiver tightened.

"This is in regard to your Visa payment," he continued.

Glancing at Caleb, now perusing the contents of the refrigerator, she walked slowly into the living room as she kept her voice low. "I made a payment last week."

"Yes, I see that," the voice on the phone answered smoothly. "But were you aware that your minimum payment has increased?"

"No," she answered as her heart picked up its rhythm. "How much?"

"It's now one hundred and fifty dollars and—"

"But that's doubled," she cried.

"You were sent a notice," he replied calmly.

"I can't afford that."

"You do have the choice of paying off the entire amount."

"Sir, if I can't afford a hundred and fifty, what makes you think that I can afford a couple of thousand?"

"I'm sorry, Ms. Weaver, but if you can't catch up on the payments, we'll have no choice but to turn the matter over to a collection agency."

A wave of nausea hit her. If the bank turned her bill into collections, it would ruin her credit rating, and make it impossible to get any loans for Caleb's college.

"Which will it be, Ms. Weaver?"

"Can't you give me more time?"

"You have ten days," he answered.

Anne hung up without replying. Walking over to the couch, she sank down and buried her face in her hands. What did she do now? So much for telling Lawrence Moore she quit. Maybe, just maybe, if she saved every dime, with her check from the Moores, she and Caleb could squeak through the summer and she could pay the extra money on her credit card. Then this fall, if she got her job back at the hospital, they'd be okay.

"Mom?"

Anne dropped her hands and turned to see Caleb standing in the doorway, holding a thick sandwich.

"Who was that on the phone?"

She couldn't let him see her fear. Schooling her face, she pinned on a tight smile. "Telemarketer," she lied. Slapping her thighs, she stood. "I'd better get going. I don't want to leave Sam alone for too—"

The jangling of the phone interrupted her again. Great, probably the bank calling back with more threats. Angrily, she grabbed it. "Yes?"

"Anne? Lawrence Moore here."

Anne rolled her eyes. The old saying "when it rains, it pours" sprang to her mind. She'd hoped to avoid discussing Sam's little mishap with her father, but evidently it was too late for that. Sam probably called him to complain the instant Anne had left the cabin.

"Mr. Moore," she said, motioning Caleb out of the room, "I'm so sorry about Samantha's fall." The words came rushing out. "It all happened so fast and—"

"What are you talking about?" he barked. "What fall?"

"Uh . . . well . . . she didn't call you?"

"No," he answered tersely. "I think you'd better explain yourself."

"Samantha's fine," she hurried on. "Just a little sprain. She tripped going down some steps and twisted her right ankle. We have ice on it and it will be okay in a couple of days. I'm on my way back over there now."

There was a long pause on the other end of the line.

"I see," he finally said. "And where were you when this happened?"

"I was there," she answered defensively, "but not close enough to prevent the fall."

"Need I remind you that you're being paid not only to help my daughter with her therapy, but also to keep her *safe*?"

"No, of course not, Mr. Moore. I assure you I don't take my responsibilities lightly, but really there wasn't much I could do. She—"

"I'm afraid, Ms. Weaver," he said, cutting her off, "that this incident will require us to seek someone else to care for Samantha."

"You're firing me?" Anne gasped.

"We can't afford to have your inattentiveness impede Samantha's recovery."

"Mr. Moore," she began.

"We'll expect you to continue you duties through this weekend," he interrupted, not letting her finish. "I'll send you a check next week."

The line went dead.

Anne stared at the silent phone in the palm of her hand. She thought back to her earlier plans to quit. Well, she didn't have to worry about that decision anymore. Lawrence Moore had made it for her. What if she couldn't find another summer job? She'd have to dip into her savings account to make it through until the hospital called her back this fall . . . *if* they called her back. And now there was that damned Visa bill. No matter how she looked at it, it meant less money for Caleb's college. After all her years of careful planning, her dreams for his future were slipping away. Tears sprang to her eyes. It wasn't fair. She'd worked so hard to give Caleb the chances that she'd thrown away when she'd been his age.

Pinching the bridge of her nose to hold back the tears, she placed the phone on the coffee table. Sitting here bawling about her problems was pointless. Maybe she had been fired, but she was still responsible for Samantha Moore at least until the weekend and she needed to get back to the cabin. She wouldn't give Lawrence Moore another reason to accuse her of being derelict in her duties. She'd start her job search tomorrow. Now all she had to do was figure out a way to convince Sam that she should stay the night.

Anne stood in the doorway of Sam's bedroom, watching her read a magazine. Finally the girl looked up and frowned.

"You're back," she stated flatly, returning her attention to the magazine. "I told you I wanted to be alone."

"Tough," Anne replied in a hard voice. "Your ankle needs to be kept elevated, so I'm here to wait on you . . ." She paused. "At least for the rest of the week. After that, you can argue with someone else."

Sam placed the magazine on the bed and cocked her head. "You're quitting?"

Placing her shoulder against the door frame, Anne crossed her arms over her chest. "No, I've been fired. Your father thinks I've been 'inattentive,' so I'm done Monday."

Sam shook her head. "No, you're not."

"Oh yes, I am," Anne exclaimed, pushing away from the door. "Your father was quite clear on that score. I'll fix you a tray then put more ice on your ankle."

Plucking at the bedspread, Sam tugged on her bottom lip. "My father changed his mind."

Anne's eyebrows shot up. "When?"

"He called after talking to you." Sam's eyes narrowed. "Why did you tell him I fell?"

"I thought you'd already told him."

Sam gave a small grunt. "Not likely. In case you haven't noticed, my father has control issues. The less he knows the better." Her mouth tightened in a grim line. "I'm trying to convince him that I can take care of myself, and telling him that I fell isn't the way to do it. I'd appreciate it if you'd keep that in mind."

"Let's go back to the part about me not being fired—" Anne stopped as a small, satisfied smile crept across Sam's face.

"It's the first time in a long time that I've won a battle with him," Sam said in a wry voice. "It was lovely." She shook her head again and the smile disappeared. "I convinced him that I wouldn't work with anyone else."

Stunned, Anne stared at her. "Why? It's not like you've enjoyed working with me."

Sam shrugged. "I guess I'd rather have the devil I know than the one I don't."

"Me being that devil?" Anne said curtly.

"Exactly." Sam studied Anne carefully. "You may be bossy and pigheaded, but at least you've been straight with me. And you don't take any bullshit." A grin tugged at the corner of her mouth. "As evidenced by the fact that you came back even though I kicked you out."

"Speaking of which—"

Sam held up a hand, silencing her. "I know. Not one bum leg, but now two. Do you have any idea how embarrassed I was? Falling flat like that? Then having a stranger cart me around like I was a baby?" Her hand dropped. "I needed to be alone for a while. I'm not stupid . . . I knew you'd be back."

Anne felt a subtle shift in power. She now owed her job to Sam. Did that mean she had to answer not only to Sam's father, but to Sam, too? If so, it wouldn't work. Based on Sam's behavior the last couple of weeks, Anne couldn't afford to let her have the upper hand. And that's exactly what she'd have. She'd be able to remind her every time she didn't want to do something that it was thanks to her that she still had a job. Anne couldn't be effective under those conditions.

"Look, thank you for convincing your father not to fire me, but maybe it would be best if you worked with someone else."

"Why? Afraid I'll hold getting your job back over your head?"

Anne grimaced. "To be honest . . . yes."

"I won't," Sam replied sincerely. "You know what you're doing, but I need you to back off a little." Her attention traveled to the window as she shifted nervously. "Before the attack, I ran my own life. Now I'm told when to get up, when to go to bed, what to eat, what not to eat. I'm sick of it."

"You want to call a truce? Is that it?"

"Yes."

Anne's gaze roamed around the bedroom. "I won't let you hibernate."

"I don't expect you to."

She thought of the pile of bills lying on the kitchen and her eyes narrowed. "The first time you threaten to go to your father, I'm out of here."

"Fair enough," Sam replied.

With a glance over her shoulder, Anne moved away from the door. Could she trust the girl? Or would she play the prima donna? Time would tell, but every dollar she earned here would be one less dollar lost out of savings—that was enough at this point. Anne took a half step before Sam called out, stopping her.

"Wait a second—who is Greg Clemons?"

Anne noticed two faint red splotches appear on Sam's cheeks. She must really have been embarrassed earlier if even the mention of Greg's name made her blush.

"If you're worried Greg will gossip about you, don't," she said with a shrug. "Greg's a good guy, keeps mostly to himself, and doesn't spread tales." Anne's thoughts flashed to Esther Dunlap and Fritz Thorpe, and she frowned. "Not like some others I could name around here."

"He works for the animal shelter?"

"Yes." Anne tugged on her bottom lip. How much should she tell Sam? Greg was a friend, and after mentally condemning Esther and Fritz for their loose lips, she couldn't very well reveal his secrets. "He not only works at the shelter, but takes in the worst cases of abuse, rehabilitates them, then finds homes for them."

Sam cocked her head. "When I knocked, I heard a saxophone."

"Yeah, that was Greg. He loves jazz."

"I've never cared for it," Sam replied, her lip curling.

"Ah, something you have in common with Fritz Thorpe. He doesn't like it either. He's been trying to get Greg to play with him for years, but Greg won't play what Fritz wants." Anne gave a small chuckle. "I think he refuses just to irritate Fritz."

"Mr. Thorpe is a musician?"

"Oh yeah," she answered with a vigorous nod. "He's a retired music professor."

"He's fairly young to be retired, isn't he?"

She hesitated. Fritz might not be her favorite person, but she didn't feel the need to relate the old stories of why he had taken early retirement.

Ignoring Sam's question, she continued, "According to some, he's even composed a few pieces." She caught the look of surprise on Sam's face. "You're shocked?"

"Well . . . yeah. I wouldn't have expected, ah, um . . ."

"Culture in the backwoods of Minnesota?"

Sam bobbed her head.

Anne turned on her heel. "You'll find that there are a lot of unexpected things around here."

A hand shaking her shoulder awoke Anne from a sound sleep. Rolling over on the couch, she opened her eyes to see Sam's face looming over her in the pale moonlight. She wiped the sleep from her eyes and sat up.

"What are you doing out of bed? Your ankle. You shouldn't be putting any weigh—"

"Shh." Sam silenced her while she leaned heavily against the arm of the couch. "She's back."

"Who?"

"The woman," Sam answered in a voice tight with fear.

"What woman?"

"There's a woman, dressed in a nightgown, standing at the end of the dock."

"Impossible," Anne said, throwing off the light blanket covering her. She swung her legs off the couch and, with quick strides, crossed the room to the patio door. Flinging the curtains open, she peered into the darkness. Nothing. She opened the door and stepped out onto the deck.

Across the lake, lights from Fritz's cabin flickered, and she heard the light notes of a saxophone drifting on the breeze. Walking along the edge of the deck, she looked over the side. Again, nothing. Rolling her eyes, she went back inside.

Turning, she locked the door to the deck and flicked on a light. Sam sat on the couch, her face white and her eyes huge. Anne shook her head. "There's no one out there."

"Didn't you hear the whispers?"

"No," Anne answered slowly. "Did you?"

"Yes." Sam lowered her head and stared at her lap. "Just like before. I heard whispers and smelled cigarette smoke." She lifted her head. "You don't smoke, do you?"

"No." Anne watched her carefully. Sam was truly afraid. "This has happened before?"

"Yes. The first night I was here alone." She drew a shuddering breath. "First the whispers, followed by the smell of cigarette smoke." Her eyes darted to the now-closed drapes. "Then I saw a woman, in a lavender nightgown, standing at the end of the dock."

"Did you see what she looked like?"

"Not her face, but she had long red hair."

It could have been a nightmare, but Sam seemed so convinced

that she had seen someone. Anne searched her mind for an explanation. *Long red hair, huh?* She wasn't aware of any redheads living at the lake this summer. Next time she ran into Fritz Thorpe, she'd try to ask him about red-haired strangers without raising his suspicions.

Her lips tightened in a frown. Caleb had told her that the rumors about Sam's nervousness had been flying. What if someone who had nothing better to do than to prey on others thought it would be funny to play a sick joke on her? Someone like Teddy Brighton.

# Ten

I stop playing and stand. Spanning my fingers wide, I admire their competence. So strong, so sure, I really do have beautiful hands. Curling and uncurling each digit, I watch the tendons expand and contract and am satisfied every muscle, every nerve is working as it should. I drop them to my side and stroll to the kitchen. Immediately my attention is caught by the window above the sink.

I'd forgotten to lower the blinds.

Frowning, I cross the room. My hand pauses on the cord as I move to lower them. Outside, I see the hulking shadows of the pine trees ringing my property. Once I roamed those woods and the hills behind them. No longer. They contain secrets, secrets dark as a cave. A small smile flits across my face at my cleverness. Dark as a cave, I like that. But then my breath quickens as I remember just how dark that is. A cold, damp dark that seeps into every pore as you lie huddled and alone, crying for your mother . . .

*No.* I yank the cord and send the blinds crashing down. My breath slows. I'm an adult, and the darkness holds no power over me now. Stepping over to the liquor cabinet, I open it and take down a glass and a bottle of Scotch. Not my beloved Glenlivet, but under the circumstances it will have to do. I dislike the way my hand shakes as I pour three fingers. Knocking it back, I let the amber liquid chase away the cold memories.

Better now, I pour another before I go back to the living room. I search for my special tape, one that I made years ago when cassettes were all the rage. Finding it, I fumble in my haste and pop it into the tape deck. Soon the melody fills the room. Closing my eyes, I sway back and forth to the music and some of the Scotch sloshes onto my hand. Normally, wasting precious drops of the amber liquor would bother me, but not now. All I want is for the music to carry me away.

He handles that particular section of the piece with such mastery that it almost brings me to tears. In a wordless salute, I lift my glass to him then down it in one gulp.

I look at my hands again. I'm good, but he was better. Such flair, such styling. He could've been one of the greats if she hadn't come along.

I try and turn my thoughts. I will not sully his work by thinking of her while his music dances around me. Angry now, I stop the tape.

She should've recognized his talent and left him alone. But no, she played with him like he was a shiny new toy. That is, until the shininess wore off. Then she cast him away, ruined and broken, and moved on to the next one.

My eyes are drawn back to the kitchen window. She deserved it, she really did. My finger taps at the empty glass. So what if it trapped me in a life I never wanted? Vengeance does have its price, and not only for its victim, but also for its avenger.

# Eleven

Sam rolled over on her back and stretched her arms high above her head. Carefully, she moved her right ankle side to side. Nope; nothing, not even a twinge. She smiled to herself. She'd been right—Anne and Greg Clemons had made a fuss over nothing. Her face sobered. She'd been lucky. The fall could've been serious and she'd need to be more cautious. Not let herself get swept up in her emotions so easily.

Turning on her side, she tucked her hands under her pillow. She'd been so humiliated by her outburst that all she could think about was getting away from Greg as quickly as possible. She'd always been in control of her feelings, but now they constantly simmered right below the surface, ready to burst forth at the smallest thing. Wonder what Dr. Weissinger would say about that? Wonder what he'd say about the mysterious woman haunting her dock at night?

Was there a woman? She burrowed deeper under the covers. Anne didn't see her, but, she argued with herself, that didn't mean the woman hadn't been there. Did Anne believe her? Probably not, because no one ever believed her. It's true that after the coma she'd had a hard time differentiating between her dreams and reality, but she thought she was better. Panic threatened to claim her. What if everyone did have reason to doubt her? What if she was again losing her grasp? No, she wouldn't allow it.

Throwing off the covers, she sat up, but dizziness hit her and she fell back against the pillows. Her gaze fastened on the pills sitting on the nightstand. She hadn't been able to slide on her meds last night. Anne had insisted that she take every single one, including the ones Jackson said would help her sleep. She gave a soft snort. Well, they weren't working, were they? She'd actually slept better on the nights she'd been too tired to take them.

A sharp rap at the door broke through her thoughts. The door swung open and Anne's head appeared in the doorway.

"Breakfast is ready," she said, stepping into the room. "How's the ankle?"

"Better," Sam replied.

"Let's see." Anne crossed the room and, kneeling, removed the bandage around Sam's ankle. "Hmm," she said, gently pressing the muscle. "The swelling's gone. Does it hurt?"

"No," Sam answered truthfully.

"Good." Anne rose to her feet and looked down at her with a twinkle in her eye. "I know this is going to break your heart, but I think we'll pass on the walk today. We'll concentrate on strengthening exercises here at the cabin."

"Inside?" Sam couldn't keep the hopeful note out of her voice.

Anne crossed her arms over her chest and studied her for a moment. "Why don't you like going outside?"

"I just don't," Sam mumbled.

Anne wasn't going to give up. "And the reason is?"

Sam tugged on her bottom lip, and her gaze traveled to the

window and the closed blinds. "It's hard to explain—" She halted. "It . . . I . . . I feel exposed."

"Exposed?"

"Yeah, as if someone is watching me." Returning her attention to Anne, she held up her hand when Anne started to speak. "Okay, I know no one is really watching me, but I can't seem to shake the feeling."

"Have you talked to your therapist about it?"

"Of course," Sam replied, her lips in a grim line. "He said those feelings would lessen in time, then he gave me another prescription."

"But they're not?"

"No, and to be honest, it's worse up here than it was in the Cities."

Anne frowned. "That doesn't make sense. I would think those feelings would be more severe in a crowded city than in the open spaces here."

"Look, I didn't say it made sense." Sam swung her legs off the bed and made a move to stand, but the dizziness hit her again and she plopped back onto the bed.

Anne was at her side in an instant. "What's wrong? Is it your ankle?"

"No, my ankle's fine. The swelling's gone and I can put weight on it," Sam answered, passing a hand over her eyes. "It's those damn pills Jackson insists I take at bedtime. They make me woozier than the last prescription."

"Dr. Van Horn prescribed them, not your psychiatrist?"

Sam waved her away and slowly rose to her feet. "I don't know whose name was on the scrip—I never looked—but Jackson thought they'd help."

Anne picked up the bottle of pills and studied them. Dr. Van Horn's name was on the label. Without a word, she placed it back on the nightstand. "By the way, Jackson called last night after you were asleep."

Sam's eyes widened. "You didn't tell him about my fall, did you?"

"I didn't have to," Anne said with a grimace. "Your father had already talked to him."

"Great." Sam took a few halting steps away from the bed. "I suppose he's rushing up here?"

"No," Anne said, following close behind. "I convinced him it was minor, but he is calling back this morning."

Sam stopped her progress across the room and turned. "When he does call, please don't say anything about the woman."

"If someone is prowling around the cabin, don't you think he should know?"

"No," Sam replied, her words short. "He won't believe me, so what's the point?" She studied Anne carefully. "Do *you* think I saw someone?"

Anne's gaze dropped to the floor. "I believe that you saw something." She hesitated. "Whether or not someone was really down there . . ." Her voice trailed away.

"I might have been dreaming?"

"I don't know." She laid a hand on Sam's arm. "But word travels fast around here. If anyone else has spotted a woman wandering around the lake at night, someone is sure to mention it."

Well, at least Anne wasn't dismissing her out of hand like her father and Jackson would've done. She supposed she should be grateful for that much, but maybe if there were more late-night visits, it would be best to keep her mouth shut.

"Do you need any help getting dressed?" Anne asked.

Sam shook her head.

"Okay. I'll set the table and we'll have breakfast."

A few minutes later, Sam joined Anne in the kitchen. She'd pulled out the chair when a knock at the door startled her. Jerking, she made a move away from the table, heading back to the safety of her bedroom, but a look from Anne stopped her. With a sigh of resignation, she sat down.

Anne swiftly walked to the door, opening it to reveal Greg Clemons and the black dog Sam had defended, standing on her porch.

She stifled a groan.

"Hope you don't mind," Greg said, stepping into the kitchen, "but Roxy wanted to see how you were doing."

Sam's attention turned to the dog sitting at Greg's side. Once again, their eyes met and the dog wiggled in response.

"I think she remembers me," Sam said in a surprised voice.

Greg bent and scratched the dog's ears. "Sure she does. Animals always remember when someone does them a kindness." He smiled down at the dog. "Don't you, Roxy?"

Roxy's eyes left Sam's and she stared up at Greg, cocking her head.

Sam gave a chuckle. "She knows you're talking about her."

"She's a smart girl," he answered, giving Roxy's ears another scratch. His attention turned toward Sam. "Would you like to officially meet her?"

Sam felt a moment of panic. She'd never been around animals much. When she was a child, her parents had never wanted a dog interfering with their lifestyle, and as an adult, she'd always been too busy for pets.

"I guess," she replied hesitantly.

He knelt beside Roxy. "Okay. I'm going to remove her leash, so just let her come to you when she's ready. And don't stare at her—dogs sometimes see that as aggression. Pretend she's not even here."

Sam turned her head away from Roxy and focused on the wall. A moment later, she felt a cold nose nudge her hand resting on her thigh.

"May I look now?" she asked.

"You bet," Greg said with a laugh. "She wants you to pet her. That's a good sign."

She lowered her gaze to the pair of brown eyes looking up at her expectantly. With a smile, she stroked the slick black head. "You're a pretty girl, aren't you," she said softly as a long pink tongue flicked out to lick her wrist.

With a pleased look, Greg pulled out a chair and joined them. "I'm glad she's making friends with you. She's been afraid of strangers and we're trying to help her get over it."

Placing a cup of coffee next to Greg, Anne watched Sam interact with the dog. "She looks like a border collie."

Greg nodded. "Plus some German shepherd and who knows what else thrown into the mix."

"What's her story?" Anne asked.

Greg frowned before answering. "We found her chained in the yard of a vacant house. No food, no water. The owners moved away and left her behind."

Sam gave a small gasp. "That's terrible."

He picked up his coffee and took a long sip. Setting it down, he glanced at the dog. "You're right. They could've at least found a home for her or turned her in to the shelter instead of abandoning her." He shook his head slowly. "But some people treat animals like they're disposable."

Sam leaned down and laid a cheek on Roxy's head. "You poor thing," she murmured, missing the speculative look on Greg's face.

Suddenly the dog jerked away from Sam, and with two loud yips ran to Greg.

Startled, Sam drew back. "Did I frighten her?"

Greg tossed a glance over his shoulder at the door. "Nope, she hears someone coming up to the porch."

The words were barely out of his mouth when a knock at the door set Roxy barking furiously from her spot by his leg.

"Quiet," he said in a firm voice as he laid one hand on her head and fastened the leash with the other. Immediately, Roxy plopped at his feet, panting.

Anne, her hand on the door, looked back at Greg. "Is it okay if I open it?"

He nodded.

"My goodness," Fritz Thorpe said, standing in the doorway. "What's all the racket?" He spotted Greg and Roxy. "Ah, Greg and one of his strays."

"Hi, Fritz," Anne said, giving Sam a cautious glance while she swung the door wider. "Greg brought Roxy over to meet Sam."

"How nice," Fritz said, stepping inside. "I hope I'm not disturbing you."

Greg tightened his grasp on the dog's leash as he rose to his feet. "I'd better be going," he said, giving the leash a light tug. "Too many people make her nervous."

Fritz stepped out of their way as they headed for the door. "I didn't mean to run you off," he said, his eyes never leaving the dog. "But wait a moment—have you given any thought to joining us for the Fourth of July?"

Greg paused in the doorway. "The quartet?"

"Yes, we'd love to have you join us."

Greg's eyes narrowed. "Are you playing any of that longhair stuff?"

Fritz chuckled. "No, simply a few rousing marches."

Greg gave the leash another tug and moved out the door. "I'll check my schedule," he called over his shoulder.

Sam reluctantly watched Roxy go. It had been calming to sit and stroke the dog's head. And in a way, she suddenly realized, she'd felt safe having Roxy at her side. Now that feeling was gone, and she looked at Fritz nervously.

Seeing the change in Sam's demeanor, Fritz quickly turned to Anne. "I really must go, but I wanted to drop by and beg you to let Caleb join us."

Anne's mouth tightened, but before she could speak, Fritz rushed on. "The boy really does want to play, but he's a good kid and he won't do it without your permission. If I promise that the rehearsals won't interfere with his schedule, would you reconsider?"

She eyed him skeptically. "Do you also promise not to fill his head with a lot of big dreams that won't come true?"

"Yes." Fritz crossed his heart. "I won't give an ounce of advice as to what his future plans should be."

"Okay," she said with a sigh. "He can play *this* time."

Fritz grasped both of her hands. "Thank you." He looked over his shoulder at Sam. "Nice to see you again, Samantha," he said, releasing Anne's hands and turning toward the door.

"Wait," Sam suddenly called out. By his own admission, Fritz kept his eyes and ears open to all the latest around the lake. Maybe he had heard about the mystery woman.

He stopped, his eyebrows raised in curiosity. "Yes?"

Sam swallowed hard. "Um—well—I was wondering—ah—last night, I—" She hesitated and looked to Anne for help.

With a shake of her head, Anne jumped in. "You know everything that's going on around here," she began reluctantly.

He held up a hand stopping her. "Please," he said humbly, "not everything."

"Have you heard anyone mention a woman, dressed in a lavender nightgown, wandering around the lake at night?"

His eyes widened in shock before he recovered himself. "In a lavender nightgown you say?"

"Yes, we spotted a woman down on the dock."

Sam felt a stab of gratitude that Anne hadn't told Fritz that she'd been the only one to see the woman.

He stroked his chin thoughtfully. "I can't say as I have, but if I do, I'll let you know."

"Thanks." Anne put out a hand, stopping him. "And I'd also appreciate it if you wouldn't mention this to Esther."

Fritz gave a dry laugh. "You don't want everyone on the lake to be discussing it, eh?"

Anne nodded.

"Don't worry, I won't," he said, walking out the door. "Samantha, nice to see you again."

After Fritz had left, Anne finished making breakfast. In a few minutes, she placed toast and now-cold scrambled eggs in front of Sam. Sam looked at her plate then up at Anne. "Thanks for not telling Fritz that I was the only one who'd seen the mystery woman."

"Ah, that's okay. Fritz doesn't need to know everything." Anne turned back toward the counter. "He—"

Another rap at the door interrupted her. "What now?" she said, striding over to the door.

Sam peered around Anne as she opened the door and saw Fritz standing on the porch again.

"Did you forget something?" Anne asked.

Not coming in, Fritz looked at them both. "Neither one of you smoke, do you?"

Sam felt a trickle of dread mingled with relief.

"No," Anne replied.

"I found these down by the dock," he said, stepping inside and holding out a clenched hand. Slowly he uncurled his fingers, revealing two cigarette butts. "You may not smoke, but your mystery woman does."

Sam's head whipped toward Anne and their eyes met. Anne opened her mouth, but before she could speak, the ringing of her cell phone interrupted her. Flipping it open, she frowned. "Caleb. Just a minute," she said, and held up one finger as she stepped out the door.

From her place at the table, Sam heard Anne's muffled voice drift through the screen door. Nervously, she pushed her plate away while her eyes darted toward Fritz. What should she do now? Escape to the bedroom? She shifted uneasily in her chair.

Fritz gave her a friendly smile and sat down across from her. "I don't mean to pry," he said quietly, placing the cigarette butts in the center of the table, "but I'd like to help if I may. I take it this woman's been here before?"

When Sam didn't reply, he glanced over his shoulder at Anne, still talking on the porch. "Regardless of what Anne might think, I *can* keep secrets."

Sam dropped her chin and stared at her cold breakfast. "I think so," she whispered. "I saw her two nights ago."

Fritz leaned back in his chair and crossed his legs. "I see. Being new to the area, I don't suppose you recognized her?"

Sam shook her head.

Fritz was silent as his gaze roamed the kitchen. "It's not changed much," he murmured. "Same cabinets, new flooring, and furniture, but it looks remarkably the same."

Sam was perplexed. "This isn't the first time you've been inside the cabin?"

"No." His face took on a hard look. "Many, many years ago." He turned to Sam, his expression softening. "May I ask how you came to choose Elk Horn Lake for your vacation?"

"I didn't," she replied with a slight shake of her head. "My fiancé rented this cabin. He spent the summer here at the lake as a teenager and thought it would be a peaceful place for me to work on my physical therapy."

"Hmm, I see." Fritz uncrossed his legs and sat forward. "A teenager, and that would've been . . . ?"

"Well . . ." She did some swift arithmetic in her head. "Jackson just turned forty and I believe he said he was fifteen that summer, so it must've been about twenty-five years ago." Sam cocked her head and studied him. "Why?"

"Too young, even for Blanche," he muttered.

"Blanche? Who's Blanche? Why all the questions? And how does this relate to a strange woman prowling around my dock?"

"Blanche was the woman who lived here back then, but I'm sure it's just a coincidence that you wound up staying in this particular cabin." He stroked his chin thoughtfully. "However, it's not a coincidence that you're seeing a woman dressed in lavender. That was Blanche's favorite color."

"She's prowling around her old home?"

"No, Blanche left the lake about the time your fiancé spent his summer here. He probably didn't even know her." He looked toward the patio door and to the lake beyond. "But plenty of others still living here did." He turned back to Sam, his face once again tightening. "I'm afraid, my dear, someone has selected you as the target of a rather cruel joke."

# Twelve

Anne came back in the kitchen just in time to hear Fritz's remark. Wonderful. She might have considered the same thing, but Anne thought back to what Sam had said about feeling exposed. Now that Fritz had planted the seed that Sam wasn't safe here at the cabin, she'd never get Sam to come out of her bedroom.

But watching them, Anne was surprised. They were chatting away like new best friends. Sam seemed relaxed and comfortable in Fritz's company. What had happened while she'd been on the phone with Caleb? Whatever it was, she was glad to see the change in Sam, and even though Fritz was not her favorite person, the interaction was good for Sam.

Noticing Anne, Fritz turned. "I think someone is playing tricks."

"Any suspects?" she asked.

Fritz cocked his head and gave her a knowing look. "One."

"Teddy Brighton," Anne stated flatly.

"Ah." He leaned back in his chair. "You've already considered the possibility."

"Who's Teddy Brighton?" Sam interjected.

"A little hooligan," Fritz replied in a clipped voice, then, with a look at Anne, shrugged. "No insult intended toward Caleb."

"Caleb is not hanging out with him," Anne shot back quickly. "For once I agree with you, Fritz, and I've told Caleb to stay away from him."

"Does he live at the lake?" Sam asked.

"For the summer," Fritz replied. "I heard there'd been a problem concerning Teddy and a missing car, so he's been banished to the lake and placed under the watchful eye of his grandmother Irene."

"Brighton?" Sam's eyes narrowed. "That name sounds familiar."

"The family is quite influential. Irene's family were lumber barons," Fritz said. "Lots and lots of lovely money that Ted Two has used to build a successful construction business."

"That's where I heard the name," Sam said with a snap of her fingers. "Jackson mentioned them. They were involved with the new wing at the hospital."

Fritz gave a slight nod. "It wouldn't surprise me. Ted Two is just a bit older than your fiancé and has his fingers in a lot of pies."

"You saw his mother and wife at the beauty shop, Sam," Anne remarked.

"The two women whispering?"

"Yeah."

"The grandmother looked a little old to be handling a delinquent teenager," Sam said.

Tipping his head back, Fritz gave a bark of laughter. "You don't know Irene. She rules that family with an iron fist. When he was alive, she kept Ted One on such a short leash, it was a wonder he didn't strangle." His attention drifted around the room. "Of course, he *was* known to slip it off occasionally. Right here in this cabin, as a matter of fact."

Anne's eyes widened in shock. "Blanche and Theodore Brighton?"

"Yes. It was—"

Sam held up a hand, stopping him. "Wait, the Blanche who lived here?"

"Yes, there was only one Blanche." He paused. "Thank God. As I said, her presence graced—if one could call it that—these four walls." Fritz settled back in his chair. "Blanche may have wreaked havoc wherever she went, but I have to give her this—she was never afraid to live her life as she saw fit. She was never afraid to go after what she wanted, even if it did belong to someone else."

"Was she married?"

"Yes, to Harley Jones, the poor, besotted fool. It's an often-told tale—old bachelor gets hooked by a much younger woman." He shook his head. "And, by God, she led him a merry chase. When she finally ran off, he sold this place and moved to the city."

"They've never been back?" Sam asked.

"No, but I'm sure wherever Blanche may have landed, she's still causing trouble."

"And now you and Anne think that Teddy is pretending to be Blanche and wandering around the lake?"

"Possibly."

"Why?"

"Who knows what goes on in that young man's head? I, for one, wouldn't care to find out." Fritz paused. "It could be that he's doing it to shake up his grandmother—trick her into thinking that Blanche has returned in order to get back at her for trying to control him. Irene's reaction to the mere mention of Blanche's name is well known. Or he might have heard about you, my dear, and decided to play a prank on you."

"Why me?"

"Everyone's been wondering about you. They've heard just enough to want to know all of the gory details."

"It's none of their business," Sam declared hotly.

"True, but it doesn't lessen their curiosity." Fritz pursed his lips. "It could be that, thanks to the rumors, Teddy sees you as an easy target. Anyone else might run him off with a load of buckshot. You, on the other hand, wouldn't."

While Anne watched Fritz talk about the Brightons and Blanche, she saw Sam's demeanor change. Her body seemed to shrink and her eyes lost their spark. She could almost see Sam's carefully constructed wall rise again to its formidable height. If Fritz would've just left well enough alone without sharing all that old gossip. But no, as always, he had to stick his nose in where it didn't belong.

Fritz pushed away from the table and rose. "Well, that's enough of a stroll down memory lane." He looked down at Sam. "I would caution you not to repeat what I've told you this morning. Irene Brighton isn't the only one who finds the subject of Blanche Jones distasteful."

But before he could leave, Anne spied the mail carrier pulling up in front of the cabin. Stepping out on the porch, she collected a large package, addressed to Sam. Excited, she held it up. "Were you expecting this?"

"Yes," Sam replied in a terse voice and with a lift of her eyebrows. "So Dan finally got around to it."

"Aren't you going to open it?"

Sam shrugged. "You can if you want."

Anne hurriedly ripped off the tape and extracted two frames. When she turned them around, her breath caught in her throat. They were paintings, cityscapes; the subject of one—Anne couldn't tell whether it was St. Paul or Minneapolis—showed the city in the early morning, before the sleeping giant had stirred. Looking at the painting, she felt the stillness, the quiet, as a hint of the morning sun began to peek over the tops of skyscrapers. The other painting showed the same scene, only at night. City life moved across the painting in a rush. Figures of people hurried down the sidewalks, while neon signs glowed above them. Cars filled the streets, and such was the immediacy of their portrayal that Anne could almost swear she caught a whiff of their exhaust.

She was amazed. When she'd first learned that Sam had been an artist, she'd assumed her painting was nothing more than a rich girl dabbling. Calling herself an artist because it sounded good. But these works, even to Anne's inexperienced eye, spoke of real talent.

"These are amazing," she cried. "I don't know much about art, but these are truly beautiful."

Fritz stepped closer and took one of the paintings from Anne. Holding it at arm's length, he studied it closely.

"These are quite good," he said, looking over his shoulder at Sam. "Is this your work?"

Sam's face tightened and she waved his question away with her hand. "Yes, but I did them a long time ago. I don't paint anymore."

Propping the painting against the cabinet, he turned. "But, my dear, you really should. It's a shame that a talent like this should go to waste."

Sam rose to her feet. "What do you know about it?" she stormed. "You live up here in the backwoods of nowhere. Hardly the seat of art and culture no matter how much you'd like to pretend differently."

Shocked, Anne and Fritz watched her stumble from the room, down the hall to her bedroom. A moment later, the door slammed.

"Was it something I said?" Fritz asked Anne in a wry voice.

Rolling her eyes, Anne grabbed Sam's plate from the table and, with a couple of angry strides, scraped the remaining food into the garbage.

"Who the hell knows," she answered, setting the plate on the counter and facing him. "She has more mood swings than any other patient I've ever dealt with." She looked back toward the bedroom and lowered her voice. "And for some reason, any discussion of her experiences as an artist sets her off."

Fritz's gaze followed Anne's and he shook his head. "That's too bad. She really is talented." He glanced down at his watch. "Look at the time. I've got to go." Pausing at the door, he smiled warmly. "Again, thank you for giving Caleb permission to play in our quartet."

Anne's eyes narrowed and she gave him a steely look. "Just remember your promise not to encourage his foolish dreams."

"Anne," he said with sympathy, "not all dreams fail."

Sam had been so angry over Fritz's comments that Anne decided to let her cool off for a bit. She needed a little time to herself, too. Taking the last of the coffee, she stepped out onto the front porch and, pulling up a chair, propped her long legs on the railing.

It had been a morning of revelations. The cigarette butts proved Sam hadn't been dreaming, and Anne was relieved. She didn't like the idea of someone prowling around at night, and the thought of Teddy Brighton playing one of his tricks made her blood boil. But at least the sightings were real. She didn't know what the solution was. They didn't have enough proof to go to the Brightons and accuse him. Anne rolled her eyes at the thought of how that exchange would play out. Irene Brighton would have a stroke if she thought her grandson was wandering around the lake dressed up as Blanche. But maybe Fritz was right and that was Teddy's intent—to enrage his grandmother.

She took a long sip of coffee, and thought about Sam's reaction to the paintings. Was Fritz correct? Had Sam's dreams failed and now the mention of them generated anger? If so, she and Sam had more in common than either of them had realized. Anne knew how it felt to have your deepest hope dashed by cruel reality. It was for that exact reason that she was so determined not to let Caleb fall into the same trap. She shook her head. She never would've thought that she had *anything* in common with Samantha Moore.

Her eyes strayed to the plant that she'd noticed growing by the porch. She dropped her legs and stood, peering over the railing. Something had happened to it. It looked like it was dying. The once-green leaves were yellow, and their edges were brown and curling. Almost as if the plant were pulling in on itself. The clusters of buds had dropped, unfurled, and now littered the ground beneath the bush. Anne shook her head. One day vibrant and alive, then the next brittle and lifeless. She reached out and plucked one of the leaves, the edges crumbling in her fingers. Kind of like Sam. She'd been a vital, successful woman, but all of it had ended in the space of a day. Hopefully Sam was strong enough to make a comeback.

Dropping the leaf, Anne moved away from the railing, and as she did, she noticed a lone figure walking down the lane whom she recognized immediately.

Setting the coffee cup on the railing, she hurried down the steps. “Edward,” she called out.

He stopped, turning toward her, but averting his gaze from the cabin.

Sprinting, Anne caught up with him. “Hey, how’s it going?” she asked, slightly out of breath. “I’ve been meaning to stop by the gas station, but I’ve been working with a new patient.”

A slight smile tugged at his lips as he moved, putting his back toward the cabin. “So I’ve heard.”

“Have you talked to Dr. Osgood?”

Edward’s head lowered. “No, I’ve been busy, too. With the fishing tournament this weekend, we’ve had a lot of customers at the bait shop.”

Anne frowned. “I understand, but you need to take care of yourself,” she chided.

He raised his head and his eyes drilled into hers. “Why?”

Years of pain and hopelessness sounded in that one word, and Anne looked away. She couldn’t bear seeing the despair in his eyes, and she wouldn’t diminish his suffering by responding with some cliché. She focused on her own limbs. Her strength had never failed her and she’s always taken it for granted. What must it be like for Edward, or Sam, to have that suddenly taken away? When even the simplest task brought pain or failure? It didn’t bear thinking about.

Raising her gaze, she saw Edward staring at a cardinal sitting in the branches of a pine. Its bright red feathers almost glowed against the dark green of the pine needles. His face, lifted to the sun, relaxed, and she caught a glimpse of what he had been. She'd heard the stories—the local superstar, the young man who was going to go far—until a car accident shattered his future. His forehead tightened and he absentmindedly rubbed his arm.

"Can pain drive you crazy, Anne?" he asked softly while his eyes met hers again.

"Edward—"

He placed a hand on her shoulder, and his expression shifted. "Forget I said that," he said with a squeeze. "You're right—I should talk to Dr. Osgood. Who knows? Maybe they've discovered some new treatment."

Anne couldn't help giving a sigh of relief that she didn't have to answer his question. "Exactly," she exclaimed.

"I've got to get back to the store." He dropped his hand and began to walk away. "Take care."

"Promise you'll call Dr. Osgood?" she called to his retreating back.

With his arm held tightly to his side, he nodded.

"You look troubled," Greg said, placing a glass of wine on the small table next to her.

Sitting on Greg's deck, Anne looked out over the lake. She'd stopped by for a breather. Sam had insisted on spending the day shut up in her bedroom, and no matter how hard Anne had argued, she'd refused to come out. Anne had tried to be understanding, but her charitable feelings went only so far. The truce they'd struck hadn't lasted long and she left the cabin frustrated and on edge. She'd hoped that stopping by Greg's for a chat would help ease some of her tension before she had to return and deal with Sam again.

"Does it ever get to be too much for you?" she asked, leaning her head back against the chair.

"What? Life? The dogs? The price of coffee?"

Lifting her head, Anne gave him a wry look. "Life."

"Oh, that," he replied, patting his leg. His golden retriever, Molly, trotted over and dropped at his side. "Sure. All the time."

"So how do you handle it?"

After downing his Scotch, he bent and stroked Molly's well-shaped head. "I'm a simple guy. My dogs and my saxophone help me keep life in perspective." Sitting back, he stretched his legs out in front of him. "What's getting to you?"

"Do you want a list?" Anne asked, arching an eyebrow. "Let's start with Samantha, add Caleb and all the bills, then finish with Edward Dunlap."

"Edward?"

Anne, picking up her glass, stared at the ruby liquid. "Yeah, I ran into him today. It's so sad." With a sigh, she ran her finger down the side. "I wish there was something I could do to help him, but I never can get him away from Esther long enough to do any therapy."

"Anne," Greg said, his voice gentle. "You can't save the world."

"I'm not trying to, but Edward's life could've been so much more. Here he is almost fifty and still at his mother's beck and call." She frowned. "If only he hadn't had that accident."

Greg shook his head slowly. "Maybe."

Her eyes widened. "What do you mean?"

"I've heard all the stories about how he was on the brink of a great future, too, but in the end, I doubt if he'd ever have made the break with his mother."

"Why?"

"Esther would've found some way to stop him. Guilt him into staying."

"I always heard she was proud of him and looking forward to seeing him succeed."

"Really? Maybe that's what you heard, but knowing Esther, I think the attention she received from being Edward's mother was what mattered most to her."

"What about now?"

"Now she has everyone's sympathy and has had for twenty-some-odd years. Poor widowed Esther and her damaged son."

"That's kind of sick, Greg," Anne exclaimed.

He shrugged. "The world's a sick place Anne." He leaned his head back and crossed his arms. "If they could talk, the two dogs we found today would tell you."

"Bad?"

"Starved, dehydrated; someone dumped them, God knows how long ago, over by Perkins Hill." His eyelids drifted shut as if he was suddenly weary. "I don't know if they'll make it through the night."

Anne reached out and placed a hand on his arm. "I'm sorry."

His eyes opened and he gave her a sad smile. "Thanks, but we're human; there's only so much we can do. Can't save them all."

"But you'd like to, wouldn't you?"

"Yup, sure would." He scratched Molly's ears. "I think most of the time, present company excluded, I'd rather be with them than with people. At least with a dog, what you see is what you get. They're faithful, loyal, and they don't have any hidden agendas."

"Not everyone has an agenda."

He gave a short laugh. "Sure they do."

"I don't," Anne declared hotly.

"Oh yes, you do—get Caleb in college and see him get a degree, whether he wants one or not."

Anne snorted. "Now you sound like Fritz Thorpe."

"I hate to say it, because I think Caleb should go to college, too, but I agree with Fritz. At some point you're going to have to let Caleb make his own choices."

"Yeah, but what if his choices are wrong?"

"You followed your dream, Anne."

"Yeah," she shot back, "and look where it got me—spending my life hustling for a dollar."

"But at least you gave it a shot."

"What about you?" she asked pointedly.

Greg sat forward. "I followed my dream."

"But when you got screwed, you gave up. Why didn't you fight back?"

"Hey, we were analyzing you, not me," he said, lightening his tone.

"Truth hurts, huh?"

Greg chuckled. "We're a fine pair, aren't we? Life threw us both a curve, and now we're where we never thought we'd be."

"Right," Anne said, setting her glass back on the table. "And where I should be right now is back at Samantha Moore's."

Greg rose and extended his hand. Grabbing it, Anne rose. "You're spending the night at her cabin?" he asked.

"Just for a couple of days."

"Not looking forward to it?" he asked, following Anne across the deck and into the house.

"Not really." Anne stopped and turned. "It was funny—earlier this morning, after you left, she sat and chatted with Fritz just like a normal person—"

Greg's chuckle broke in. "Whatever that is."

"Right," she said with a lift of her brow. "But after two of her paintings arrived, she turned back into the ice queen and stayed that way." Anne puffed out her cheeks and blew out a long breath. "I hope by now the nicer version has reemerged."

Greg nudged her arm playfully. "Good luck."

"Thanks," she said, and with a wave headed down the lane.

The sun was sinking lower on the horizon and the long shadows stretched across the path. To her right, Anne saw the calm surface of lake. Above her, birds flew, searching for their nightly roost. She paused and took a deep breath, attempting just for a moment to lay her worries aside and enjoy herself. Releasing her breath slowly, she tipped her head back and closed her eyes.

Everything would work out, she told herself. Just get through this summer and into the fall, then Caleb would be back in school, and she'd be working at the hospital again. Samantha Moore would be long gone, back to whatever life she wanted in the city. Life would be normal again.

Suddenly the back of her neck prickled. Someone was watching her. She could feel it, feel their eyes on her, but as she scanned the woods for something . . . there was nothing there.

"Stop it," she whispered. "You're beginning to act as paranoid as Sam."

To her left, the snapping of a branch broke the stillness. Someone was lurking there. She turned and hurried in the direction of the cabin—all the time feeling the unknown presence following her. She fought the urge to cast a worried glance over her shoulder. Her pace increased. More sounds came from the woods, but not from behind her—in front of her. Whoever it was—they were outdistancing her. Would they cut her off just as she reached the cabin? She began to trot, her breath coming in pants. Part of her brain ridiculed her silliness, but another part urged her to hurry.

When she was just yards from the cabin, the crashing of branches erupted from the woods, and Anne skidded to a halt as a ten-point buck leaped from the woods, landing in the center of the road. For a moment she and the deer stared at each other in surprise, both shocked to find the other.

The deer was the first to recover. With an angry toss of his antlers, he bounded across the road and down the hill, heading for the lake.

Laughing at her unfounded fear, Anne strolled to the cabin, missing the sudden flash of red as her watcher turned and pulled deeper into the forest.

# Thirteen

A curl of steam rose up from the bowl of oatmeal sitting in front of Sam.

"I don't like oatmeal," she said, pushing it away.

"Look," Anne said, towering over her. "I let you slide yesterday, but not today. We have a deal and I expect you to live up to it. Now eat your breakfast."

Sam stared down at the bowl in front of her and contemplated flinging it across the room. Her lips formed a smile as she imagined the bowl hitting the wall and splattering globs of oatmeal everywhere. Childish, but it would show Anne that she couldn't keep bossing her around. Her hand inched across the table. *Don't be an idiot*, she thought, drawing back. Anne was right; they had a deal, but did it mean she had to eat the oatmeal?

"I doubt I would've made that deal if I'd known it included oatmeal," she grumbled.

Anne chuckled and moved over to the counter. She returned and placed a plate with a poached egg and toast next to the bowl of oatmeal.

"At least taste it. It's an old family recipe, and you'll insult my long-dead grandmother if you don't."

Sam snorted. "What's to making oatmeal? You open the package, pour it in a bowl, and add hot water," she said, stirring the thick glop with her spoon.

"This isn't instant."

"Bet it still tastes like wallpaper paste," she replied, shoving a spoonful in her mouth.

Not bad, but she wasn't going to admit it to Anne. She took another spoonful as Anne placed a glass of milk next to the egg and toast.

Sam shot her a quick look.

"Let me guess . . . you don't like milk." Anne's lips twisted in a wry grin. "Drink it anyway."

"Thought you were supposed to back off on the bossiness," Sam replied indignantly.

Anne's eyebrows lifted. "Oh, I'm so sorry, Ms. Moore," she said with a slight bow. "Would you care for a glass of milk?"

Sam rolled her eyes. "Fine. I get it. I'm being a brat."

Anne shrugged. "Yup, and I've never been very good at letting someone steamroll me." She crossed her arms and cocked her hip. "So if I'm too bossy, how do you want me to act?"

Sam placed her spoon next to the bowl. "You might try asking me what I'd like to eat. Minor, but it would be nice to be able to make a few decisions for myself, even if it's only what's for breakfast."

"Fine," Anne said, dropping her arms and returning to the stove. "I'd planned on grocery shopping today. You can go with me and show me what you want."

"Wait a second," Sam cried, her voice full of dismay. "Can't I make a list?"

Anne shook her head. "Nope. It will do you good to get out."

"You know being around people makes me nervous."

"And the best way to get over fear is to face it." Anne turned and leaned against the counter. "It'll be a short trip, I promise. And if it turns out you can't handle it, you can wait in the car."

Chewing her lip, Sam thought about it. At one point in her life, she'd thought nothing of standing in front of a roomful of people, giving a presentation. And now the thought of a simple trip to the grocery store set her nerves jangling. Maybe Anne was right. The best way to get over it was to take it in small steps. She had to do this if she ever wanted to get her life back.

"Fine. Whatever. But if I feel panicky, I'm going to the car."

"Fair enough."

An hour later, Sam questioned the wisdom of her decision while she walked slowly alongside Anne. Pushing the cart did help her keep her balance, but in every aisle, she felt people watching her. With curious glances in Sam's direction, several people had made conversation with Anne, forcing her to make introductions. Part of Sam did want to run to the car, hide from all the prying eyes, but if she did this, she'd be giving in, acting like a coward. And, honestly, she was tired of being a coward. She steeled herself against the speculative glances and kept moving, concentrating on keeping her balance.

When the ordeal was over, Sam couldn't help feeling that she'd accomplished something—maybe minor—but the important thing was that she hadn't given up and gone to the car. Now, if she could succeed once, she could do it again. Feeling happy with herself, she sat up straight as they pulled into the driveway.

Jackson's car was there, and Jackson himself stood on the porch talking with Fritz Thorpe. He was early. As the thoughts of all the issues between them came crashing down on her, some of her happiness dimmed. Pasting a smile on her face, she got out of the car and walked slowly to the cabin.

Jackson, spotting her, came rushing down the steps and across the yard. "Samantha," he cried, grasping her shoulders and holding her away from him. "You look wonderful." He reached up and lifted a few strands of her hair. "Did your mother send Renaldo up here?"

Self-consciously, Sam batted his hand away. "No, Anne took me to a beauty shop in Pardo—um—Alice's Beauty Barn."

He took a step back with a derisive snort. "You've got to be kidding me! Alice's Beauty Barn?"

Sam's chin shot up as she smoothed her hair. "I think she did a great job. Every bit as good as Renaldo would've done."

He threw an arm around her shoulder and led her toward the cabin. "Ha, well, I never would've expected someone that talented to be living up here."

Out of the corner of her eye, she studied him. Did she come across as being as snobby as he was? Her attention shifted to Fritz, who was still standing on the porch. What had she said to him yesterday? That the community up here wasn't a seat of art and culture? Chagrined, she lowered her chin. At the first opportunity, she'd apologize for her remark.

"Um," she said, clearing her throat. "I went grocery shopping with Anne."

"That's wonderful," he said, then paused, his eyes going back to her hair. "I can't get over how much better you look. Your father is going to be so pleased."

Irritated that all Jackson could think about was her new haircut, Sam dodged out from underneath his arm and continued walking toward Fritz.

"Fritz, nice to see you again," she called out.

His eyes widened in surprise. "After yesterday, I wasn't sure I'd be welcome."

Taking one step at a time, Sam climbed to the porch. "About that," she said softly to avoid Jackson's overhearing her. "I'd like to apologize for my behavior. You were trying to be kind and my reaction was rude."

"Not to worry," he said with a wave. "We all say things we regret, and I understand that you have many things on your mind. Shall we forget it and move on?" He extended his hand.

Remembering that Fritz had been the one to find proof of the existence of her late-night visitor, she smiled and took the offered hand. "I'd like that," she replied, giving it a quick shake.

"Good." Fritz glanced at Jackson, who was helping Anne unload the groceries. "I was telling your fiancé that I'm having a little get-together—nothing elaborate—tomorrow night, and I'd love for you both to attend."

"Gee, Fritz," she stuttered, "I don't know—I—ah—"

"Now, Samantha, we're friends," he said with a twinkle.

"Yes, but—"

Before she could finish, Jackson came up the steps carrying an armload of groceries. "Did Fritz tell you about his party?"

"Yes—"

"I'm looking forward to it, Fritz," Jackson continued as he opened the cabin door and motioned them both inside.

"But, Jackson—"

He cut her off as he placed the sacks on the kitchen table. "It will be good for us, Samantha. It's been too long since we've done anything *fun*." He looked over his shoulder at Fritz. "It seems that Fritz and I share a love of music. In fact, he knew my mother."

"Small world," Sam muttered, surprised at the mention of his mother. Usually it was a topic he avoided.

"Yes, it is," Fritz said, hearing Sam's remark. "In fact, Dr. Van Horn—"

"Please, it's Jackson," Jackson said with another glance at Fritz. "*Jackson's* mother sponsored a couple of my more talented students while they were trying to get their musical careers started."

Out of the corner of her eye, Sam saw a faint blush spread over Jackson's face.

"That must've been during the time I was living with my father," he said quickly.

Fritz, noticing the other man's discomfort, abruptly changed the subject. "Do you play?"

"A little . . . the piano—and only for my own enjoyment," Jackson replied.

Fritz laid a hand on his shoulder. "Why don't you join me and a few other musicians for one of our Sunday jam sessions?"

"I don't—" Jackson began with a shake of his head.

"It's strictly amateur," Fritz said, cutting off Jackson's objection. "And only for fun."

"Okay—well, maybe some weekend, I will."

Sam shot a look at Anne. Although it appeared that she wasn't paying attention to the conversation, Sam noticed her lips were tightly shut, as if she were fighting the urge to speak out. Sam would love to know what she was thinking. Did she approve of this sudden camaraderie between Jackson and Fritz? Sam had figured out that Anne had a bone to pick with Fritz over his involvement in her son's life. Maybe that was it? Or maybe Anne resented Jackson strolling in and usurping her position as boss-in-charge?

Sam gave a mental shrug. Either way, it didn't make a difference. She was still the pawn.

Suddenly Jackson stopped unpacking groceries as his attention traveled to her paintings, now propped up in a corner of the living room.

Striding over, he picked one up. "Where did these come from?"

A heavy silence filled the room. Sam looked first at Fritz and then at Anne. It was as if they were both holding their breath, waiting for her to fly off the handle.

"Dan sent them," she said smoothly, and arched an eyebrow. "Dan's redecorated my office, and Dad was planning to donate them to charity. Know anything about that?"

Jackson flushed, letting Sam know her question had hit the mark. "I'm sure it would've been to a good cause," he answered defensively. He picked up the other painting and started down the hallway. "Since there isn't any place to hang these, why don't we put them in the closet, out of sight," he said, opening the hall closet and stuffing them inside.

Sam looked at Fritz and Anne again. Anne's mouth was so tight, her lips had disappeared.

"Are you looking forward to Fritz's party tomorrow night?" Anne asked as they walked down the gravel path.

Jackson, needing to contact his office, had stayed back at the cabin instead of joining them. And all Sam felt was relief.

"What do you think?" Sam asked snidely.

"Not so much," Anne replied, "but it might do you good."

"I'm not going."

"Dr. Van Horn wants to go."

"Fine. He can go without me."

"How are you going to get out of it?"

Sam chortled. "In case you haven't noticed, I'm pretty good at getting out of stuff if I really try."

"I *have* noticed," Anne replied with a grin, "but I still think it would be good if you at least tried."

"I don't have anything to wear."

"I'll take you shopping tomorrow. There are a couple of shops in Pardo that will have something suitable."

Sam shuddered. First shopping for groceries, now clothes. "I don't think so."

"Oh, come on. It won't kill you."

Sam stole a glance her way. "Will you be there?"

Anne gave a snort. "Not likely. In case you haven't noticed—I'm one of the hired help around here. I don't get invitations to parties."

"Well, I'm not going in any case," Sam said stubbornly, then stopped. "Fritz has never mentioned it, but is there a Mrs. Thorpe?"

"Nope. He's never been married." Anne kicked a pebble with the toe of her shoe and sent it flying down the road.

Sam resumed walking. "Girlfriend?"

"Not that I'm aware of," Anne replied, falling in step with Sam.

"As charming as Fritz is, one would think he'd have someone special in his life."

Anne stopped short and placed a hand on her hip. "Why all the questions about Fritz?"

"I don't know—habit I guess. I'm accustomed to knowing the details." Sam shrugged. "I've always had a closed circle of friends—people I've known since childhood."

"Okay," Anne relented, "according to the story, he had an unhappy love affair."

"Really?" Sam's thoughts focused on Fritz's stories about Blanche. "Anyone from around here?"

"I don't know—if someone mentioned a name, it didn't stick." She shook her head. "I've got enough going on in my own life without spending time speculating on the lives of others and wondering about what happened in their pasts."

"Is that why you didn't tell me that this cabin has a notorious reputation?"

Anne fluttered a hand. "Nothing more than a lot of old rumors."

"Aren't you curious?"

"No. Are you?"

Sam stopped walking and thought about it. Yes, she was, she realized with surprise. For so long, her repertoire of emotions had consisted of apathy, fear, anger, self-pity, and panic—there hadn't been anything else.

"Yeah, I am. I'd like to know if Blanche was as wicked as Fritz suggested."

Anne shot her a stern look. "Fritz told you about Irene Brighton and how she reacts whenever anyone mentions Blanche. You've got to know that she isn't the only one. People around here still pale at the mention of Blanche's name. I wouldn't go around—"

The chirping of her cell phone interrupted her. Taking it out of her pocket, she flipped it open. "Yeah, Caleb." She listened to his response. "Right now?" She paused, her lips curving into a frown. "Can't you stay?"

After hearing what Caleb said, she snapped the phone shut. "Damn. The repairman's here to fix my washer. I've been waiting on him for two weeks, and he had to choose this morning to show up." She looked back toward Sam's cabin then down the road in the other direction. "I just live a short distance down that trail," she said as she gestured toward a path leading off the left. "It will only take a few minutes to explain what's wrong with the washer." Pointing to a log lying off to the left of the road, she took Sam's arm and began to lead her toward it. "Why don't you wait here and I'll be right back?"

Sam jerked her arm away. "No. You know how I feel about being outside. Let's walk back to the cabin."

Anne shoved her hands in her pockets. "Caleb has to leave for his summer job, and I don't have time to walk you back to the cabin. If I don't go now, the repairman will leave and it will be another two weeks before my washer's fixed. Do you know what it's like having a teenage boy, and no washer?"

The thought of Anne abandoning her terrified Sam. She'd be alone, out in the open. "I'll walk back by myself."

"No, not after the fall you took a couple of days ago. Come on," Anne said, tugging at Sam's arm again and leading her toward the log. "I'll be right back."

Realizing it was pointless to argue, Sam let out a long sigh and eased herself down on the log. She'd wait until Anne was out of sight and walk back to the cabin. Satisfied that her charge was settled, Anne spun on her heel and took off at a run down the path.

Sam watched with envy as Anne's long legs covered the distance. Would she ever be able to move like that again?

She had begun counting to ten when a sound in the brush startled her. Her attention flew to the nearest pine, and she let out a shaky breath as she watched a squirrel scamper up the tree. He disappeared from sight, and silence fell around her. She glanced over her shoulder while a chill crept up her bare arms as though she felt someone watching her.

Alarmed, Sam decided she'd waited long enough. Pushing to her feet, she took a faltering step in the direction of her cabin.

The howl of an animal in pain suddenly split the silence.

Turning, she hurried as fast as she could toward the sound. As she rounded the bend, she saw two teenage boys—a blond and a redhead—standing by Greg Clemons's fence, laughing and focused on what lay on the other side of the fence.

Craning her neck, she peered around them, but didn't see anything.

The red-haired boy nudged the blond with his shoulder as he nonchalantly tossed a small rock in the air. Stopping, he grasped the rock and, cocking his arm, hurled it over the fence to a spot in the corner.

"Missed," the blond called out.

The redhead lifted one shoulder in a careless shrug and bent to pick up another rock. As he did, Sam noticed Roxy cowering in a corner of the fenced-in area.

The dog had scooted as close to the fence as possible. Her pink tongue lolled out of her mouth as she panted, her thin ribs moving like a bellows. Terrified brown eyes met Sam's across the distance.

The boy cocked his arm again.

"No!" The word tore out of Sam's mouth before she could stop it.

Both boys whirled around and two pairs of eyes watched her with speculation. She felt her own breath suddenly come in rapid gasps. *Teenagers . . . one holding a rock . . .*

Roxy howled again, drawing their attention away from Sam.

*Now*, said a voice in her head, *get away while you can. Go get Jackson.*

The redhead laughed and drew back for the pitch. Sensing his intent, Roxy ducked her head and whimpered, waiting for another rock to strike her.

She didn't have time to hobble back to the cabin. These boys were torturing the dog, and if a rock hit her the wrong way, she could die before Sam returned with Jackson. Sam had no choice . . . she had to act.

"Drop the rock," she called out, struggling to keep the fear out of her voice.

"Who the hell are you?" the blond boy asked.

"She's the gimp living at the old Jones place," replied the redhead sarcastically as he rolled the stone around in his hands.

Sam swallowed hard and took a step back. A triumphant smile lit the red-haired boy's face.

*No—don't back down now; don't let these two little jerks scare you.*

Squaring her shoulders, Sam stepped forward. "I'm going to tell you one more time—drop it."

The redhead cocked his head. "Oh yeah? What are you going to do if I don't?"

"I'll march—"

"Limp, don't ya mean?" the redhead broke in, his lip curling.

"Doesn't make a difference how I get back to my cabin," Sam shot back, "but once I'm there, I'll call the sheriff and report you."

"Ooo, I'm scared." The red-haired boy took a half step toward her, still rolling the rock around in his hand, as if he were testing its weight.

*My God, he's going to throw the rock at me!* Sam stumbled back. "*Run*," cried part of her brain, but she couldn't, not with her weak leg.

The redhead took another step closer and Sam inched away, her feet sliding on the loose gravel. A desperate bark from the other side of the fence stopped her cold.

Sam knew all about desperation.

Fighting to remember what it felt like to live without desperation, without fear, she pulled around her whatever shreds of courage she had left. She narrowed her eyes and glared at the teenagers. "I'll also call Greg Clemons. He doesn't strike me as the type who'd appreciate two punks throwing rocks at his dog."

The blond's face lost its grin. He grabbed his friend's arm. "Come on, Teddy—"

"You dope," the redhead exclaimed, shaking off the blond boy's hand. "Now she knows my name."

"The sheriff would've figured it out," the blond muttered as he turned toward Sam. "Look, lady," he pleaded, "don't turn us in, okay? We didn't hurt the dog—we only scared it."

Teddy spun to face the blond. "You are *such* a pussy. Even if she does call the sheriff and Greg, they're not going to do anything to us," he scoffed.

The blond scuffed the toe of his dirty tennis shoe across the gravel. "Maybe your folks won't, but mine will. And if Greg talks to my dad . . ." His voice trailed off as he shoved his hands in the back pockets of his frayed cutoffs. "He's already told me that if I get into trouble one more time—"

He was interrupted by the door of the cabin slamming open. Greg Clemons stood, framed in the opening with his hands on his hips as he sized up the situation.

The boys froze.

"You little shits," he yelled, spying the rock in Teddy's hand. With two long strides, he was off the porch and headed toward the boys.

Teddy dropped the rock and, without a glance toward his friend, took off at a dead run into the woods. The blond sprinted with just as much speed in the opposite direction.

Greg caught Sam as her knees buckled.

# Fourteen

Anne jogged down the trail leading back to where she'd left Sam. The discussion with the plumber had taken longer than she'd expected, and she had a feeling Sam had freaked out while she was gone. She rounded the bend and stopped. There was the log, but no Sam.

Terrific. Now what did she do? Go back to the cabin? What if Sam hadn't gone back there? She'd have to admit to Jackson—who, after this morning, she confirmed, was a direct pipeline to Daddy Dearest—that she'd lost Sam. She was beginning to think all the remarks Sam had made about her family were true. Dr. Van Horn had appeared so charming during her interview with him, but as he nattered on with Fritz he'd come across as a first-class asshole. He hadn't even acknowledged the courage it took for Sam to brave going to the grocery store. All he seemed to care about was her new haircut. Brushing a stray hair out of her face, she scanned the road. It was empty. She was getting canned for sure. She had to find Sam.

"Damn it," she exclaimed, kicking a rock down the road.

With reluctance, she turned and started toward Sam's cabin.

The sound of barking and a woman's laugh stopped her. Sam? Whirling, she took off at a run toward Greg's.

The sight she saw in Greg's small side yard stopped her dead. Sam sat in a lawn chair underneath a shade tree while Greg leaned nonchalantly against its trunk—both of them watching the dogs, Roxy and Molly, cavort around the yard. The expression Greg wore reminded Anne of a proud father witnessing his child's antics.

Rolling her eyes, Anne walked to the gate and, opening it, entered the yard. "I told you to stay put," she said, her words echoing her irritation.

"I—" Sam began, but Greg cut her off.

"It's good that she didn't, Anne. She rescued Roxy from Teddy Brighton."

Anne's eyes flared. "What?"

Sam gave her a shy nod. "I don't know if I really rescued her—Greg was the one who ran them off."

Greg laid a hand on Sam's shoulder, and Anne noticed that she didn't flinch. "Teddy and Joey Wiggins were throwing rocks at her, but Sam stopped them long enough for me to get out here."

"Where were you?"

He jerked his head toward the lake. "Down at the dock. I'd gone down to check the moorings on my boat. I only intended to be gone a short time, but then Duane Parker came by with a stringer of fish." He frowned. "I shouldn't have left Roxy alone. I got back in time to see Sam squaring off with the two of them."

"Have you called the Brightons and the Wigginses'?"

His frown deepened. "Not yet, but I will. Joey's basically a good kid, but Teddy's a bad influence. And once Joey's dad finds out about this, I think Teddy's going to be looking for a new friend." He gave a derisive snort. "He was the last kid on the lake whose parents would allow him to hang out with Teddy."

Anne walked to a lawn chair next to Sam's and sat. "Caleb said Teddy had friends from the Cities with him."

"Humph, not anymore," Greg said. "They got caught buzzing the loons' nesting area with their Jet Skis, and Irene sent his friends packing." He picked up a ball and tossed it to Molly. "I suppose now he's bored and looking for trouble."

Anne thought of her suspicions regarding Teddy. No friends, left to find ways to amuse himself—yup, in that kid's mind, wandering around the lake at night, stirring up trouble would be a great idea. She decided not to mention her conjectures to Greg. He was pissed, and she knew he'd be giving Irene an earful about her grandson's behavior. If they were lucky, she'd send Teddy packing, too.

Roxy, tired of no longer being the center of attention, grabbed a ball and shoved it on Sam's lap. Backing up, she stood perfectly still, waiting. Only her eyes moved—first to the ball, then to Sam's face.

With a laugh, Sam took the ball and held it high. "Oh, so you want this, do you?"

Excited, Roxy began to dance in circles.

With another laugh, Sam threw the ball, and Roxy flew after it, her back paws throwing grass in the air. Catching it midair, she trotted back to Sam and, with a sigh, plopped down on Sam's feet. Sam bent and scratched her ears, earning her a look of pure adoration from the dog.

Watching Roxy and Sam play, Greg suddenly gave a wide grin. "I think Sam should adopt Roxy."

"Huh?" Anne's head whipped toward him.

From what she'd learned about Samantha Moore, Sam's life was all about her work. Not the best candidate for a dog owner.

Greg read the disbelief on her face. "Oh, come on, Anne, you've used my dogs in your therapy before."

"Yeah," she spluttered, "to help with the patient's exercises. No one has ever adopted one."

Anne looked over at Sam petting Roxy. Her face held a slight smile as she stroked the dog's head, and her body, normally tight with tension whenever she was outside the safety of her cabin, was relaxed.

"What do you think, Sam?" Anne asked.

"I've never had a pet," Sam said, straightening. "It might be fun." She glanced down at Roxy, lying at her feet. "She's had it tough . . . I think I can give her a good home."

"What would you do with her once you return to the city? You live in an apartment, don't you?"

"Yes, but I'll be moving into Jackson's family home. It's big and in a wooded area. There'd be plenty of room for her to run around."

"What about Jackson? How will he feel about you adopting her?"

Sam shrugged as if it didn't matter. "He likes dogs," she said, reaching down and patting Roxy's head. At Sam's touch, the dog rolled over on her back for a tummy scratch. Laughing, Sam gave her what she wanted.

Dr. Van Horn might be fond of dogs, Anne thought, but he struck her as the type who'd want his pet to have a pedigree dating back to the beginning of time, with at least a few show champions thrown in for good measure.

"When would you adopt her? When you go back to the city?"

Sam looked at Anne with a devilish glint in her eye. "Why

not today? I can take her back with me now. Greg told me that the shelter picked up two more dogs that need fostering. If I take Roxy, he'd have room for them."

Anne held up her hand. "Wait a second—you can't go 'poof, I've got a dog.' You need to think about this. They're a responsibility." She looked over her shoulder at Greg for help. "They need training, discipline, food, bedding—isn't that right, Greg?"

"What Roxy needs right now is love and a home." He placed a hand on Sam's shoulder. "I think Sam is more than capable of giving her that."

Sam preened at his words. There wasn't even a shadow of the cranky, embittered woman Anne had seen over the past weeks.

Greg continued. "I can drop over some dog food and Roxy's bed later." His hand fell away from Sam's shoulder. "They can have the weekend to get better acquainted, then next week I'll help Sam with Roxy's training."

Training? Visions of piles and puddles scattered throughout the cabin and herself armed with a roll of paper towels and a bottle of disinfectant flashed through Anne's mind. Her eyes narrowed. "She *is* housebroken, isn't she?"

Greg's laugh rang out as he squatted next to the dog and took her head in his hands. "Yes," he said emphatically. "You're a proper lady, aren't you, Roxy?"

A swipe of the tongue was her answer.

A short time later, the three of them headed back to Sam's cabin. Anne still wasn't convinced that adopting Roxy was the best idea, but she had to acknowledge the bond Sam and the dog had already formed. Roxy pranced happily at Sam's side, never getting too far away. It was as if she understood Sam's limitations. When they neared the cabin, Anne spotted Jackson sitting on the porch, drinking a glass of wine.

Seeing them, he placed his glass on the railing and bounded off the porch. He halted abruptly when he noticed the dog. Taking in Roxy's bald spots, her thin appearance, his face hardened. "What in the hell is that?" he asked, pointing.

At the sound of his harsh voice, Roxy rushed away from Sam's side and threw herself in front of Sam, barking.

"Quiet!" Jackson yelled.

Roxy barked louder.

Sam bent, placing a hand on Roxy's head. "Shh, shh," she soothed. "It's okay. He won't hurt you." She lifted her eyes and glared at her fiancé. "You frightened her." Returning her attention to Roxy, she continued murmuring soft words until the dog calmed. "There," she said with satisfaction, "she's fine now."

Even though the dog quieted, she refused to relinquish her protective position between Jackson and Sam.

"What are you doing with that dog?" Jackson asked, struggling to keep his voice even.

Sam straightened and squared her shoulders. "I'm adopting her."

"You've got to be kidding me," he sputtered. "Look at her—she's mangy—"

"She is not," Sam huffed in a voice that reminded Anne of a mother defending her child. "She may have a couple of bald spots, but her fur's growing back."

"Sam, honey," he wheedled, "if you want a dog, let's get one from a breeder."

*I knew it*, Anne thought.

"No," Sam said with a lift of her chin. "I want this one."

"She's a mutt."

"But she's *my* mutt."

"Samantha—"

"Anne," Sam interrupted, handing her Roxy's leash, "would you please take Roxy inside while I explain the situation to Jackson?"

"Sure thing," she replied, grasping the leash and giving it a light tug. "Come on, Roxy."

The dog looked up at Sam and refused to budge.

"It's okay," Sam said softly as she gave Roxy a quick pat.

Slowly the dog followed Anne, glancing back at Sam. Once inside, Roxy planted herself by the screen door and stared out at Sam and Jackson.

With a chuckle, Anne smiled at the dog. "I don't blame you—I want to see this, too," she said, crossing to the kitchen window and pretending to be busy at the counter. She wasn't an expert on body language, but she didn't have to be to tell what was going on in the front yard. Jackson stood with his hands on his hips, leaning forward while he made his case. Sam faced him, her head high and her arms crossed tightly across her chest. Whatever he was selling, she wasn't buying it. Finally, Jackson nodded, gave Sam a hug, and took off down the road.

A smile of satisfaction wreathed Sam's face as she made her slow progress the remainder of the way to the cabin while Roxy's tail thumped a steady beat on the floor.

Turning, Anne grinned at the dog. "Looks like you're home."

The next morning, Anne stood with Sam in the third clothing store they'd visited. For a woman who'd been uncomfortable leaving her cabin, Sam seemed to have made a rapid recovery. Anne didn't know if it was from winning the argument with Jackson or rescuing Roxy, but she had a new confidence about her.

A thousand questions filtered through Anne's head and she'd pondered all morning how to ask them. Finally, she spit one out. "Not to be snoopy, but what happened between you and Jackson after I went inside with the dog?"

Sam glanced away from the white knit top she was holding up. “With Jackson?” she asked, shaking her head and placing the top back on the rack.

Anne nodded.

“Not much,” she replied, examining a navy-blue shirt. “He agreed that I could keep her.” She grimaced. “But I might get a call today from my father.”

Anne thought about how happy Sam seemed when she was with Roxy. “You’re not going to let your dad talk you out of adopting the dog, are you?”

“Absolutely not,” Sam said vehemently. “She might not be the designer dog he’ll think I should have, but I don’t care. She’s mine.”

“Um—” Anne began, “why did you want to drop her off at Greg’s before we came shopping?”

Sam moved over to the next rack of shirts. “I’m sure Jackson and Roxy would’ve been fine,” she rushed to say, “but they didn’t exactly bond last night. Roxy was really skittish around him. Besides, at Greg’s, she’ll have Molly to play with.” She ran her hand down one of the tops.

“What are you going to do if that doesn’t change?”

“It will. They’ll get used to each other eventually and I’m sure Jackson will grow to love her, but for now . . .” Her voice trailed away.

Anne wasn’t so sure, but she kept her opinion to herself as she busied herself looking at a price tag. These clothes weren’t high end, but even so, she couldn’t afford them. She dropped the tag and moved to the next rack. She couldn’t remember the last time she’d bought something for herself. Necessities always came before desires, but someday . . .

Sam suddenly turned, breaking into her thoughts. “I’m not finding anything here either.”

Anne bowed her head and sighed. "The only store left is one that handles used clothing."

Sam perked up. "Vintage?"

"I don't know if you'd call it vintage," Anne replied with a chuckle, "but it's the only store left."

Five minutes later, Anne found herself going through the dress rack at the used-clothing store with Sam.

Grabbing one of the garments, Sam held it against her body. The light lavender dress, covered with tiny, dark violet flowers, had a fitted bodice and a skirt that floated down to her knees.

"What do you think?"

Anne looked down at her shorts and T-shirt. "I'm not exactly a fashion plate—I think you'd better ask one of the clerks their opinion."

"You're certainly tall enough to be in fashion," Sam answered with a grin. "You could've been a model."

Anne felt herself blanch and turned quickly away. "Oh, look at these," she said, swiftly changing the subject. She picked up a dark purple shawl, lying on a table near the dresses. "How would this look with that dress?"

Sam took the shawl. "Terrific. I'll take it." She started to move away, but stopped. Moving to a rack of tops, she picked out an ice-blue tunic and held it up to Anne. "This looks great with your blond hair and blue eyes. You should get it."

"What? No," Anne said, with a shake of her head as she took the hanger from Sam, meaning to place it back on the rack. She paused and her fingers played over the slinky material. Silk, it had to be silk. She stroked the material with longing. She had never owned anything this nice.

Sam glanced at the price tag. "It's a real steal—only seventy-five."

"Seventy-five *dollars*?" Anne quickly moved to hang the tunic back on the rack. "That's about seventy-five more than I have to spend on something I'd probably never wear."

"I'll buy it for you," Sam said, and grabbed the hanger from Anne. Turning, she headed for the counter. Anne's hand shot out, stopping her.

"No you won't," she stated in a flat voice.

"Why not?"

"I don't need your charity."

"It's not charity."

"Yes, it is."

"No, it's *not*." Sam pulled away, still clutching the tunic. "I'm buying it, so quit arguing." Her face softened. "Look, I know I've been difficult. Getting this for you is a way to make up for it." She smiled. "Maybe then you won't think I'm such a bitch."

Anne lifted her chin. "My regard can't be bought."

Sam's brows shot up and she eyed Anne with a smug look. "I know. And frankly, if it were for sale, I wouldn't want it."

# Fifteen

I stroll along the lane, smiling at the people I meet. Vacationers. I lower my head so they can't see the amusement on my face. They remind me of ants scurrying this way and that without purpose, looking for any morsel to cart back to the anthill. They try to make memories, try to find excitement, something that they can trot out once they've returned to their mundane existence to convince themselves that their sad little lives have some sort of meaning. But they're wrong. Their lives have no passion, and without passion there is no life.

I lift my head, the walkers now safely away from me. My smile fades. That's one thing I have to give her—at least she had passion. Maybe it led her and those around her to destruction, but she did live her life. She didn't run or hide from it. Not like Samantha.

Ah, Samantha—that little mouse, hiding away, thinking she's safe. She wouldn't know passion if it hit her on the head. Oh, wait, that already happened, only it was a tire iron. I smirk. It's too bad that she survived. It would've been better if her sorry life had ended then. But again, her life had already ended. It was over when she allowed her art to be stripped away from her. Since that time, as far as I'm concerned, she's only been going through the motions, and her actions only show how powerless she is.

I'm near the cabin now and I stop and take stock. Yes, Samantha is weak, but I'm not. I'm strong. The weak exist as prey for the strong. And prey on her I will. She is worthless, but Lawrence Moore isn't. The way I was treated was so unfair and I resent my forced retreat into a life I didn't choose. I allow myself a sly smile. But with a man like Lawrence Moore backing me, no one would stand against me. If I could only figure out a way to take Samantha out of the equation.

A frown replaces my smile. I see a problem—a six-foot blond problem. Anne Weaver is gaining an influence over Samantha. And that just wouldn't do. In order for any kind of a plan to work, I need Samantha to be dependent on me, not on Anne. So how can I squelch this?

An idea comes to me. I may not know Anne well, but well enough to know her vulnerable spot. Her son, Caleb. Caleb could be the tool to undermine Samantha's trust.

Hmm. I turn and walk back the way I came. Not ready to go home yet—I need to think. The seed of a plan begins to take root, and I hum to myself as I consider the possibilities.

# Sixteen

When they arrived at the lake, Anne and Sam picked up Roxy and drove the short distance to Sam's cabin. Anne hadn't mentioned the tunic since they left the store and Sam hadn't either. Sitting next to Anne, Sam slid her eyes toward her. She had surprised herself. The anxiety that she'd felt for so long hadn't been present during their shopping. She'd had fun. Had Anne? Her whole attitude over the tunic perplexed Sam. It was only seventy-five dollars, not as if she'd offered to buy her some designer bag for thousands. She really hoped that once they reached the cabin, Anne wouldn't insist that Sam take it back.

Pulling up in front of the cabin, Sam gathered up her purchases and turned to Anne. "Greg's well informed about dogs. How long has he worked for the animal shelter?"

Anne lifted a shoulder. "About five years."

"What did he do before that?"

"Um," Anne said, squirming, "he was a vet."

"Really? Here?"

"No, in the Cities."

"Does he have a practice up here?"

"No."

"Why not?"

Anne hesitated as she pushed the car door open. "You'll have to ask him."

Getting out of the car herself, Sam opened the door for Roxy and, grabbing her leash, followed Anne. "You make it sound like it's a secret."

"No, it's not," Anne said, her voice short, "but it's Greg's story to tell, not mine."

Subject closed . . . together they walked to the cabin. Once inside, Sam carried her new clothes back to her bedroom with Roxy hot on her heels. She'd opened the closet door when Roxy wheeled and ran barking down the hall. Sam hurried after her. She rounded the corner to see Jackson and Fritz standing in the kitchen. Fritz's face wore an amused look as he watched Roxy carry on while Jackson, his expression tight, admonished the dog to be quiet. Noticing Sam, Jackson pointed at Roxy.

"Get her to shut up, will you!" he exclaimed.

"Shh," Sam said with a snap of her fingers. The dog immediately stopped her barking and came to Sam's side. Sam gave Jackson a triumphant look.

"You'd better teach her some manners," he grumbled. "We can't have her carrying on every time we have guests."

Fritz chuckled and held out his hand for Roxy to sniff. She approached him cautiously. "I'm sure she'll adapt, Jackson," he said. Squatting, he stroked her head. "Greg's very particular about his strays and he wouldn't have let Sam adopt this one if he hadn't thought she'd provide a good home."

Jackson eyed the dog skeptically, while Sam felt a rush of gratitude toward Fritz. It seemed that someone, other than Greg, had confidence in her.

"One thing about having a dog," Fritz continued. "No one will approach the cabin without Sam being aware of it."

"Lawrence isn't going to like this," Jackson muttered under his breath, but Sam caught it.

She cocked her head, her eyes drilling into him. "What did you say?"

"Nothing," he muttered, still staring at the dog. Suddenly his demeanor shifted and he lifted his head, smiling at her. "Did you have fun shopping?"

*Okay,* she thought, *he's making an effort. I will, too.* Relaxing, she smiled back at him. "Yes, and I found the perfect dress for tonight."

His eyebrows raised in surprise. "Really? I wouldn't have thought there'd be much of a selection around here."

Sam's irritation sparked. "Why? Because we're not in the Cities?"

Before Jackson could answer, Fritz broke in, turning to Anne, leaning against the counter. "Are you available tonight?"

Sam grinned. Anne was invited.

"See? Aren't you glad—" she began.

"Megan can't help serve tonight, so I'm shorthanded," Fritz interrupted, dashing Sam's excitement. "Would you be able to come at six?"

Anne opened her mouth to answer, but Sam didn't give her a chance. "Fritz, I invited Anne to accompany us," she said, smiling sweetly. "You said 'the more the merrier,' didn't you?"

"Well, yes—"

Sam crossed to Jackson and linked her arm through his. *You'd better back me up on this,* she thought, keeping her attention on Fritz. "I haven't been out much and I tire easily," she explained. "With Anne there, Jackson can enjoy the party without worrying about me. Isn't that right, dear?" she finished looking up at him.

Jackson hesitated, then looking down at Sam, he smiled. "I always worry about you, darling, but I think it's an excellent idea," he said, returning his attention to Fritz. "Not for my sake, but for Sam's. She hasn't had a chance to get acquainted with that many people around the lake, so I think having Anne at her side will make her more comfortable." He turned on a charming smile. "That is, if you don't mind?"

Pleased and grateful for his support, Sam gave his arm an affectionate squeeze.

"Of course not," Fritz said graciously. "It will be fun having you as a guest, Anne."

"Thank you, Fritz," Anne replied, shooting Sam a knowing look. Shoving away from the counter, she glanced at the clock. "I'd better get home."

"I think I left one of Roxy's toys in the backseat," Sam said smoothly. "I'll walk you to the car."

Once they were off the porch and out of earshot, Anne whirled on her. "Why did you do that? I've never been to one of Fritz's parties as a guest."

Sam snorted. "It's about time that you were, then."

"I don't move in Fritz's social circle," Anne argued.

"Greg will be there, won't he?"

"If he doesn't change his mind at the last minute," Anne grumbled.

With a wink, Sam gave her arm a friendly poke. "Make sure he doesn't." Her tone grew serious. "Please come—I haven't been among strangers for a long time, and it would be nice to have at least a couple of friendly faces there."

"Jackson will be with you."

Sam shook her head. "Jackson's like a butterfly at these things—

flitting from group to group. And now . . ." Her voice trailed away as her attention moved down to her leg. "I don't know if I'm up to that."

Anne stopped at the car and placed her arms on the roof. "Okay, I'll go, but I'm going to be nervous the whole time."

Sam chuckled. "Good—we can be nervous together."

In the bathroom, Jackson stood in the doorway watching Sam as she applied her makeup. His eyes met hers in the mirror. A lazy smile lit his face, and in the mirror, Sam saw that he was holding both hands behind his back.

Pushing away from the door, he strolled toward her.

She turned and returned his smile. "What?" she said with a teasing note in her voice.

He took a strand of her short hair and rubbed it between his fingers. "It's been a long time since we've gone to a party." Withdrawing his other hand from behind his back with a great flourish, he presented Sam with a long, black velvet box.

"Jackson," Sam said with a sigh, "you didn't need to buy me a gift."

"I thought the occasion needed a little something special."

Quickly Sam opened the box and her eyes widened. A bracelet made of tiny interlocking gold leaves nestled inside. Sam held it up to the light with trembling fingers.

"The pattern is so delicate," she gasped. "It's gorgeous."

Jackson took the bracelet from her and fastened it on her wrist. He finished by pressing a kiss to the soft skin above the clasp.

"Thank you," she said with a quick peck to his cheek.

Pleased, he smiled more widely. "Do you remember last fall, when we were at my old house, going over the restoration plans with the contractor?"

"Yes," she replied, staring at the bracelet. "After he left, we took a walk through the hills behind the house—through the woods. The leaves had turned, and I remember how beautiful and peaceful it was." She looked up at him. "We were so happy."

Jackson ran a finger over the tiny leaves. "When I saw this, it reminded me of that day." Placing a knuckle under her chin, he lifted it. "We can be that way again."

"I hope so."

"I know so. Now," he said, and gave her bottom a playful slap, "finish getting ready and let's go party."

She moved away from the mirror and headed toward the bedroom. Jackson followed.

"You surprise me," he said abruptly.

Sam halted. "How?"

"Your relationship with Anne. A short time ago, you didn't want her here, and now—"

"I thought you and Dad wanted me to cooperate," she interrupted.

"We do, but your turnaround is unexpected. Not that we aren't pleased, of course."

"Of course," she repeated, and continued to the bedroom. Jackson stopped at the doorway, watching her.

Sam went to the closet and removed her dress. Laying it out on the bed, she stole a glance at Jackson over her shoulder. "I know my change of heart seems abrupt, but Anne really is good at her job and she doesn't let me slide."

"That's good, I suppose."

Sam whirled in surprise. "You suppose?"

Jackson leaned against the door. "We weren't happy that she let you take that fall. Your father—"

She held up a hand, stopping him. “That wasn't her fault.”

“She should've anticipated what happened.”

“Don't be silly,” Sam scoffed, tightening the belt of her robe.

“And I'm sure your father is going to hold Anne responsible for your adopting that dog,” he grumbled.

“Anne had nothing to do with it,” Sam answered, tossing the rest of her clothes on the bed. “And Roxy isn't *that dog*—she has a name.”

Jackson pushed away from the door and took a step. “You know, if your father does object to *Roxy*, it isn't too late to give her back. I know a breeder of cute little Pomeranians,” he said hopefully.

“Like Marcy Crane's dog?”

Jackson missed the note of warning in Sam's voice. “Yes.” Smiling, he took another step. “A dog like that might fit into our lifestyle better,” he said, his attention moving to Roxy, lying on the bed.

Sitting down next to the dog, Sam laid a hand on her head. Roxy's tail beat the mattress. “Marcy's dog snarls and nips every time anyone gets close.”

“And your dog doesn't?” he asked.

Catching the tone in Jackson's voice, Roxy lifted her head and stared at him for a moment. Then, with a sigh, she laid it back down and her eyes closed. Sam had the impression that the dog didn't think Jackson's comparison mattered. She agreed. Marcy's dog was aggressive, but Roxy barked only when someone surprised her, and she had never tried to bite.

Rising quickly, Sam felt her vision suddenly blur as black dots danced across her line of sight. Plopping down, she rubbed her forehead.

Jackson hurried to her side. "What's wrong?"

"Nothing." She let her hand fall and stood again, more slowly this time. "A dizzy spell. I'm okay now."

He stepped aside, allowing her to cross to the dresser. Opening the drawer containing her underclothes, she sighed. "Roxy's going to be fine. She'll quiet down, and once she gets over her nervousness around you, you're going to love her as much as I do."

Jackson eyed the dog skeptically.

With a shake of her head, Sam selected her underwear and moved back to the bed. Sinking down, she threw an arm over Roxy. "She makes me feel safe," she said defensively. "So safe that I didn't have nightmares last night."

Jackson strolled over to the nightstand and picked up Sam's bottle of medication. "Did you consider it might be the meds, and not the dog?"

"I know it's not the pills," she argued. "I forgot—" She slapped her hand over her mouth.

His eyes narrowed as he opened the bottle and, shaking them out in his hand, quickly counted them. "You haven't been taking them," he accused as he returned them to the bottle.

"I have a couple of times," Sam answered, stretching the truth. In reality, she hadn't taken one since the night she'd seen the woman on the dock.

"Samantha, your agreement with your father included taking you medication," he lectured.

"But I don't need them. And," she stressed, "they make me groggy."

Smacking the bottle back on the nightstand, Jackson frowned. "You can't simply stop taking them—your body needs to be weaned away from them." His frown deepened. "Otherwise, you'll suffer side effects."

"I haven't. If anything, I've felt better, stronger, and—"

"You will continue to take them until we have a chance to discuss this with Dr. Weissinger," he said in a firm voice.

Leaning over, Sam grabbed the bottle and, rising, moved to the dresser. Opening a drawer, she tossed the bottle in and shut it. "Okay, so I take the pills." Wanting to change the subject, she turned and leaned against the dresser. "Do you think you'll know anyone at the party tonight?"

"The Brightons. Maybe a few old faces from the summer I spent here as a teenager."

"How old were you?"

"Fifteen. It was the year before Mother died." He crossed the room and lifted the blinds. "I remember this cabin, actually. We stayed across the lake, down a bit from where Fritz lives."

"Really? Did you know the couple who lived here?"

Dropping the blinds, he turned and a sly smile stole across his face. "I didn't know them, but I remember the wife. She'd sunbathe every afternoon down on the dock." He hung his head sheepishly. "And put it this way, spotting her as I cruised by in my fishing boat was the high point of my day." He lifted his head and shrugged. "You know how teenage boys are."

Sam's thoughts shot to Teddy Brighton and the young men who'd hurt her. Unconsciously, her hand stole to the scar now covered by Alice's haircut and she felt a moment of anxiety. Yeah, she knew all about teenage boys.

Jackson noticed. "Has Anne mentioned her son?"

"No—no." Sam dropped her hand. "Why? Is there something I should know?"

Jackson shook his head as he glanced at the clock. "I'd better get changed," he said, crossing to the door. He stopped. "It was something Fritz said."

Sam's breath quickened. "What?"

"I guess the kid had been in some trouble while they lived in the Cities."

"Anne mentioned it," Sam said in a tight voice.

"Did she mention that he'd been picked up for possession?"

"Drugs? He was into drugs?"

Jackson lifted a shoulder. "I don't know if he was using, and Fritz did say that the kid was straight now." Pivoting, he caught the look on Sam's face and went to her quickly. He gathered her in a hug, and for once she didn't push him away. He placed a light kiss on the top of her head, his arms tightening.

"I'm sorry—I've frightened you," he murmured in her ear. "I spoke without thinking. Fritz said the kid was okay now." Releasing her, Jackson stood and looked down at her. "Really, I am pleased that you're getting along so well with Anne."

She looked up at him with doubt in her eyes.

"Darling," he said, bending and lifting her chin, "don't look so worried. Even if her son was still trouble, it's not like he has keys to the cabin."

Placing another kiss on her head, he turned and left the room, leaving Sam alone with Roxy.

Sam looked down to find the dog staring up at her with her head cocked to one side. Leaning over, she threw her arms around Roxy's neck and exhaled slowly.

"You'll protect me, won't you?"

# Seventeen

Anne's eyes roamed the room. She'd never been at one of Fritz's parties as a guest, but she had worked at them before and knew how much emphasis he placed on details. Tonight was no different. His large living-room and dining-room area glowed with soft candlelight. The lilting notes of one of his favorite piano concertos floated under the buzz of voices. Large vases of fresh wildflowers dotted both rooms. And along one wall, there was a buffet table spread with appetizers. Two local high school girls circled the room bearing trays holding glasses of wine, iced tea, and lemonade. From where she stood, she could see bright paper lanterns strung along the deck railing. The whole atmosphere, both inside and out, was a study in casual elegance.

Anne fingered one of her tiny, gold hoop earrings and tried not to feel out of place. She didn't look out of place—she knew that. The tunic that Sam had insisted on buying her shimmered down her body in graceful folds and the white linen pants she'd dug out of the back of her closet still fit. She'd even worn makeup. Dropping her hand, she felt her lips curl in a small grin. When she'd exited her bedroom, Caleb had been so surprised at her appearance that he'd jokingly asked what she'd done with his mother. What a switch—for him to see her as a person and not just his mom.

Spying one of the girls approach a cluster of people, she watched as they took the beverages the girl offered without so much as a glance in her direction. To them, she was as much a part of the decor as the candles and flowers. And without Sam's interference, that would've been her. Instead of standing here, all dressed up and exchanging greetings with people she'd known for years, she'd have been as invisible to those people as the high school girl.

It was nice not just being a mother. It was nice not being invisible. And she had Sam to thank for it. Still, the thought troubled her. On the one hand, she did appreciate Sam's kindness, but on the other, she didn't want to feel beholden to her. In the past, she'd been the one doing favors for people. Having the roles reversed made her squirm.

Turning her head slightly, she looked over at Sam. The lavender dress and purple shawl set off the young woman's coloring perfectly and the sickly paleness of weeks ago was gone—banished by the hours Anne had forced her to spend outside. With her new haircut disguising some of the gauntness in her face, she'd also lost that brittle look she used to have.

It was clear to her that she wasn't the only one who'd noticed the change in Sam. Dr. Van Horn did, too. It was evident in his expression when he looked at her. Attentive and smiling—his condescending attitude had disappeared. Anne's eyebrows knitted together. But maybe there was more to it than the way she looked on the outside. Sam had shown real spunk when she'd stood up to him about keeping Roxy, and the whole incident appeared to have given her confidence. Hopefully, that's what he was responding to.

Suddenly she was yanked out of her thoughts by a gasp and the sight of Sam's body turning rigid. Anne's gaze darted to what had caught Sam's attention. The Brightons had made their entrance, and not only was it Kimberly, Irene, and Ted Two, but they had Teddy in tow. Dressed in a casual sport shirt and pressed khakis, with a supercilious grin across his face, Teddy was nonchalantly gazing around the room while his parents and grandmother greeted a new arrival who was standing near the door. When his eyes found Sam, his grin dropped and he leaned close to his father. Too far away to hear his words, Anne watched Ted Two nod and, taking his mother by the arm, begin to lead the group straight toward them.

"Get me out of here," Sam hissed.

"Don't you dare turn and run," Anne replied, her voice stern. "You stand your ground."

"I can't."

Tugging on Sam's sleeve, Anne angled her body toward her. "Yes, you can. That little sociopath would like nothing better than to see your fear. Do not give him the pleasure."

Conflicting emotions shadowed Sam's face. Finally, she inhaled sharply and drew her shawl around her shoulders. Exhaling slowly, she lifted her chin and prepared to meet the enemy. Anne moved aside as the Brightons reached them.

Ted Two was the first to speak. "You must be Samantha Moore," he said, extending his hand. "It's nice to finally meet you." Turning, he drew his mother forward. "My mother, Irene, and my wife, Kimberly."

Smiling stiffly, Sam gave his hand a light shake and acknowledged each introduction with a quick nod, saying nothing and keeping her attention carefully centered on Teddy.

Stepping back, Ted Two threw an arm around his son's shoulder and maneuvered the boy until he stood directly in front of Sam.

Anne's breath caught while she waited for Sam's reaction, but instead of shrinking back as she'd expected, Sam remained motionless.

Ted Two's manner suddenly became more formal. "I believe you've met my son, Teddy." Focusing on his son, he squeezed the boy's arm. "He has something to say, don't you, Teddy?"

Teddy's head dipped, and when he lifted it, his face wore an expression of humility. "I'd like to apologize for my behavior the other day, Ms. Moore." His eyes darted to his father before returning to Sam. "It was inexcusably rude and I hope you can forgive me."

At his side, Ted Two gave a satisfied nod and dropped his arm from around Teddy's shoulder.

Sam opened her mouth to reply, but before she could answer, Jackson joined the group and introductions were made once again. Teddy's apology was forgotten, and Anne caught the sly look he shot at Sam before focusing on Dr. Van Horn.

"I'm so happy to meet you, Dr. Van Horn," Teddy said, grasping Jackson's hand firmly in his own. "I've heard some of my mom's friends talk about what a terrific surgeon you are."

Taken by surprise, Jackson beamed. "Thank you."

"In fact, Irene," the boy continued with a nod toward his grandmother, "thinks plastic surgery might be a good career for me." He smiled broadly. "She's always wanted a doctor in the family."

For the next five minutes, he peppered the doctor with questions concerning his practice while Jackson was all but preening at the young man's interest.

Watching Teddy suck up to Dr. Van Horn, Anne wanted to gag. She didn't know what the boy's game was, but whatever it was, Dr. Van Horn was falling for it. Hadn't Sam told him about the incident with Roxy? She glanced at Sam, standing rigidly at her fiancé's side. A brittle light haunted her eyes as she plucked at her shawl, clearly unnerved by Teddy's performance, and Anne felt her anxiety growing. She had to figure out a way to get her charge away from the group before she crumbled.

"Um," she began, interrupting Teddy.

"Wait," he said before she could speak. "I see you don't have any refreshments. May I get you something?" He looked expectantly at Sam and Anne.

"How thoughtful of you, Teddy," Jackson interjected. "Wine, Anne?" he asked with a glance her way.

Anne gave a quick nod.

Linking his arm with Sam's, Jackson smiled. "Sam will have lemonade."

After Teddy left, Jackson turned to the Brightons. "What a nice young man."

A stunned silence ensued until Irene broke it. "Humph," she snorted, drilling her son and daughter-in-law with a knowing glance. "My grandson has his moments." Taking Kimberly's arm, she gave Jackson a gracious smile. "We haven't said hello to our host. If you'll excuse us?"

"Of course," Jackson replied.

As the Brightons made their way across the crowded room, Teddy returned with the two glasses. After handing them to Sam and Anne, he glanced around the room for his parents and grandmother. "Thank you for answering all my questions, Dr. Van Horn," he said, "but I'd better join my family."

"My pleasure, Teddy. And, please, if you think of more, stop by the cabin."

Anne heard Sam's soft gasp.

"I'll be happy to answer them," Jackson continued, oblivious to Sam's reaction.

Sam, her face drained of color, took a step away from Jackson and Teddy. Lifting her glass, she downed the lemonade in one long gulp. "Anne, it's getting close in here. Would you come out on the deck with me?" she said, passing her hand across her forehead.

Jackson's focus shifted to Sam. "Wait, are you feeling ill?"

She gave a quick shake of her head. "No, I just need some fresh air. Anne can go with me—you stay and make the rounds."

Anne followed Sam across the room, until she paused at the French doors leading to the deck. Sam hesitated, as if bracing herself, then, taking a deep breath, she slid open the door and stepped outside. In the pale light of the lanterns, Anne saw her eyes dart to the shadows before crossing to the railing.

"He won't come to the cabin, will he?" she asked in a low voice.

Anne didn't have to ask who "he" was. "I don't know," she replied.

She drew her shawl tightly around her shoulders. "I don't want that kid near Roxy."

"I don't blame you." Anne tugged on her bottom lip. What could she say that wouldn't escalate Sam's fears? "I don't know what Teddy was trying to prove. Maybe he was putting on an act for the benefit of his grandmother in hopes she'd loosen the leash?" She stepped closer to the railing and looked down at the water. "I take it you didn't tell Dr. Van Horn about your confrontation with Teddy."

"No."

"Why not?"

"In case you haven't noticed, my family doesn't take my concerns very seriously. If I would've told Jackson about the incident, he would've minimized it. Accused me of being paranoid."

"When is Dr. Van Horn going back to the Cities?"

"Early Monday morning."

Angling away from the railing, Anne laid a comforting hand on Sam's arm. "Hopefully, Teddy won't stop by tomorrow. After Dr. Van Horn leaves, he won't have a reason to stop by." Her mouth tightened in a grim line. "But if he does show up while I'm there, *I* won't let him in."

Sam gave a quick shake of her head. "But what if you're not?"

"Don't worry about it. There's no sense in borrowing trouble."

Turning away from the railing, Sam staggered slightly forward. Her shawl slid down her arms as she ran her fingers through her hair. "Whew," she said abruptly. "I'm hot. Are you hot?"

"No, but if you—" A figure stepping into the light startled her. "Edward," Anne exclaimed. "I'm sorry. I didn't see you."

"I came around from the front," he replied, motioning toward the steps at the side of the deck. "I didn't want to brave the crowd. Mother's inside."

Suddenly, from her place next to Anne, Sam giggled and moved forward. "Aren't you going to introduce me to your friend, Anne?" she asked in a coy voice.

Anne whirled toward Sam in surprise. The young woman's tenseness had disappeared as she stood directly in front of Edward with her head cocked. If Anne hadn't known better, she would've sworn she saw Sam wink at him.

"Um—" she stuttered in confusion. "Edward Dunlap. He and his mother own the little gas station at the four corners."

"Edward," Sam said, stepping closer and extending her hand. "I'm Samantha Moore."

Edward grasped her hand reluctantly. "Samantha."

She moved in closer without letting go of his hand. "I'm staying at the old Jones place. Maybe you know of it?"

"Yes," Edward answered in a tight voice.

Moving her hand up Edward's arm, Sam smiled at him. "Did you know Blanche?"

Anne shook her head in disbelief while Edward shifted uncomfortably. Fritz had warned Sam—she herself had warned Sam—that talking about Blanche made people nervous. What did she think she was doing? Taking a step closer, Anne opened her mouth to interrupt, but before she could get the words out, Edward jerked back, his head whipping toward the crowd inside.

"Excuse me, but I see my mother waving at me."

He turned on his heel, clutching his arm tightly to his side, and left them alone on the deck.

Taking Sam's shoulder, Anne spun her around. "Fritz and I both warned you not to ask about Blanche," she hissed.

"So?" Sam replied with a toss of her head. "I'm curious. If I know more about her, I might be able to figure out who's wandering around my dock at night." She glanced over her shoulder to where Edward now stood at his mother's side. "Was he one of Blanche's 'friends'?"

"There've been stories—" Anne stopped, watching Edward with his mother. "But I don't want you asking him a bunch of questions. Edward's life isn't easy. He's in constant pain and he doesn't need you bugging him."

Sam fluffed her hair and Anne felt her lack of concern. What was with her tonight? She'd never seen Sam act this way. First Teddy schmoozing with Dr. Van Horn, now Sam acting like she didn't have a care in the world. It was as if she'd stepped into an alternate universe. No one was acting the way Anne expected.

"Oh, forget it," Sam said, fluttering her hand at Anne. "This party's a drag. Let's see if we can juice it up."

*Juice it up?* What in the hell did she mean by that?

An hour later, Anne understood what Sam had meant. Once she was back inside the cabin, Sam had flitted from group to group, introducing herself, smiling and laughing at old jokes, and even mildly flirting with some of the men. At first, Anne had followed in her wake, but had finally given up when Sam started verbally sparring with Irene Brighton. She now leaned against a wall watching Sam carry on. For someone who claimed to have a problem with crowds, Sam certainly knew how to work a room.

"Has she been drinking?" a voice next to her asked.

Anne's attention slid to Greg, who'd come up silently beside her. "As far as I know—just lemonade. With all the medication she's taking, she can't have a drop of alcohol."

She looked back at Sam, who had her hand on old Mr. Abernathy's arm as she . . . My God, was she fluttering her eyelashes at him? Anne's eyes sought out Dr. Van Horn. Had he noticed Sam's behavior? Yup—from the tight-lipped expression on his face, it looked like he had. She shoved away from the wall.

"This might get ugly," she whispered over her shoulder to Greg. "I'm getting her out of here."

Anne made her way to where Sam had been standing only to find her gone. Casting her eyes around the room, she spotted her by Fritz's baby grand piano, whispering to him. Fritz's eyes flew wide open in what looked like surprise as he shook his head. Sam persisted, leaning in close. Finally he slowly nodded, and pulling out the bench, he sat down and began to play.

With a satisfied nod, Sam tossed her shawl on the bench and moved to the side of the piano. Spreading her arms wide, she clutched the edge, swaying to the rhythm of the music. The guests' voices stilled and all attention was on her. Her eyelids drifting shut, she opened her mouth and began to sing.

She had a rich alto voice as she crooned an old song that Anne recognized as one her mother used to play back in the mid-seventies.

When Sam reached the chorus, a startled gasp came from the direction of Esther Dunlap, and Anne saw Edward's face flush bright red. He turned suddenly and rushed out the door with his mother following him closely. Anne heard the front door slam over Sam's singing.

Sam's eyes opened and focused directly on Teddy Two. Strolling over to him, she ran her hand up his arm as she sang the next line. She leaned toward him.

Abruptly the music stopped as Dr. Van Horn approached them. Taking Sam's arm, he led her through the stunned crowd and out the door.

Returning to Greg's side, Anne placed her fingertips at her temples and shook her head. "Can you take me home?" she asked, letting her hands fall to her side. "Looks like I just lost my ride."

# Eighteen

W*hat a party*, I think, grinning to myself. Stirred everyone up good and proper, didn't it? Irene had been so pleased. Made her night—until Samantha Moore started singing. She didn't like that—I know she hates that song—know it reminds her of a time she'd rather forget. And to witness Samantha singing it to Irene's son—how dare she? I'd watched Irene silently fume, drilling both her son and Samantha with a look that would drop a horse. It had been so funny, and I had to fight the laughter boiling inside of me. It had been almost impossible to hide my feelings.

It was amazing really that Samantha had chosen that particular song. What a strange twist of fate. Or had she been asking questions? Had she heard the stories and decided to play a little trick on the partygoers?

And Edward Dunlap—he stormed out of there like the hounds of hell were nipping at his heels. Of course, in a way, they had been. That thought sobered me. In the recesses of what I suppose I could call my heart, I feel sorry for Edward. I know he had been a young man with a bright future until *she'd* destroyed it.

I walk down to the end of the dock and stare out over the dark water. It always comes back to her, doesn't it? Twenty-five years is a long time for someone to haunt the memories of so many people. Who would've thought that someone so insignificant would have such an impact on so many lives?

My eyes travel to the boards beneath my feet. *Insignificant?* I ask myself. She hadn't been insignificant, lying here in this very spot, dressed or undressed, depending how one looked at it, in her minuscule bikini. She'd been rather impressive. Every male on the lake had found a reason to run their boats by during the hours of one and three. Disgusting, really, when I stop and think about it, and feel my hands clench at my side. Cheap, that's what she'd been. A common tramp who'd almost ruined my life. I should've learned my lesson from her—never trust a woman. What if she had persuaded old Ted to run off with her? Would my life have been different? Would Edward's?

I turn slowly and walk back toward the cabin. Reaching the edge of the dock, I hear the sound of a dog barking and quickly I duck into the trees.

That damn dog! How can I possibly engage in these nightly strolls undetected when that dog carries on like that? It was a mistake for her to adopt it.

A small grin tugs at my lips. There are ways to make the animal disappear.

# Nineteen

Sam knew she was dreaming. The feeling was all too familiar—dreams, never ending, looping over and over in her mind, with her unable to stop them up. *Oh my God*, a tiny part of her brain screamed. Was she in a coma again? She wanted her eyes to open, needed her eyes to open. She fought to regain consciousness and to rise above the darkness that was sucking her under.

Useless. A tear leaked out from the corner of one eye as she surrendered and slowly sank into the abyss.

The dream opened with Sam lurking in a corner of a room filled with people. Okay, she could handle this—not a nightmare, simply a dream triggered by Fritz's party. In fact, it *was* Fritz's party: she spotted his baby grand sitting in the center of the room, but something was off. The cabin didn't look the same. The furniture had changed and the decor was different.

The people were different, too—she didn't recognize anyone. And they were dressed funny. Hawaiian shirts; blouses with huge shoulder pads; miniskirts. One woman was wearing a shiny blouse that broadened her shoulders and tight skinny jeans. Earrings the size of fifty-cent pieces bobbed from her earlobes, while her hair rose straight up from her forehead and fell in a cloud of curls around her head.

Sam's attention turned to the man at the piano. Wearing a white sport coat over a neon-pink T-shirt, jeans, and loafers with no socks, he sat with his head down as his hands played softly over the keyboard. A woman with red hair cascading down her back leaned against the piano listening. She was dressed as oddly as everyone else—a purple miniskirt and a sheer lavender blouse. She held a cigarette in one hand, waving it through the air as she talked with the piano player. Something she said caused the man to suddenly lift his head.

Fritz. A much younger Fritz.

Before he could reply, their heads turned in tandem as a distinguished-looking man with silver hair joined them. The woman turned slightly and pushed away from the piano. Stealing a hand up his arm, she stood on her tiptoes and whispered something in his ear. Amused, the man threw back his head and laughed. Smirking, Fritz lowered his head once again and began playing louder.

Sam recognized the song. It was one she'd heard on a golden oldies station in the Cities, but she couldn't remember the lyrics.

The woman had no problem with the words. Stepping away from the man, she stubbed out her cigarette and began to sing seductively, allowing her body to slither against the piano. Her companion looked on, an approving smile on his face and lust in his eyes.

Another watched her, too. A lone man sitting on the couch. He was dressed roughly compared to the others in the room, and his long face was marked with unhappiness as he stared at the redhead standing by the piano. His knees were pressed together tightly while he clutched a highball glass with both of his work-worn hands. Sam didn't think she'd ever seen a man more miserable and she felt drawn toward the couch.

The dream shifted and she found herself outside. Was it the same night? Was she still dreaming about the lake?

She cast her eyes upward. A crescent moon shone in the night sky and cast a pale light on the woods surrounding her. Moving in the dream, her feet crunched on fallen pine needles while a cool breeze caressed her bare arms and rustled the leaves around her. *Summer, it must be summer*, she thought.

Peaceful, but she didn't feel peaceful. The shadows of tall pines crowded her, and in her hyperalert state she was aware of the creatures skittering through the brush. It felt as though a thousand eyes were watching while the stench of decay hid beneath the scent of the wild honeysuckle. In the distance, she heard the angry buzz of voices. Turning, she went toward the sound.

A cold sweat formed on her forehead as she stepped away from the trees and saw the black water of a lake. The voices stilled.

A figure knelt at the end of a dock stretching out over the dark water. A woman who was unrecognizable in the dim light clutched her hands tightly to her chest; her sobs rose and fell with the rhythm of the water lapping the shore.

The breeze carried a soft *please* to Sam's ears, and made her stomach burn with acid. She'd been that woman. Begging and sobbing for her life while the cold of the concrete floor seeped into her joints. Sorrow and empathy poured out of Sam's heart as if her soul were trying to reach out and touch the crying woman.

Abruptly the woman stopped. Her head lifted and the shadow of one hand moved to wipe away her tears. She shifted slowly and Sam knew that any moment their eyes would meet.

Pain—fast and hard—hit the back of her skull, driving her to her knees. Pebbles, lying on the ground beneath her, ripped at her flesh, while a silent scream tightened her throat. She knew what was coming next. The dream would change. She'd be back—back in the deserted garage. She'd be surrounded by the harsh smell of exhaust fumes. She'd hear the taunts and jeers of the young men circling her. Pain . . . so much pain . . . enough to blind her fear.

She had to wake up.

With a jolt, she shot up in bed, only to collapse back against her pillows, her head throbbing with each thump of her heart. Rolling onto her side, she clutched at her pillow as she bit back a whimper. Awake now, she willed her muscles to relax and tried to conquer the waves of hurt rolling through her head.

A warm body suddenly pressed against her and the pain eased. When a cold nose tentatively touched her hand, Sam looked at the head close to hers. Two brown eyes surrounded by black fur stared at her as Roxy edged closer, her nose nudging Sam repeatedly. With great effort, Sam lifted her hand and let it fall on the dog's head. Sighing, she closed her eyes . . . and she slept.

The warm rays of sunshine slanting across Sam's face stirred her to consciousness. Slowly, like a deep-sea diver, she rose to the surface. Disoriented, she threw her forearm over her eyes and took a deep breath. Okay, her name was Samantha Moore, she was at Elk Horn Lake staying in a cabin, and what she had experienced last night was nothing more than a weird dream, she thought. In the end, she'd pulled herself free of the nightmare and she was fine. Maybe *fine* was too strong of a word. Her head throbbed dully and her body ached. Was she coming down with the flu? The dreams might have been caused by a fever. She placed her hand on her cheek. No, her skin felt normal, not hot to the touch.

Scooting away from Roxy, who still lay curled at her side, she sat up and swung her legs off the bed. With bones creaking, she rose and hobbled into the bathroom. She flipped on the faucet and splashed her face with cold water. It trickled down her neck and dampened the front of her nightgown. Ignoring the cotton sticking to her chest, she stared at herself in the mirror. Dear Lord, she looked like a rabid raccoon. Smeared mascara ringed her eyes, deepening the dark circles already there, and her hair was sticking out in spikes. Frowning at herself in the mirror, she turned and headed back to the bedroom. It must have been some party.

She stopped and gripped the doorjamb, leaning against it. The party. She couldn't remember the party. She glanced down at her wet nightgown. She couldn't recall putting it on. Staggering back to the bed, she dropped down and buried her head in her hands.

*Think, Samantha, think.* What happened last night? Her memory spun in circles and all she could recall clearly was the dream. *No, you went shopping, you got ready, you and Jackson picked up Anne, you—* Muted voices from the kitchen caught her attention and stopped the litany of her thoughts. Slowly she stood and crossed the room to the door. Opening it a crack, she pressed her ear against it.

Jackson and Anne.

"Are you sure she didn't have any alcohol?" Jackson was saying in a curt tone.

"Yes," Anne declared. "Lemonade and that's it."

A long pause followed.

Jackson broke the silence. "Did you know that she hasn't been taking her medication?"

"I knew she'd missed a couple of times, but I made sure she took the pills when I was here."

A small smile cracked Sam's face, causing her to wince. Anne didn't know that she'd palmed them and then flushed them down the toilet.

"Was she suffering from withdrawal last night?" Anne continued.

"Possibly." Sam heard the exasperation in Jackson's voice. He sighed. "I don't know how I'm going to explain her behavior to Fritz."

"Aren't you more concerned about why Sam acted that way?" Anne blurted.

Another long pause followed, punctuated by footsteps pacing the kitchen floor. "Of course I am," Jackson replied irritably, "but did you see Irene Brighton's reaction?" The footsteps stopped. "The Brightons are an influential family and Irene is on the board of several hospitals. I don't need her carrying tales about Sam back to any of the boards' members. I don't need my colleagues—"

"Have you checked on her this morning?"

The pacing resumed. "She was curled up in bed with her dog," he answered, spitting out the words.

Anne's response was too low for Sam to hear, but she did hear her quick steps crossing the kitchen. Shutting the door, she crossed to the bed and crawled in. As she pulled the sheet up around her neck, she concentrated on feigning sleep. A moment later, she felt more than heard the door open softly. It stayed that way for what felt like several minutes, but finally she heard it snick quietly shut.

Rolling over on her back, she stared at the ceiling while she absentmindedly stroked Roxy's head. Searching her mind, she tried to recall last night moment by moment. She remembered walking into the party, remembered how strangely everyone was dressed—no, that was the dream. She tucked that thought away. What happened next? Meeting the Brightons and the anxiety Teddy had caused. Then she'd gone out onto the deck with Anne.

The next clear memory was the dream. But there had to be more. How long had they stayed at the party? She couldn't remember. Her mind was like a defective long-playing record—it played up to a certain spot and then the needle skipped. She heard the beginning and the end, but missed the middle.

Frustrated, she climbed out of bed and moved restlessly around the room. *Admit it, Samantha, you had some kind of a blackout.* That had never happened to her before and the thought of it terrified her. And what was worse, both Jackson and Anne had known something was wrong with her. She gave one of her shoes an angry kick and sent it flying across the room. She'd been so sure she was getting better. She'd felt she was finally conquering the emotional aftermath of her attack. Stopping at the window, she pulled back the curtain and stared out over the lake. What if she had another one? No. She dropped the curtain. She was getting stronger and she wasn't going to let what happened undermine her confidence. So what if she couldn't remember a portion of the evening right now? It might eventually come back to her. And as far as Jackson and Anne's concerns? She'd find a way to dance around them.

A soft whining at the bedroom door caught her attention.

"You need to go out, don't you?" Reluctantly, Sam shoved her arms into her robe and belted it tightly. When she opened the door, the dog shot out and took off down the hallway. Sam followed and, after rounding the corner, saw Jackson and Anne seated at the kitchen table. Simultaneously their heads turned. Neither spoke, and by the shuttered looks on their faces, Sam knew that their conversation had continued to be about her.

Anne broke the silence. "How are you feeling?" she asked, rising to her feet. "Would you like some coffee?"

Sam shook her head and grabbed Roxy's leash off the counter.

"I think I might be coming down with the flu, so I'd rather have orange juice."

"Here, I'll trade you," Anne said, filling a glass from the pitcher on the table and handing it to her. She took the leash from Sam's hand. "I'll take the dog out."

Accepting the glass, Sam joined Jackson at the table. She drank the juice while he silently studied her. Placing the glass on the table, she licked her lips and tried to smile. "Did you enjoy the party?"

"Are you being sarcastic?" he sputtered, jerking back in his chair.

"No—no—but—"

"After the way you acted last night? I certainly hope you're going to apologize to Fritz."

"Yes, of course," she murmured, lowering her head. She bit the inside of her lip. That might be tough since she didn't know what she'd be apologizing for. She'd either have to wing it or confess that she couldn't remember. She stole a glance at Jackson. Did she dare tell him about her lack of memory? If she did, how long would it take him to call her father and share the story with him? A strong sense of self-preservation cautioned her to keep her mouth shut.

Jackson leaned forward and clasped his hands on the table. "What were you trying to prove?" he asked in a low voice. "I know you've felt unattractive since the accident, but haven't I tried to reassure you that it didn't matter?" He shook his head. "Wasn't that enough? Did you have to flirt with Ted Brighton last night?"

Her cheeks grew hot. "I didn't flirt with Ted Brighton," she declared.

"I don't know what else you'd call it," he answered with a snort.

She stared at him blindly as the fear she'd felt earlier returned. No, Jackson had to be wrong. It was one thing to have a memory lapse, but to act out of character? Impossible. Even before the attack, she'd never been the type of woman to come on to men. It wasn't her style. Jackson had to have misconstrued her behavior.

"I don't know how you could put me through something so shameful. You reminded me of *her*," he spit out. "How many times have I told you how her behavior embarrassed me?"

"Jackson—I know your relationship with your mother—"

Jerking back, Jackson crossed his arms over his chest and glared at her. "If you don't want to acknowledge the flirting, will you at least explain whatever possessed you to sing?"

Sam's jaw dropped and she quickly snapped it shut. "S-s-sing?" she stuttered.

His eyes narrowed and he looked her over carefully. "You don't remember, do you?" His voice rang with suspicion.

Hanging her head, she considered trying to bluff her way out, but it wouldn't do any good. He'd know she was lying. "No," she whispered.

He stood suddenly and came to her, kneeling beside her chair. With a sigh, he took her hand in his and softly stroked his thumb across her knuckles. "Samantha, darling," he said gently, "I was afraid something like this would happen when I learned you'd stopped taking your medication." His other hand lifted her chin and he stared into her eyes. "You have to trust that I know what's best for you."

Her head turned away. "I do."

"Do you?" he asked, placing a palm on her cheek and forcing her to look at him. "I hope so. I am a doctor, you know," he finished with a trace of humor in his voice.

Sam tried to smile, but her lips trembled. If she did as Jackson said, she'd spend her time drifting through the days in a haze. "But the pills make me feel so sluggish."

Noticing the strain on her face, Jackson sobered and placed both hands on her shoulders. "You need them," he insisted. "Now, no more arguments." Leaning forward, he kissed her forehead. "And don't worry, my darling," he said in a whisper. "I'll take care of you."

Later that afternoon, still shaken by her promise to continue her medications, she said a muted good-bye to Jackson while Anne stood on the sidelines and watched. Once he'd left, Anne turned to her.

"Are you hungry?" she asked with false cheerfulness.

"Not really." Sam stole a glance at the other woman as they crossed the yard. "Did Jackson tell you that I don't remember the party?"

Stopping at the edge of the porch, Anne plucked one of the leaves off the dying shrub. "Yes, and I'm glad he did. If I'm to help you, I need to know what's going on."

"Do you think I'm losing it?" Sam asked in a small voice.

"No," Anne replied with a confident shake of her head. "Dr. Van Horn said it was the effects of withdrawal. We'll just make sure you take your meds."

"But I hate the way they make me feel," Sam argued.

"Would you rather have blackouts?" Anne asked, crumbling the leaf in her hand.

"No."

"Then I think you'd better do as he says."

Reluctantly, Sam nodded as she followed Anne into the cabin. Once inside, she leaned against the counter and studied the other woman for a moment. "I made quite a spectacle of myself last night, didn't I?"

Anne shrugged. "I don't know—I've seen worse." She gave her a quick smile. "You did surprise me, though. I didn't know you could sing. You have a lovely alto voice."

"No, I don't. I'm a soprano."

Anne snickered. "Not last night you weren't. You were an alto."

Sam looked confused, and her gaze traveled to the floor. "That's odd," she muttered.

"Well," Anne said, placing her hands on her hips. "Are you up for some exercises?"

"Could we go for a walk?" Sam asked, looking up at Anne.

Surprise showed on Anne's face. "You want to go outside?"

"Yeah. We can take Roxy with us. She needs a walk, too."

"You won't feel uncomfortable?"

Glancing to where the dog lay stretched out in the sunshine pouring through the French doors, Sam smiled fondly. "I don't know what it is, but when I'm with her, I feel safe."

"Good, let's get going before the bugs come out."

A few minutes later, the three of them headed out the door and up the road. They'd gone a short distance when they heard the sound of a rousing march coming from Greg's cabin.

"The quartet for the Fourth," Anne offered in way of explanation. "Do you want to stop by and listen?"

"I guess."

The music became louder as they approached Greg's, but stopped when Anne knocked loudly on the screen door. Seconds later, Greg appeared in the doorway.

"Hi," he said, swinging the door open. "Come on in. We're practicing."

"We heard," Anne replied, arching an eyebrow.

"Hey, what good is a march if it isn't loud?" Greg joked.

Anne and Sam followed Greg into the living room, where he quickly introduced Sam to Caleb and George Roberts, the flutist for the group. Meeting Caleb for the first time, she remembered Jackson's warning and eyed him suspiciously. He didn't look like a gang member or a druggie. He looked like an average, normal teenage boy—all angles and loose limbs. Out of the corner of her eye, she saw Anne watch him with pride and love written on her face. Roxy's reaction was the one that surprised her. After giving Caleb's leg a good sniff, she plopped down at his feet and rolled over onto her back.

Noticing her, Caleb laughed and squatted beside her. "Ah, so you want a belly rub, do you?" Scratching her stomach, he laughed again when her back leg pawed at the air. "She must be ticklish," he said, smiling up at Sam.

"Must be," Sam answered, returning his smile. Looking away from Caleb as he played with Roxy, she noticed Fritz eyeing her with speculation. *Oh, great*, she thought, *he's thinking about last night. Well, now is as good a time as any.* Squaring her shoulders, she walked over to him.

"May I speak with you privately?" she asked, her voice quivering.

"My pleasure," he replied easily. "Greg, let's take five, shall we?" With a wave of his hand, he motioned Sam toward the door. Walking across Greg's deck, he leaned against the railing and waited.

Sam shifted uncomfortably as she struggled for the right words. Finally she gave up. "I'm sorry," she blurted.

Fritz jerked in surprise. "For what?"

"My behavior last night at your party. I'm sorry if I caused a scene."

"Nonsense," he said with a smile. "You didn't cause a scene. If Jackson would've simply let you finish your song, no one would've thought a thing about it."

"Really?"

"Yes, most of my guests were enjoying your performance," he assured her. "You have a lovely voice. I've always enjoyed a strong alto."

"Soprano," she mumbled.

"Pardon?"

"Nothing," she said with a brush of her hand. "I appreciate your graciousness, Fritz, and all I can say is that I wasn't myself last night."

Fritz chuckled. "No, you weren't. In our short acquaintance, I don't think I've ever seen you that relaxed. And isn't that what a party is supposed to be about? Letting loose and having a good time?" He arched an eyebrow. "And I will say that whatever you imbibed certainly made you let loose."

"Lemonade."

Fritz pressed his hand against one ear. "George's playing must be affecting my hearing. I could've sworn you said 'lemonade.'"

"I did," she replied tersely.

"Hmm," he said, brushing his fingers across his chin. "Did it taste odd?"

"What do you mean?"

"Well, it wouldn't be the first time someone spiked the punch, so to speak."

"It wasn't spiked. I would've tasted the liquor."

"Did you feel well this morning?"

"You mean did I have a hangover? No." Sam thought about the muscle aches and her pounding head. "I did feel like I was coming down with the flu, but that feeling is gone now."

Fritz pursed his lips and looked at her thoughtfully. "Just out of curiosity, did one of the girls serve you?"

"No. Ted—" She broke off with a gasp. "Teddy Brighton gave it to me. Do you think—"

"That Teddy slipped you a mickey?" His lips twisted in a frown. "It wouldn't surprise me. When I taught at the university, we had quite a problem with some young men slipping 'roofies' to the young ladies."

"The date-rape drug?"

"Yes. I don't mean to overstep my bounds, but did you suffer a blackout?"

Sam choked. "Yes. How did you know?"

"A common side effect, along with a reduction in one's inhibitions, which could account for you bursting into song."

"Is there a test?"

"There is, but I imagine too much time has elapsed."

Sam's face fell at his words, then brightened. In a way, she was angry that the little shit had drugged her, but in another way she was relieved that there was a reason for her behavior other than withdrawal.

Observing the emotions play across her face, Fritz cocked his head. "You seem almost happy that you were drugged . . ."

"I'm not," she said with a shake of her head. "It's just—" She gave a rueful laugh, but it ended with her voice cracking. Clearing her throat, she continued: "Anne has told me how fast the stories fly around here. How much do you know about my injuries?"

"I heard you were attacked and suffered a head injury," he answered gently.

"Yes . . . and it put me in a coma." Sam gnawed on her bottom lip and grasped the porch railing. "And when I woke up . . . nothing was the same. My left leg didn't work right; I couldn't go outside without feeling like I was being watched; I've had nightmares—"

Fritz placed his hand over hers, but said nothing.

"But lately, I've been getting better," she continued in a firm voice. "My leg is stronger; I'm not as afraid as I was; and the nightmares aren't as frequent—" Her voice dropped and her eyes filled with tears. "When Jackson told me how I'd acted at your party and I couldn't remember doing any of the things he said, it scared me." She swiped her eyes. "I thought I'd had a relapse."

"But if Teddy drugged you, there's an explanation."

"Exactly," she replied with a sniff.

He looked at her with sadness in his eyes. "You poor dear. You've suffered so much." His face tightened. "And now that young man plays an evil trick on you—it's inexcusable. I'll speak to Irene."

Sam's hand shot out. "No, please don't. We can't prove it."

"Are you sure you don't want me to say anything?"

"Yes," she said, letting out a long breath.

She felt as if a weight had been lifted from her shoulders. Thanks to Fritz, she could stop taking her nightly medication without guilt. Jackson was wrong—the blackout hadn't been caused by withdrawal—she was sure of it. But the mistake wasn't his fault. Teddy had made a good impression on him. He would never have expected that kid to drug her. And she couldn't wait to tell him—he had to be as relieved as she was when he learned that there was a logical explanation.

# Twenty

Walking back to the cabin, Anne noticed the change in Sam's mood. She gave her a sideways glance. "I'm guessing that you apologized to Fritz?"

"Yeah, and he was very kind about it," Sam said with a frown, then related the whole conversation. Finished, she looked over at Anne. "You look skeptical. You don't agree?"

Anne waited before speaking. "It's possible. I wouldn't put anything past Teddy—but Dr. Van Horn seemed so convinced it was a reaction—"

"Anne, I only took the nightly pill sporadically at the beginning, and now I haven't had any for days," Sam insisted. "And while I'm being honest, I've quit taking the antidepressants." Her chin went up a notch. "*And* I've felt better without them."

"But—"

"Can we give it the rest of the week and see what happens?" she pleaded. "If I have another episode, I'll go back on them."

Anne tugged on her lip. She believed a patient's input was an important part of her recovery, but not to the point of disregarding her doctor's orders. And Dr. Van Horn had been insistent that Sam continue the medication. Her memory went back to the first day she'd met Sam. She'd wondered if Sam's lethargy had been a result of the medication.

"Please? If you're worried it will get you fired, don't," Sam said, rushing the words. "I'll take full responsibility."

With a sigh, Anne made her decision. "Okay, you can skip the pills tonight, but you have to agree to an appointment with one of the doctors at the hospital. Then, if they say it's okay—"

"Thanks."

"I'll try and get you in tomorrow."

"Okay," Sam replied, wandering over to the dying plant by the porch steps.

As she neared the plant, Roxy let out a low whine, but Sam ignored her.

Surprised, Anne followed and watched as Sam bent and stroked one of the dying leaves.

"Poor thing," she said softly while her eyes seemed to lose their focus, "you've been neglected, haven't you? Love Lies Bleeding—so beautiful . . ." Her voice trailed away as she continued to finger the leaves.

"What did you say?" Anne asked, lightly touching her arm.

Sam snapped back from her reverie. "Nothing. I—ah—just wondered what kind of a bush this is."

Anne cocked her head. "You called it Love Lies Bleeding."

"I did?" She fingered Roxy's leash. "Oh, I probably saw a picture in some magazine and recognized it." Sam took a small step onto the porch, her eyes avoiding the plant. "I'm hungry. Are you hungry? Why don't we—"

She stopped abruptly at the sound of a car coming down the road. Anne turned and, shading her eyes against the setting sun, watched a black Town Car slowly roll to a stop in front of the cabin. Sam groaned when the driver exited the vehicle.

"Dad," she hissed. "Jackson didn't waste any time calling him."

With purposeful steps, Lawrence Moore crossed the yard, his eyes hidden behind aviator sunglasses. At the bottom of the steps, he stopped and whipped off the glasses. "Anne," he said tersely before turning his attention to Sam.

"Hi, Dad," Sam said with false brightness. "What a surprise."

The air grew heavy with tension as his lips curved down in a frown. "Is it?"

Sam stiffened, and Roxy, sensing her unease, moved closer to her side while a low growl rumbled deep in her chest.

Lawrence, noticing the dog's reaction, took a step back. "I heard about *that*," he said, waving a finger at the dog. His eyes shifted to Sam. "Really, Samantha. Tomorrow you'll take it back to wherever you found it."

"No, I won't."

His eyes flared at Sam's defiance. "What?"

She stood her ground. "I said no. I love that dog and I'm not giving her up. I'm keeping her whether you like it or not."

"Fine. We'll discuss the dog later," he said, striding past Anne and his daughter and into the cabin.

The two followed him, but once they were inside, Anne was struck by Lawrence Moore's presence. It was as if he filled the small cabin, sucking the air right out of the space. She dreaded what was to come.

Pulling out a chair, he sat down and, leaning back, glared at Sam. "Do you want to explain what happened last night?"

"Why? I'm sure Jackson has already told you. It's why you're here, isn't it?"

"Jackson is concerned. He told me that you're not living up to your end of our agreement. You're not following through with your medications and no one's guaranteeing that you are." Leaning forward, he raked Anne up and down with his eyes. "I'm worried we made the wrong choice in your therapist."

Anne's stomach dropped. Great—she was getting fired for sure. She opened her mouth to defend herself, but Sam's hand on her arm stopped her.

"I think I was drugged last night, Dad," she spit out.

He snorted derisively. "That's not the story I heard from Jackson."

"Jackson didn't know all the facts—"

"Which are?" he interrupted.

Sam crossed her arms over her chest. "I had a run-in with a teenager—Teddy Brighton—and I believe he slipped—"

"Wait." He held up a hand, stopping her. "Ted Brighton's son?"

Sam nodded.

"Nonsense," he answered dismissively. "I know the Brightons and they're a fine family."

"Have you met Teddy?" Sam asked, arching an eyebrow.

"No, but I know Ted, and his son wouldn't do that."

"His son is a juvenile delinquent."

"You have proof?"

Sam squirmed. "No, but I've been told—"

"Gossip," he said with a jeer. "You're judging a young man based on rumors."

When Sam sagged against the counter at her father's dismissive words, Anne felt the need to step in.

"Mr. Moore," she interjected, "it's not rumors. Sam's right—"

A look from Lawrence Moore stopped her in her tracks. Helplessly she turned toward Sam. Lawrence Moore had made up his mind before he'd reached the cabin and he intended to bully Sam until she agreed to whatever his demands were. Dropping her chin, Anne stared at the floor. Sam had come a long way during the past week, but she didn't think the girl had the strength to stand up to her father. Hell—Anne wondered if *she'd* have the guts if she were in Sam's position.

Satisfied that he'd quashed the both of them, he sat back in his chair. "Since you're not making the progress *we'd hoped*," he began, slipping in a dig at Anne, "Jackson has suggested that we try a residential facility that specializes in helping people with your type of problems."

Sam gasped, bolting away from the counter. "You want to have me locked up?"

"Really, Mr. Moore, I don't think that's neces—"

"You weren't hired to think," he broke in, focusing on Anne. "You were hired to take care of my daughter, and by not monitoring her medications, you have failed."

The blood rushed to Anne's face. Who did this guy think he was? Question her professionalism? Her hands clenched at her sides, she took a step forward and a deep breath, ready to let him know in no uncertain terms exactly what she thought of him and his heavy-handed ways. But before she could take a second step, Sam's arm blocked her.

"You seem to have forgotten I'm an adult, Dad," Sam said in a calm voice.

Anne's attention flew to her charge's face in surprise. Sam looked composed and her thin body seemed to be relaxed as she stared at her father.

"You can't force me," she continued. "Ever since I came out of the coma, I've allowed you to control my life, but the control stops now, Dad." Her eyes shifted to Anne. "I'm staying here. *Anne* and I will decide the best course to take from here on out."

Lawrence Moore jerked back in his chair. At first, shock was written on his face, but his expression shifted suddenly. He gave

Sam a conciliatory smile. "Princess, I'm only thinking of what's best for you," he said smoothly. "We can't have you suffering another blackout and hurting yourself."

"I'm not going to have another blackout." She bent and patted Roxy's head, who'd stayed glued to her side. "I'm staying here, I'm keeping my dog, and I'm working with Anne." Straightening, she cocked her head and met her father's stare. "Any questions?"

His smile vanished. "Humph," he choked out in a tight voice. "And how are you going to pay for this?"

A wry grin appeared on her face for an instant before she sobered. "You forget—you've paid me very well over the years. I can afford to stay here as long as I want."

"And you forget you gave Jackson power of attorney over your affairs after you came out of the coma."

"Yeah, I can change that," she blurted.

Mr. Moore swiftly rose to his feet. "If you expect to resume the life you had before your accident, you'd better listen to me," he threatened.

"Or what? You'll fire me?" She shook her head as she turned toward the door. Crossing to it, she opened it and motioned for her father to leave. "I have a degree. I can find another job."

"Making a pittance compared to the salary I've given you," he shouted, striding over to her.

Squaring her shoulders, she stared up at him. "I can sell my artwork."

Placing a hand on her arm, he leaned toward her. "Samantha, don't be difficult," he said softly. "I'm your father and I love you."

"I think I'd be happier if you loved me a little less," she said, dropping her gaze to the floor.

His hand rubbed her arm. "I can't let you throw everything you've worked for away. I want nothing more than to have you back at my side at the agency, where you belong, but right now you're not thinking straight and you have to listen to me."

Sam's head lifted. "I *am* thinking straight. Go back to the Cities, Dad."

His hand dropped. "Samantha," he said sternly, "I know what's best for you."

Swinging the screen door open, Sam glared at him. "That's what everybody has been saying. No more." She tapped a finger on her chest. "From now on *I'm* the one calling the shots."

He drew back as if she'd struck him. Taking his sunglasses from his pocket, he shoved them on his face. "Samantha, you are clearly not in a state to have a rational, *adult* conversation. This discussion isn't over," he said as he stomped out the door.

Anne was speechless. She shook her head in amazement. She never thought Sam would take on Lawrence Moore like that. "Wow," she began before noticing that Sam's legs had started to tremble. Rushing over, she grabbed the girl's arm and guided her to the nearest chair. Sinking down, Sam looked up at her, her eyes wide.

"Oh my God," she said breathlessly as she covered her face with her hands, "I just kicked my father out of my house."

"Yeah," Anne replied, still stunned. "And how does it feel?"

Sam's hands fell away and her lips curled in a smile. "Good." Her smile dropped. "But I think I just lost my job."

"Do you care?"

"At the moment, no." Rising, Sam walked down the hallway and opened the closet door. Taking out her paintings, she propped them against the wall and studied them for a moment without speaking. Finally, she glanced over her shoulder at Anne. "Is there an art store in Pardo?"

* * *

The examination was over and together they sat waiting for the doctor's verdict. Sam had cooperated, patiently answering his questions. She'd been uncomfortable talking about her attack, but Dr. Douglas had gently prodded her into giving a description of that horrific day. It was the first time Anne had heard the story in such detail and from Sam's perspective. No wonder the poor girl had problems, she thought, feeling a stab of guilt over the times she'd minimized Sam's fears. To have your life stripped away like that. To have any sense of safety ripped away. Anne felt she now had a better understanding of why Sam had been so paranoid, so reluctant to leave the cabin, and vowed to be more patient with her in the future.

"Do you think I was drugged?" Sam asked, her voice rising with hope.

"Hmm," Dr. Douglas said, scanning his notes. "How long have you been off the sertraline?"

"The one to help with depression and anxiety?"

"Yes."

Sam gave Anne a sheepish look. "I can't remember the exact date, but it's been at least a week."

"And you'd been on it for several weeks, prior to staying at the lake?"

"Yes."

Tapping his pen on the clipboard, he looked over at Sam, sitting on the examination table. "Your fiancé is correct—one really should taper off this kind of medication. What about the diazepam? How—"

Sam broke in. "The sleeping medication?"

Dr. Douglas nodded.

Her lip curled. "I didn't like the way that made me feel, so I only took it a few times."

"And you were also taking the sertraline?"

"Yes."

"Other than the blackout, how have you felt?"

"Good," Sam replied quickly. "I've felt stronger and had more energy."

"No dark thoughts?"

"You mean of suicide?"

"Yes."

"No."

"Hallucinations?"

Sam paused. Was she remembering the late-night visitor on the dock? Anne wondered. She was so sketchy about when she'd gone off both of her medications that Anne couldn't tell if the visit coincided with her failure to take them. She thought about the cigarette butts Fritz had found by the dock, but they could've been left there by anyone. With a mental shrug, Anne let it go. She had faith in Dr. Douglas. He'd come up with the right diagnosis.

He stood and placed the chart on the counter. "If you're feeling better, I don't recommend resuming the medications. If you start feeling anxious again, or have trouble sleeping, we'll take another look." Crossing to the door, he turned. "Anne, why don't you step out in the hall with me while Samantha gets dressed? Samantha, if you have any more questions, give me a call."

Stepping out into the hall, Anne shut the door behind her and looked at Dr. Douglas expectantly. "You think she was drugged, don't you?"

"It's possible," he answered, rubbing his chin, "but it's too late now to test for flunitrazepam. The medication Dr. Van Horn prescribed?" He hesitated. "Since I haven't seen Sam's entire case history, I don't like to question another doctor's choice of treatment." He shook his head. "But I usually don't prescribe a combination of those two particular medications."

"Are they out of her system now?"

"Again, hard to say. Every patient is different. Keep an eye on her and call me if she has any problems."

Anne watched Dr. Douglas enter the next examination room. Leaning against the wall, she took a deep breath. Who would've thought this job would come with so much drama? She'd never found herself being so drawn into a patient's life. In the past, she'd done her job then gone home. Not this time. With every passing day, she was becoming more embroiled in Sam's struggles, and not only the one Sam was fighting to regain her physical strength. Thanks to the last two days, she was now aligned with Sam in her battle to overcome her family's control. Pushing off from the wall, she moved to the door, but paused before opening it to say a little prayer that this was a fight she and Sam would win.

They were almost to the car when a voice called out Anne's name. Turning, she saw Edward Dunlap hurrying toward them. She stopped and waited for him.

"Edward," she said, surprised, "are you here to see Dr. Osgood?"

As he rubbed his arm, his gaze slid toward Sam then quickly away. "Just did."

"And?" Anne asked with a hopeful note in her voice.

"He wasn't encouraging," he answered with a shake of his head, and Anne felt her hope plummet.

"I'm sorry," she replied, placing a hand on his arm. "Did he have any recommendations?"

"Not really. He suggested that I try a pain management program." He shuffled his feet. "But I'd have to drive down to the Cities."

"Okay, then drive down to the Cities."

"I can't. Too much to do here."

Exasperated, Anne dropped her hand. "Edward, I've told you before—you need to take care of yourself. Your mother can get along without you for a few hours."

He gave a bitter laugh. "I'm sure you're right. Most of the time I think I'm more of a hindrance than a help, but it's no use, Anne."

"That's not true!" she exclaimed.

He ignored her statement and turned toward Sam. His shuffling stopped as he studied her face. "You remind me of someone." His voice dropped to almost a whisper. "Why did you sing that song at the party?"

Sam shifted uncomfortably and her eyes sought Anne's.

How could Sam answer Edward's question when she didn't remember her performance? Anne tried to think of a way to cover for her, but came up empty.

"Ah, I don't know," Sam said awkwardly.

Edward looked past Sam while his hand stroked the arm hanging uselessly at his side. His face took on a faraway expression. "It was her favorite song."

Anne's eyes narrowed. Whose favorite song?

"Edward," she said softly, trying to draw him back to the present. "Who are you talking about?"

His expression didn't change. "Blanche." He bit out the name.

"Blanche Jones?"

"She loved 'Make Me Your Baby.'" His attention returned to Sam, and he took a step toward her. "She sang it at parties, too."

His words had a strange effect on Sam. Her face paled and she backed away.

Anne's eyes darted from Sam to Edward as she tried to figure out what was going on. It was as if they were both thinking about something of which she knew nothing, but how could that be? They'd never laid eyes on each other until Fritz's party.

Edward continued to stare at Sam. "You're back to cause trouble, aren't you?" Suddenly his shoulders slumped and he pivoted on his heel. With his head down, he shambled across the parking lot.

Anne made a move to go after him, to ask why he seemed so beaten. Dr. Osgood hadn't given him the answer she'd hoped for, but she knew the key to helping him was out there. She simply had to find it. She stopped, glancing over her shoulder at Sam then back at Edward, who was now on the far side of the lot. Her attention returned to Sam. She looked shaken, and it was pointless to chase after Edward. He had his pride and he wouldn't appreciate her pushing him toward another type of treatment. She'd go to Dunlap's tomorrow, and if she could get him away from Esther, she'd convince him not to give up. And even though the subject of Blanche was taboo, she'd like to understand why he had suddenly mentioned her.

Anne turned back to Sam. "What was that about?"

"I—I—don't know," Sam answered, hurrying to the car. She yanked the door open and slid inside. Anne followed and, once in the driver's seat, shifted toward Sam.

Eyes closed, Sam sat with her head resting against the back of the seat.

"Did you recognize the song I sang?" she asked without opening her eyes.

"Not really—it was an old one, I think."

Sam lifted her head and sat forward, looking out the windshield. "One thing I do remember from that night is the dream I had." She hesitated and gave a small shudder. "I was at a party—at Fritz's—but things were different."

"In what way?"

Sam shook her head. "Everyone was dressed differently—like they were all back in the eighties or something. And Fritz was there, but he looked a lot younger." Rubbing her forehead, she shut her eyes again as if she were trying to remember. "A woman was flirting with some man I didn't recognize and then she began to sing."

Anne wondered if she had told Sam that this was exactly how she had acted at Fritz's. No, she'd wait and hear the rest of her story.

Sam's eyes popped open and she leaned back. "The dream shifted and I was in the woods, by the lake. A woman was crying on a dock, but in the dark I couldn't see who it was." She let out a long breath. "That's it." She fell silent.

Tapping on the steering wheel, Anne tried to think of an explanation. Unable to think of one, she turned on the ignition and backed out of the parking space.

"Don't you think it's odd?" Sam asked.

Anne shrugged, pulling out onto the street. "Most dreams are odd. And after everything that you've been through . . ." She let her voice trail away.

"But it's as if I dreamed of something that happened in the past. And haven't you noticed how Blanche Jones keeps popping up? Fritz mentioned her—Edward mentioned her."

"Look, the cabin's been empty for a couple of seasons," Anne said with a glance Sam's way. "Now you're living there and it's stirred up some memories."

"But even Jackson mentioned her."

Anne cocked her head. "Dr. Van Horn knew Blanche?"

"I don't think he really knew her. From what he said, the summer he stayed here she simply fueled a few of his teenage fantasies."

"Is that why he rented her old cabin?"

"I don't think so," Sam replied.

"I wouldn't worry about it." Anne gave Sam a confident look. "Forget about the dream. If what you suspect is true and you were drugged—chalk it up to that. Concentrate on getting stronger."

Sam pulled on her bottom lip. "I suppose you're right. It could be that the talk about Blanche filtered into my subconscious and it came out in the dream."

Anne breathed a sigh of relief. Sam had enough problems without becoming obsessed with a woman who was long gone from the lake. The next time she ran into Fritz, she'd drop a couple of hints about not regaling Sam with any more stories about the "good old days" and specifically any dealing with Blanche Jones.

# Twenty-one

Sam's fingers tapped a rapid beat on the car seat as Anne drove back to the lake. Bags of art supplies, which she hadn't purchased in years, filled the trunk. The small store hadn't had a great selection, but she'd bought more than enough to get started. If she found that she needed more, she'd call down to the Cities and have additional supplies shipped to the cabin. It had been exciting wandering around the store and making her selections. The lingering aroma of turpentine and oil paints had carried her back to happier times and college days spent lost in her work. The world had seemed full of possibilities back then. In those days, she'd dreamed of exhibitions, not meeting ad campaign deadlines. She'd envisioned having her own studio, one she had designed. As she thought about it, her fingers stilled and curled into a fist. But those dreams had died in the face of reality and the need to earn a living. Was it too late to see them reborn? It had been so long since she'd created anything. What if she'd forgotten every technique she'd learned in college? What if—

Anne's voice broke into her thoughts. "What's wrong?" she asked with a quick glance toward Sam. "You looked worried. Aren't you pleased with your purchases?"

Sam's fingers resumed their tapping. "It's not that." She looked down at her restless hand and swiftly tucked it under her leg. "I just haven't painted in years." Turning her head, she stared at the tall pines whizzing past the car window before returning her attention to Anne. "What if I've lost it?" she finally asked in a small voice.

"Lost it?"

"Yeah." Sam shook her head, trying to put her thoughts into words. "When I was a kid, all my mother had to do to keep me occupied was hand me a box of crayons and a piece of paper. I'd spend hours drawing whatever struck my fancy, and I grew up taking that ability to create for granted."

"And now you're worried that it might have disappeared? I'm no art expert, but Fritz was really impressed by your work."

Sam brushed away Anne's words. "I did those two paintings straight out of college and haven't worked on anything since."

Anne frowned. "It seems to me that talent isn't something that goes away from lack of use. You may be a bit rusty at first, but I would think either you have it or you don't."

"There's a little more to it than that," Sam answered in a wry voice. "It takes practice to learn how to use light against dark, to create emphasis, to—" She broke off with a frustrated shake of her head. "There are a million tricks that an artist uses to get his point across."

"Okay," Anne answered reasonably, "so maybe you won't be happy with your first piece, but in time, I'm sure you'll remember those tricks."

"What if I can't?"

"What do you mean?"

"What if I can't remember? Thanks to that crack on my skull, what if that part of my brain's been damaged?" Sam's voice rose in desperation. "What if I've been robbed of more than just the strength in my leg?"

Pulling into the yard at the cabin, Anne stopped and shut off the engine. "There's one way to find out," she said, reaching into the backseat and grabbing one of the bags. She plopped it on Sam's lap. "Here. Let's get everything inside, and while I'm putting it away, you can sit on the couch and sketch."

Keeping her hands clenched at her side, Sam fastened her eyes on the sack lying in her lap. A sketch pad. It might have been fun buying all this stuff, but the reality of using it terrified her. Unless she made the concessions he wanted, her father wouldn't let her eventually come back to the agency. And things were dicey with Jackson. All she had left was her artwork that she'd abandoned years ago, she thought, staring at the sketch pad in her lap.

Anne's sudden nudge startled her. "Oh, stop—that sack isn't a snake, and quit being a wuss."

Sam's eyes widened. "I beg your pardon," she exclaimed. "I'm *not* a wuss."

"Then tackle your fear head-on." Anne opened the car door and stepped out. "Get in there and get going."

A few minutes later, Sam sat curled up on the couch with Roxy next to her while Anne stood in the middle of the room with her hands on her hips.

"Where do you want the easel?" she asked.

Sam's eyes scanned the room, noticing the play of light throughout the cabin. "I think over there," she said, pointing, "close to the French doors."

"Alrighty, then," Anne replied, rubbing her hands together.

While Anne went to work setting up the easel, Sam opened the sketch pad and, picking up a piece of charcoal, gazed at the pure white paper. Her hand, poised above the sketch pad, trembled. Where to begin? *Let your mind go*, she told herself. Taking a deep breath, she made a swift line then softened it with the pad of her thumb. After glancing up at Anne, who was now studiously reading the easel's assembly instructions, she made a second line, followed by another, then another. Her shoulders relaxed and the world fell away as an image began to appear on the paper. She paused and rubbed her nose. *No, too harsh—more shadow.* Sam smeared the outline. Another swoop of the charcoal, and the image gained definition. A smile tugged at her lips. *Not bad—the focal point is good, but the balance is a little off.* She concentrated on adding more emphasis on the left. She was adding detail when a shadow fell across the sketch pad. Tearing her eyes away from the pad, she looked up to see Anne towering over her.

"Here, have some iced tea," she said, extending a glass. "You look like you could use it."

Like a diver emerging from the ocean, Sam needed a moment to get her bearings. With glassy eyes, she scanned the living room. An easel sat in the corner with brushes laid out neatly on the tray. Other art supplies were arranged within easy reach on the shelves next to it. She noticed the shadows creeping across the floor. What time was it? Her eyes flared as she noticed the clock. She'd been at it for over an hour. Dropping the charcoal and flipping the sketch pad shut, she flexed her fingers before accepting the glass from Anne.

"Thanks," she said, and drained the tea in one long gulp. Uncurling her legs, she groaned softly as blood rushed to cramped muscles.

Anne shook her head. "You can't stay in one position for so long. You need to stretch every so often."

Placing the glass on the coffee table, Sam slowly rose to her feet and arched her back. "You're right," she replied, but Anne wasn't listening. Her attention was focused on the sketch pad lying on the couch.

With a chuckle, Sam lifted it. "Do you want to take a look?"

"May I?"

Sam tugged on her bottom lip and hesitated. She wasn't completely happy with the piece, but for a first attempt after such a long spell, she supposed it was okay. Flipping the pad open, she handed it to Anne and waited nervously for her reaction.

"It's me," Anne said in a hushed voice.

Sam let go of the breath she didn't know she was holding. "I'm glad you think so," she said lightly.

Anne took her eyes off the drawing and looked at Sam in surprise. "Are you kidding? This is terrific."

"Here," Sam said, taking the sketch pad away from Anne and picking up a pencil. With a flourish, she signed the drawing and, removing it from the pad, handed it to Anne.

"Seriously? I can keep it?"

"Sure," she said, flushing with pleasure. "It's the least I can do. You've paid me the highest compliment an artist can receive. You're happy with—"

Roxy's loud bark as she shot off the couch interrupted her. Running to the door, the dog stood on her hind legs and peered out the window. Her fur stood in a ridge along her spine while a soft growl rumbled deep in her chest.

"Looks like someone's here," Anne said as she placed her portrait on the easel. Crossing the room, she grabbed the dog's collar and used her knee to ease Roxy away from the door. "It's Dr. Van Horn," she said with a glance over her shoulder at Sam.

"He wasn't supposed to come until Friday." Sam sank to the couch. "Dad called him." She buried her head in her hands. "Great—now I'll have to listen to his lecture, too."

Not letting go of the dog's collar, Anne reached over to the counter and picked up Roxy's leash. "Why don't I take her for a walk and give you some privacy," she said, snapping on the leash.

Sam lifted her head. "Coward," she said in a wry voice.

"You'll be okay. If you can handle your dad, you can handle Dr. Van Horn."

Anne swung the door open and Sam heard her greet Jackson over Roxy's barking as she stepped out onto the porch. With a sigh, she settled back on the couch and waited for the inevitable.

Without speaking, Jackson strode into the cabin and walked over to the couch. Sitting next to her, he gathered her in his arms in a tight hug.

"Samantha, I'm so sorry," he murmured into her ear.

Stunned, Sam pushed away from his hug. "For what?"

"Lawrence talked to me. I've been wrong about so many things and I can only hope you'll forgive me."

"What things?"

He pulled his fingers through his hair. "Where do I begin? I misjudged what happened at Fritz's party . . . I allowed your father to convince me that you should be in residential treatment . . . I've ignored all your concerns and treated you like a child instead of the woman I love." He gave her a wry grin. "How's that for starters?"

"Pretty good," Sam replied, and held up her hand, "but let's back up. You said that the residential facility was *Dad's* idea?"

Jackson drew back. "Yes. Why?"

"He claimed it was your idea."

"He must have misunderstood. He did ask me about such places and I told him what I knew, but he was the one who brought it up and suggested that a facility might be the best place for you."

Sam's eyes narrowed as she studied him. His expression was

guileless. He could be telling the truth. It wouldn't be the first time in her experience that she'd seen her father twist the facts to suit his needs.

Picking up her hand, Jackson planted a soft kiss on her knuckles. "You believe me, don't you?" His voice rose on a hopeful note. "Please say you forgive me."

"Jackson, I—"

He lightly touched her lips with his finger, silencing her. "No, there's something else I need to explain . . . I thought about it driving up here." He dropped his hand and leaned back, giving her space. "In my desire to keep peace between you and your father, I haven't been as supportive of you as I should have been. I can see now how it must've appeared that I was always siding with your father."

"Well, I know Dad—"

"It was a mistake," he interrupted. "And all I can say in my defense is that I let my own family's dynamics overrule what should've been my main priority—*you* and the life we can build together."

She felt her heart soften as she thought about the stories Jackson had told her about his childhood—stories about how his parents had used him as a weapon to hurt each other. About how they'd treated him more like a prize to win in their battle with each other than a child to love in his own right. About the demands that they had placed on him.

When Sam said nothing, Jackson tentatively scooted closer. Just like Roxy did when she knew she'd been naughty. She relaxed against the couch as memories of what her life with Jackson had been like before her attack came flooding back. They'd been *so* good together. Shared interests, shared passions—he had been not only her lover, but her best friend. Since the attack, though, the dynamics of their relationship had shifted. Instead of partners, they'd been playing out the roles of caretaker and patient. Somewhere along the line, mistrust had crept in. She glanced over at him. So handsome . . . so sincere. She felt the love she'd been unable to show for so long flicker back to life. Could they go back to the beginning? Without her father's constant interference, she felt that maybe they could.

"Jackson," she began, leaning toward him.

"Sam!" he suddenly exclaimed, and stood. Walking over to the easel, he picked up her charcoal drawing of Anne. "This is wonderful." He held it at arm's length as his eyes roamed over the portrait. "You've captured Anne's strength, her determination, yet at the same time shown the vulnerability she tries to hide." Shaking his head, he propped the portrait back on the easel and returned to the couch. "I've always thought it was wrong for you to give up your art."

"Really? You did?"

He nodded. "It's a shame for a talent like yours to go to waste. I'd love to see your work shown at a gallery someday." He dipped his head shyly. "It's always been a secret dream of mine for you, but I knew how your father felt, and didn't want to interfere."

Moved by his confession, Sam threw her arms around his neck. She felt the old passion for him begin to spark. It had been so long. Staring into his eyes, she lifted her mouth to his and pressed it firmly against his lips. He gave a start of surprise, but then relaxed into her, deepening the kiss. Sam's belly clenched and her grip on his neck tightened. Leaning back, she pulled him down on top of her while his hand stole up her side. A long sigh escaped.

Abruptly, footsteps on the porch made him jerk away, ending the kiss and the embrace. Sam sat up quickly just in time to see

Anne and Roxy stride through the door. She felt her face flush in embarrassment, but smiled when Jackson gave her a conspiratorial wink.

"Later," he mouthed.

Later never came. Thanks to an incident involving Roxy and one of Jackson's Gucci loafers. He'd been furious to find it lying on the bed with teeth marks marring the expensive leather. He'd yelled at Roxy, at Sam, and had insisted he'd had it with the dog. He'd frightened the dog and she cowered at Sam's side during his entire tirade. When Sam had refused to accede to his wishes, he'd stormed into the guest room, slamming the door behind him.

How could he be so unyielding and arbitrary? Sam fumed to herself as she paced her bedroom. Roxy was just being a dog—he shouldn't have left his shoes out where she could get to them. Sure, they couldn't have her going around eating shoes, but hadn't Greg said it takes time to train a dog properly? She walked over to the window and pulled the curtains back. If he really loved her, he'd understand how much Roxy meant to her. How Roxy gave her back the feeling of security that she'd lost that day in the parking garage. She'd tried to explain it, but he wouldn't listen. Dropping the curtains, she crossed to the bed and sat next to Roxy, who'd been watching Sam pace with a bewildered look in her eyes.

"It's okay," she said, burying her face in the dog's fur. "I won't let him send you away."

Roxy's tail thumped the bed in response.

With a smile, Sam stood and patted the dog's head. "Let's go to bed. We'll sort it all out in the morning."

* * *

Hours later, a crash of thunder had Sam bolting upright. Instinctively, she reached for the dog, but Roxy wasn't on the bed. Leaning sideways, she fumbled with the bedside lamp. Once it was on, the room filled with a soft glow and Sam noticed the door to her room. It was open and a stiff breeze was blowing through it, whipping the curtains.

"What the hell," she muttered, struggling out of bed. Throwing on her robe, she stumbled out of the room and down the hall. As she did, she heard a thumping sound above the storm raging outside the cabin. Rounding the corner, she gasped. The kitchen door stood wide open, and the thumping was caused by the screen door hitting the side of the cabin. Her easel lay on its side and papers were scattered across the floor. Tightening her robe around her, she crossed the room and shut both doors against the pouring rain.

"Roxy? Roxy!" she called, her voice rising with apprehension.

She went back to her bedroom. Maybe the storm had driven the dog under the bed in fear. Using the side of the bed for balance, she knelt and peered underneath. No dog. Shoving herself to her feet, she went back to the living room.

"Roxy," she shrieked.

Jackson, his hair tousled, suddenly appeared behind her. "What's going on?"

Sam whirled on him. "The door wasn't locked and the storm blew it open. Now Roxy's gone," she cried, emotion choking her. "We have to go look for her."

Jackson walked past her and threw the lock. "Don't be silly. Just because your dog's stupid enough to go out in a storm doesn't mean we are."

Sam stamped her foot in anger. "You won't help me find her?"

Jackson's hands fisted on his hips and he shook his head. "We'll find her in the morning."

"That might be too late," she exclaimed.

He shrugged. "Samantha, sometimes things work out for the best. If we find her, we find her. If not . . ." His voice trailed away as he held his hands wide in a helpless gesture.

Turning away, Sam marched down the hallway. "That is *not* good enough," she called over her shoulder.

He followed. "I'm not going to let you go out in this storm."

Pulling on a pair of sweatpants, Sam hiked up her nightgown around her waist and used the elastic waistband of the pants to hold it in place. She grabbed a sweatshirt and shoved her arms into the sleeves. Sliding her feet into her tennis shoes, she picked up the flashlight from the dresser and shoved passed Jackson, down the hallway toward the kitchen door.

He beat her to it. Standing with his back against the door, he crossed his arms and stared down at her. "I'm not letting you out in the storm."

"You're not going to stop me, Jackson," Sam replied in a low voice.

"Samantha, darling . . . be reasonable." He spread his hands wide and took a step forward. "I can't in good conscience allow you out in weather like this. What if something happens? What if you have a panic attack? Alone . . . in the dark . . . with the storm raging." He shook his head. "We'll look for the dog tomorrow."

Her resolution wavered as she remembered the terror she'd felt during those attacks—the feeling of eyes watching her, the way her heart raced, her desire to crawl into a hole and hide. She took a step back as the picture, painted by Jackson's words, formed. She'd be surrounded by darkness with only the feeble illumination of her Maglite to guide her. She wouldn't know what lurked beyond that light.

*They could hurt you again*, a voice inside her began to whisper.

Suddenly the image of Roxy, looking up at her with trust in her eyes, drove away Jackson's words and the whisper died. Roxy had known fear, too, and she had counted on Sam to protect her.

Her grip on the Maglite tightened. "Get out of my way, Jackson."

"I can't believe you're acting this way," he said, his nostrils flaring in anger. "I'm trying to take care of you and all you care about is that mangy dog."

"Roxy needs me."

"I need you, too," he argued. "With you, I can have the kind of family that I've always wanted." The anger on his face turned to reproach. "My childhood—"

No, she wasn't going to let tales of his parents distract her.

"We can talk about that later," she interrupted. "If you want to protect me, then fine, come with me and help find Roxy."

He shook his head slowly. "No. That dog's been nothing but a pain in the ass. We're better off without her."

Taking a step back, Sam looked him up and down while a nasty suspicion began to form in her mind. In her panic to find Roxy, she'd forgotten her last act before retiring to her bedroom.

"I locked that door before I went to bed. Care to explain how it came to be *unlocked*?"

He flushed and turned away from her. Crossing to the kitchen cabinet, he opened a bottle of Scotch and, grabbing a glass, poured a drink. "Samantha . . . really. You sound just like my moth—"

"I want an explanation, Jackson," she demanded.

He drained his glass, then faced her. "Maybe you just think you locked it? You know your memory plays tricks on you."

"It's not going to work this time, Jackson. You're not going to manipulate me by bringing up your rotten childhood and you're not going to convince me that I *didn't* lock the door." She stopped and felt sadness squeeze her heart as the spark she'd felt earlier that day died once and for all.

Not able to stand the sight of him, she looked down at the floor. "You unlocked the door and tried to get rid of my dog," she said in a weary voice.

"I did not," he said indignantly. "If I'd wanted to get rid—"

She held up a hand to stop him. "I'm done." Pulling the ring off her left hand, she raised her eyes and shoved it at him. "When I come back, I want you gone."

He said nothing and just stared at the ring in her outstretched hand.

With a frown Sam tossed it on the counter and dodged around him. She threw back the lock and, opening the door, stepped out into the storm.

# Twenty-two

I stand at the window and watch the rain sheeting down the glass. Jumping at every clap of thunder, I hug myself and turn away, but the violence occurring outside calls to me. I cover my ears, but it only muffles the sound of the storm. I would like to run, to crawl under the bed as I did as a child. But I'm not a child—I'm a man. My hands drop and my lips twist in a bitter smile.

Take it like a man—isn't that what I've always been told? Childish tears *will not* be tolerated. And if I fail? If I can't control my emotions—punishment will follow. Isolation. Darkness. The cold and damp pressing down on me as I curl into a small ball and pray for rescue.

But there is no rescue. No one hears my pitiful cries for help.

My back is to the window, my gaze traveling around the room. Such a fine, upstanding family everyone says, but they don't know the secrets behind the facade. The violence hidden under the surface—more frightening than any storm nature could manufacture.

I was only six when it happened the first time. Shaking my head, I can't even remember what caused the incident. A broken toy? A temper tantrum over not being allowed another cookie? "*Stop it, stop it,*" he screamed into my tearstained face. "*Real men don't cry,*" he admonished.

And her? She stood by and watched him grab my thin arm and march me out the door. He pulled me toward the black, gaping gash in the side of the hill. In my innocence, I had no idea what was to follow. I'd witnessed his anger focused on her, but he had never directed it at me. I had no thought that the man who was supposed to protect me would throw me in that dark hole then leave me. How long had I lain there? Minutes? Hours? Whimpering in terror until finally he brought me out into the light, my soul forever marked.

With trembling hands, I pour a drink. I don't even care that it's the cheap stuff. Downing it in one gulp, I slam the glass on the counter and, bowing my head, try to banish my dark thoughts.

My attention steals to the window. It had been a night like this, hadn't it? My last visit to my own personal hell. All I'd asked for was understanding and a little kindness. Wasn't that my right? Didn't I deserve it? My hands tighten into fists. Didn't she *owe* me?

But she'd mocked me, questioned my manhood, used the same words he'd used. As I look back, it all seems like a bad dream now. Stumbling up the hill on the rain-slick slope.

I stagger over to the window and press my palm against the cool glass. As I stare across the dark water, the tears begin to gather. It's so unfair—this dream that haunts me. Is there no escape? I wipe my eyes. Samantha was to be my ticket to freedom. I would have used her and her father to achieve the life I deserve. Lawrence Moore's patronage and all that money would've made the difference. Old scars and wounds would've been forgotten and forgiven.

But now? I feel it slipping away.

"No!" I cry above the thunder. Squaring my shoulders, I slap my hand against the window. I'm a man. A man meets his challenges head-on. A man strikes at the heart of his enemies and takes that which they value most. Divide and conquer.

I smile. No. I haven't lost yet.

I stare out the window and plan—my mind spinning ways that I can salvage the situation while in the distance a light bobs through the storm.

# Twenty-three

Tears streamed down Sam's face, indistinguishable from the raindrops pouring all around her. Above her, bolts of lightning crisscrossed the sky, while thunder pounded. In the distance, over the thunder, she heard the wind whipping the waves against the rocks lining the shore. What kind of man would send a defenseless animal out in a storm like this? She swiped a wet sleeve against her dripping nose. Not one she'd want to spend the rest of her life with, that's for sure. A lie—it had all been a lie. The person she thought she knew so well had been false, nothing more than a front.

*Don't think about it now*, she chided herself. *Find Roxy.*

Her flashlight beam bounced through the trees as she desperately called out the dog's name. Would Roxy hear her over the thunder? She prayed she would. The thought of losing her tightened Sam's throat and caused fresh tears to run down her cheeks. Thankfully, in her frantic search, she forgot to be afraid.

She'd passed Greg's place and made it to the end of the road before she stopped. Ahead of her nothing but the churning water of the lake. Her shoulders drooped and her hand holding the flashlight sagged. It was no use. Roxy was nowhere to be found. Her only hope was that the dog could find her way home on her own. Discouraged, Sam turned and began to slog her way through the mud, back to the cabin. She'd never forgive Jackson for this, she thought, anger stiffening her spine. He'd better be gone when she arrived.

She was halfway there, when a hand on her shoulders spun her around as the smell of liquor hit her. *Jackson*. She raised her flashlight in defense and the hand dropped away. Shining the light upward, she was astonished to see Greg standing in front of her.

"Hey," he said, raising his hands to shield his eyes. "You don't need to blind me."

"Sorry." Sam lowered the light. "What are you doing out here?"

"I might ask the same of you, but I already know." Taking her arm, he started to lead her back toward his cabin. "I saw your flashlight from my window and figured you were out looking for your dog." He paused. "She's at my house."

Sam halted, the soles of her tennis shoes skidding in the mud. "Roxy? You found Roxy?"

Greg chuckled. "More like she found me. I was enjoying a hot toddy when I heard her over the storm, scratching at the front door." His voice lost its humor. "What happened? You didn't put her out in this, did you?"

"Of course not," Sam replied, not keeping the anger out of her voice. "Jackson did."

"Ah." He paused. "You know, Sam, since Jackson feels so strongly about her, maybe it would be better if I kept her."

"No!" Sam cried, pushing the wet hair back from her face. "You can't take her back. I won't let you."

Greg held up a hand. "Easy now. It's only a suggestion. I simply think that with Jackson—"

She spun toward him, cutting him off. "Jackson is gone."

"For now, but what about when you move—" He stopped when Sam wiggled her left hand in front of his nose.

"I mean gone as in *permanently*," she insisted.

"You broke up with him over Roxy?"

Sam shook her head. "What he did was mean and dirty, but there's more to it than that." She hesitated, thinking back over the relationship. "Jackson changed after I was attacked, or maybe it was that I changed. I don't know, but I wasn't the same person he'd asked to marry him." She looked down at her weak leg. "I'm not a trophy he can parade on his arm any longer."

"A trophy? You're more than just a beautiful woman."

*A beautiful woman*—she hadn't been called that since her attack, and her cheeks grew warm with pleasure. But before she could thank Greg for the compliment, a crack of lightning flashed overhead.

Taking her arm, Greg started toward his cabin. "Come on, let's get out of the rain."

She allowed him to guide her up the steps, and they both stopped on the porch, watching the storm roll around them. Sam let the silence lengthen.

Finally she glanced over at him and smiled. "I've learned something over the past few days—I don't want to be a princess and I don't want to be a trophy."

Greg stepped forward and braced his hands on the porch railing. "Life has a way of changing on us, doesn't it?" he asked, and Sam heard the sadness in his voice.

"It changed on you, didn't it? Anne told me you were once a veterinarian."

"*That*," he said, the single word speaking volumes.

"What happened?"

He jerked his shoulders. "An old story—young man falls for a gorgeous woman, only to find said woman is more interested in the money than the man. She took me for everything I had." He laughed caustically. "Last I heard—she and her boyfriend were living quite well."

"Why haven't you opened a practice up here?"

He turned and leaned against the rail, the rain running off the porch roof and forming a curtain behind him. "I discovered it's more rewarding to give animals a second chance at a home than to treat some rich woman's pampered pet." His eyes strayed beyond her to his small cabin. "I also learned I really don't need much—a warm place to live; food on the table; my saxophone; and my dogs." He clicked his tongue. "Life's good."

"You didn't mention a woman on that list."

His eyebrows shot up. "Are you kidding me?" he exclaimed. "Once bitten, twice shy."

"So you've given up?"

"Some might see it that way," he answered wryly, "but *I* prefer to think of it as simply using good judgment."

Sam shook her head. "Every woman isn't like your wife."

"Ex-wife," he interjected quickly.

"Okay, ex-wife, but—"

Greg's chuckle stopped her. "You sound like Anne." His face grew serious. "Maybe you're both right, but after the wringer I went through, I find it hard to trust those of the female persuasion." His smile returned as he glanced back toward the cabin. "Except Molly, of course." He left his post by the railing and crossed the porch until he stood directly in front of Sam. Looking down, his eyes questioned her. "After what's happened with your fiancé, don't you feel a little betrayed? Are *you* going to rush into a new relationship?"

Sam's heartbeat picked up and she stepped back. "Well, ah, yes . . . a bit, and no, I don't want a new relationship *tomorrow*." She glanced out at the storm. "Someday I'll find someone, but first I have to figure out who Samantha Moore is."

"Not a trophy or a princess?" Greg asked, his eyes twinkling.

She chuckled in response. "Right." With a nudge to Greg's arm, she turned and headed for the door. "Now give me back my dog."

The next morning, Sam slowly turned on her back and gave a long stretch. What was that corny old saying? "Today is the first day of the rest of your life"? Sitting, she pulled her knees up to her chest and grinned. Corny or not, it described how she felt at the moment. Sure, she thought, resting her chin on her knees, there was a little bit of sadness involved whenever she thought about Jackson, and she knew there'd be more battles with her father. He wasn't one to give up easily, especially when he believed he was right. Which was most of the time, she thought, snorting inwardly. But for now, she couldn't help feeling like she'd been let out of jail. And it made her almost giddy.

Scooting to the edge of the bed, she swung her feet onto the floor and leaned back. Propped on her elbows, she lifted her right leg and held it. Now for the left leg. Her brow knitted in a frown as she began to raise her left leg. She crossed her fingers. Slowly her left leg rose until it was the same height as her right. Scrunching her eyelids shut, she waited for the spasm to hit. When it didn't, her eyes shot open and she started counting.

*One . . . two . . . three . . . four . . . five.* Sweat gathered on her upper lip and her belly tightened, but she felt no pain. *Six . . .*

*seven . . . eight . . . nine.* Her leg began to quiver. *Come on—just one more. Ten!* Falling back against the mattress, she rested half in, half out of the bed.

"Yes," she cried, pumping her fist in the air. Sitting up quickly, she lifted her nightgown high enough to see the muscle in her left thigh. Maybe it was her imagination, but she could swear that it looked thicker, more toned. She threw her arms around Roxy's neck.

"Greg's right—life is good," she said to the bewildered dog.

Quickly Sam rose and crossed to the window. The lake below sparkled in the morning sun and the world looked fresh after last night's storm. A wild idea flitted through her brain. With a nod, she grabbed her jeans, a T-shirt, and a pair of sturdy shoes. Hurrying into the bathroom, she dressed, then quickly brushed her teeth and splashed water on her face. After running a comb through her hair, she was ready. She wrote a hurried note to Anne giving her the morning off, and she and Roxy took off for a leisurely stroll.

As she carefully took the steps, she spied a flash of red out of the corner of her eye. She stopped. Son of a gun—the dying bush at the corner of the porch had come to life. The buckets of rain must have revived it. Not only were the leaves now a dark green, but the stalks were covered with heavy clusters of bright red flowers, hanging downward like grapes. She moved toward it, but Roxy gave a tug on her leash and pulled her back.

Stepping onto the gravel in front of the cabin, Sam felt a beat of panic. Setting off alone was a little bit crazy. What if she lost her balance and fell? Her leg was stronger, but would it be enough to get her back on her feet after a fall? Or would she lie there like a turtle flipped over on its back?

*Stop it*, said a voice in her head. Remember the first day and all that. Did she want fear to be part of her new vocabulary—her new life? No, she didn't and she wouldn't allow it. Suddenly her spirit felt lighter. Wow, was it that easy? What other words would be banished from her life? Hmm, *deadlines* . . . definitely *deadlines*. From now on the only deadline she'd meet would be of her own making. No more having her father harangue her about meeting the client's needs. No more endless chatter about corporate goals. She'd pick out her own goals, thank you very much.

Committee meetings should be nixed, too. She thought back on the endless ones her mother had made her attend. Talk, talk, talk, but no action. Sitting with people whose idea of charity was writing a big check to ease their conscience so that they could go about their business. Well, not her. She needed to be careful with her money—at least until she knew how successful her career as an artist would be—but it didn't mean that she couldn't do charitable things. She looked down at Roxy, trotting happily at her side. Such an excellent dog and look at the difference Roxy had made in her life. Here she was, strolling down the road, without a care, no anxiety, no panic. Roxy had given her back a measure of confidence, but without Greg, the dog probably would have been euthanized. That's what she'd do—she'd give her time and volunteer at a rescue shelter. Help other dogs—and people—get a second chance at life.

Sam lifted her head and was shocked. She'd been so lost in planning her new life that she hadn't realized how far she'd walked. She was halfway around the lake. Moving to retrace her steps, she halted when the sound of music drifted through the trees. So beautiful, but Sam didn't recognize it. She walked a few yards toward the sound and stepped into a clearing. Fritz's cabin sat a short distance away. He must be listening to his stereo.

Sam stood quietly for a moment, letting the lilting notes wash over her, but before she could turn away, Fritz stepped out onto his porch with a garbage bag in hand. Seeing her, he called out.

"Samantha, have you come for a visit?" he asked in a delighted voice.

Caught, Sam faltered. "Ah, it's a lovely morning, so I decided to take a walk."

Dropping the bag, Fritz lifted his face to the sun filtering through the trees. "It is, isn't it? A storm always seems to clear things." Returning his attention to her, he peered past her. "Where's your chaperone?"

"Anne?" Sam shook her head. "Roxy's my only companion today."

"Good for you. A little independence never hurt anyone." He waved her forward. "Come in. Join me for coffee."

"That's kind, but I wouldn't want to disturb you."

"You're not disturbing me," he said, nudging the bag with his foot. "You're rescuing me from mundane housework."

Sam gave Roxy's leash a light tug and joined Fritz. After ushering her into the cabin, he moved toward the stereo. Sam stopped him.

"No need to turn it off. It's lovely, but I don't recognize the composer. Who is it?"

Fritz placed a hand over his heart and bowed slightly. "Me."

Sam's eyes widened. "You composed that?"

"Yes," he answered, his face wreathed in pleasure. "For that reaction to my music, you deserve more than coffee. A Bloody Mary perhaps?"

"No thanks," Sam said, waving her hands. "Too early in the day for me, but don't let that stop you."

"We'll both have coffee," he replied with a wink, and went to the cupboard. After removing two cups and saucers, he had started to pour when a knock interrupted him. "My, my, today is my day for visitors."

Fritz crossed to the door and opened. Edward Dunlap stood on the other side of the threshold.

Grabbing his arm, Fritz drew him inside. "Edward, join us for coffee," he said as he led him into the kitchen.

Spying Sam, Edward hesitated. "I can come back later."

"Nonsense." Fritz dropped Edward's arm and quickly filled one of the cups and handed it to him.

Edward stared at the full cup as if he didn't know what to do with it. Setting it on the counter, he glanced down at Roxy, curled up by Sam's feet. "I heard that you adopted one of Greg's strays."

Sam smiled down at her dog. "Yes, she's become a great companion."

"I always wanted a dog," Edward said wistfully, "but Mother's allergic."

"That's too bad."

Edward's attention shifted and he cocked his head as if suddenly hearing the music. He placed his uninjured hand on the counter, and his fingers began to play along with the invisible pianist. His eyes took on a dreamy look while his lips curled in a half smile.

"Edward, do you—" Sam began, but stopped when Fritz rushed past her.

He strode over to the stereo and with one quick, angry movement shut it off.

As if stunned by the abrupt silence, Edward shook his head, dazed. His eyes flew to Fritz, still standing by the stereo.

"I—I—have to go. Excuse me." Edward whirled and headed for the door.

"Edward, wait," Fritz called after him, but Edward didn't hesitate. "Edward, I'm sorry. I thought—"

The slamming door cut him off.

Fritz bowed his head for a moment before joining Sam at the kitchen bar.

"I suppose you'd like an explanation," he said grimly.

"Only if you want to give me one," Sam replied in a soft voice.

Taking a deep breath, Fritz exhaled slowly. "At one time, Edward was one of my students and that piece was one of his favorites." He slammed a hand on the counter, startling Roxy. "Damn it, I should've shut it off the moment I saw him standing in the doorway."

Sam lightly touched his hand. "Fritz—"

"No, don't say anything. It was inexcusable of me to even inadvertently remind that poor boy of what he's lost."

"Don't be so hard on yourself. You couldn't have known Edward would drop by." Sam paused. "I know Edward was in an accident, but no one has ever said what happened."

"Car accident," Fritz answered, his tone short.

"And his arm was injured?"

"Yes, his shoulder. Alone, late at night, out on a gravel road—Edward ran a stop sign and was hit broadside. The force of the impact sent his car into the ditch." Fritz took a step back, leaning against the counter. "He has never regained use of his arm. Due to the injury, he developed some sort of syndrome that affects his nerves and causes constant pain." He shook his head. "I don't have a medical background, so I don't understand what all his condition entails, but I do know he's been tormented by it ever since."

Sam thought of her own medical problems, slight in comparison to Edward's. She *was* lucky. She knew that her recovery was possible. Edward would never have that same gift—the gift of hope.

"How sad," she murmured. "I wonder how he's kept his sanity."

"I don't believe he has," Fritz answered slowly.

# Twenty-four

"What are you doing home?" Caleb called from the living room as Anne walked in the front door. Joining him, she sprawled in one of the chairs.

"Sam gave me the morning off."

"Cool," he answered, not looking up from the magazine lying in his lap.

Anne studied him closely. He sat, leaning back against the couch with his long legs stretched out, resting on the coffee table. From her position, she couldn't see the article he was reading, but whatever it was, it was engrossing. She sat forward. With a yip, she jumped up and ran over to stand behind him. Throwing her arms around his neck, she kissed the top of his head.

"Oh, Mom," he said, ducking to the side. "It's just a catalog."

"For St. Michael's University," she exclaimed as she peered over his shoulder at the brightly colored pages. "It's an excellent school." Moving around the corner of the couch, she sat next to him and propped her feet on the edge of the coffee table. She leaned close and tapped the page. "Just look at the campus. Isn't that beautiful? And there," she said, pointing to another picture. "Those dorm rooms look really comfortable."

"Here," he said with a lift of his eyebrow, and handed her the catalog. "Would you like to look at it?"

"If you insist," she replied with a wry grin and quickly began to thumb through the pages. "Caleb, are you seriously considering St. Michael's?"

Leaning his head back against the couch, he closed his eyes and sighed. "I don't know. A state university would be cheaper."

Dropping her feet, Anne curled her legs under her as she did some swift calculations in her head. She'd hoped her job with Samantha would last all summer, but the way it was going, she doubted it. Sam had been making remarkable progress, both mentally and physically, especially since she'd stood up to her father. Eyes focused on the pictures, Anne couldn't help but wonder how much one played into the other. Had Lawrence Moore's tight control over his daughter's life been impeding her recovery? Shaking her head, she returned her attention to the catalog. Attitude, it was all about attitude.

As she flipped to the last pages of the catalog, her eyes widened at the sight of the cost per college credit. She'd managed to keep Caleb's college fund intact, but that payment to the bank was looming. If Caleb was set on St. Michael's, even with her paychecks from Sam, it wouldn't be enough, and she wanted to avoid applying for student loans. She needed to get a second job at the care facility in Hankton. She could work for Sam during the day and the night shift part-time in Hankton.

A knock at her front door startled Anne out of her silent planning session.

"Caleb, answer the—" she began, turning to where he'd been sitting. He was gone. When had he meandered off? With a sigh, she uncurled her legs and, rising, crossed the room. Through the door's window she spied a Scott County sheriff's car sitting in her driveway, and Duane Parker, one of the deputies, standing on her front porch. Her stomach instinctively clenched only to relax at once when she remembered that Caleb was somewhere in the house.

Holding the door open, she smiled. “Hey, Duane.”

“Anne,” he said, twisting his hat nervously in his hands. “Miss seeing you at the hospital.” He peered over her shoulder into the house. “Is Caleb around?”

Her stomach tightened again. “Yeah,” she replied, glancing over her shoulder toward the kitchen. “Come in. I’ll get him.” Letting the door swing shut behind him, she turned and strode toward the kitchen. Caleb was in his usual position, hanging on the refrigerator door and staring blindly at its contents.

“Caleb, Deputy Parker is here to see you,” she hissed. “What have you been up to?”

Caleb shut the door, his eyes widening in surprise. “Nothing.”

“Then why does he want to talk to you?”

“I don’t know.”

“You’d better be telling me the truth,” she replied in a low voice.

“I am. I swear.”

She sighed and jerked her head toward the hall. “Let’s go see what he wants.”

With Anne right behind him, Caleb shuffled out of the kitchen and into the hall, where the deputy waited.

She cast a narrow glance at Caleb as she motioned him and Deputy Parker toward the living room. “Shall we go in there?” she asked, trying to keep her voice bright.

Once Deputy Parker was seated on the couch and Caleb had plopped into an armchair, Anne seated herself in another chair and waited for the deputy to begin.

"Quite a thunderstorm last night, wasn't it?" he asked, directing his question to Anne.

"Sure was," she replied, leaning back in the chair. "Why do you want to talk with Caleb, Duane?"

He tugged at his collar as he pulled a small notebook out of his jacket pocket. Scanning it quickly, he cleared his throat. "Ah, Caleb, we've had a complaint last night from a Dr. Jackson Van Horn—"

Anne drew back. "Dr. Van Horn?"

The deputy nodded. "I know you work for his fiancée, Anne." He glanced down at his notes. "As he was leaving his cabin last night, he saw two kids running down the road in the storm. Then, when he stopped at Dunlap's to get gas, he noticed someone had keyed the passenger side of his car." He snapped the notebook shut. "Anything you'd like to tell me, Caleb?"

"No."

"Okay—well, when one of the boys passed under the neighbor's yard light, Dr. Van Horn saw he was wearing a red sweatshirt." He paused. "Still don't have anything to say?"

Caleb's chin dropped. "No."

"The sweatshirt had 'Weaver' printed on the back."

"Caleb!" Anne gasped, shooting forward.

Caleb's head whirled toward his mother. "I know this looks bad, but it wasn't me . . . honest," he cried.

Anne's lips tightened. "But you know who it was, don't you?"

He seemed to shrink in the chair. "No—ah—I lost that sweatshirt a couple of weeks ago."

"Where?" she asked, her eyes drilling into his.

Shrugging, he looked down and shook his head. "I don't know."

"Okay, let's try this," Deputy Parker said in a calm voice. "Where were you last night?"

Caleb shot a nervous glance at Anne. "It was raining so hard that I pulled over at Dunlap's to wait it out."

"Did anyone see you?"

"Ah—no."

*He's lying*, Anne thought as her temper began to flare. "If you know anything about what happened to Dr. Van Horn's car, I suggest you tell Deputy Parker . . . immediately."

"I can't—I don't," he declared.

Deputy Parker slapped his legs and rose. "I guess if you can't help me out, Caleb, I'll just have to write up my report based on what Dr. Van Horn said." He lifted a shoulder. "Then, if he wants to press charges, it'll be up to the judge to decide."

Anne, her mind numb, showed Deputy Parker to the door. When they reached it, he turned.

"Sorry to see you again under these circumstances," he said softly. "Caleb's a good kid and it's hard for me to believe he keyed Dr. Van Horn's car." He shook his head. "But I do think he knows who did. If he wants to talk about it, give me a call. I'm on duty all day."

Anne laid a hand on his arm. "Thanks, Duane. I'll let you know if I find out anything."

After shutting the door, she marched back to the living room and over to where Caleb was still sitting. Towering over him, she fisted her hands on her hips. "Unless you want to be grounded for the rest of your life, you'd better start talking."

He shot out of the chair. "I can't—I won't—I'm not a narc." Pulling his fingers through his hair, he walked around her and headed for the kitchen.

Anne followed, stopping at the doorway. "You can be charged as an adult."

"I'm sorry someone did that to Dr. Van Horn's car, Mom, but

it is just a misdemeanor," he said, yanking a cabinet door open. "If Deputy Parker doesn't find out who did it and they blame me, all a judge would do is give me community service."

"Have you got shit for brains? Allowing yourself to be charged for something you didn't do?" Anne screamed, then thought of Sam's reaction. "I could even lose my *job* over this!"

Caleb slammed the cabinet shut and rested his forehead against the door. "I'm sorry, Mom."

Taking a deep breath, she crossed the distance between them and laid a hand on his shoulder. "I'm sorry, too. I shouldn't have sworn at you," she said, trying to keep her voice gentle, "but if you know who did this, you have to tell the authorities. If you're found guilty, it will be on your record."

Caleb lifted his head. "I don't know for sure if he did it."

Anne's fingers gripped his shoulder. "Who?"

He spun away from the counter and began to pace. "I gave a couple of guys a ride home from Dunlap's last night." He hesitated. "I think my sweatshirt might have been in the backseat."

"And one of them took it?" she prodded.

"Maybe—I didn't check."

Placing her palms on her cheeks, Anne shook her head. "Who were the guys?"

He stopped his pacing and stared down at his feet.

"Who were they, Caleb?" she asked again.

"If I tell, you're going to call Deputy Parker, then they'll know I ratted them out."

"You'd rather face charges?"

"I like having friends, Mom, and if I get branded as a rat, I won't." He pulled out a chair and flopped down. "I don't want my car keyed and I don't want the inside of it smeared with Limburger cheese." He buried his head in his hands. "That's what happened to Joey last year after he told them that Te—" He clamped his lips shut.

"That Teddy was the one who set the boats adrift," Anne said, finishing for him. "You gave Teddy a ride home from Dunlap's. Was Joey the other guy?"

He nodded.

"And Teddy took your sweatshirt?"

"Probably—Joey was in the front with me."

She crossed to the table and placed both hands on its top, leaning forward. "Look at me, Caleb," she commanded. "You're old enough to do the right thing, but if you don't, I will." She glanced up at the clock. "I'm going to Hankton to see about a job. You've got until I get back to think about it."

The interview had taken place in the administrator's office, and Anne thought she'd made a good impression. The job itself was up in the air. Her availability was in question, but to determine that, she needed to tell Sam of her plans. Surely Sam wouldn't object to her moonlighting. And that's exactly what it would be, since she'd be working the night shift. She hated leaving Caleb alone every night, but he was a big boy. He *should* be able to take care of himself. If only she could trust him to stay away from Teddy Brighton.

She gave her head a quick shake. She had to trust him. This second job meant sending him to St. Michael's—the first college Caleb had shown any interest in. She'd have faith that he'd behave, and she'd make the sacrifice of working eighteen-hour days. After all, who needed sleep?

Anne had reached her car and was unlocking the door when a blonde walking across the parking lot caught her eye. She'd recognize that bouffant anywhere.

"Alice," she called out to the woman.

The woman gave a hurried glance over her shoulder then picked up her pace.

"Alice," Anne called again, but the woman kept walking.

When she reached a small car, she unlocked the door and got in. In a moment she was wheeling out of the parking lot.

With a shake of her head, Anne opened her door and started her own car. She could've sworn the woman had been Alice, but Alice would have acknowledged her. Settling her sunglasses on her face, she forgot about the woman and set her mind on calculating once again how much it would cost to send Caleb to St. Michael's.

Confident that Caleb would tell the truth to Deputy Parker, she allowed images of the next four years to dance through her mind—Caleb finally going off to college. A frown played on her lips. That would be hard, watching him walk out the door and into a new life. A life in which she didn't play a daily role. But that was okay. Hadn't Greg pointed out that she would have to loosen the strings at some point, and really, she didn't mind. If it meant that Caleb was moving toward a secure future, it would all be worth it. She pictured herself a few years from now, standing proudly with the other parents, watching Caleb receive his degree. A thrill of happiness filled her. Caleb would have the chance that she'd thrown away.

Promptly at one o'clock, Anne pulled up in front of Sam's. Looking at the cabin, she hoped that the mess Teddy Brighton had created for her son had been straightened out. Surely, by now Caleb had called Deputy Parker and confessed what he knew.

When she'd stopped by earlier and read Sam's note giving her the morning off, both Dr. Van Horn and Sam had been gone. Maybe they'd gone for a drive. Or maybe they were engaged in something else, she thought with a little smirk. They'd been pretty chummy when she walked in on them yesterday. It had taken her aback. She'd never witnessed any kind of affection between them, but now it looked like the situation was changing. She hesitated. Should she make a racket when she walked in the door? Should she knock first? No, Dr. Van Horn's car was still gone, so the danger of interrupting them was slim.

Anne walked the rest of the way to the cabin and opened the door. Nope, no Dr. Van Horn—just Sam standing in front of the easel with one brush in her mouth and another in her hand. She watched as Sam made a few quick strokes with the one in her hand. Amazed, she saw a pine tree appear in the painting. Switching brushes, Sam made a few more strokes and the rough outline of the shore appeared.

Anne cleared her throat.

Sam jumped at the sound, the brush falling from her hand as she pressed it to her heart. "You startled me!" she exclaimed.

"Sorry." Anne stepped inside and motioned over her shoulder. "Is Dr. Van Horn at the sheriff's?"

Sam gave her a puzzled look. "Sheriff's?"

Quickly Anne explained Deputy Parker's visit and Caleb's confession.

When she'd finished, Sam frowned. "I'm sorry Jackson accused Caleb."

"It's understandable. Teddy *was* wearing his sweatshirt, and maybe now Caleb will finally stay away from him." Anne looked around the room. "So where is Dr. Van Horn?"

"He left last night," Sam replied, rinsing out her brushes.

"Short visit."

Sam picked up a towel and began drying the brushes. "Last visit."

"What?" Anne exclaimed.

Placing the brushes back in the tray, Sam crossed to the couch and, after sitting down, related last night's events. Dumbfounded by Sam's story, Anne joined her on the couch.

"Don't you think you might be overreacting?" Anne hesitated. "The wind could've blown the door open. It *was* quite a storm."

Sam's lips tightened and she shook her head. "No, I distinctly remember locking it." She picked at a cushion next to her while she stared off into space. "Ever since I stopped taking those damn pills, my memory's been sharper." She turned toward Anne and her eyes narrowed. "I almost wonder if they weren't slowing my recovery."

When Anne didn't answer, Sam slapped her thighs and rose. "Moot point now." Looking down at the other woman, she smiled. "What do you have planned for me today? I've already taken a walk."

Anne looked toward the sun streaming in the French doors. "Let's try something new. It's a beautiful day. How do you feel about going for a swim?"

Sam's nose wrinkled as her attention drifted down to her left leg. "I'd have to wear a bathing suit."

Standing, Anne laughed. "You can't very well swim in sweatpants."

Sam's hand drifted down to her left thigh. "My leg," she began with reluctance in her voice.

"Oh, don't worry about that," Anne said, waving away her fears. "You can wear your sweats over your suit then take them off right before you get in the water. No one will see your leg."

"You're sure?"

"Trust me. It will be okay."

With that, Sam went back to her bedroom to change while

Anne slipped into her suit in the guest room. Together they carefully made their way down the steps to the dock. Once there, Sam took off her pants and quickly waded into the lake. She stopped when the water lapped around her waist. Looking up at Anne, she cocked her head.

"You know you look great in a bathing suit."

Blushing, Anne smiled. "Thanks." She waded in to join Sam, handing her one of the "noodles" she'd hauled down to the lake.

"Have you ever thought about modeling?" Sam asked suddenly. "With your figure and height—"

Anne launched herself into the water, cutting Sam off. She swam briskly to the end of the dock. Straightening until her feet hit the bottom, she wiped the water out of her eyes. Sam, wearing a perplexed look on her face, still stood where Anne had left her.

"Use the noodle and swim out to meet me."

"You didn't answer my question."

Her eyes downcast, Anne moved her arms through the water. "I know."

Sam swam over to Anne. "I'm serious—I worked with plenty of models at the ad agency, and half of them don't have your presence. I know you're not in your twenties, but there is a niche for older women. You should give it a try."

"Like I haven't heard that one before." She gave a furious shake of her head. "No."

"Why? What's the deal?"

Anne grabbed the edge of the dock and let her legs float upward. "What's the expression? 'Been there, done that.'"

"You modeled?"

Anne gave a sharp snort. "I tried it—all the folks around here told me I was perfect—but the modeling agencies in New York thought differently."

"When did all this happen?"

"A long time ago. I was young and stupid." Anne let her fingers trail through the crystal-clear lake water. "I took every dime my parents had saved for my college education and wasted it on trying to break into the business." She dropped her chin. "I came home with my tail tucked between my legs. The only good thing to come out of the experience was Caleb."

Sam laid a hand on her wet shoulder. "I'm sorry."

Anne brushed her away. "Don't be. I got over it. Now the only thing that's important is that Caleb doesn't make the same mistake I did by chasing after some foolish dream. He's going to get an education."

"But is that what Caleb wants?"

"No. He thinks he can make a living working as a musician." Anne scoffed. "But I'm not going to allow it."

Sam moved to the end of the dock and grasped the edge. "Kind of like my father didn't allow *me* to see if I could make it as an artist?"

Anne felt her temper rise. "No, it's not like that at all," she declared hotly. "You've always had money. We haven't. You can afford to fail. Caleb can't. He needs an education to be successful."

"There are more ways to fail than just financially. I know people who have lots of money, but I wouldn't say they have successful lives."

Anne kicked away from the dock and swam into deeper water. "Yeah, try living from paycheck to paycheck and see how successful you feel."

Using the noodle for buoyancy, Sam paddled toward her. "If my paintings don't sell, I might—"

The sudden roar of a Jet Ski cut off her words. A teenager, with the sun turning his red hair orange, rode high in the seat as he headed straight toward them. At the last minute he cranked the steering hard toward the left, creating a big wave. As the wave rolled toward them, Anne made a grab for Sam, but the girl's wet arm slipped from her grasp. She watched helplessly as the force of the water yanked the noodle out Sam's hands and carried her back toward the end of the dock.

With a dull thump, Sam's head met the dock's metal pylon. Her eyes closed while her body slumped back in the water. In two long strokes, Anne had reached her and, supporting her shoulders, lifted her face clear of the water.

Sam's eyelids fluttered open, and with a groan, she raised a hand to her head.

"What happened?"

"Are you okay?" Anne asked as she took a firm grip on Sam's upper arm.

"Yeah," she said, allowing Anne to pull her back into shallow water. When her feet touched the bottom, she rubbed the side of her skull.

Anne looked beyond Sam to the Jet Ski disappearing in the distance. "The force of the wave carried you into the side of the dock. Can you make it up the hill to the cabin?"

Sam dropped her hand and nodded. "I'm fine. I was stunned for a moment, that's all." She glanced over her shoulder. "Who was on the Jet Ski?"

"Do you really have to ask?" Anne's face flushed in anger. "Teddy Brighton."

## Twenty-five

When they reached the cabin, Anne helped Sam into one of the kitchen chairs and called Dr. Douglas. After taking the phone, Sam sat patiently and answered the doctor's ridiculous questions.

"Are you nauseated?"

"No."

"What day is it?"

Sam grimaced. "Monday."

"Do you have any ringing in your ears?"

"No."

"On a scale of one to ten, rate your pain."

"Five."

"Okay," Dr. Douglas said. "May I speak with Anne, please?"

Anne accepted the phone and listened intently. "You're positive you don't want to see her?" she asked in a voice weighted with skepticism.

Sam shook her head vigorously at Anne's question and mouthed the word *no*.

With a frown, Anne turned her back on Sam and continued

listening to the doctor's instructions. "Sure, I'll spend the night," she replied. "Okay, thanks, Doctor."

Anne placed the phone on the counter and crossed over to Sam. After helping her to her feet, she guided her toward the hallway. "Dr. Douglas said to rest and take ibuprofen. Do you need help getting out of your swimsuit?"

Sam pulled her arm away. "Don't treat me like an invalid. I took a little bump on the head. I'm fine."

"Okay, but I'm staying. I'll call Caleb, make sure he did talk to the deputy sheriff, and let him know that I'm spending the night."

Before Sam could answer her, a knock interrupted them, followed by Fritz appearing in the doorway.

"I don't mean to intrude," he said self-consciously, "but I have a gift for you, Samantha—a CD of my compositions. I thought you might enjoy listening to it."

She made a half turn and moved toward him, but Anne stepped forward and blocked her.

"This really isn't a good time, Fritz," she said, not hiding the irritation in her voice.

He looked flustered as his attention shifted to Anne.

"Sam's had an accident," she continued.

"Oh, my dear," he cried, stepping over the threshold. "Is there anything I can do to help?"

"No," Anne answered for Sam. "I've called the doctor and he said the best thing for her is rest, so I'm staying the night."

"But, Anne, aren't you concerned about Caleb?"

"Um—not at the moment."

"Oh," he said, not hiding his surprise. "I'd heard Duane Parker paid you a visit."

"I'm sure that the matter has been straightened out by now," she replied gruffly. "I want to get Sam to bed, so if you'll excuse us . . ."

Fritz reached around Anne and shoved the CD case toward Sam. "Here, my dear, you can listen to this while you're resting."

Sam glanced at the case and shook her head. "Not now. I think I'd better do as Anne says." She waved toward the counter. "If you'd put it over there, I'll listen later."

Fritz glanced down at his hand. "Yes—yes," he muttered. "I'm sorry to have bothered you." Placing the case on the counter, he left.

"I think we hurt his feelings." Sam sighed after the door had softly closed. "It was sweet of him to make me a CD of his music."

"You can thank him later," Anne replied. "My job is to make sure you follow the doctor's instructions, not worry about Fritz's feelings."

Muttering under her breath about Anne's bossiness, Sam deliberately shut the bathroom door in her face and quickly changed. Such a fuss about nothing. Okay, so a feeling of panic had flashed in the instant her head made contact with the pylon, but it had happened so fast that she didn't have time to react. The thought of another head injury nagged at her, but she had no intention of wearing a helmet for the rest of her life, so what was the alternative? She thought back to her walk earlier that day. She'd decided fear would no longer be in her vocabulary. This was a perfect time to put her new resolution in practice. She'd follow the doctor's orders and all would be well by morning. Satisfied, she went to the bedroom and curled up on the bed. A moment later a rap sounded and Anne entered with a glass of water and a bottle of ibuprofen. She shook a couple out and handed them, along with the water, to Sam. Sitting up, Sam popped the pills while Anne crossed to the window and adjusted the blinds, sending the room into semidarkness.

At the door, Anne paused. "Rest, and if you need anything, holler."

Yawning, Sam nodded. She was tired, she thought, scooting down in the bed. She shut her eyes and waited for sleep to claim her, but every sound seemed magnified. She could hear Anne rustling around in the kitchen, a boat speeding by down on the lake—even her bedside clock seemed to click away the seconds. Giving up, she sat up in bed. Her sketch pad lay beside her, but she didn't feel like drawing. Her eyes spied a book on the dresser. Getting out of bed, she went over and picked it up. It was the book Jackson had been reading—*The Minnesota Guide to Haunted Locations.* She thumbed through it as she walked back to the bed and climbed in.

She scanned the pages, reading the usual tales of ghostly Native American princesses wandering the shores of misty lakes; lost miners still digging in abandoned mines; cabins plagued by poltergeists. It was the last entry in the book that caught her attention.

The story told of a cabin located not far from Elk Horn Lake where for years vacationers had been tormented by the pesky ghost of a young woman. This mischievous spirit seemed especially to enjoy playing pranks on the unwary visitors by hiding objects that belonged to them and startling them out of a sound sleep.

*Hiding objects?* Isn't that what happened to her brush and the photo Jackson had given her as a gift?

She snorted softly. In a way, it would be comforting to believe that it was some restless spirit that was haunting her, instead of her own mind not functioning as it should. With a grimace, she tossed the book to the side and eased down in the bed. She placed her forearm over her face and shut her eyes.

The dream that was unfolding was like watching a movie. She was present, but removed from the scene, like a spectator. The green light from the dashboard was casting eerie shadows on the faces of a man and woman as their car sped down a lonely gravel road. Warm humid air rushed into the open window of the passenger side, where the woman sat. With her red hair tumbling around her face, she extended her arm out the window as if she were trying to catch the wind. In front of her, the headlights lit the dark strip of country road. Turning with a laugh, the woman scooted closer to her companion and threw an arm around his neck.

The man's profile revealed a strong chin, high cheekbones, and a straight nose, but the color of his hair and eyes were hidden in shadow.

"What's my surprise?" the woman cooed.

The man's lips moved in a faint smile. "It wouldn't be a surprise if I told you."

She inched closer and nuzzled his earlobe. "Please?"

"Behave," he said, shifting his body away from her.

Lifting her head, she sat back. "But you like it better when I don't." Her hand stole up his arm and across his chest, her fingers playing with the buttons on his shirt.

"Knock it off—not while I'm driving," he said as he brushed her hand away.

Flopping back in her seat, she crossed her arms over her chest while her lips formed a pout. "Aren't we about there?"

"Almost."

"I don't have all night, you know," she said in a querulous voice. "I need to be home before he gets back."

The man didn't speak for a moment. "Why don't you leave him? You're miserable." One hand left the steering wheel to grasp hers. "I could make you happy."

She jerked away. "How?" she scoffed. "Living upstairs in a two-bedroom apartment?" She tossed her long hair. "I've got bigger plans than that."

Both the man's hands gripped the steering wheel until his knuckles whitened. "He's not going to change his life for you."

"Yes, he will," she answered with a firm nod.

"I'd treat you better," he argued back.

"Oh, baby," she crooned, leaning in until her full breasts were pressed tightly against his side. "You know this is just for kicks and giggles."

He shifted his upper body to the side, creating a gap between them. "Right. Until something better comes along," he replied in a bitter voice.

The woman slid closer, and the car filled with the scent of lavender. "Don't be this way," she said, moving her hand to his lap and letting her fingers wander up and down the zipper of his jeans.

He gasped.

She lifted her chin and pressed her lips to the tender spot below his ear and his gasp turned into a groan. His lower body arched, pressing into her open palm. The headlights wove an erratic pattern across the road. Laughing, the woman licked the side of his neck and his eyelids drifted shut for a moment.

Suddenly his body slammed into hers, throwing her against the passenger door. The car careened wildly into the ditch while clouds of dust poured in the open window. Bouncing over the rough ground, they were tossed like a couple of rag dolls. Finally the car came to a stop with its headlights pointing into the night sky at a crazy angle.

The woman tried sitting up, but the man's heavy body was sprawled across her. She pushed him away and her hand found the door handle, which she wrenched open. Half crawling, half tumbling, she slithered to the ground. Getting to her feet, she staggered back while she drew a hand across her mouth. It came away wet and sticky. She held it in front of her face. Bleeding, she was bleeding. Still staring at her bloody hand, she jumped when a voice called out.

"Hey, are you hurt?"

The words were followed by the sound of heavy boots crashing through the weeds.

Without a backward glance at the man still lying in the wrecked car, the woman crouched and slipped off into the dark before the other man could see her.

Sam woke up curled on her side with her hands fisted into her pillow. What a dream—had it been triggered by Fritz telling her of Edward's accident? Fritz had said Edward was alone that night, but in her dream, he hadn't been. Blanche? Why had her subconscious inserted Blanche? Sliding over, she felt a body pressed up against her back. *Thank goodness for Roxy,* she thought, smiling as she rolled over. The dog was always there to comfort her. Still smiling, she turned her head to pet the dog.

The breath froze in her lungs as her smile fled. Her eyes widened and terror like she'd never known ignited a scream. Rolling away, she fell onto the floor and then jerked to her feet. Without a backward glance at the terrible visage in her bed, she half limped, half ran down the hall.

"Anne, Anne!" she shrieked.

Coming to a halt in the middle of the living room, she spun around. Alone . . . she was alone. Except for the awful thing lying in her bed.

She darted to the kitchen door and was ready to fling it open when Anne suddenly stepped in from the deck.

"What's going on?" she asked, crossing to Sam.

Sam sagged against her in relief and, with a trembling arm, pointed to the bedroom.

"Back there," she said, her voice quivering, "in the bed—"

Anne quickly moved her to the couch. "Stay here," she said, pivoting, then taking off toward the bedroom. A few moments later, she returned and sat next to Sam.

"Whatever you saw, it's gone now," she said.

Sam covered her face with her hands and tried to catch her breath. "It can't be—I saw it—I know I did."

"What did you see? A snake? A bat?" Anne glanced over her shoulder. "Bats can find their way into these old cabins, but they're nothing to be afraid of."

"No, not a bat." Sam dropped her hands and stared at Anne blindly. "It was so real—"

Anne gave her arm a little shake. "What was so real?"

"A corpse," she said, choking on the word.

Anne sat back in disbelief saying nothing.

"A body—a woman—with her face battered in and rotting."

Anne shot to her feet. "I'm calling Dr. Douglas."

"No, wait." Sam grabbed at her hand and forced herself to breathe evenly. "I must've still been dreaming and the body was part of the dream." She shuddered and let her head drop back against the couch.

"What were you dreaming?" Anne sat back on the couch.

"Edward—I think I know what really happened to Edward."

"He was in a car accident. Everyone knows that."

"But everyone thinks he was alone." Sam lifted her head. "He wasn't. Blanche was with him, and she caused him to run the stop sign."

"Sam, that's cra—"

"Crazy?" Sam finished the sentence for her. "Do you know for sure that Blanche wasn't with him?"

"The farmer who went for help said he was alone."

"What has Edward said?"

"Not much—he doesn't like to talk about it, and I don't want to pry."

"Did he ever explain how he came to run the stop sign?"

"He believes he dozed off for a second."

"Look, I know this sounds unbelievable." Sam paused. "At first, I thought meeting Edward at Fritz's this morning triggered the dream, but now I'm not so sure." Tugging on her lip, she stared off into space. "It's almost as if someone is trying to tell me something. First the dream about a party at Fritz's." Her eyes slid toward Anne. "Now this dream. It was the same woman in both dreams, and I know it's Blanche."

"What?" Anne's eyebrows rose. "You think you're being haunted by Blanche Jones?"

Sam sat up. "There've been cases of this . . . I found a book about ghosts . . . Jackson was reading it . . . it talks about stuff like this."

"When were you reading it?" Anne asked in a skeptical voice.

"This afternoon, before I—" Sam stopped.

"Before you fell asleep?" Anne gave her a knowing look. "Sam, you suffered a traumatic experience this afternoon. Old fears might have surfaced—"

"No," Sam interrupted, "the dreams haven't been about me. They've been about Blanche."

Anne rose to her feet and looked down at her. "I knew all this talk about Blanche wasn't good. You've never even seen a picture of her, have you?"

"No."

"Then you can't know that she's the woman in your dreams." She held out her hand to Sam and helped her to her feet.

"You think I'm losing my grip on reality, don't you?"

"Like I said, I think you had a bad scare this afternoon." She guided Sam down the hallway. "From what I know, Blanche Jones was the type to land on her feet, and right now she's probably living the high life with her latest love. Not haunting you." She stopped at the door to the bedroom. "See? Everything's fine—nothing in this room has changed. Why don't you try and rest again?"

Sam drew away from the door. "I'm not sleeping in there."

"Okay, then how about the guest room?"

Sam nodded. "I suppose you're right." She looked over her shoulder at the bed. She wanted her sketch pad, but couldn't seem to force herself to step inside the room.

Anne noticed her looking at the bed. "I'll get it," she said, crossing to the bed and grabbing the pad and the pencil lying next to it. "Here," she said as she handed them to Sam. "Maybe sketching will help you relax."

With Anne following her, Sam entered the guest room and sat down on the bed.

"Would you like something to eat?" Anne asked from the doorway.

"No . . . thanks . . . maybe later." Sam swung her legs onto the bed and lay back against the pillows, the closed sketch pad resting on her lap.

After Anne left, softly closing the door behind her, Sam opened the pad and stared at the blank paper. Twiddling the pencil between her fingers, she tried to empty her mind of the awful sight she'd thought she'd seen. Anne was right. Her subconscious had been playing a nasty trick on her, but she wasn't going to let it get away with it. She'd had enough of that when she'd first come out of the coma. And she wasn't going through that torment again. She was better, stronger, she thought as her grip on the pencil relaxed. She'd forget about Blanche and everything would be fine.

The tickling sensation of drool running out of the corner of her mouth woke her. She wiped the side of her mouth. Man, she'd slept hard. She'd probably been snoring, too. Still, she thought, it was better to drool and snore than hallucinate about lying in bed with a corpse.

Reaching over, Sam turned on the nightstand light and glanced at the clock. It was past eleven—she vaguely remembered Anne coming in periodically to check on her, but she'd fallen back asleep each time. Wide-awake now, she sat up in bed and looked around the room. What was she going to do to kill time? Watching television would disturb Anne, and she figured she'd put her through enough for one day without interrupting her sleep. Reading was out of the question. She didn't want any more tales of ghoulies and ghosties slipping into her head. She could try sketching. She'd fallen asleep without making a single mark.

Sam picked up the sketch pad and opened it. The page she'd been staring at before she'd fallen asleep wasn't blank. The face of a woman looked up at her. Her heart hitched. She didn't remember drawing this, but it was definitely her work. Another blackout? *Please, no,* she thought, fighting the urge to rip out the page and tear it into a thousand pieces.

Her gaze was drawn back to the drawing. The woman's face wore a half smile as she sat, with her legs curled beneath her, on a grassy lawn. Sexuality oozed from every line of her body, from the way she held her head to the tilt of her shoulders. A profusion of flowers lay in her lap.

Sam's eyes narrowed and she studied the flowers. There was something familiar about them. Pushing the pad off her lap, she suddenly remembered. She quietly left the bed and padded over to the door in her bare feet. Opening it, she peered into the hallway. The cabin was dark, and from across the hall, she could hear the rustling of bedcovers. Anne must be sleeping in her, Sam's, room. Good, she thought as she stole out of the room. Reaching the kitchen, she eased the dead bolt back and unlocked the door. With a quick look over her shoulder, she stepped out onto the porch.

The rising moon hung above the pine trees and cast the yard in shadows. In the distance an owl hooted while Sam crept across the porch. Sitting on the top step, she leaned toward the bush that was growing there. The red blossoms seemed to glow with a light of their own as she bent and plucked one of the heavy stems. Cupping the crimson flowers, she raised them to her face and softly stroked them across her cheek while tears gathered in her eyes.

Love Lies Bleeding.

# Twenty-six

Anne heard the kitchen door lightly close and was on her feet immediately. On her way to the kitchen, she checked the guest bedroom. No Sam. No Roxy. She found the dog lying with her nose pressed up against the base of the door. With a soft whine, the dog lifted her head and her soft brown eyes seemed to implore Anne for help.

"Is she outside?" Anne whispered, moving the dog out of the way and opening the door. She expected her to follow, but Roxy plopped on the floor with a sigh and refused to budge.

Once outside, Anne saw Sam sitting on the top step, swaying from side to side in the moonlight. Dropping down next to her, she waited for Sam to speak, but she remained silent. Great, was she sleepwalking?

Finally Sam spoke. "See my plant?" Sam asked in a dreamy voice. "See how pretty it is?"

Anne decided to play along. "Yeah, I noticed. I thought it was dying but the rain last night brought it back."

Sam stopped her swaying. "I planted it from seeds."

"Really?"

"Uh-huh." Her head bobbed. "Alice gave me some from her

plants." Sam giggled. "I didn't think she would after Pumpkin tried to dig one up. Alice was so angry."

"I didn't think Alice ever got mad at her dogs."

Sam's gaze shot to Anne's face. "Pumpkin isn't Alice's dog. She's mine."

"Your dog's name is Roxy," Anne said carefully.

"No, my dog's name is Pumpkin," Sam insisted in an even voice. "Ted bought him for me." She gave Anne a wink. "Harley thinks I got him in a pet store."

*Damn it all to hell—she is sleepwalking and she thinks she's Blanche.* Anne tried to stay calm, but inside she was scared. Very scared. The blow to the head had caused more damage than she thought. She had to get Sam to the hospital. She could have a seizure or a stroke.

She stood and gave Sam a reassuring smile. "Hey, what do you say we go for a drive?" she asked, reaching down.

Sam inched away from the outstretched hand. "No, I have to wait right here."

"Why?"

Sam looked up at her with an expression that said, *Isn't it obvious?* "Ted promised he'd come by tonight."

"Ted?"

"Theodore Brighton the First," Sam said proudly. "He's crazy about me, you know." She gave a happy laugh as she lifted her face to the sky. "What that man can do." Lowering her face, she gave Anne a sly look. "You'd never know he's on the downhill side of forty. A twenty-year-old would be lucky to keep up with him."

When Anne didn't comment, Sam pointed down the road. "You can't tell anyone, but he pulls off right over there and flashes his lights."

"Then you run out to meet him?"

Sam hugged her knees to her chest and grinned. "Sure do."

Anne was losing her patience. She had to get this woman medical attention. Bending down, she made a grab for Sam's arm. "Come on, Sam, let's take a ride."

Sam dodged her by rising to her feet. Moving past Anne, she paced to the far side of the porch. Anne noticed she was moving without a limp.

"I don't know who Sam is," she declared. "My name is Blanche." She gave a short bark of laughter. "Terrible name, isn't it? I don't know why my ma couldn't have named me something more mysterious . . . like Cassandra . . . instead of plain old Blanche." She turned and cocked her head. "I don't think it suits me at all, do you?"

"Come on, let's go inside."

Sam turned with a wiggle of her hips and leaned against the railing. "I told you I can't. Ted's coming."

"No, no, I don't think he is."

With a sigh, Sam straightened and turned. "You're probably right." She fisted her hands on her hips. "Isn't that just like a man? Promises, promises, but they never come through." She jerked her head toward the cabin. "Harley promised me the world, but look what I got—a stinking shack in the middle of nowhere." She whirled, staring out at the empty road. "Ted has to take me away from this," she cried. "Lordy, I don't think I can stand another winter up here. Day after day cooped up with him."

Anne had had enough. Striding across the porch, she grasped Sam's arm and gave it a shake. "We're going inside. Now."

Sam's posture suddenly changed. Her shoulders fell and she took one limping step forward. Her head whipped from side to side until her attention stopped on Anne. "What are you doing out here?"

Anne released her arm. "What are you?"

"I—uh—came out to look at that bush."

"And then?"

Sam shrugged. "I guess I dozed off."

"You don't remember our conversation?"

"No." Sam's voice rose in panic. "What conversation?"

Anne slung her arm around Sam's shoulders and guided her toward the door. She noticed Sam's limp was more pronounced than it had been in days. Had she had some kind of a stroke?

When they entered the house, Roxy jumped to her feet and pressed her black nose into Sam's palm. Kneeling, Sam brushed her face against the dog's neck.

"I had another blackout, didn't I?" she murmured, not lifting her head.

"I don't know what happened, but I'm calling the emergency room and taking you in."

"No, please," Sam cried in a desperate voice. "I'm okay. It's Tuesday night—"

"Monday," Anne said quietly.

Sam fluttered her hand nervously. "Okay, so it's Monday. My name is Samantha Moore; I'm thirty-five years old," she said, rattling off statistics. "See, I remember. I'm okay." A tear rolled down her cheek. "Please, don't take me to the hospital."

Anne's heart broke for her. The Sam she'd seen the last couple of days had vanished, and the woman, kneeling on the floor and clutching her dog, needed help that was beyond Anne's skills. She walked over to her and helped her to her feet.

"Sam," she began gently, "I'm afraid your head injury is more serious than we thought. You must see a doctor."

"Do you promise that you won't let them keep me?"

"We'll do whatever the doctor thinks best, and—"

Sam struggled away from her. “No.”

“Sam,” she said, laying it on the line, “during the blackout, or whatever it was, you thought you were Blanche.”

Sam’s eyes flared and she held up her hand, stopping Anne. “Wait.” She turned and fled down the hall.

Anne took the opportunity to grab the phone and quickly dial a number.

“Yeah?” Greg’s sleepy voice sounded in her ear.

“It’s Anne.” She glanced over her shoulder. “I’m at Sam’s and I think I’m going to need your help,” she whispered into the receiver. “Would you please come over right away?”

Not waiting for an answer, Anne disconnected before Sam caught her on the phone. A moment later, Sam came rushing into the kitchen, waving a piece of paper.

“Here. Take a look at this.” She held out the paper. “It’s Blanche.”

Anne stared down at the paper and remained silent.

“Don’t you get it?” Sam asked as she tapped at the sketch. “Blanche is holding a bouquet of Love Lies Bleeding.”

“You’re not making sense,” Anne replied, not trying to hide the weariness in her voice. “What does this prove?”

“It’s Blanche, I tell you,” she said as she furiously shook the paper in Anne’s face. “The woman from my dreams.”

“Sam—”

Anne broke off as Sam’s attention flew to the door then back to her. She saw the mistrust written on Sam’s face.

“Who did you call?”

Before Anne could answer, Greg appeared in the doorway. Roxy ran to him in delight and he paused to scratch her head. When he looked up, his eyes went first to Sam then to Anne. “What’s going on?”

“Greg,” Anne said calmly, “Sam had an accident this afternoon. She hit her head on a pylon at the dock and she needs to see a doctor."

"No," Sam exclaimed, "I did hit my head, but she thinks I'm nuts." She rushed over to Greg and tugged on his sleeve. "She's going to have me committed. You can't let her do that." She quickly gave him a garbled version of what had happened that afternoon and finished by waving the picture at him.

"Sam, calm down and let me see your sketch," he said gently. He took the picture and studied it. "I was a kid, so I barely knew Blanche, but this does kind of look like the way I remember her."

"See?" Sam threw Anne a triumphant look.

"But," Greg continued, "whether or not this is a drawing of Blanche, you still need to see a doctor."

Sam took two steps back. "You're siding with her," she cried. "I thought you were my friend."

Greg stepped forward. "I am."

"No, you're not."

"Sam, don't be angry with Greg. He's as worried about you as I am." Anne stepped forward. "Please, let me take you to the hospital."

Sam lowered her head. "What about Roxy?"

Placing a hand on her shoulder, Greg smiled at her. "I'll take her home with me." He placed the picture on the counter. "I'll bring her back tomorrow."

"You promise?"

"Yes, Sam, I promise. Now, will you go with Anne?"

"Just for them to check me out. I'm not staying," she said with a hitch of her chin. Whirling, she went back to the bedroom to change.

After watching her leave, Anne lifted her hands and rubbed her face. "Thanks," she breathed between her fingers.

"What do you think is wrong with her?"

Exhaling, Anne shook her head. "I don't know. When I described her symptoms earlier, Dr. Douglas thought she'd be okay. He did say to watch her in case problems showed up later."

"What kind of problems?"

"Seizures, confusion." She looked back over her shoulder at the closed bedroom door. "She hasn't had a seizure as far as I know, but she's definitely confused." Anne gnawed on her bottom lip for a second. "I'll have to call her father."

"Can't it wait?"

"No." She pinched the bridge of her nose. "It's a mess and the last thing I need is Lawrence Moore trying to sue me for dereliction of duty."

Anne paced the hospital corridor with long strides as she waited for the technician to finish Sam's CAT scan. On admittance to the emergency room, Sam had sat silently and let Anne explain her symptoms to the nurse. Anne had been honest and described Sam's confusion, her blackout, but she'd left out any references to Blanche. She stopped her pacing and took a slug of the bitter coffee from the Styrofoam cup she carried in her hand. She grimaced at the acidic taste. What was taking so long? She resumed her lonely walk. She'd called Lawrence Moore, but he hadn't picked up. Unwilling to give too many details in a voice mail, she tried to sound reassuring while she explained that Sam had been taken to the hospital for tests. He hadn't called back.

She drank the last of her coffee and tossed the cup in a wastepaper basket. Walking over to the window, she stared out at the parking lot. The image of Sam battered her heart. She'd seemed so small, so defenseless, as Anne had checked her in. Anne knew her actions had damaged the trust between them, but she'd had no choice. Hopefully the tests would show what had caused Sam's aberrant behavior, and the prognosis would be something simple like bed rest. Whatever the result, Anne would do all she could to help her.

"Anne?"

She whirled to see Dr. Douglas standing in the waiting room.

"Sorry it took so long. We had an emergency that took precedence." He lowered his eyes to the clipboard in his hand and scanned the report. "The tests came back normal," he said, lifting his eyes to meet hers.

"Normal?"

He nodded. "There was no evidence of swelling or bleeding, but I'd like to keep her in the hospital overnight for observation."

Puzzled, Anne cocked her head. "If everything looked normal, then what's causing the blackouts?"

"It could've been sleepwalking. Has she ever had a problem with that in the past?"

"Not that I'm aware of."

"Has she been anxious? Had any additional stress?"

"She broke off her engagement to Dr. Van Horn."

"How has she been handling that?"

"She seemed sad that it hadn't worked out, but also relieved. The past few days, she's been making plans for her future and her attitude appeared optimistic."

"Overly?"

"What do you mean?"

"Has she been manic?"

"Are you wondering if she's bipolar?"

"The blackouts concern me. Based on the CAT scan, there doesn't appear to be a physiological reason for them." He made a few notes on the clipboard. "I'd like to run a few more tests to see if there's anything we might be missing." He shoved his pen in his pocket. "I'd also like Dr. Crane to do an evaluation."

"A psychiatrist?"

"Yes, and we'll need her medical records."

"Sam can give you the names of the physicians who treated her after her attack."

Dr. Douglas frowned slightly. "Something else you should know. Samantha refused to list her parents on her release-of-information form. Evidently she doesn't want her father involved in her care." He paused, waiting for Anne to explain. When she didn't, he continued: "You're the only one she named."

Anne looked down. Lawrence Moore wasn't going to like that. Hopefully, the doctors would be the ones explaining it to him, and not her.

"May I see her now?"

Dr. Douglas nodded. "She should be in her room." He pointed down the hall. "They can tell you her room number at the nurses' station."

After stopping by the nurses' station, Anne rode the elevator up to Sam's floor and found her room. The door was partially closed, and she peeked in.

Sam was reclining in the bed with her face toward the window. She turned as Anne swung the door open. When she saw her, her face flushed with anger. "You promised you wouldn't let them keep me," she spit out.

"No," Anne said firmly as she entered the room and crossed to Sam's bed. "I said we'd follow the doctor's orders."

Sam snorted and faced away from her.

"You're only in for observation and a few tests. Dr. Douglas is planning on releasing you tomorrow." Placing a hand on Sam's shoulder, she drew Sam's attention to her. "Did he go over the CAT scan with you?"

"Yes." Her lips curled. "They said my brain is 'normal,' whatever that is."

"Did he tell you that he wants you to talk to someone?"

"Someone?" she barked. "Another shrink, you mean."

"Sam, Dr. Douglas just wants to help you."

"That's what they all say."

"But," Anne argued, "Dr. Douglas is good. I'd trust him if I—"

"Samantha," a voice cried from the doorway. Anne's head jerked toward the sound. With her heart sinking, she saw Lawrence Moore silhouetted in the doorway, with Jackson Van Horn hovering right behind him. She rolled her eyes as Jackson pushed past Mr. Moore and rushed to stand next to Anne at Sam's bedside.

Sam's reaction was to scoot to the far side. "What are you doing here?"

Before he answered, Lawrence Moore broke in, addressing Anne. "Step outside with me. I want to speak with you," he commanded.

Anne didn't budge.

"Now," he said.

She looked down at Sam and saw a silent plea in her eyes. "I'm not leaving Sam."

"I'm warning you, Ms. Weaver. Don't make me call security."

"It's okay, Anne, go," Sam said, her eyes shifting from Anne to Dr. Van Horn.

Once they were out in the hallway, Anne pulled the door shut and spun on Lawrence Moore. "You're not my employer and I don't take orders from you," she hissed, firing the first salvo.

His response was to arch an eyebrow. "I'm not going to engage in a scene with you, Ms. Weaver." He pulled out a leather-covered checkbook. "How much do we owe you for services rendered?" He named a figure that made Anne's eyes bulge.

"You're trying to pay me off," she spit out.

"No," he said, tapping the checkbook. "I'm simply paying you your wages plus a bonus." He frowned. "I doubt that you deserve the latter—my daughter *was* injured twice while in your keeping—but Samantha seems rather attached to you."

"Sam doesn't need a keeper."

His lips curled in a sneer. "You've been acquainted with my daughter for barely a month. I've known her for thirty-five years. I believe I'm in a better position to—"

Anne cut him off. "I don't think you know your daughter at all. If you did, you'd know how strong she is."

"Really? Then what is she doing in the hospital, and why does her doctor suspect an underlying mental illness?" Noticing the surprise on Anne's face, he smirked. "We spoke with Dr. Douglas."

Confused, Anne shook her head. "But he told me Sam wouldn't include you on her release of information."

"She didn't include me, but we had proof that Jackson is one of her treating physicians."

Anne glared at him and crossed her arms over her chest. "Yeah, about that—what's a plastic surgeon doing prescribing anti-anxiety medications for his fiancée? How ethical is that?"

He smacked the checkbook in his open palm. "It's none of your concern. If my offer isn't enough, how much do you want?"

Anne stood tall and locked her gaze on him. "Nothing, Mr. Moore. I want nothing from you."

Spinning on her heel, she marched off down the hall.

# Twenty-seven

*Take a deep breath*, I tell myself. Her anger is still niggling at me. How dare she treat me that way? She is nothing—less than nothing. Hadn't I been kind and sweet to her? Hadn't it been enough? No, with women, it is never enough. I've tried to please my entire life, but it has never been enough for them. Passed over and ignored—that has been my fate.

The injustice stuns me.

If only I could punish them all. The desire to hurt something, anything, threatens to overwhelm me, but I regain control. That's what it's all about isn't? Control. Maintain my control. Maintain the facade. I smile to myself. If they only knew who they were dealing with. If I allowed the mask to slip, they'd be trembling with fear. I'm delighted at the thought. To stand tall, to stand like a man, to be recognized for who I truly am. I brace my shoulders in response only to sag as the next thought courses through my brain.

They always stop me. Knock me down and step on me. My anger surges at their unfairness and I'm forced to battle my rage again. I know what might happen if I loosen the leash that holds it at bay. I'm still paying for the only time it slipped from my control.

I carry on a dialogue with myself while the world goes on around me; no one suspects what's really going on inside my head. On the outside, I appear as I always have. Concerned, only wanting what's best for those I care about. Care? Ha, when has anyone ever cared about me?

You must quiet your emotions. Think. You were rejected, true, but there are ways to turn the situation to your advantage. Isn't the true measure of a man the ability to take a disadvantage and turn it into an advantage?

And who is she to stand against me? *Pour on the charm*, I tell myself; you know her weakness, use it. Manipulate her and her father. Make yourself indispensable. Do whatever it takes to achieve your goals.

# Twenty-eight

Sam felt like a trapped animal. Jackson and her father stared down at her with identical expressions. Benevolent and condescending—like she was some five-year-old in need of their wisdom. This couldn't be happening to her. She rolled on her side away from them. Her father appeared in her line of vision. With a sigh, she moved onto her back and flicked on the TV. When her father reached down and killed the power, she continued to stare at the blank screen.

"Samantha, we need to talk," he said.

"No, we don't," she replied, her attention never leaving the black screen.

He reached down and turned her chin until she faced him. "Yes, we do. You're in the hospital again."

She jerked her chin out of his fingers. "I know I'm in the hospital. I had a minor accident and I'll be released tomorrow."

Her father gripped the side of the bed. "I don't think so. These doctors are fine for cuts and bruises, but you need specialists to handle your condition. You can't find them in a rural area like this."

"What condition, Dad?"

"Your blackouts." His eyes left hers and went to Jackson, standing across from him. "We've found a residential facility up by Duluth that can help you both physically and mentally."

"Duluth? Are you sure that's far enough away from the Cities? Why not Canada?" she shot off sarcastically. "I'm sure no one's ever heard of Lawrence Moore in Canada. A damaged daughter wouldn't affect your reputation up there."

"That's enough," he insisted. "The decision has been made."

Tears threatened while her panic rose. Taking a deep breath, she shoved it down. Any sign of weakness would be fatal. "No."

"Yes," he insisted.

"I'm an adult—you can't force me."

Again, her father looked at Jackson. Her body stiffened. What did they have planned?

She didn't have to wait long for the answer.

"We've petitioned for a competency hearing."

"No," she gasped, "you can't do this to me. I am not crazy!"

Her father took her hand in his. "Of course you're not. You're simply going through a rough patch and need a little extra help in dealing with it."

"Rough patch? Then why do you want to lock me up?" The tears began to run down her cheeks and she angrily swiped them away.

"Princess, I'm worried," he said, squeezing her hand. "I want my perfect baby girl back, and everything else we've tried has failed."

She pulled her hand away. "No, it hasn't," she argued. "I was doing pretty good until this afternoon."

"Jackson disagrees."

She shot Jackson a withering look and he retreated back a step. "I don't care what Jackson thinks. We're through."

"Darling, I know you're angry over what happened with that silly dog, but you don't mean that."

"Don't tell me what I mean," she exclaimed. "You can drug me, you can badger me, from now until hell freezes over, but it won't make a difference." She clutched the bedcovers tightly in her hands. "I want you out of my life, and I'd appreciate it if you'd . . ." She took a deep breath. "Get. Out. Of. My. Room."

Jackson's attention flew to her father, who gave a slight nod. Without a word, Jackson turned and left.

Her father waited until the door shut softly. "Princess—"

"Don't call me 'Princess,'" she spit.

"Fine, if you object." He leaned in closer and said in a conspiratorial tone, "I'm beginning to understand why Jackson lost your affection, but we'll deal with that later. Right now we need to get you well."

Sam lowered her eyes and tried to think, but it was hard with her father hovering over her. She didn't doubt that her father would make good on his threat of a competency hearing, and right now she wasn't so sure that he wouldn't be able to persuade a judge he was right. She knew how persuasive her father could be. No, she had to come up with a plan. If not, by this time tomorrow she'd find herself bundled up and on her way to lockup. She glanced up and saw her father staring at her with an all-knowing look in his eyes. She had to get him out of her room so she could think.

Faking a yawn, she stretched her arms over her head. "I'm so tired," she said, forcing her voice to slur while she let her arms fall. Through slitted eyes, she saw a look of victory flash on her father's face.

"I understand. Get some sleep, Prin—er, Samantha," he said, stroking her hair. "We'll talk after you're rested."

Sam remained motionless until she was sure her father had left the room. Sneaking out of bed, she crept over to the door and placed her ear against it. She heard her father's low voice talking with Jackson.

"She can be held for seventy-two hours?" her father asked.

"That's right, and during that time a judge will hold the hearing."

"I don't know." Sam heard the hesitancy in her father's voice. "I think it would be better if she went willingly."

"But she won't," Jackson insisted. "You can't allow this to continue, Lawrence. That Weaver woman has too much influence over her. I've done a little research and Anne Weaver is in serious financial trouble. She's not about to let the golden goose slip through her fingers. She wants to milk Sam for whatever she can, and she'll persuade Sam to fight you."

"I thought you vetted this woman," her father said with a hint of anger in his voice.

"I did. She came highly recommended."

"Humph. If she thinks she can manipulate my daughter, she's sadly mistaken. I'll make sure she never works again."

Their voices became fainter, and Sam assumed they were leaving. Leaning against the door, she thought of the unintended irony of her dad's last remark. He wouldn't let Anne try to manipulate her, but he didn't have qualms about allowing Jackson . . . or himself . . . to give it a shot. Her lips tightened with determination. He was wrong on all counts. *She* wouldn't allow herself to be manipulated.

With legs trembling, she crossed to the closet and pulled out her clothes. Thank God they hadn't taken her shoes. Dressing, she plotted what she'd do. She couldn't go back to the cabin in case her father and Jackson had taken up residence there. And

Anne's? She frowned as she pulled her shirt over her head. Her father already had Anne in his gun sight; going there would only cause her more trouble. No, it had to be somewhere they'd least expect.

She stole over to the door and carefully opened it. Peeking out, she saw the nurses gathered at their station down the hall. She directed her attention in the opposite direction and was relieved to see a bright red exit sign at the other end.

Ducking her head down, she shoved her hands in her pockets and stepped out into the hallway.

*Calm, even steps,* she cautioned herself. *Don't draw anyone's attention.*

Without a backward glance, she walked slowly toward the exit sign and freedom.

Sam stayed in the early-morning shadows as she crept to the door. She'd hitched a ride with a trucker not far from the hospital, and the driver had dropped her off at Dunlap's. She hesitated for a moment before exiting the cab. The parking lot was full of cars. Probably not enough time for a search party to gather to hunt her down, right? Steeling herself and keeping her back toward the station, she scurried for the cover of a copse of nearby pines. By the time she'd hiked that last mile to her destination, the muscles in her left leg were trembling from exertion. She doubted that she could walk another step.

"Please, please be here," she prayed as she lifted her hand to knock. Greg had claimed to be her friend. Crossing two fingers on her other hand, she hoped he'd meant it.

Her light rap set off a barrage of wild barking from inside, followed by the stern command "Silence." The barking ceased.

The door opened and she looked up into Greg's puzzled face.

Stepping back, he motioned her inside. "Hey, Sam, told you that I'd bring Roxy back this morning."

"I know, but I need to talk to you," Sam replied with a nervous glance over her shoulder.

As she stepped inside, Roxy greeted her and Sam paused to crouch and rest her chin on the dog's head. Then she rose and followed Greg into the living room. Gratefully, she sank down onto the couch.

Instead of joining her, Greg eyed her. "Rough night?"

"You might say that."

"Like some coffee?"

"Love it." She sighed.

He left the room and returned a few moments later bearing a steaming cup.

Gratefully she accepted the cup and took a careful sip. As soon as the coffee hit her throat, the warmth spread through her body until it hit the cold spot that had lingered inside ever since she'd heard the words *residential facility*. It remained like a chunk of ice that refused to melt.

"Everything okay?" Greg asked cautiously.

"Not really," she replied with a grimace, then hesitated. "I need your help." Quickly, she related everything that had happened at the hospital. A hard look crossed his face when he heard Jackson's opinion of Anne.

"She doesn't have a mercenary bone in her body."

"I know, but I can't ask her for help. Dad's already mad, and she doesn't have the means to go up against him. To involve her further would only bring her more trouble."

Greg shook his head slowly. "I'd like to help you, but I don't know what I can do."

"I'm not crazy, Greg."

"I believe you, but—"

"I don't understand what's happening to me—the dreams, the blackouts—but if I could know for sure that it's Blanche, it might help."

He sat next to her and pulled his fingers through his hair. "I was just a kid when Blanche lived up here and I don't remember much about her. I know my mom didn't like her, and I overheard a few conversations between her and my dad about her doings."

"What did she say?"

"She didn't approve of the way Blanche was carrying on with Ted Brighton."

"Did she ever mention Edward Dunlap and Blanche being an item?"

He rubbed his chin. "No." He paused. "But Mom didn't like Esther either, and I vaguely remember her saying something about how Esther resented the way Edward followed Blanche around."

Sam shifted toward him. "So they were involved," she said, the excitement apparent in her voice.

"Sam," he cautioned, "an offhand remark made years ago doesn't prove anything. You know how gossip flies around here."

She sat back. "The old adage—'where there's smoke, there's fire.'"

"Only in some people's imaginations."

"Okay, so who was the man Blanche ran off with? We know it wasn't Ted Brighton or Edward Dunlap."

"No idea." Greg leaned back against the couch and propped his long legs on the coffee table.

"No one ever heard from her again?"

"No."

"What about Harley?"

"No—he sold out and moved shortly after Blanche left."

"What about friends? Did she have any friends?"

He arched an eyebrow. "You mean other than her boyfriends?"

Sam nodded.

"I remember her hanging out over at Fritz's."

"Really." She leaned forward in surprise. "I didn't think he liked her."

"That's probably true. Since I became an adult and heard the stories about her, I've wondered if Fritz didn't hang out with her solely because of the trouble she caused. He likes seeing people squirm, especially Ted Brighton. He hated old Ted when he was alive—*that* I remember very well."

"Do you know why?"

"Fritz was involved in some kind of scandal at the college where he taught, and he was forced to leave."

"What does that have to do with the Brightons?"

"Ted was on the alumni board, and since they'd grown up together here on the lake, Fritz expected him to help save his job. Ted refused, according to gossip." Greg shook his head. "You're asking me to remember things I haven't thought about in years." He turned toward her. "And, Sam, I don't know how any of this old gossip will help you and I don't have any clue about how accurate it is."

Sam bent and stroked Roxy's ears. "You're right," she said, discouraged. "I should be thinking of ways to outfox my father and Jackson." She sighed and sat back, leaning her head against the couch. "I'm so tired right now that I can't think straight."

Greg turned toward her and leaned closer. "Don't worry, Sam. You'll figure a way out of this."

She lifted her head, surprised at his confidence in her. Her eyes widened. It had been so long since anyone had thought her capable, and here was Greg, telling her that she could succeed. The coldness inside of her shrank as she stared into his brown eyes, warm with concern for her. His strength, his raw masculinity, seemed to reach out and wrap around her. Unconsciously, she inched toward him.

He met her halfway, and when his lips brushed hers, the last of the coldness disappeared. She snuggled closer, seeking more of the heat surrounding him. Her arms went around his neck as he whispered her name against her mouth then deepened the kiss. The warmth inside her built until she felt like every nerve in her body was glowing. A satisfied sigh escaped her lips.

Suddenly Greg drew back, ending the kiss. A puzzled look pinched his face.

"Wow," he said in a shaky voice while he ran his fingers through his hair. "I—I'm sorry, Sam. I don't know where that came from."

He was sorry? She wasn't. Sam felt the blood rushing to her face. "Me either."

"You've got enough problems without me—" A brittle laugh cut off his words while he put distance between them. "Um, let's say that wasn't very 'gentlemanly' of me, but honest, I wasn't trying to take advantage of you."

She rested a hand lightly on his thigh. "It's okay, Greg," she said gently. "We're friends, right?"

He nodded.

"So what's a little kiss between friends?"

"Uh-huh . . . a little kiss," he muttered.

Lifting her hand, she plopped it back in her lap. "If only I could prove at least to myself that Blanche has been haunting my dreams," she said quickly, trying to steer the conversation back to a safer topic.

Greg suddenly snapped his fingers and sprang to his feet.

"Wait a second—I'll be right back." He left the room, and soon Sam heard him opening and shutting drawers, then the sound of rustling papers. He returned a few minutes later with his arms full of what looked like photo albums. He dumped them on the couch next to her and smiled.

"There—take a look at those," he said, pointing to the pile. "Maybe there's a photo of Blanche in one of them. If there is, you can compare it to your sketch."

"Good idea," she said as she eyed them, "but I don't have the sketch. I left it at the cabin and I don't dare go back in case Jackson and my father are there."

"Not a problem. Remember you gave it to me last night?" He crossed to the bookcase and came back holding her sketch. "I brought it home with me."

Sam opened the first album and began to thumb through the pages, examining each faded photo one by one. She saw a teenage Greg, recognizable by the cocky smile, dressed in cutoffs and mugging for the camera. She saw a younger Fritz, much the way he had appeared to her in her dream, sprawled in a lawn chair and toasting the photographer with a bottle of beer.

But the woman from her dream was missing.

Not willing to give up, she picked up another album and browsed through it. One picture caught her attention.

She held it out to Greg. "Is this Irene Brighton?"

"Yeah, I think so," he said, after studying the picture of a woman with a haughty look about her.

"Is that Ted Brighton standing next to her?"

"Probably, but with his face in the shadows, I really can't tell. Why?"

"In the first dream, the woman was flirting with a man. This might be the same man."

"Let's see," he said, digging through the albums. "Mom and Dad threw a Labor Day party every year and Mom kept all the photos in the same album." He held one up triumphantly. "Here it is." Laying it on his lap, he opened it and began scanning the pages. Finally he stopped and tapped one of the pictures. "This is old Ted."

Sam pulled the album over onto her lap and stared at the picture. "That's him," she said, not hiding her excitement. "Now, if we can only find one of Blanche."

Greg grabbed the album back and flipped the pages. The room was silent except for the sound of the turning pages. He stopped and let out a low whistle. "Dad must've taken this one," he murmured. "I'm surprised Mom didn't burn it." He shoved the album onto Sam's lap. "That's Blanche."

Sam looked at the picture. It showed a woman standing at the end of a dock, and if Sam wasn't mistaken, it was the dock at her cabin. The woman was wearing a purple bikini that revealed her voluptuous curves. Both her arms were lifted as she held a mass of red curls on top of her head. The photographer had been standing at the top of the hill, so her features weren't sharp, but even at that distance, Sam saw the half smile lighting the woman's face.

"What do you think? Is this the same woman?"

Sam let her breath out slowly before answering. "To be honest—it's hard to say. The bone structure looks similar, but I can't say for certain."

"Let's take it out of the album," he said as he peeled back the yellowed plastic and held it up. "Still can't tell?"

She shook her head.

"I've got a magnifying glass in the desk. Wait and I'll get it."

When he returned, he handed it to Sam, along with her sketch. She held the glass over the photo then studied her drawing. Her excitement rose. She gave them to Greg. "Tell me what you think—and be honest. Don't just say what you think I want to hear," she cautioned.

He was quiet while he carefully looked at the picture and her sketch. His face grew serious and he placed both images faceup on the coffee table.

Sam's emotions dipped and she sank back against the couch. "You don't think it's the same woman, do you?"

He turned to her, his face still somber. "No, as a matter of fact, I do." Placing his arm across the back of the couch, he rubbed his chin. "But this brings up another question."

"What question?"

"How is it that you're dreaming of a woman you've never met?" He hesitated. "And why?"

# Twenty-nine

"Mom, what are you doing home?" Caleb asked as he meandered into the kitchen. "I thought you were spending the night at Ms. Moore's."

Anne's lips turned downward. "No, Sam had to be hospitalized."

"Is she okay?" he asked, grabbing a box of cereal and a carton of milk.

"Yeah, they wanted to keep her for observation." She leaned against the counter and watched her son eat his breakfast while her mind flashed back to her insulting conversation with Lawrence Moore. She wanted to help Sam, but she knew Mr. Moore wouldn't let her near his daughter now. Maybe later she'd talk to Greg . . . Suddenly a mad idea popped into her head. Maybe together, she and Greg could spring Sam, just like an old-fashioned jailbreak. Immediately she shook her head at the silly notion. She'd worked at that hospital and hoped to do so again. Attempting anything as foolish as sneaking a patient out would ruin her career . . . and she expected Lawrence Moore already had plans to ruin it without her assistance. She needed to protect herself.

She had Caleb's future to consider. She'd have to come up with another way to help Sam.

Caleb and his future . . . now was as good a time as any to tell him that without the income from her job at Samantha's, St. Michael's was a pipe dream.

"Hey," she began, as a preface before dropping the bomb about St. Michael's, "I'm proud of you for telling Duane the truth."

Caleb lifted one shoulder. "You were right. Why should I take the heat for Teddy Brighton?"

Coming up behind him, she wrapped her arms around his shoulders and propped her chin on the top of his head. "You know I love you, right?"

"Yeah," he mumbled with a mouth full of cereal.

"And there's nothing I wouldn't do for you?"

He nodded, making her head bounce.

Letting go, she moved around him and took a seat at the table. "So here's the way it is. I'm not going to be working for Samantha anymore. I do have a job lined up at the care facility in Hankton, but it's for a lot less money." Tracing a finger across the table, she couldn't look at him while she delivered the blow. "I'm afraid St. Michael's is going to be out of the question. We can't afford it."

She stole a look and was surprised at his reaction. He was reading the back of the cereal box. "Aren't you upset?"

He shrugged carelessly. "Nah."

"But I thought you wanted to go to St. Michael's? They have one of the best prelaw—"

"I'm not going into prelaw, Mom," he said, laying the cereal box to the side. "I wanted to go to St. Michael's because of their music department." Catching the look on her face, he held up his hand. "You're right about needing a college education, but why can't it be in something I love? I love music, Mom."

Anne shot to her feet, knocking her chair over. "If you think I'm going to waste all the money I've saved over the years so you can chase after some crazy—"

"It's not crazy. People with a degree in music earn a living."

"At what? Teaching?"

"What's wrong with that?"

"Nothing, but I wanted more for you."

Red-faced, Caleb rose. "What about what I want for myself?" He began to pace the kitchen. "I don't want to be crammed in some stuffy office, writing wills, handling divorce cases. I want music in my life."

"It can be a hobby," she insisted.

He whirled on her. "You don't get it, do you? I'm not a kid anymore and you can't tell me how to live my life."

Anne glared at him. "Oh yes I can, Caleb Weaver. As long as you're under my roof, *I*," she said, stabbing a finger at her chest, "make the rules."

"I won't be under your roof if I'm away at college," he argued back.

"But I'll be paying for the roof you *are* under."

"If it means getting to make my own choices then I'll pay for college myself," he spit at her.

She crossed her arms and tried to stare him down. "How?"

"Scholarships, part-time jobs, loans. It may take me longer to finish, but I can do it." He spun on his heel and stomped toward the door. Reaching it, he stopped. "In fact, Mom, why don't I start supporting myself right now. I'm eighteen. I'll move out. You won't have to worry about paying for a damn thing!" He yanked the door open, then slammed it behind him, leaving Anne standing alone in the kitchen.

She righted the chair and sat down hard. Dazed, she couldn't believe Caleb's reaction. He'd never talked to her like that. Oh, sure, he argued, but she'd never seen him so vehement about a subject. He'd grouse and grumble, but in the end, he did what she thought best. *Thought best?* Anne groaned. Those were the exact words she'd heard Lawrence Moore say to Sam. No, she didn't treat Caleb the same way Sam's family treated her. She respected his opinion.

*As long as his opinion agrees with yours,* said a little voice inside her head.

Suddenly weary, Anne laid her head on the table and began to cry. She hadn't meant to bully her son. She'd only wanted to see him have a better life than hers had been. Deep sobs shook her shoulders while guilt racked her heart. How could she have been so stupid, so blind? Hadn't both Greg and Fritz tried to talk to her? Caleb was a good kid, a smart kid. She should've trusted him to know what would make him happy. Now he was going to move out, go off on his own. He'd never be able to earn enough to meet his expenses while going to school. He might talk himself into dropping out. After working all these years to make sure he had a shot at a good life, she'd lost him.

Raising her head, she picked up a napkin and blew her nose. Sitting here blubbering and having a pity party wouldn't solve anything. When Caleb calmed down, they'd talk. And for once, she'd listen. She blew out a shaky breath and rose to her feet. She needed to keep busy until she could talk to him again, but she was at a loss about what to do with herself. Her eyes roamed the kitchen, searching for something to do.

*Guess I'm unemployed.* The thought felt strange to her. She'd gone to work every day she possibly could, seldom, if ever, taking any time off. She'd dreamed of having a day all to herself, and now that she had one, she didn't know what to do with it. Shoving her hands in her pockets, she jumped when the phone suddenly rang.

*Caleb, calling to apologize.* She ran to pick it up. She wouldn't let him—she'd tell him how sorry she was before he had a chance.

"Caleb," she cried with the phone to her ear. "I'm sor—"

"It's not Caleb, Anne. It's Fritz." His voice sounded tight, strained. "Have you heard anything about Edward? I know you're friends and I was hoping you had news."

"News? What news?" Anne's grip on the phone tightened. "Has something happened to Edward?"

"You don't know?"

"No," she exclaimed.

"Edward had an accident last night. His car . . . he wrapped it around a tree."

"Oh no." Anne gasped.

"They took him to the hospital in Pardo, then by air ambulance to the Cities, but that's all I know."

Anne remembered Dr. Douglas mentioning an emergency delaying Sam's CAT scan. Had Edward been the subject of that emergency?

"I've tried calling Dunlap's but the line is busy."

"I'll run down there right now and see if I can find out."

"Will you keep me in the loop?"

"Yes." Anne slammed the receiver down and, grabbing her bag, rushed out the door.

When she whipped into the parking lot at Dunlap's, she saw all the cars. Surely someone inside could tell her about Edward's condition. Jumping out of her car, she ran up the steps and opened the door. She skidded to a halt. Instead of being at the hospital with her son, Esther was sitting on her stool behind the counter as if she were holding court. A couple of local women, friends of Esther's, stood next to her making comforting sounds while Esther whimpered into a handkerchief.

All eyes turned to Anne, standing in the doorway. An uncomfortable silence settled on the room. Ignoring it, Anne crossed to the counter.

"Esther," she began, "I'm so sorry to hear about Edward. How is he?"

"He'll live," Esther barked in a tear-roughened voice. "No thanks to that woman you're working for."

Stunned, Anne took a step back. "What does Samantha Moore have to do with Edward's car accident?"

"It's her fault," Esther sniffed as she wiped her face. "Living in that cabin, asking him questions about *her*, bringing back memories best left buried."

"Now, Esther," said one of her friends as she rubbed the woman's shoulders, "don't get yourself all riled up again."

Anne lifted her hands in a silent question as she looked at Esther's friends.

One of them shifted back and forth nervously. "He done it on purpose," she said in a hushed voice, as if she could keep Esther, sitting next to her, from hearing.

"That's right," Esther said, sliding off her stool and shaking a plump finger at Anne. "He tried to kill himself." She took a deep breath. "I saw the way she acted at the party. Just like that woman did. Cut out of the same cloth, those two are. Singing the same song she always sang, flirting with men she had no business making up to, just like she did." She folded her arms over her ample breasts. "He's been stirred up ever since."

"Esther, really," Anne began in a calm voice, but Esther cut her off.

"I tell you, that cabin's cursed. I wish it would've burned down years ago," she yelled at Anne.

Anne started backing out of the store. Esther was hysterical and not making any sense. But she'd learned what she needed to know—Edward was going to live—she'd have to rely on the grapevine for any information about his condition.

She pulled out of the parking lot. It was all too much. Sam, Lawrence Moore, Caleb, Esther's ranting. If she went home, all she'd do would be to pace like a wild thing. She needed to talk. Shooting a look at the dashboard clock, she decided to stop at Greg's. It wouldn't be easy admitting that he'd been right about the way she'd been dealing with Caleb, but Greg would help her come up with a way to make peace with him. What's eating a little crow if it led to reconciling with her son? And Sam—Greg would want to know what had happened with her.

It wasn't until she stopped her car in front of his cabin that something Esther had said finally sank in.

Edward had mentioned the same thing that day in the parking lot, but it hadn't registered. Sam had sung Blanche's favorite song at Fritz's party.

# Thirty

A wet nose touching her cheek startled Sam out of a sound sleep. She opened her eyes to see Roxy's face inches from hers. With a smile, she stretched and patted the dog's head. She sat up and glanced at the clock. Eleven A.M. At least she'd had some sleep. Once they'd discovered Blanche's picture, Greg had insisted that they forget about it for a while and get some rest. Sam had curled up on the couch and gone to sleep immediately. Now it all came rushing back. Her father, his threat of a competency hearing, the weird dreams, Blanche—she'd thought that confirming the identity of the woman in her dreams as Blanche would solve everything, but it hadn't. As Greg pointed out, it only raised more questions.

She picked up her sketch and stared at it. *What really happened to you, Blanche? Did you run off?* Blanche's smile seemed to mock her.

Placing the sketch on the coffee table next to Blanche's photo, Sam folded the blanket she'd used and thought about her father. Instead of worrying about a woman from the past, she had to create a plan to deal with him. She couldn't stop him from petitioning the courts, but she could plan a defense. She'd ask Greg to recommend an attorney.

Greg—the way he'd kissed her. He was right—she had more pressing problems to consider. A slow grin tugged at her lips. *But it had been very nice.*

The grin vanished when a sudden rap at the door set the dogs barking. Was it the sheriff looking for her? Alarmed, Sam thought about trying to hide, but before she could take any action, Greg walked into the living room.

He held up a hand. "It's okay. It's Anne," he said, opening the door.

"Hey," Anne said, smiling, until her attention drifted beyond Greg and she saw Sam standing in the living room. Her expression changed as her mouth formed an O. Recovering her composure, she brushed past him. "What happened? What are you doing here?"

"I guess you could say I've run away from home," Sam said in a wry voice.

Anne sat suddenly in one of the chairs. "Your dad—"

"Nope," Sam answered with a shake of her head. "He doesn't know I'm here, and I'd like to keep it that way until I have a chance to talk to a lawyer."

"Why didn't you come to my house?"

Sam sat on the coffee table facing her. "I heard what my father said to you, Anne, and I don't want him causing you more trouble."

Anne gave a snort. "I'm not afraid of Lawrence Moore."

Sam chuckled. "I'm sure you're not, but I don't want him making your life miserable."

"Oh, I think he already plans to do that," Anne replied sarcastically.

Sam gave Anne's knee a pat. "We won't let him."

Anne's eyes moved to the albums stacked behind Sam. "What are those?"

Sam glanced over her shoulder. "We were looking for a photo of Blanche."

"And?"

"And we found one," Greg said, striding over to the coffee table. "Take a look at this." He handed Anne both the sketch and Blanche's photo.

Anne studied them for a moment then shook her head. "I don't understand how this happened."

"Neither do we, but it proves Sam really was dreaming about Blanche."

"Do you think Blanche did cause Edward's—" Anne slapped her hand over her mouth. Dropping it quickly, she stared up at Greg. "Edward was in another car accident."

She told Greg and Sam about her call from Fritz and her visit to Dunlap's. "One last thing: Esther is blaming you, Sam."

Sam jerked. "Why? I barely know Edward."

"She said all the talk about Blanche upset him." She leaned forward. "Here's something else that I should've thought of before—the song you sang at Fritz's party?"

"The one I don't remember?"

"Yeah, that one." Anne frowned. "Edward mentioned it first, but I blew it off. Esther said that Blanche sang the same song at parties, too."

"You're kidding?"

"Nope."

Sam tugged on her bottom lip. "I remember Edward saying something about a song, but he was acting so strange and I was upset." She looked up at Greg. "What do you think?"

"I don't know," he said, combing his fingers through his hair. "Too many things have happened for it to be a coincidence." He studied Sam for a moment. “Before you moved into the cabin, had anything like this ever happened to you?”

Sam hesitated before answering. Right now Greg was on her side, but if she told him the truth, would he still believe her? If she told him about how tenuous her grasp on reality had been after waking up from the coma? She decided to take her chances and be honest.

After she finished telling her tale, Greg studied her carefully. “But what’s been happening to you now is different, right?”

Seeing that he understood, Sam sighed with relief. “Yes,” she declared. “The dreams that haunted me before were ones tied to the attack . . . Someone was watching me; intruders were in the house; I was being chased . . . I always played the starring role.” She looked off into space. “But in these dreams, I’m an observer.”

Greg sat on the couch and picked up the sketch. “Do you think there’s anything significant about your drawing of Blanche?”

“What do you mean?”

“I don’t know—I’m grasping at straws—but maybe there’s something about the way she’s dressed, the location, the flowers—”

Anne stuck out her hand. “Give me that,” she demanded. Taking the sketch, she looked it over for a second. “The flowers,” she said, tapping the picture. “They look like the ones blooming on the bush by the step.”

“I know that. I recognized them, too. It’s why I wandered outside.”

Anne’s eyebrows arched. “But do you know Blanche planted that bush?”

“Who told you that?” Sam asked with a frown.

“You—when you were rambling. You also said Alice gave her the seeds.”

"Alice? Alice at the Beauty Barn?"

"Must be." Anne slapped her thighs and rose to her feet. "I say we go have a chat with her. What do you think?"

Sam looked up at her. "To be honest—I don't see the point. What difference does it make who planted the bush? Or if it *was* Blanche, where she got the seeds?"

Greg leaned forward. "Sam, last night you said you wanted to prove that it was Blanche who was haunting your dreams. If Alice can confirm what you told Anne, it's one more piece of evidence."

"Evidence that I'm not crazy," Sam murmured with her eyes downcast.

Anne grasped Sam's arm and pulled her to her feet. "Come on, let's go."

Sam stared out the window while Anne parked the car in front of the beauty shop. Signs announcing specials decorated the windows, and beyond them, she saw a beautician working on a client. She didn't spot Alice's signature hairstyle.

"I don't think she's here," Sam told Anne warily.

"Do you want to wait in the car while I run in and check?"

"I don't know—I think my time would be better spent talking to an attorney."

"Why are you so reluctant to talk to Alice?"

She didn't know what to say. Part of her wanted to learn why she was having these dreams. Another part of her was afraid. What if the answers only confirmed that something was seriously wrong with her? What if her dad was right and she should be committed? She couldn't handle another stint of confinement in a hospital.

Without waiting for Sam's answer, Anne hopped out of the car and returned in a few moments. "You were right," she said, getting in the car. "Alice didn't come in today—she's at home." After starting the car, she pulled out into traffic. "It's not far. We'll be there in a minute."

True to her word, a short time later, Anne stopped in front of a small ranch-style house. Sam knew instantly that the house belonged to Alice—poodle lawn ornaments were scattered across the yard, and by the door, two Love Lies Bleeding bushes bloomed profusely.

Reluctantly, Sam got out of the car and followed Anne to the door. Alice answered the knock right away and, not masking her surprise, invited them in.

"What can I do for you ladies?" she asked, leading them to the back of the house.

"Um—well—" Sam stammered, not knowing how to begin.

Anne saved her. "We want to ask you some questions about Blanche Jones," she said bluntly.

*That's right, Anne,* Sam thought, *get directly to the point. Don't ease into it.*

Alice's eyes widened. "Blanche? She hasn't lived around here for years."

Anne tugged Sam forward. "You know she's staying in the old Jones cabin and we're curious. Someone mentioned you'd been friends."

"People don't like talking about Blanche," Alice mumbled.

"Why is that, Alice?" Anne asked.

"She could be . . ." Alice paused. "Well, difficult."

"But you two were friends?" Anne persisted.

"Yes." Alice's attention moved to the kitchen clock. "This isn't a good time. I don't want to rush you off, but I have an appointment." She crossed to the counter and began fussing with some papers that were stuck behind the telephone.

Sam stepped toward her. "We won't keep you, but I have to ask you a question. Did Blanche plant the bush growing at the cabin?"

"That old thing still alive?" Alice asked, obviously without thinking.

Sam nodded. "You gave her the seeds, didn't you?"

Alice shoved the papers into a drawer. "I really have to be going."

"I've one more question," Sam said, edging closer. "Was Blanche with Edward the night of his accident?"

Alice's hand flew to her throat. "How did you know?" Her head wobbled back and forth in confusion. "I've never said a word." Her eyes narrowed. "Did Edward tell you?"

"No."

"Then how—"

Sam cut her off. "Where's Blanche now, Alice?"

"How should I know? I haven't talked to her in years."

She was lying; Sam was sure of it. A terrible suspicion crept through her mind. The bloody corpse in her bed. She knew the truth. She knew why Blanche had been literally haunting her.

"Blanche never left the lake, did she, Alice?" she demanded.

Alice tried to dodge around her, but Sam blocked her.

"She's dead, isn't she?"

Anne gasped while Alice suddenly crumpled into a nearby chair. She covered her face, her shoulders beginning to shake. Kneeling in front of her, Sam placed her hands on Alice's legs.

"What happened, Alice?" she asked gently.

Alice's hands fell away from her face and she stared at Sam with her eyes full of tears. "She's not dead, but she might as well be."

Sam sat back on her heels in shock. She'd been so sure.

"He should've just taken a gun and shot her," Alice continued with passion. "It would've been a mercy."

Standing, Sam looked down at her. "I don't understand—"

Alice surged to her feet. "No? I thought you had all the answers."

"Calm down, Alice," Anne said, rushing over and taking her by the arm. She guided her back to the chair. "Now tell us what happened."

All the breath seemed to leave Alice's body as she dropped to the chair. Lifting her eyes, she looked first at Anne then at Sam. Turning her attention to the window, she stared blindly at the poodles cavorting in the backyard. "My first Pumpkin was her dog, you know," she said, her voice trembling. "Pumpkin was the one who found her."

"Found Blanche?" Sam prodded.

Alice bobbed her head and sighed. "I suppose it won't make a difference now . . . he's dead and they say she soon will be."

Sam felt as if she'd fallen down the rabbit hole.

"Alice—"

"Sit down, sit down," she said. "I can't keep staring up at you."

Sam and Anne both pulled up a chair and quickly sat.

Watching her two visitors, Alice took a deep breath. "Blanche isn't dead. She's in the care facility over in Hankton."

"It was you I saw in the parking lot, wasn't it?" Anne exclaimed.

"I was afraid you had recognized me. I visit there once a week and have for the last twenty-five years."

"Did Blanche have some sort of a breakdown?" Sam asked.

"No." Alice's face tightened with anger. "Ted Brighton beat her half to death."

"What!" Sam and Anne cried simultaneously.

"Think he was too respectable to lift a hand to a woman?" Alice didn't hide the bitterness in her voice. "Well, he wasn't. Not when Blanche threatened to ruin him if he didn't divorce Irene and marry her."

Anne shot a glance at Sam. "How was Blanche going to do that?"

"Blanche knew about some of his double-dealings and said she would expose him if he didn't give her what she wanted." Alice shook her head sadly. "I told her to be careful, but she wouldn't listen."

"So he tried to kill her?"

"He went to his grave thinking he had. Beat her bloody then stuffed her in a cave where no one would find her." Alice bit her lip. "I was supposed to meet her, to help her sneak away from Harley, but when she didn't show up, I went out looking for her. That's when I heard the racket Pumpkin was making," she recounted in a flat voice. She shuddered and raised her gaze to the ceiling. "Lordy, I'd never seen anyone so bad off. I don't know how I ever got her down that hill and to the hospital in Hankton."

"Why didn't you go to the sheriff?"

"I couldn't. Blanche was barely conscious when I found her, but she was afraid. All the way to the hospital, she kept begging me to hide her. And in the end, it would've been my word against his. Who'd have believed me over Theodore Brighton?"

"Blanche could've testified against him."

"Weren't you listening? I told you he beat her bloody, so bloody her brain was damaged. Then she had a stroke while she was still in the hospital." Her eyes filled with tears again. "Blanche hasn't been in her right mind for the last twenty-five years and now she's finally going to die." She swallowed hard. "She's been in a coma for the last month and the doctors say it won't be much longer now."

"Are you sure you don't want me to go with you?" Anne asked Sam as they sat in the parking lot of the care facility.

"I'm sure," Sam replied, nervously picking at her seat belt.

“This probably won’t accomplish anything, but I want to see the woman who’s been haunting me face-to-face.” She turned toward Anne, unhooking the seat belt. “Isn’t it ironic that after what I’ve been through, I’m visiting another coma patient?”

Anne made a move to open her door. “I’m going with you.”

Sam stopped her. “No, this is something I need to do by myself.”

Reluctantly, Sam climbed out of the car and walked into the care facility. Alice had given them Blanche’s assumed name—Cassandra Collins—and her room number. Alice didn’t explain how she’d managed to establish a fake identity for Blanche and Sam and Anne didn’t ask. In the end, it didn’t matter. What mattered to Sam was that her dreams were validated. And she knew that seeing Blanche in the flesh would do just that.

With a smile and a nod to the aide behind the desk, Sam headed down the long hallway toward Blanche’s room. The smell of disinfectant tickled her nose, while her heartbeat kicked up a notch. Would there be a shadow of the woman Sam had drawn in the sketch left in the Blanche of today? Or would she find a battered husk? With sweaty palms, Sam grabbed the door handle to Blanche’s room and pushed. The door swung wide and she stepped inside.

The blinds had been lowered against the afternoon sun, making the room dim, but Sam could see a still form lying in the center of the bed. She slowly crossed to it and looked down.

The sheets were pulled up to Blanche’s chin, but Sam saw the slow rise and fall of her chest. Her hands lay at her side. Next to the bed sat a nightstand, and on it was a bouquet of Love Lies Bleeding. Alice’s offering to her dying friend.

Finally, Sam allowed her eyes to travel to the woman’s face. She gripped the bed railing and leaned in close. Yes, she could see a bit of Blanche in the woman's face, but not much. The vibrancy, the sexuality that had been so much a part of Blanche, was gone. Her red hair had even lost its shimmer. Shot with gray, it hung in straggles around her face, a face that sagged on one side, twisting her mouth downward.

A sense of sadness filled Sam. This woman had been so beautiful, but her beauty hadn't brought her joy. It had been a tool in her hands. Something she used to achieve her goals. From all accounts, Blanche hadn't been stupid. Why hadn't she used her brains instead of her beauty? She could've gotten what she wanted on her own instead of looking to someone else to provide it for her. Sam gripped the railing tighter and sank into a chair, still holding on to the railing. *So tired*, she thought, resting her head between her hands.

Suddenly she felt a clawlike hand shoot out and grab her wrist. Two green eyes, gleaming with malevolence, stared over at her from the face lying on the pillow. No, this had to be a hallucination, she thought as she tried to pull away from the hand holding her.

The fingers tightened, and Sam swore she felt a foreign energy slither up her arm. Her eyes clamped shut while images flitted through her mind.

Kneeling on a dock in the dark . . . the rough boards cutting into her knees . . . a woman begging for mercy . . . a man's angry voice, somehow familiar, screaming obscenities into the night . . . shattering pain as blows rained down on her . . . darkness followed by a damp coldness settling into her bones . . . finally . . . nothing. A big well of nothingness.

She felt herself sinking deeper into the hole. As a sense of panic overwhelmed her, she knew that if she didn't fight back, it was a place from which there'd be no return. Sam struggled to open her eyes, to tear her wrist away from the grip that had turned vise-like. Her energy was fading and she felt her hands loosen on the railing. She was sliding forward, sliding into oblivion.

Her eyes flew open when her knees hit the hard tile floor. Taking a deep breath, she focused on regulating her breathing. *My God, what a dream!* She knelt on the floor for a minute, shaking. Finally, she gripped the railing again and slowly pulled herself to her feet. To her dazed eyes, the room hadn't changed. She was still in Blanche's room. Then her focus settled on the bouquet of Love Lies Bleeding.

The once-vibrant crimson flowers now appeared faded, while the green leaves draped lifelessly over the side of the vase. In the space of minutes, the whole arrangement seemed to have wilted.

Her eyes flew to what had once been Blanche, lying in the bed.

She hadn't moved. The covers were still up to her chin and her hands were neatly at her sides. But the chest was no longer rising and falling.

Hesitating, Sam finally allowed her gaze to travel to the head of the bed.

Blanche's eyes were closed and her face was smooth. Her mouth was no longer twisted. Instead, her lips stretched across her dead face in a smile.

# Thirty-one

*It's done*, I think as the weariness overcomes me. There is no way out. The past repeats itself and the theme of my life continues. As it has been many times before, success was almost within my reach, the sweet taste of it lingering in my mouth. I felt it just outside of my grasp, but once again, cruel fate has snatched it away at the last moment. And my life crashes around me in a thousand slivers. But this time, I don't have the strength to pick up the pieces and go on.

I see my reflection and am shocked. Haunted eyes; disheveled hair. With a harsh laugh, I pour another drink.

Did I say fate destroys my dreams? I shake my head and down the glass. Wiping the back of my hand across my mouth, I pour another. No, not fate—her, always her.

Crossing to the stereo, I turn it on and crank it up until music fills the room, but not even music can bring solace to my soul. I make it softer. Feeling imprisoned, I roam the room aimlessly, looking for escape. There is none.

I return to the window and look beyond my reflection and see the truth.

I killed once . . . I can kill again.

# Thirty-two

Sam sat on the deck with a cup of coffee in her hand and Roxy curled up at her feet. A veil of mist was rising dreamily above the smooth surface of the lake, and above it, gray skies masked the rising sun. A stillness seemed to surround Sam as if the entire world were holding its breath. She didn't know why, but she couldn't escape the prickling sense of anticipation. It had to be an effect of the last twenty-four hours. She'd managed to convince her father to return to the Cities and take Jackson with him. It had taken the threat of a nasty court battle spread across of the front page of *The Minneapolis Star*, but finally he'd backed off. At least for now.

All she wanted to do today was to look to the future. A plan was forming in her mind. After what had happened between her, Jackson, and her family, there was no way she was moving back to the Cities. She'd extend her lease on the cabin and stay here, at least for now. If it worked out, maybe she'd eventually open a small art gallery. She'd display her work and that of other artists. Sam frowned. One problem. Running a gallery wouldn't leave her much time for painting. She'd need someone she trusted to handle the day-to-day management.

Her frown fell away. Anne. She loved managing. Handling hesitant customers wouldn't be much different from managing unwilling patients.

Pleased at her new idea, she smiled down at Roxy. "See—everything is going to be fine."

At the sound of her voice, Sam felt the dog lift her head, and looking down, she saw her staring up, as if asking a question.

"We should be happy, right?" she said aloud. "The past is finished." Returning her attention to the lake, she realized that what she'd said was true. When she'd described her experience in Blanche's room to Anne and Greg, she'd felt a sense of completion. It was over. Whatever connection she'd had to Blanche had ended with her death. She could move forward with confidence, haunted by no one. All she had to do was ditch the antsy feeling crawling up her arms and all would be well.

Sam glanced over her shoulder at the half-finished painting, visible through the French doors. If she wanted to move forward, she should go finish that painting. Tilting her head back, she studied the sky. Not in this light. If she was serious about painting, she needed to make a few alterations to her work area, and lighting was at the top of the list.

That's what she'd do, she thought, standing, make a list. Then she'd call the art supply store in the Cities and have new supplies shipped to her. It would be another step forward. Entering the cabin, she grabbed a pencil and piece of paper and, sitting at the kitchen table, began to consider what supplies she'd order. She drew a blank.

Tapping the pencil, she stared at the empty page. A soft whimper drew her attention to the door.

"I get it. You want to go for a walk," Sam told the dog, rising to her feet. "Maybe you're right. Some fresh air would do us both good."

Sam slipped on her tennis shoes and, after fastening Roxy's leash, was out the door. She'd made it to the last step when she glanced over at what she'd forever think of as "Blanche's bush." Her steps faltered. The bush was dead.

Not wanting to contemplate the significance of this, she tugged on the leash and set off down the road. She tried not to think about Blanche as she walked, but couldn't avoid it. Something that happened yesterday was hovering on the edge of her mind, but she couldn't quite bring it into focus. She took a deep breath and let it go. *Keep walking and don't think about it,* she told herself. *It will come to you.*

The self-talk failed and the sense of apprehension increased. She felt a moment of fear. She wasn't going to have another panic attack, was she?

"No," she whispered firmly. "You're just nervous about beginning a new life," she finished, pleased that she could find a place for her emotions.

She was so lost in her thoughts that she didn't hear the footsteps behind her until Roxy darted away from her, barking loudly. Sam spun to find Jackson blocking the path between her and her way back home.

Holding up both hands, he took a step back. "I just want to talk to you. Could you get your damn dog to shut up for a minute?"

At Sam's light tug on the leash, Roxy quieted, but wouldn't move from her position between Sam and Jackson. He took another step back.

*Good Lord, he looks terrible,* Sam thought. His clothes appeared as if he'd slept in them and his normally groomed hair was tousled.

"Jackson, leave me alone, or I'm getting a restraining order," she said in a firm voice

He eased a bit forward. "You can't do it."

"Why? Afraid it will hurt your practice? I will if you keep harassing me."

He stared at her blankly and shook his head. "You can't walk away from me. You have to marry me, Sam."

Sam spun on her heel. "We've been through this," she called angrily over her shoulder. "I'm not going over it again."

"Wait!" he cried out. "I'm no good without you, Sam."

She hesitated and turned to face him. "Jackson, I'm sorry, but we're not right for each other. We do not want the same things anymore."

*Did you ever?* asked a little voice in her head.

"Yes, we do," he said petulantly. "I'll want whatever you want."

"I wouldn't expect that of you."

He came forward. "But I'd do it, I would," he said with an intense light burning in his eyes.

He was beginning to scare her. Glancing around, she tried to get her bearings. If she wasn't mistaken, Fritz's cabin was around the next bend, but she knew that she couldn't outrun Jackson.

She began to inch backward, her eyes never leaving Jackson. At her side, Roxy tensed. "I don't want—"

"Me!" he exclaimed. "You don't want me. You're just like her," he said in disgust.

"Who?" Sam asked, still slowly backing away.

"Mother," he blurted. "I wasn't good enough for her either."

Sam stared at him in shock. "Your mother's been gone a long time. I'm sorry. I know you still feel—"

"Why does the past keep repeating itself?" he asked, his chin lowering.

From his expression, Sam had a feeling that his question wasn't addressed to her. She moved a little faster, increasing the distance between them.

Jackson lifted his head. "There's someone else, isn't there?" His eyes raked her up and down. "You've been cheating on me with that guy living down the road."

"Greg is a friend."

He waved a hand in the air dismissively. "I'll forgive you, but only if you come back to the Cities with me."

Sam forgot her fear as her anger flashed. Grasping Roxy's leash, she looped it around her hand tightly while she prepared to try to make it to Fritz's. "Get away from me," she cried, spinning, and hurried off toward her neighbor's cabin.

Her unsteady gait made it hard to run fast and she fought the urge to peek over her shoulder. She feared that she'd see Jackson only a few steps behind her. Concentrating on keeping her balance, she rounded the bend. *Almost there*, she thought with relief. She stumbled up the steps and pounded on the door. *Hurry, hurry,* she prayed, ignoring the music drifting through the open window. Finally the door opened, and she almost fell inside.

"Oh, thank God you're home," she panted. "Jackson is following me. I need to use your phone."

"Phone?" Fritz asked in a slurred voice.

It was then that Sam noticed the confused look on his face, the rumpled clothing. He wasn't in much better shape than Jackson.

Crossing to him, she placed a hand on his arm. "Fritz, what's wrong?" She got a whiff of booze. "Are you ill?"

"Not ill," he replied, moving away from her. "Edward—don't you know about Edward?"

Sam wasn't following what he was trying to tell her. Anne had told her about Edward's accident, but she hadn't expected Fritz to take it this hard.

"Yes," she answered in a calm voice. "I know he's in the hospital, but I thought he was stable. Has his condition worsened?"

Fritz's face took on a shrewd expression. "You don't understand, do you?"

"No, Fritz, I'm sorry. I don't." Wrapping Roxy's leash around the table leg, Sam moved to the window to see if she could spot Jackson. It looked like he'd disappeared. Was it safe to walk back home? No, he could be waiting for her. She'd call either Greg or Anne and ask them to pick her up. But first she needed to help Fritz.

"Fritz, why don't you explain to me about Edward? I know he was a former student, but I didn't realize you were such close friends."

"Friends? Pupil?" Fritz said, swatting the air with his hand. "We were more than that." He leaned forward and peered at her with bloodshot eyes. "Do you hear that?"

"Yes, that's the piece you were playing when I stopped by a few days ago."

He snorted and weaved his way over to the stereo. "That's Edward playing," he exclaimed. "Brilliant, brilliant. How a woman like Esther ever produced a boy with Edward's talent, I'll never know." He squinted one eye and tapped himself on the chest. "But I—me—it took *me* to awaken that talent."

"I'm sure you were a very good teacher," Sam murmured.

"Good? No—no—more than that," he said, his head wobbling back and forth. "Edward needed me. He needed me to survive as a concert pianist. Without me, he would've been nothing. Just another country boy who could play the piano." His eyes filled with tears. "We had such plans. I was to be his impresario, his agent. Together we would've played the capitals of the world."

"I'm sorry," Sam said with feeling.

Fritz sank down on the couch, hanging his head. "I would have been vindicated—those who turned their backs on me would've been forced to acknowledge my gifts." He lifted his face, the tears flowing freely now. "I would've finally, finally received the recognition that I deserve," he cried, his voice rising.

Sam watched him crying on the couch. She didn't know how to respond. She'd never seen anyone behave so irrationally. She couldn't understand it. It had been twenty-five years since Edward's career had been ruined. Had this bitterness been boiling inside of Fritz all these years? She'd better call Anne.

She moved to the phone, picked up the handset, and began to dial Anne. Fritz was beside her in an instant, tearing the phone out of her hand and slamming it down.

"No."

Sam stepped away. "I think it would be best if I came back when you're feeling better."

"Samantha, Samantha," he said in a stronger voice. "I think you should stay."

Something in his tone told her that she shouldn't argue with him. "Okay, but let's invite Anne over, too, shall we?"

"We shall not. She was rude to me."

"I know, and I want to apologize for that," she said, trying to placate him. "It was so nice of you to make those CDs for me."

"Have you listened to them?"

"Well, no . . . I haven't had the chance yet, but I will."

"And will you use your connections to help me?"

Sam was taken aback. "Help you? How? I don't have any connections."

"Sure you do," he replied. "You can pull some strings with the symphony. Your mother's on the board—I checked. They'll play my work if you recommend me." He frowned. "I would've liked something more prestigious, but it will be a start."

"Fritz, I don't think my mother has any influence over the symphony's selections."

"You mean you won't help me?" His face flushed.

"I don't see how I can."

He came toward her with his eyes narrowed. "You're refusing me. You're ruining my plans just like she did."

"Fritz," Sam cried, "I'd help you if I could, but—"

"You're lying!" he exclaimed.

Backing away from him, Sam held up a hand to stop him. "I'm not."

"Yes—you can't fool me." He pointed a shaking finger at her. "You're just like Blanche. She ruined my life and now you're doing the same thing."

"Fritz," she said, hoping to reach through his alcoholic haze, "Blanche is dead."

"I know."

"I didn't expect the news to get out this soon."

Fear flashed across his face as her words seemed to bring him up short.

He shook his head as if trying to clear it. "What?"

"Blanche—she never ran off. Ted Brighton beat her half to death, causing irreparable brain damage. She's spent the last twenty-five years in the care facility in Hankton."

"Impossible." He began to laugh while his eyes roamed the room. "I was afraid, so afraid what I'd done would be discovered. I made this my prison. And for what?" His laughter suddenly died. "For nothing. There was nothing to find."

Whirling, he ran to the stereo and, with one pull, sent the entire shelving unit crashing to the floor.

For a moment Sam was frozen in place. The voice she'd heard in her mind, the one screaming obscenities as she witnessed Blanche's attack. It was not Ted Brighton—it was Fritz. She didn't understand what exactly had happened twenty-five years ago, but she knew she didn't have much time before he turned his rage on her. Moving to the table, she tried to unhook Roxy's leash, but it was wrapped around the leg. Looking over her shoulder, she saw Fritz coming toward her and redoubled her efforts.

Too late, a painful grip on her shoulder sent her sprawling away from the table. Roxy went crazy, straining and snapping, as she tried to reach Sam.

Fritz towered over her while she struggled to get to her feet. One swift kick to her left leg, and he sent her tumbling to the floor. Her muscles seized and she writhed on the floor in pain.

He watched, his lips curled in a smirk. "You know. I can see it on your face."

"You, not Ted," Sam gasped, grabbing her leg.

"Yes. It is rather amusing that whoever found her suspected him. I wish I would've known that. I might have been able to use it to my advantage." He smiled down at her. "It would have been only fair that Ted finally paid for siding with that bitch. That college student who accused me of drugging her." He sighed and shook his head. "They forced me to retire, you know."

"But Blanche? Why—"

"Did I try to kill her?" He finished her sentence and shrugged. "I hadn't intended to, at least not in the beginning." His hands clenched and unclenched. "It was her fault really. She shouldn't have made me so angry. She wanted me to help her get back at Ted for abandoning her, but she refused to give me a share of the goodies."

Rubbing her leg, Sam scooted toward the coffee table with Fritz following close behind.

"She was such a selfish bitch. She was the one who destroyed my plans."

"And caused Edward's accident."

"My, my, for someone new to the lake, you certainly know a lot. Did Edward tell you?"

Sam shook her head, edging closer to the table. If she could only get to her feet, she might stand a chance.

She'd almost reached it when he suddenly grabbed her arm and hauled her to her knees. Without letting go, he yanked the heavy lamp off the coffee table. He released her arm and stood above her, weighing the lamp in his hand as if it were a baseball bat.

"Poor Samantha, so defenseless." He threw a glance at Roxy, who was barking wildly. "Not even your dog can help you. I do suppose I'll have to get rid of her, too."

Sam clutched at the coffee table and attempted to stand, but he forced her back on her knees.

"My plan would've worked, but she was too stupid to see it. When we disagreed, she insulted me. Questioned my manhood, made me plead for a chance to get back at Ted. Beg as so many other men had begged for her favors. She sickened me. In the end, she was the one who begged and cried for her life." His eyes raked over her. "And now it's your turn, little Samantha."

Her mind flashed back to the scene she'd witnessed while standing at Blanche's bedside—Blanche kneeling on the dock and crying for mercy before the blows began to fall. Another image was superimposed over the first. One of herself, months ago, in a lonely parking garage. She heard the words in her head: *"Okay, pretty lady, start begging."*

She heard her own choked reply. *"Please, please, I don't want to die."*

*No, not again, never again.* Nausea churned in her stomach. She wanted to live, but she'd be damned if she'd beg. No, if she was going to die, she'd die standing. Sam shoved against Fritz's legs with all her strength. He tumbled backward. Using the coffee table, she clawed her way to her feet and dodged past him. She felt the air move by her head as Fritz took a swing at her with the lamp, but missed. Not attempting to untangle the leash, she unclipped it and dragged the dog by her collar toward the door.

Roxy let out a sudden bark and Sam whirled in time to see the lamp descending toward her again. But before it could touch her, Roxy launched herself at Fritz and grabbed his pant leg, shaking it like a rat. It threw him off balance. His arms windmilled while he fought to regain his balance. He failed and fell back.

Sam grabbed Roxy's collar and, pulling the dog along with her, moved as fast as she could. Out the door and up the hill—all the time listening for the sound of chasing footsteps. She'd made it halfway up when she heard them. Closer now, gaining on her. With her weak leg, she couldn't hope to outrun Fritz. Hide, she had to hide.

A few feet above her she spied a break in the hillside. A cave—was it where Fritz had stashed Blanche's body? If it had hidden Blanche, maybe it could hide her.

She scrambled toward it and ducked inside. Crouching in the shadows, she pulled Roxy close to her chest. "Shh," she whispered in her ear.

The footsteps stopped, and Sam held her breath. A shadow crossed the entrance and Sam shrank back farther into the cave. The shadow passed by. She waited. Silence. Leaning her head back against the damp cold rock, she prayed that Fritz had given up his pursuit. She was still trapped, but the longer she lasted, the better her chances were of getting away.

“I know you’re in there,” he suddenly called out, his shadow once again blocking the light.

She didn’t answer.

“I won’t hurt you . . . I’m sorry . . . I was drunk.”

Unbelievable—did he really think she was that stupid, that weak?

“Samantha, come out right now,” he commanded. “If you don’t, you’ll regret it. It gets very unpleasant in that cave at night. There’re bats and they swoop down on you in the dark. Things will creep over your feet and land in your hair.”

Sam realized that Fritz was afraid to enter the cave. How could she use that fear against him? Her hand found a rock, lying next to her. She weighed it in her hand. Heavy enough to knock a man out. If she could lure him into the cave, she could hit him from behind. It was worth a try. What had he said? Blanche had insulted him? Questioned his manhood?

“What’s wrong, Fritz?” she called out. “Aren’t you man enough to come in and get me?”

He failed to answer.

“I don’t believe it,” she scoffed. “Someone like you afraid of the dark? Did Blanche know that? Did she know you were a coward? Is that why she spurned you?”

“Shut up,” he cried. “I was better than her, better than everyone. It’s not my fault I didn’t have the advantages that I needed to succeed.”

“Oh, please,” Sam called back, letting her voice fill with sarcasm. “All the breaks in the world wouldn’t have helped you. You needed Blanche and you needed Edward. Without them, you were nothing but mediocre.”

“I am not,” he answered in a childlike voice.

“Yes, even your work is nothing. It was Edward who made it

soar." She forced herself to chuckle. "I bet Edward could play the scales and make them sound like a concerto."

"No, it was me—I made Edward."

"No, you didn't." She paused and let the silence lengthen. "In the end, once he saw the real you, Fritz, he would've rejected you, too."

With a scream, Fritz hurled himself into the cave. Sam slipped back and let him rush past her. She raised the rock, but before she could bring it down, Fritz fell to his knees. Curling on his side, he began to whimper.

With one hand trailing along the damp rock and the other still clutching the dog, Sam backed away from Fritz's prone body. At the entrance, she released the dog and pointed down the hill. "Go," she ordered.

Roxy took two steps, stopped, and turned.

"Go on. I'm right behind you."

"Don't go," a voice whined from behind her. "Don't leave me, please. I'll be good. I promise."

Sam glanced at the figure lying on the floor. The shadow was shaped like Fritz, but the voice was that of a child. Wherever Fritz was, he wasn't here.

Dropping the rock, Sam stepped out of the darkness and into the light.

## Thirty-three

The lawn in front of the small stage was littered with blankets and lawn chairs while the neighbors around the lake gathered to listen to the Fourth of July trio. Since Fritz was not available, the program selection had fallen to Greg. There wasn't a march or a classical piece listed. Instead, he'd picked a nice mix of pop tunes and jazz.

Sam sat in her lawn chair next to Anne and surreptitiously watched her glow with pride while she focused on Caleb, who stood center stage practicing a few riffs on his guitar. Fritz may have been emotionally stunted, and more than just a little bit off balance, but he could spot talent. And Caleb's gift was obvious even to Sam's untrained ear.

Leaning over, she touched Anne's arm. "Everything okay now?"

Anne smiled in response. "Yeah, we had a long talk. He agreed to live at home while he finishes his senior year, and I agreed to let him plan his own future." Her expression turned serious. "Everyone deserves that, don't they?"

Sam gave a small snort and settled back in her chair. "Yeah, and hopefully one day my father is going to reach the same conclusion."

Anne gave a low chuckle. "It's funny. When I first met you, all you cared about was getting your old life back. Now he's begging you to come back and you won't go."

Sam grimaced. "I know, but I've realized my *old* life wasn't ever mine. It was the life my father chose for me. And I permitted it to trap me."

"You're not the only one. I've done a lot of thinking." Anne's gaze traveled again to the stage. "My ambition for Caleb was a trap, too. For both of us." Turning toward Sam, she grinned. "But not anymore."

"Does that mean you're going to accept my job offer?"

Anne hesitated. "I really don't know anything about selling art."

"But you have a real presence." She leaned forward and nudged Anne's shoulder. "And, dahling," she said in a phony accent, "don't you know appearance is everything?"

Anne rolled her eyes, laughing.

Sam suddenly sobered. "Come on, it would be fun. You'd be terrific at handling our budget, and I already know you're great at talking people into things. The rest you'd learn."

Anne looked thoughtful. "I don't think I'll be working at the hospital this fall." She smiled. "Working in an art gallery does sound better than waitressing or cleaning bed pans."

"Does that mean you'll do it?"

Anne gave a small nod.

"Wonderful!" Sam exclaimed, then narrowed her eyes. "One thing—you have to agree not to bully the customers," she said, her voice teasing.

"Trust me," Anne replied, placing the flat of her hand over her heart. "My bullying days are over."

Sam's eyes sparkled. *Yeah, right,* she thought. In spite of her declarations to the contrary, Anne hadn't quite let go of her bossy ways. For the last several weeks, she'd been pushing Sam and Greg together whenever the opportunity presented itself. If Sam was honest about it, she really didn't mind. *Who knows,* she thought, looking at the stage and the group gathered there, *maybe someday.* But right now she was happy to have him as her friend.

Her attention settled on Greg and found him watching her. He *was* pretty sexy holding that sax. With a smile, Sam lowered her head and slid her gaze to Anne once again.

*Lucky,* she sighed to herself. Instead of the life she thought she wanted, she'd found the life she really needed. Her father had backed off a bit. When he'd learned of Jackson's waylaying of her along the road, his fatherly protectiveness had kicked in. Maybe with a little time and a lot of distance, they might someday have a good relationship.

Her thoughts finally wound around to Blanche as they did less and less these days.

Sam's happiness dimmed. When the sheriff had found Fritz in the cave, he'd been wailing like a child. It wasn't long before Dr. Crane learned that when Fritz was a child, his father had confined him to the cave as a form of punishment. Sam shuddered at the thought. What kind of monster would do that to a child? In view of his battered psyche, Dr. Crane felt that Fritz would probably spend the rest of his life in a state mental hospital.

It was ironic. Blanche had spent the last twenty-five years of her life confined, and now Fritz would do the same.

Sam looked over to the horizon as the trio launched their first number. The setting sun had hung a banner of rose, mauve, and gold above the pines. It was over. Whatever had caused the connection with Blanche didn't matter.

What mattered? She was free and so was Blanche.

And over the sound of the bluesy notes, Sam heard the call of a loon, echoing like a woman's laughter.

# Acknowledgments

The creation of a book truly is a journey, and I'd like to thank those who made this trip a little easier!

As always and as already mentioned . . . Emily Krump and Stacey Glick. I appreciate your guidance and your investment in this project more than I can say. I'm also thankful that not once have you ever reminded me that e-mails are supposed to be direct and to the point! Thanks for reading *and* answering all my ramblings!

The staff at William Morrow—from the cover artist to the copyeditor (sorry about all the danglers!) to the proofreaders. Thanks for catching my mistakes, smoothing it out, and putting it all into a nice package.

Dr. Robert Weissinger—thank you so much for all the free advice and the use of your name.

And speaking of names—thanks to my granddaughter, Kassidy, for naming some of the characters, a job I always find difficult.

June Steinbach. Thanks, June, for answering my questions concerning head injuries and drug interactions.

Valerie Allen of Expression's Photography. You did a great job,

Valerie, and I appreciate all the effort you put into making sure the shots were "just right."

As promised . . . Jack and Jamie. Thank you for very kindly allowing us the use of your living room for the photo shoot. (There, Jamie, your name is now in print!)

Sara Anne McConkey—stylist, personal assistant, and most of all, daughter. Thank you for designing old Mom's new look!

And last but not least, the rest of my family and friends. You are the blessings in my life!

Valerie, and I appreciate all the effort you put into making sure the shots were "just right."

As promised . . . Jack and Jamie. Thank you for very kindly allowing us the use of your living room for the photo shoot. (There, Jamie, your name is now in print!)

Sara Anne McConkey—stylist, personal assistant, and most of all, daughter. Thank you for designing old Mom's new look!

And last but not least, the rest of my family and friends. You are the blessings in my life!

Jess McConkey

Valerie Allen

**JESS McCONKEY** (aka Shirley Damsgaard) is an award-winning writer of short fiction. She lives in a small town and is currently working on her next novel.